Canadian **Dani Collins** knew in high school that she wanted to write romance for a living. Twenty-five years later, after marrying her high school sweetheart, having two kids with him, working at several generic office jobs and submitting countless manuscripts, she got The Call. Her first Mills & Boon novel won the Reviewers' Choice Award for Best First in Series from *RT Book Reviews*. She now works in her own office, writing romance.

Emmy Grayson wrote her first book at the age of seven, about a spooky ghost. Her passion for romance novels began a few years later, with the discovery of a worn copy of Kathleen E. Woodiwiss's *A Rose in Winter* buried on her mother's bookshelf. She lives in the Midwest countryside with her husband—who's also her ex-husband—their baby boy, and enough animals to start their own zoo.

HER IMPOSSIBLE BABY BOMBSHELL

DANI COLLINS

HIS BILLION-DOLLAR TAKEOVER TEMPTATION

EMMY GRAYSON

MILLS & BOON

First Published in Great Britain 2021
by Mills & Boon, an imprint of HarperCollins*Publishers* Ltd,
1 London Bridge Street, London, SE1 9GF

www.harpercollins.co.uk

HarperCollins*Publishers*
1st Floor, Watermarque Building,
Ringsend Road, Dublin 4, Ireland

Her Impossible Baby Bombshell © 2021 Dani Collins

His Billion-Dollar Takeover Temptation © 2021 Emmy Grayson

ISBN: 978-0-263-28247-4

05/21

MIX
Paper from
responsible sources
FSC® C007454

This book is produced from independently certified FSC™ paper
to ensure responsible forest management.
For more information visit www.harpercollins.co.uk/green.

Printed and bound in Spain
by CPI, Barcelona

HER IMPOSSIBLE BABY BOMBSHELL

DANI COLLINS

MILLS & BOON

For my son, Sam, who takes it in stride when his mother texts him out of the blue asking, "Why would a young man your age get a vasectomy?" and later brainstorms some scenes with me when I'm stuck. Thanks, dude. You're the best.

PROLOGUE

LOVE. *YUCK.* IVY LAM was over it.

She wasn't cynical by nature, but she'd only come to this engagement party to be polite. A DM to an old work colleague asking if she could buy him coffee to discuss a career shift had resulted in the invitation from Kevin.

If you're in town, come to our party. Lots of leads will be there.

So she'd picked up a bottle of wine and spent way too much money on a dress. It was a "casual" afternoon barbecue in one of Vancouver's most upscale neighborhoods, celebrating a society engagement, but she needed to make a good first impression on potential employers. Easy-peasy.

She had settled on a dusty pink knee-length floral dress that had a 195f0s Sunday school vibe to it, but the darts and pleats gave it a tailored look and the scooped neckline made the most of her modest bosom.

For all the good the effort had done her. Most of the women were in daring halter tops with bohemian skirts and eyelet sundresses that hugged their curves. Ivy was both a sore thumb that stuck out and a wallflower to be overlooked.

It was the story of her life. Ivy was neither an introvert nor an extrovert. She was middle-of-the-road, which made her too boring to be the center of attention but perfect for filling out background laughter.

Kevin had been right about the guest list, though. It was brimming with Vancouver's top commercial real estate developers, stock traders and financial investors. Even a real, live billionaire—if the hushed remark she'd overheard was to be believed.

Tsai Jun Li was—well, it didn't matter that he'd made her blood heat when Kevin had seemed to make a point of introducing them. Ivy wasn't here to find a man.

Therefore, it hadn't bothered her a bit that Jun Li had been drawn away seconds later by a stacked blonde. Blondie was welcome to him. Ivy refused to get hung up on a man who didn't want her. Not again.

Even if he might be, without exaggeration, the most beautiful man she'd ever seen.

No. Either way she sliced it, there was nothing here for her. Trying to network at such a celebratory event would be tasteless and Kevin's effusive love for Carla only reminded Ivy of how spectacularly she had failed when it came to happily-ever-after.

Thirty minutes after she arrived, she quietly exited the Point Grey mansion without saying goodbye. As she emerged onto the stoop, the April sunshine made her sneeze.

Allergic to love, she almost said to the valet who blessed her.

"I'm ordering a ride share," she said in answer to his offer to fetch her car.

She didn't hurry to bring up the app, though. She wasn't anxious to go back to her father's. His new relationship was also loving and sincere and hard to be around. Ivy was happy for him, but she felt like a dupe for believing she had had anything like it.

What a waste! But no more kidding herself. She was moving on. That's what this trip was about.

She went down the steps to stand in the shade of an ornamental plum tree, trying to read her email. She was hoping for an impromptu request for an interview, but there was nothing because it was Saturday afternoon and the sun was shining. The entire city was outside enjoying a startlingly beautiful and unseasonably warm spring day.

Ivy stepped into the sun and turned her face up, letting the warmth and brightness shine down on her with all its might. She was coming home. It wasn't so much a do-over as the launch of a new and improved Ivy. One who wasn't so gullible. One who made her own decisions. Bold, self-serving ones.

"It's false advertising," a male voice said.

The valet made an "eep" noise and said, "The Pagani?" He snatched up a key from his board and hurried away.

Ivy looked up the steps, and there *he* stood, surveying her the way an emperor assessed his domain.

According to Kevin, the thirtyish Chinese billionaire had been his "roommate from our time at UBC." That made Jun Li sound very tame when he actually moved like a predator, gliding down the stairs in a panther-like lope.

Ivy didn't mean to stare, but seriously, she forgot to breathe, he was so good-looking.

He had short black hair with just enough length on top to be rakish. His brows were stern, his beard trimmed to a thin line that framed his square jaw and somber mouth. His cheekbones were so high and sharp, they should have shattered the screen on her phone. His skin held a warm golden hue set off by the lime-green color of his pullover.

How was that loosely knit but closely worn sweater not wearing him?

Ivy only noticed his clothes because they so elegantly hugged his muscled shoulders and accentuated his athletic build. He'd skimmed up his sleeves to reveal his forearms, adding to his air of being utterly unaware of how stunning he was. He was like a snapshot out of a men's magazine. He only needed to tuck a hand into his bone-colored chinos and point at something off camera.

What would he look like in his underwear, she wondered sinfully.

He kept coming toward her, and her admiration sharpened to something more visceral. A tightness of danger with a thrill of excitement.

Lust.

It was a testament to how anemic her last relationship had been that she had never experienced anything like this surge of anticipation for the man she had wanted to marry, but heat built in her throat as Jun Li closed in on her.

Just as she wondered if he would overwhelm her completely, he stopped in the shade of the tree.

"The weather," he clarified. His mouth might have twitched as though he was laughing at how mesmerized she was. "An arctic outflow will come through tomorrow and kill all these flowers." He nodded at the planter pots filled with cheerful pansies. "Or a pineapple express from Hawaii will dump a metric ton of rain and drown them. Everyone who visits thinks this is what it's like to live here. It's not."

He was making her feel exactly how she didn't want to feel—like a tongue-tied adolescent with her first crush. Like a woman who allowed men to tell her things she already knew. She wanted to be one of those sophisticates like that blonde who hadn't been afraid to make a play for a man who was clearly out of her league.

"I know" was all she managed to say. "I grew up here."

His brows went up slightly. "I misunderstood. I thought Kevin said he knew you from his time in Hong Kong."

"We worked together there, yes."

Kevin had a very similar background to Ivy's middle-class, second-generation immigrant upbringing. As a fellow Chinese Canadian boosting a banking career with a stint in Hong Kong, he'd taken her under his wing for the year she'd worked in his department, offering her a sibling-like bond of outward teasing and underlying support.

"I took his job when he left." That felt very braggy, but she was trying to overcome years of allowing herself to be reduced. "Six months ago, I took a transfer to Toronto." Huge mistake careerwise, but at least it had forced her to confront how poorly she was allowing herself to be treated and put a stop to it once and for all. "My father still lives here, so I'm moving back to enjoy the smooth traffic and affordable cost of living. Fabulous weather is not this city's only selling feature," she punctuated with a facetious smile.

"I would have sworn it had none, but I stand corrected." His mouth curled with equal irony. The flick of his gaze to her shoes and back suggested male notice. The crinkles beside his eyes suggested he appreciated what he saw. "Do you need a lift?" he asked as a growling engine approached.

Her heart skipped, and she thought, *This is it. This is what it's like to be single.*

The tendrils of attraction within her were sliding and coiling with possibility. A flattered blush warmed her cheeks, and she felt the rush of preparing to take a big leap.

At the last second, old habits had her stupid mouth stammering, "I'm in Richmond. It's too far out of your way." Because he couldn't possibly want to spend a second longer with her than he had to. This was exactly how she'd wound up in a dead-end long-distance relationship for *eight years.*

"I'm looking for an excuse to drive," he said as a cobalt-blue convertible roadster stopped before him. It was a two-seater with fins and muscles and spoked hubcaps. There was a hawklike beak down the hood. The windshield was slanted to an acute, aerodynamic angle, and the mirrors swept out like antennae.

Ivy couldn't help biting her lip in temptation. "It

looks like something a crime-fighting duo would use to chase supervillains."

"Blame me for the crime rate, then. I forgot I owned it. I had to have it tuned up before I could drive it, but now that I have, I've decided to ship it home. I'm hardly ever here." He opened the passenger door. "Are you really going to make me save the city all by myself?"

Ivy stifled a snort at anyone owning a car like this— likely worth seven figures—and not only forgetting about it, but having it sent around the world like an overnight package.

This man was not only out of her league, he was from a different planet. But when would she get a chance like this again?

"If the city *needs* us…" She dropped into the low-slung seat, feeling like a racecar driver must. She dug in her bag for her sunglasses, a cheap pair of cat-eyes that she'd grabbed while picking out this dress.

He put on a pair of designer wraparounds that made him look even more sexy and inscrutable. As he pulled away, she felt like one of those daring women who got on the back of the bad boy's motorcycle. She felt sexy and self-possessed just by being next to him in this wicked car on this glorious day.

They wound down the hill through tree-lined streets, but when he reached the main road that would have taken them south, there was a detour arrow.

"This looks like a sign," he said.

"Are you being literal? Or do you mean it's a warning that I shouldn't move back here because this is what I'll be up against?"

"I'm saying we're being offered a chance to seize

this rare, fine day. How do you feel about taking the long way home?"

She waved her hand, silently deferring to him, bemused that she was here at all.

He proved his familiarity with the side streets, and they were soon across the bridge and skirting English Bay, heading into Stanley Park. From there, he took the Lion's Gate bridge and ran through the gears up the Sea to Sky highway.

Her skirt fluttered as he picked up speed. Her heart pressed back into her spine and her hair snapped her cheeks. She grinned with delight as the music blared and he smoothly whistled past sedans and minivans. It was a sensation of absolute freedom and she should have let them both enjoy it, but she wound up ruining it.

"You know they'll impound this car if you go too far over the speed limit?"

"They'll have to catch me first," he said cockily, but he eased off a little, glancing at his speed and the sign they passed.

"I've been working in compliance," she said by way of apology. "Job hazard."

"You're still in banking?"

"Yes." She understood he was asking because Kevin had left the bank in Hong Kong to take a private-sector position in asset management here in Vancouver. "What do you do?" She had an idea but wondered how a man like him answered such a question.

"The bulk of my work involves international infrastructure projects. We have a lot of contracts around the Belt Road Initiative. I'm president of a conglomerate with a diverse portfolio, though. My father started

it with medical devices, and we're still a global manu-
facturer for those. My aunt has a handbag supply chain
that does ridiculously well."

"Why is it ridiculous? Every woman needs something trendy in which to carry her husband's wallet."

It was a silly joke, a dig toward all the men who
complained about holding purses in shopping malls but
didn't want to carry their own wallet.

Jun Li's expression grew more alert. "I assumed you
were single because you were at the party alone."

Whose wallet do you carry? he seemed to be asking.

*A man who led me on for years and never really
wanted me. That wallet has been sent to the secondhand store.*

A worldly woman with confidence in her own worth
didn't blurt out a sob story about being taken for granted
and rejected, though.

"I'm consciously uncoupled as of last Christmas,"
she said in the most laissez-faire tone she could manage. "You?"

"Consciously uncoupled as a lifestyle choice."

"Ah. Noted," she said dryly, hearing the underlying
warning. It stung more than it should, but she was still
raw from her breakup. She didn't need another man
telling her she wasn't good enough for forever. Kudos
to Jun Li for being up front about it, at least.

She made herself enjoy the moment and they were
halfway to Whistler before she realized it.

"How far are we going?" he asked and her heart
lurched as the words 'all the way' sprang into her mind.

She didn't have the nerve to say it and he wound up

taking the next exit off the highway. It led to a tourist attraction with a gondola to summit and a dining lodge.

"I've never gone up there. Have you?"

"No."

"Is today the day?"

"When will we have another?"

Minutes later, they were ambling along an interpretive path enjoying spectacular views of the mountains and the sound below.

"I don't care if it is false advertising," Ivy said as she stood at the rail of a platform that jutted out into thin air. "When it's beautiful, it's really beautiful. To me, that's worth suffering the bad days."

"I'd rather avoid the bad days and accept the good ones as the gift they are." He turned to her.

He wanted to kiss her. She knew it and she wanted that, too. She turned and lifted her gaze to meet his. They were both smiling.

She didn't let herself wonder what any of it meant. This day was a gift for both of them.

When his mouth settled on hers, lips firm and smooth and hot, her whole body grew charged with electricity.

This was her chance to take another step toward moving on, she realized with a flash of possibility. Indulging herself with Jun Li was liable to wipe her memory clean all the way back to her first kiss in grade school, but that was exactly what she needed.

The conscientious woman inside her, the one still longing for love, marriage and a baby carriage, warned that a man like him could set a bar that no other man could reach. He could destroy her without even meaning to.

She told that fearmongering voice to pipe down and kissed him back.

They kissed until they were both breathless. When he lifted his head, she discovered they were pressed together, arms wrapped tight around each other.

He licked his lips.

"How do you feel about being used in a rebound situation?" she asked before she could think twice.

"I feel great about it." His expression relaxed into one of sensual anticipation. "I leave tomorrow morning." His eyes narrowed as he gauged her reaction to that.

"So do I."

"Let's enjoy this day, then."

CHAPTER ONE

Four months later, Singapore

EXACTLY AS SHE had back in April, Ivy accepted a flute
of champagne with no intention of drinking it, even
though her mouth was a desert. She held the glass to
blend in while she got her bearings at a party where she
only knew one person.

Actually, zero. Her quarry wasn't here yet. She gave
the dimly lit piano bar another nervous skim of her
gaze—as if Jun Li was a man anyone could miss.

She belonged even less at this five-star Singapore
hotel than she had at Kevin's party. Jun Li's guests were
VPs and CEOs whose net incomes made Kevin's circle
look like burger flippers at a fast food joint.

Instead of her prim pink dress, she wore a cheongsam-
inspired sheath with cap sleeves, its red shoulders fading to indigo at the knee-length hem. Was it noticeably
tight around her middle? Yes, but it had always served
her well at the banking functions she was forced to attend, so she'd worn it as a security blanket.

She had hoped it would work for what was essentially
a corporate event, but it was too demure for a trophy wife

and not chic enough for a female executive with stock options. Any minute she expected a caterer to hand her a tray of canapés and ask her to serve them to table five.

Everything about this was *awful*. She was bordering on stalking, coming all this way to ambush a man in front of his employees, but in the three weeks since she'd discovered her pregnancy, she'd had little luck reaching out through normal channels. Jun Li hadn't given her his number, and his privacy settings on social media were locked down tight. A gauntlet of personal assistants and low-level managers had fobbed her off and shut her down, clearly judging her a schemer of some kind. She'd even asked a headhunter to nose around for jobs that might grant her an interview with him, but that process took forever, and this felt urgent. For both of them.

Truth was, she was still in shock and denial, somehow convinced it wouldn't be real until she told Jun Li. She had to tell him before she revealed it to anyone else, but getting to him was nearly impossible.

She had resorted to calling Kevin. Aside from sending a wedding gift and regrets, she'd been avoiding him, not wanting to know whether Jun Li had told him they'd spent a night together. She wasn't ashamed of their brief affair, but it was private. She'd done it for herself and wanted it to be a special memory that was between the two of them. She wasn't up for any teasing over it. She wasn't running around bragging that she'd bagged a billionaire. She'd be devastated if Jun Li was boasting about conquering her.

With all other avenues exhausted, however, she had

screwed up her courage and invited Kevin for coffee, supposedly to discuss her career.

"You haven't found the right fit yet?" he asked with surprise.

"I've been offered a position, but I'd like your take. I don't know if it will be flexible enough in the long run." That was true enough. Her entire life was changing, and she needed a position that would adapt to the needs of a single mother.

They sat down a few days later and warmed up with small talk about his upcoming wedding. It provided the perfect opening to bring up her real reason for seeing him.

"Who's your best man? Jun Li?" She already knew he wasn't.

"My brother. Jun Li can't make it. Annual strategy meeting in Singapore." Kevin had set down his coffee to side-eye her. "Why? Were you hoping to see him again? Carla thinks you two hooked up because you both left our party early."

Ivy suffered an appalled moment of realizing she was being gossiped about, but it was obviously a joke. He didn't really believe they had connected.

"Oh yeah, right," Ivy scoffed after the longest, most agonizingly culpable silence. She hoped he read her nervous, blushing laughter as unrequited attraction, not guilt. "Every woman was throwing herself at him, but Tsai Jun Li, the Chinese *billionaire*, went home with *me*. Five minutes after we met." She added an eye roll to really sell how outrageous the suggestion was.

Whether Kevin believed her or not, she didn't know. She didn't have the nerve to look him in the eye after that.

She should have confessed all and admitted, *I really need help*, but it felt like a gross breach of ethics to air one man's private business to another.

After a moment, he had said, "You could do worse. You *have* done worse." His voice was a lot more compassionate than his words. He knew all about her woes with Bryant.

Kevin had segued into asking about the job she'd been offered, and Ivy lost her chance to ask how Jun Li might react to her news.

She knew how he was going to react—with complete and utter disbelief. That's why this felt like such a personal, delicate matter that needed to be discussed in person. A text or voice mail wouldn't convince him and ran the risk of an assistant getting the news first.

If this wrap-up party had been more difficult to sleuth out, Ivy might have gone back to Kevin, but things had fallen into place very easily. The itinerary for the entire week had been on the corporate website, including the fact Jun Li was scheduled to present some awards tonight, recognizing the most innovative suggestions from the week's meetings.

Ivy had extended the start date for her new job in Vancouver, finished moving and used points to book a package, arriving in Singapore yesterday.

At least she was getting a final vacation before settling into single motherhood, she thought dourly as she glared into her flattening champagne. Because it was looking as though Jun Li wouldn't even show up—

A stir in the crowd brought her head up. She glimpsed him through the throng, and her heart stalled. Her knees went soft. She shifted so she had a better view of him, and her shoulders tensed so hard with nerves and jubilation, she could hardly breathe.

He seemed to stop time, pausing to survey the milling guests. He was still the most beautiful man Ivy had ever seen, and it was his superpower to seem completely unaware of his impact. In this faux candlelight, his complexion held a godlike bronze sheen. He wore a striped shirt, open at the collar, and a pair of tailored pants with a cuff, casually elegant and completely untouchable. Beyond her.

How had this pregnancy even happened? That's what she was thinking as her shoes from the outlet mall pinched her feet and a woman approached him, curvaceous and stunning in a peacock-blue cocktail dress and an abundance of jewelry that Ivy instinctively knew was real.

Ivy couldn't compete with that. Her gaze glued itself to him as she waited for him to notice her, half terrified, half thrilled to merely be in his orbit again while her heart tripped over itself with jealousy and loss. Her instinct was to crawl away. The last thing she wanted was a humiliating rejection in front of all these people.

If only she could take heart from the fact Jun Li's aloof expression didn't change as he spoke to that other woman, but she'd found him very hard to read when she'd spent an afternoon and evening with him. As it turned out, he'd been seducing her the whole time, so he might be doing the same to that woman right now for all she knew. Perhaps he already had.

A small choke of agony left her at the thought. She felt tangled in barbed wire as she stood there. She wanted to rush away and hide, but if he was romantically involved with anyone, he ought to know what *she* knew.

There would be no convenient time to approach him. No easy way to say what had to be said. She had come all this way, and it was time to wade in before he was completely surrounded or disappeared.

As she started forward, her situation hit her as very tawdry. Not the one-night stand part. She had agreed to that and, even though it had stung that he hadn't made any effort to reach out to her afterward, she accepted their time together as merely a fling.

No, the fact they'd been intimate but she was forced to go to these lengths so he could disbelieve and disregard her was eating her alive.

She was so focused on Jun Li, a touch on her arm made her jolt in surprise. A young man gave her a pained smile. "You're not on the list."

She could only stare blankly. He repeated it in Mandarin.

"You don't know who I am," she said, using her own flawless Mandarin.

"Exactly. I know every face except yours. Can you come with me, please?"

"No, I—" She glanced at Jun Li, digging in her heels. His attention was turned on that other woman, and he wasn't even looking this way.

"Please don't make a scene," the young man said. His hand on her arm firmed.

Ivy had the panicked feeling of someone being pulled beneath the surface of a lake, certain she was about to drown.

She yanked her arm free and hissed, "Go tell him Kevin Chow's friend Ivy needs five minutes."

Dropping Kevin's name gave the young man pause. After a wavering second, he said, "Wait by the elevator."

She did, begrudgingly, and watched as he went to Jun Li to speak in his ear.

Jun Li's head came up. His gaze seemed to hit her like a spear from across the room, deafening her to the din of conversation and the patter of piano keys. She couldn't read anything in his body language. Was he pleased? Appalled? She didn't know, but a hot sting of adrenaline shot to the ends of her fingers and toes, urging her to run while another part of her melted under his gaze.

She didn't understand why she reacted to him this way, and it was ten times stronger now they had shared a night of passion. *More.*

Her hand twitched, wanting to protectively cover her middle, but that would be far too telling when people were turning their heads, picking up on where his attention had gone.

Jun Li flicked his hand in an unspoken, *I'll handle it.* He left his group and wove unerringly toward her, expression inscrutable.

As he closed in, her lungs compressed and her insides began to tremble. His profound effect on her was not the thrill of catching a handsome, powerful man's attention. It was a painful sting of raw fear because she sensed his irritation at her turning up this way.

This was a far more daunting man than the one she'd met in Vancouver—which she hadn't realized was possible—but he still made her blood move like lava under her skin. Instead of basking in the glow of his attention, however, she felt spotted by an eagle. Picked apart. Naked.

It struck her that she'd gone to these ridiculous lengths so she could experience the soaring feeling of being in his presence again, but that had been a mistake. He was about to shoot her down, and the fall would be crippling.

"Ivy." There was no warmth in his voice. There was no hostility, either, which made it worse. He conveyed annoyance that she was bothering him at work, but otherwise he was indifferent to her being here.

She had the sudden, horrifying sense that he wouldn't have remembered her at all if she hadn't just given her name to his PA.

It was a plunge into reality from a fantasy she hadn't acknowledged. Deep down, she had imagined he might want to see her again. How incredibly foolish of her. He was supposed to have *cured* her of yearning for a man to bolster her sense of self-worth.

She cut off her anguished thoughts. The backs of her eyes were hot, and her throat wanted to close, but she forced herself to adopt her boardroom demeanor, the one she used when she had to deliver bad news. She was the person on staff everyone loved to resent. She had learned to wear a dispassionate veil to protect herself.

"I'm sorry to bother you," she said in a level voice. "It was difficult to reach you without revealing why I need to speak with you. It's a personal matter."

His brows came together with genuine concern. "Kevin?"

"No."

Just as quickly, comprehension washed over his expression along with weary cynicism. "If I gave you a wrong impression when we—"

"You didn't." She'd done that to herself and would scream her mortification into a pillow later. "I only need five minutes, but I have information you should have. It's private," she added as his assistant hovered behind him.

Jun Li drew a skeptical breath, looking like he wanted to rebuff her, but his gaze flickered over her. She was watching him so closely, trying so hard to read him, she caught the flash of something—memory? Hunger?

Whatever it was disappeared so quickly, it left a void inside her the way a detonation left a scorched crater in the earth.

He withdrew a card from his pocket and loomed close to her.

She was so disconcerted, so buffeted by his dynamic energy, she took a step back, not realizing he was only touching the call button near her hip. She practically fell through the doors when they opened behind her.

He caught her arm to steady her. "I'll escort you down." He guided her into the empty elevator and shook his head when the young man would have joined them. "How did you get up here?" he asked her as the doors closed.

By riding the elevator until she was motion sick and slipping into the ladies' room ages before the greeters with their tablets and their gift bags had arrived. "Does it matter?"

"It's my hotel. I'd like to know how my security was bypassed, yes." He touched his card to the panel.

His hotel. Right. He wasn't just some guy she'd slept with. He was the head of a Chinese infrastructure conglomerate with projects and investments worldwide. He didn't have time for a lowly one-night stand to bend his ear. She ignored his question to blurt what she had come to say.

"Look, I know my coming here seems extreme, but—"

The floor didn't drop. It went up, causing her to stagger again.

"Are you all right?" He frowned, and his hand returned to her elbow.

"I thought you were taking me downstairs."

"I will. You said this was a private matter." The doors opened almost immediately. He escorted her across a small foyer into a two-story mansion of a penthouse.

It was the kind of over-the-top luxury she'd only seen in reality shows about the rich and famous. He walked her down a spiral staircase made of glass into a living area where the wall of windows looked onto the colorful lights of Singapore against the night sky.

She was completely taken aback by the astonishing view and understated opulence of white leather sofas arranged to enjoy a fireplace that peeked through to an elegant dining room. There were modern art sculptures and abstracts on the walls, an area rug that had to be silk and chandeliers that had to be crystal.

"Drink?" he invited.

"I can't, thank you." She cleared her throat and dug deep in search of the woman she'd pretended to be that day with him. Experienced. Detached. This was a compliance error, she reminded herself. That's all. "I'm not here to attempt an extension of our…" Relationship? "Association," she decided in a strained voice. "I only thought you should know that I'm pregnant."

Her heart pounded so hard, she thought the whole building must be pulsating with the sound. Her skin felt hot, but clammy with sweat.

His expression didn't change. "Congratulations?"

"It's yours."

His breath hissed out in a humorless snort while his shoulders slanted with fatalism. He gave a small shake of his head that asked *Why are you wasting my time?*

"Hear me out." She held up a hand, noticed it was trembling and tucked it under her elbow, folding her arms defensively. "I broke up with my boyfriend last Christmas. You're the only man I've been with since. Does this look like a full-term pregnancy to you?" She opened her arms to indicate the subtle curve in her middle.

It was nearing the end of July. She was seventeen weeks along, looking more like she'd been indulging at an all-inclusive buffet than pregnant.

"Whether you're pregnant or not I couldn't say…" His attention traversed all over her, like a paintbrush making several long, thorough strokes to leave a thick coat. When he dragged his gaze back to hers, his was sparking with heat that was smothered with cynicism. "You're not the first woman to make a claim like this, you know. They don't usually have the information I confided to *you*—"

"Don't," she warned, heart wrenched by the contempt she could hear in his tone. The one that censured her against being desperate and foolish. The one that said she had grossly overstepped by coming here.

She was used to powerful men dismissing her. The truth was often inconvenient, but this wasn't a gray area in a policy or regulation that she was suggesting he abide by. It was way more personal than that. And even though she'd known he would react this way, it hurt to be accused of dishonesty. She might tell white lies, but she was dead honest when it came to life, death and tax implications.

She swallowed and hugged herself again.

"I'm not here to ask for money or a ring. I'm telling you because it's information you deserve to have. I'm perfectly capable of raising this baby on my own and plan to."

"Great. Consider me informed. I'll escort you to your room."

It was a bluff. She could tell he was testing her resolve to see how she would react to such a callous dismissal.

She wanted to cry. Everything about this was going exactly as she had expected—except for the fact he had the power to cut her in half with a few dispassionate words. She wouldn't beg him to believe her, though.

"I'm not staying here." She spoke with as much poise as she could muster, biting back pointing out his hotel was way beyond her budget.

"I'll ask the doorman to cover your taxi fare, then." He waved at the stairs.

"That's not necessary," she murmured, hesitating.

She wanted to ask one more thing, but it was such a blood-chilling worry, she could barely give voice to it.

His brows went up with exaggerated patience. A muscle pulsed in his jaw, betraying he was finding this interaction disturbing. He was probably already thinking he ought to take a test to be sure and probably annoyed with her for making him think it.

"These things are very easy to disprove, Ivy," he said, but she didn't take any comfort in having read him correctly. "Even if you go to the press, I'll be vindicated very quickly. There's nothing for you to gain. We had a nice time. I'd like to remember it that way."

"They are," she agreed. "Easy to disprove." The sting of adrenaline in her system intensified as her head whirled. All she'd been thinking for three weeks was a replay of, *I have to tell him. He won't believe me. But I have to tell him...*

"And that's what you want?" he asked in a clipped voice. "For me to do a pointless paternity test? I've had a *vasectomy*," he reminded.

"So you said." It was a petty retaliation to let her skepticism hang in the air with such disdain. She added lofty, skeptical brows out of pure malice.

He snorted, and a brief flare of outrage in his expression warned her it was unwise to provoke such a powerful man.

With a shiver of apprehension, she looked to her unpainted nails. "All I'm saying is, if you're having sex, you should be careful."

"I *am* careful," he shot back. "I always wear a condom."

"Do you?" Because after the first one had broken, they hadn't bothered using one the second time.

He swore under his breath. "You want me to believe the *one* time I had unprotected sex, my vasectomy spontaneously reversed itself and I made a baby?"

"Believe what you want. I'm telling you there's a baby inside me and there's only one man who could have put it there. But listen—" She held up her hand, striving to remember what she'd told herself when she had made her plans to seek him out. "It's obvious you had the procedure so you wouldn't become a father."

It took everything in her to speak with equanimity. In the space of a single night, he had changed her life irrevocably, and yes, on some level she felt betrayed by his assurance she had nothing to worry about. She was pregnant, overwhelmed and frightened of the future. His disbelief crushed her, but—

"I'm not here to obligate you. I felt you should know the risk you're taking with future partners. That's all." She conjured her hard-truth smile, the one that said, *I know it sucks, but this is the law of the land.*

He stood very still, sharp gaze picking her apart as though he was trying to find her ulterior motive because there was no way she could be telling the truth.

"I also want to know..." Her quavering voice trailed off. This was so hard. Her hands were so cold and numb, she nearly dropped the handbag she'd forgotten she was holding. Her heart was in her throat. "Why did you have a vasectomy?"

"My body, my choice," he threw back at her.

"It wasn't a concern about...birth defects? Or anything medical that could affect a baby?"

His brows slammed together. "No."

She let out a shaken breath, one she'd been holding

since she'd learned she was pregnant by a man who had taken a drastic step while seemingly young and fit. His reasons were his business, but a grave health concern had seemed a strong possible motive. She hadn't been able to sleep, wondering what she and her child might face.

Her knees wanted to sag as that weight of apprehension lifted. Exhaustion was catching up to her. She nodded, all of her feeling as though she more floated than stood.

"Okay. Thank you," she said faintly.

It was done. Her chest felt hollow, but tears of reaction were gathering in her throat. Definitely time to leave. She would go back to her hotel and blame pregnancy hormones for her breakdown, not her own poor judgment in getting involved with another man who was leaving her feeling used and unworthy, but at least she had done what she thought was right.

"Enjoy your party." Moving to the stairs was a walk across hot coals into an unforgiving shower of icicle daggers.

She didn't listen for him to call her back. He didn't believe her and was leaving her to raise their child alone.

It was exactly how she had expected this to go and exactly what she wanted.

CHAPTER TWO

IT WASN'T POSSIBLE. It couldn't be.

That was all Jun Li could think. He'd been in this position before, and it had turned out to be false alarms. He'd made sure after the first time that it would *never* be possible again.

But her question about birth defects and her profound relief at his answer dragged cold fingers of apprehension down the insides of his rib cage.

Jun Li didn't know one way or another if he was a carrier for anything. He'd had the procedure to ensure he would never conceive any children, healthy or otherwise.

The sound of the door opening above him snapped him out of his stasis.

"Ivy."

Calling her back was an instinctive reflex. A man in his position developed enormous cynicism. He had learned to always be on guard against people looking for an angle to take advantage. Despite one night of intimacy, her claim was outrageous and not something his logical brain wanted to give credence to.

Even so, a barbed hook seemed caught in his flesh,

one that was being tugged as though it was attached to her. He couldn't let her leave. Not yet.

Not now that he'd seen her again.

What was this disturbing reaction he had to her? He'd been warring with himself for the last two weeks, ever since his PA had told him she'd reached out, asking him to get in touch.

He'd been tempted. Very tempted. They'd had an incredible night four months ago, the kind that had burned to the ground all his previous experiences. But they wanted different things. She was moving to Vancouver, and he hated the place. There hadn't seemed any point in returning her call.

Maybe it had been arrogant to assume her call had been an attempt to rekindle their brief romance, but what other reason would there be? He'd had a quick screen for STIs, and all his results were clean.

A pregnancy hadn't occurred to him because it wasn't possible.

The silence above had gone on so long, he reached for the house phone, lifting it with the intention of asking the concierge to stop her in the lobby.

As the phone gave a beep, he heard the door click closed upstairs. She came to the rail of the loft, very pale and looking at her hands, not at him.

He could taste her defensiveness from here. It made his chest itch with premonition, the kind that warned of an approaching danger. All his sinews felt taut, as though they pulled his organs out of place.

It's not possible, he kept insisting, but there she stood, waiting for him to tell her how futile this was. He couldn't make himself say it. The knowledge that she'd been about to leave without asking him for anything was pounding in his head.

Maybe she'd realized it was a lost cause?

He never wasted words, but he was never at a loss for them, either. He didn't know what to say to her, though.

"I need to use a bathroom," she murmured.

"There's one up there."

She disappeared, and a tiny part of him relaxed at having space to think while she remained within reach.

He replaced the phone and pushed his hand through his hair, forcing himself to drink in oxygen as he tried to make sense of this.

He was normally unshockable. Even the news that Ivy had turned up here hadn't been much of a surprise. Women went to ridiculous lengths to pursue him. Not because he was some sort of player who led them on. He had been very clear to Ivy that he was only offering one night. She could have turned down his invitation to come to his room. He loved sex, but he never pressured women into it. Too many wanted the one thing he would never give them.

But he possessed a stupid amount of money and knew how to groom himself into something women found attractive. Tsai Jun Li was a catch. All the headlines said so.

He didn't wish to be caught. He had enough responsibilities without a wife and child. As such, he was judicious about when and where and with whom he had affairs.

Ivy had been a spontaneous few hours outside his normal caution. He hadn't even wanted to be in Vancouver, the city where he'd spent much of his youth, none of it happy. One of the few people he trusted had become engaged, though. Jun Li knew he wouldn't make it to Kevin's wedding, so he'd attended the engagement party and used the visit to check in on some investments and sew up a few loose threads of his old life there.

Like him, Ivy had been slipping away early. She'd emerged ahead of him, so she hadn't been trying to run into him. In fact, she'd flushed with surprised pleasure when he'd appeared.

She wasn't the most glamorous or fashion-forward woman, more fresh-faced than conventionally pretty. Her curves were subtle and her height average, but she had projected an innate confidence that appealed to him. She had amused him with her little asides.

But even before she'd asked if she could use him to get over a breakup, he'd blown off meetings and other obligations to drive her up the highway that skirted Howe Sound. He never shirked his duties. That had been the tipoff that she was dangerous to him, but they'd wound up necking in a gondola and the passion that had flared between them had emptied his head of his usual guardedness.

When they broke apart, breathless and heavy-lidded, the tone of their day had shifted. The slow-burn sensuality was a tangible entity that had imbued every word and glance. He had touched her as he drove, setting a hand on her knee and playing with her hair. She had traced patterns on the back of his hand and sent him smoky looks of anticipation.

They'd gone to his hotel for dinner, and the walk to his room afterward had felt natural. Inevitable. By then, Jun Li had told her he was leaving early the next day and wouldn't be back. Ivy confessed to recently ending a difficult relationship. She was nervous to be with someone new but wanted to move on from her ex.

He'd done his best to ensure that night was the best sex she'd ever had. If he was honest, it had been the best of his experience, too. He recalled it far too often and in far more detail than was comfortable. It had taken every ounce of discipline he had to slip away in the early hours as scheduled, the image of her naked body burned into his retinas.

He'd been tempted to stay. He'd been tempted every single day to go back to her. Tempted to turn his back on his family and duties and contracts so he could immerse himself in the pleasure she gave him.

That's why he hadn't called her back. He couldn't afford those sorts of distractions.

Now he wondered if his night with her had been a gross misjudgment. Had he involved himself with an obsessive person who chased a onetime lover around the world to make an absurd accusation? Because if she wasn't that…

His chest tightened. He'd rather think that's exactly what she was.

What did that make him, though? He hadn't stopped thinking of her and was fighting a resurgence of lust now that he'd seen her again.

Does this look like a full-term pregnancy to you?

No. It had looked like breasts straining against silk, a hint of voluptuousness across her stomach and hips. Legs that went on for miles. Oh, he'd enjoyed those legs. His groin was prickling and twitching as he recalled how her knees had hugged him. Her thighs had been hot and soft against his lips when—

Stop it.

He gave his hair another rumple as perspiration rose on his scalp. This was the reaction she was looking for—off balance and distracted by carnality.

Was she that conniving, though? Kevin wouldn't have introduced them if Ivy was an opportunist. That meant Ivy had come all this way to tell him she was pregnant, and she genuinely believed he was the father.

"It's not possible," he insisted aloud.

He would have to prove it. To himself and to her. Muttering imprecations, he called his physician.

"Failed vasectomies aren't common, but the human body can heal itself in surprising ways," the doctor said, not reassuring him at all.

Jun Li made arrangements for a test and ended the call.

In a rare fit of temper, he shouted a profanity that echoed back at him from the vaulted ceiling.

Ivy heard Jun Li release a loud, blunt curse and continued to cower in the powder room.

When he'd called her back, tears had been pressing at her eyes. She'd barely managed to face him again and had been trying to regain her composure since. Everything was catching up to her, though. One train car of emotion was piling onto another until the pressure in her chest was threatening to explode.

From the moment she'd learned she was pregnant, she'd thought only about informing Jun Li. Getting herself into a room with him had required concentration and strategy, and maybe she'd used the challenge so she could focus on that instead of the reality of being pregnant by a stranger.

It was hitting her now though. Like a wrecking ball. Her pregnancy. His doubt. The fact she was on her own when she had allowed herself the most ridiculous fantasies, ones where he greeted her warmly and claimed this was what he'd always wanted.

What a silly fool she was!

And even though she had known he would have trouble accepting what she had told him, she felt deeply scorned by his skepticism.

"Ivy." A double rap of knuckles hit the door, sending a zing of adrenaline through her. "Are you all right?"

"I'm fine." *Liar*, she accused her reflection. She was ghost-white, skin going hot and cold. She was trembling in reaction and barely able to speak because her mouth was so dry. "I'll be right out." She dabbed a wet facecloth beneath her eyes, erasing the mascara leaking from the dampness that kept gathering on her lashes.

"I'll wait for you at the door." He wanted to escort her out after all, probably to ensure she didn't sneak into any more parties uninvited.

Her sinuses pooled with unshed tears, and she tried to swallow away the lump in her throat. There was no reason to be this upset. She would be fine. Other single mothers were in far worse circumstances than she was. Once she got home and told her father, she would be able to put her life in order.

She ruthlessly pushed her emotions into a knot behind her breastbone and walked out.

Jun Li's brows came together as he looked up from

his phone and saw her. He'd thrown on a suit jacket with a silvery sheen to it, making him seem all the more armored against her.

"Jet lag is catching up to me," she said to excuse her wretched appearance, even though she'd already slept off the worst of it and had only been awake for about five hours.

His mouth tightened briefly, and his gaze raked her as though her pregnancy bump was the size of a watermelon. "Will you allow a blood draw?"

"For a paternity test?" Her heart lurched. She had thought there was a reasonable chance he might ask for one. "I signed a release form with my doctor at home."

"My doctor will do it." He opened the door. "He's on his way back to his clinic."

"At this hour?" She'd lost track but thought it must be around nine o'clock.

"This can't wait. I need to know." He was watching her closely, giving her the impression he was offering her one last chance to change her story.

She nodded agreement, and his expression grew even more remote.

They rode the elevator in silence. A car was waiting as they exited the revolving doors of the hotel lobby. The tropical night air slid across her bare arms and legs like cool silk, then the quiet of the luxury sedan closed around her as she settled into the leather seat beside him.

As it pulled away, she tried to reassure him. "Jun Li, I was serious when I said I'm not asking you to *be* a fath—"

He held up a hand. "One step at a time."

He sounded so grave, she clenched her numb hands

on her handbag and let her mind empty. Gold and blue and red and purple lights flashed by. It might have been five minutes or an hour later when they were let out in front of a skyscraper. A security guard put them onto an elevator, and they were whisked up to an eerily silent foyer, where they were greeted by a man and a woman.

"Ah-Pei is our lab technician," the doctor said to Jun Li. "She'll show you where you can provide your sample." As Jun Li followed her down the hall, the doctor waved Ivy toward a lounge. "May I offer you tea?"

"I'm sorry, I thought we both had to—?" Comprehension struck. Jun Li was not providing a *blood* sample. Not yet.

Don't laugh. None of this was funny. But hysteria was ballooning outward from the emotions she was suppressing, trying to find release in one form or another, tickling and leaking between her ribs.

"Tea. Yes, please. Thank you," she accepted in a strained voice.

The doctor showed her into a comfortable lounge with a number of tea and coffee options. She kept it simple and chose a bagged herbal tea that she dropped into a cup while he started the kettle.

He chatted about his relatives in Toronto, but all Ivy could think about was Jun Li stroking himself to orgasm in another room. She recalled his shape in intimate detail. The heat and hardness against her palm. His swollen head against her tongue. The way he'd thrust with lazy purpose when he filled her and made love to her, telling her how good she felt squeezing him. The way he'd watched to ensure she was getting as much pleasure as he was. How he had waited for her to grow tense and breathless beneath him before he'd increased his speed and power so they shattered in unison...

From the depths of the corridor, she heard Ah-Pei say something that might have been, "Thank you." Was that what someone said under these circumstances?

Jun Li came into the room on a wave of energy that struck with hurricane force. The one glance Ivy dared send him noted a fading flush across his cheekbones. She went back to staring into the bottom of her cup.

"The results won't take long," the doctor said. "I'll be back shortly." He left behind a dense silence.

"There's tea," Ivy murmured, though she was only holding hers to warm her hands.

Jun Li ignored her and stood at the window, hands in his pockets, looking so remote she wasn't sure he'd heard her.

"I'm sorry if that was difficult," she was compelled to say.

"I practice. It was easy." He bit off the words, leaving no humor in the sarcasm.

She set aside her tea and covered her face with her warmed palms, leaning her elbows onto her knees, trying to hold everything *off*. The walls were closing in anyway.

"I didn't mean for this to happen."

"Nor I. Obviously."

His subdued fury shrank her farther into herself. She had convinced herself she would feel only an air of superiority at having done the right thing by informing him, not this squirm of anguish as though she'd caused him some kind of injury. Not this sting of being blamed for something that wasn't her fault.

"All these moving parts *and* you happened to be fertile? You'll forgive me for being incredulous."

"So was I." She straightened and folded her arms across her middle. "The signs were there right away, but you'd said it wasn't possible. I thought I was missing cycles because I was moving and interviewing for a new job." She'd been exhausted and nauseated, breasts sore, emotional. "When I finally went to the doctor, she looked at me like I was a complete idiot for not suspecting sooner."

"You're keeping it, obviously." His tone was ruthlessly neutral.

"Yes." Ivy had always wanted children. Her vision of a family had always included a loving spouse, but the fact this wasn't her perfect scenario hadn't given her any pause when she discovered she was pregnant. In fact, there was a certain relief in not having to wait until Mr. Right came along.

"Have you had any tests?" He turned to pin her with a penetrating look.

"Routine bloodwork and a scan to confirm my dates. Everything is normal. I'm not really a drinker and I take a decent multivitamin, so there doesn't seem to be any problem with my having taken so long to realize…" She trailed off as she heard footsteps approaching.

The doctor wore an unreadable expression as he entered. He looked to Jun Li.

Jun Li nodded to indicate he should speak freely.

"You are not sterile. If you were having difficulty conceiving, we would make a more thorough study of count and motility, but the fact sperm is present and appears viable leads me to conclude your vasectomy has failed. It's possible you're responsible for this pregnancy."

Responsible. Yes. That was the avalanche of emotion befalling Jun Li to the point he could hardly breathe. It was exactly as all-encompassing as he recalled from the first time.

"Shall we move on to the paternity test?" The doctor's voice came to him from a thousand miles away.

Jun Li nodded. His heart was thrashing so hard, he could barely breathe. His head felt as if it wasn't even attached. He moved with Ivy into a room where the technician poked them both in the arm. He barely felt it. This part was only a formality. If he could make babies, he had little doubt he was the father of Ivy's.

Condom?

What's the point?

A kick of fury with himself struck deep in his belly.

Ivy was watching him with a wary expression, perhaps anticipating some kind of blowup.

He wanted to point fingers and shout blame. He had never wanted to be in this position again. He'd taken the ultimate step to avoid it. Old betrayals and streaks of loss were fueling his anger, but he tamped all that down.

The only emotion that seeped through the cracks was guilt. Jun Li's life was one of enormous pressure and responsibility. He had never wanted to put that burden on his own child. It was a secondary reason he had made the decision not to procreate, and he'd always been comfortable with the action he'd taken.

A pregnancy had happened anyway. His baby, his *heir*, was on its way. There was no point in railing over how things were supposed to be. His energy would be far better spent working out how to fit two new people into the life he already lived.

"Paternity results will take a day or two," the doctor said as Jun Li closed his elbow over the cotton ball inside it.

He ensured the doctor had his direct number and escorted Ivy to the car.

"What hotel are you booked into?" he asked Ivy as he placed a call to his PA.

She told him, and he relayed an instruction to collect her luggage.

"What are you doing?" she blurted, cutting off a yawn she couldn't stifle. "*No.* I'm tired. I want to go to bed."

"I'm saving you the trouble of packing. You'll be more comfortable with me."

"You don't know that! My hotel is fine. I have to be up early for a cruise anyway."

"To *where*?"

"Around the harbor. I'm on a package." Whatever astounded look was on his face made her brow crinkle defensively. "It was the cheapest way to book a flight and accommodation. It's my last chance for a vacation before the baby."

He couldn't tell if she was joking or serious. "You really think I'm going to drop you and my *unborn child* at a three-star hotel and wave goodbye?"

"I assure you the baby's current accommodation is top-notch," she said snippily. "But I'm ready for bed. If you want to talk after you get the paternity results, text me." She took out her phone and offered it for him to put in his number.

He took it and pocketed it.

"Hey!"

"You didn't come all this way to talk me into a fertility test so you could trick me into believing I'm the father of a baby that isn't mine. I believe you. We have made a baby."

"Okay. Don't you have other women to check with, though? I'd rather not hang around listening to that." She kept her hand out.

"Are you trying to make my head explode?"

"Oh, were you a virgin that night? I'm the only woman you've ever slept with?"

She was serious. For some reason it infuriated him, probably because he hadn't been able to look at another woman since her.

"That night with you is the only time I've ever skipped a condom. I don't sleep with legions of women." And he'd already done a quick mental review. Of the handful of women since his last test three years ago, one was married with a baby of the wrong age and the other two were childless. "I'm confident you're the only woman I need to worry about."

"But you *don't* have to worry about me," she insisted. "You don't even *want* children!"

"That doesn't mean I don't want this one," he shot back, tearing a small hole inside himself with the admission.

Duty required him to claim his child, but he wanted their baby in ways he couldn't articulate. It was a disturbing sensation of something in him reaching out to her, *feeling* the connection that had been forged.

"You and I are inextricably linked now." It was unsettling. He kept thinking of the way she'd tilted him off his axis once. She was doing it again, this time in a far more jarring way. "We have a life to plan."

It bothered him that he didn't know what that would look like. It bothered him that he couldn't control any of this. She had stepped back into his life and had effortlessly thrown everything into chaos. Perhaps it wasn't intentional, but that was the deeply unnerving part of it. She wasn't trying to hurt him, but he was at her mercy.

The rational side of him was reminding him to proceed with caution, to work through this methodically. Other parts were taking leaps and bounds into the future, trying to anticipate every possibility and create contingencies.

That scattered approach wasn't helpful in the long run. He knew that. He couldn't let this turn him inside out. That's why they needed a plan.

"*We* don't."

He frowned at her. "I don't remember you being argumentative."

"Gee, I wonder what got into me."

That would have been a solid gold comeback if he wasn't straining to hold on to his patience.

Tension crept into her expression as she read his mood. Her mouth tightened.

"I keep telling you I didn't come here to obligate you. *We* don't have to make a plan because *I* have one. I'm starting a new job and will live in my father's house. It's probably not *your* version of five-star—" her brow lifted with derision "—but it's cozy and in a good neighborhood with lots of young families. My father is remarrying so I'll have a stepmother and two stepsisters who already have children ready to give me lots of advice and support. You don't have to be involved at all."

He was affronted by her desire to sideline him from their child's life. From hers.

"If you didn't wish for me to be involved, you shouldn't have involved me."

"That's not fair! We each had information we needed."

"So you thought I'd book a fresh vasectomy and that would be my last thought on the matter? What kind of man do you think I am?"

"I don't know, do I? *I don't know you.*" She slouched into her seat, reminding him starkly, "But that was the deal we agreed to. One night, no strings. So yes, I expected to inform you and go home to raise this baby alone."

"The strings are there whether we want them or not. Neither of us can walk away now."

CHAPTER THREE

"THAT WASN'T WHAT we agreed," Ivy insisted, but she was so dizzy from everything that had happened she couldn't work up a stronger retort.

When she had considered all the ways this might unfold, the most likely scenario had been that Jun Li would disbelieve and reject her. Perhaps he might have taken a test at some later date to reassure himself. When he realized he could cause a pregnancy, he might have reached out for a paternity test.

In her most romantic fantasies, she had let herself dream he would welcome the news with excitement and tell her he had been thinking of her all this time, the way she had been thinking about him. But if he hadn't sought her out to continue their relationship by now, she knew it was ridiculous to imagine he had any feelings for her beyond a nice memory.

No, she had expected that once he got over the shock and got some test results, he might take some financial responsibility while they proceeded with their separate lives. He didn't want children, so why exactly did he want this one?

"Look, I'm willing to talk about you having a place

in our child's life," she said tentatively. "But you understand I'm having this baby in Canada and raising it there, right?"

"No." His expression was grave. "We're marrying and raising this baby together. Here. Or Shanghai. Maybe both if the expansion is approved. We'll work that out later, but Canada is too far away."

"Exactly! That's where my life is. My family." Actually, only her father. The rest were in Hong Kong, but his decree was sending her into a tailspin. "I can't move here— Where are we going?" she asked as she realized they were crossing a bridge.

"My home."

"I said I wanted to go to my hotel. You can't *kidnap* me."

"I'm not." He gave her the annoying look men gave women that said she was overreacting.

"Well, you're taking me somewhere against my will. What else do you call it?"

He held up a hand as his phone rang. "I have to take this."

He accepted a call while she huffed and sat back again. He told someone in Mandarin that he would not be returning to the hotel. "Ask Mutya to make the closing remarks tomorrow. Let the board know I'll be in touch in the next few days regarding the expansion." He ended the call.

"Don't let me keep you. You seem busy."

"I am. But we have a lot to work out."

"Not tonight. I'm far too tired. And now I'll have to book a car to take me all the way back…" She opened her purse before recalling, "You have my phone."

"Ivy." He took the hand she held out.

Each time he touched her, helping her in and out of cars and elevators, he realigned the polarity in her, so she felt magnetized toward his stainless-steel core. Drawn to him.

She ought to pull away. *Don't let him take you over*, she warned herself, but her hand stayed in his while she quivered like a compass arrow.

"Did you not see the people photographing us in the lobby when we left the hotel? My staff is already fielding inquiries about who you are and why we looked so serious. It won't take any time for reporters to find you and begin pestering you. I'll take you on a day cruise if it's important to you, but everything has changed. You can't wander around anymore."

"I don't *wander*." She jerked her hand free of his, voice a jagged thing that she tried to steady. "I want to live my life. No one bothered us in Vancouver."

"Because I slipped in without my usual entourage or any publicity. I've been making headlines all week with this event. That means anyone with bills to pay will sell our image to the highest bidder along with whatever story they can make up to go with it."

"You don't know that."

"I do know that. It's happened when I've had completely innocuous lunches with female colleagues. That's why I'm careful about whom I date and how serious we get."

Her heart gave a little stumble at hearing he was discerning, even though it was more convenient to think of him as a promiscuous playboy who'd added her to his notched bedpost and forgotten her. At the same time, he was making it sound as if she would be treated like one of those poor women who dated a royal and became fair game for gossip sites.

Tears of frustration welled in her eyes. She wanted to insist on going to her hotel but was nervous now that she would be accosted. Besides, the car had arrived at a pair of gates.

"Why were you in that sky mansion if you have a house here?"

"Convenience. I took several meetings, and I don't like strangers in my personal space."

"I'm a stranger." An unwanted houseguest. A harbinger of life-changing news.

"You're family."

"I haven't agreed to marry you."

"You will."

She opened her mouth to accuse him of conceit, but he wasn't being cocky. No, his confidence was more that of a negotiator who would hammer out a deal however he had to. It was a lot harder to argue against that sort of certainty. It set a heavy rock in the pit of her stomach, because she wanted to insist there was nothing he had that she wanted while the firmness in his profile told her he would dig until he found something.

They parked, and the driver opened her door. Jun Li came around as she was straightening to her feet.

He was doing it again, standing there all effortlessly gorgeous and disconcerting, lights throwing mysterious shadows into his face. He seemed to take up all her vision and consume her thoughts. Despite her annoyance with him, she couldn't help thinking, *Now I'm here, will we sleep together?*

No.

She tamped down on her yearnings and made herself look past him so she wouldn't be so dazzled. She took in the modern architecture with its flared, pagoda-style roof over half walls dripping with greenery. Recessed lights emphasized the breezy openness of the home while creating a warm, inviting glow.

She'd always been a fan of reality shows about home makeovers and house hunting in exotic locales. Despite her misgivings about being here with him, she was intrigued.

The house was surrounded by flowering trees and twelve-foot walls disguised by vertical gardens, but who needed a backyard when there was a stunning courtyard in the middle of the home?

She goggled as she entered a high-ceilinged space where a slate pathway led between two shallow pools, one narrow and trickling with a wide waterfall that poured out of the wall, the other a much larger square pond.

"The housekeeper is off since I was planning to be in the city."

They were alone? She ignored the way her skin tightened with even more acute awareness of him.

"Your house has an island," she noted as she took in the circle of greenery in the bigger pool. It surrounded the trunk of a tree that grew toward a large rectangular hole in the roof. Posts made of warm, honey-colored wood contrasted beautifully with the tiles in the water that formed a muted mosaic of ivory and pale blue.

"This is a terrible house for a baby," she added, even

though she imagined a crawler would be in heaven, paddling about in that inch of water.

"I have others."

Houses? Well, that's what she got for being rude, she supposed.

On the far side of the tree, they arrived in an open-concept kitchen of stainless steel, clean lines and bar seating.

"I can't tell if we're inside or outside," she said as he guided her past a fireplace with a cozy lounge before it.

"This is outside." He walked her out to a backyard that was mostly water with a small strip of lawn at the base of the property's enclosure walls. The pool was for swimming, but the surface picked up the surrounding gardens and soft lights to become a reflecting pond. It was so serene, she could have cuddled into a corner on a lounger and fallen asleep right here.

"There's a dining room that way, and I use the guest room at the end as a home office." He led her up a flight of stairs.

Ivy felt as though she had climbed into the most luxurious treehouse ever built. Covered breezeways surrounded the courtyard. More greenery spilled off the ledges around her. When she went through a guest room to the balcony, she saw only a slope of trees and the boat lights on the dark sea beyond, giving the illusion they were the only house for miles.

He showed her two more guest bedrooms before waving her into the master bedroom.

"Help yourself to the jet tub if you want to relax." A huge bed dominated the center of the room, and an oval-shaped window over the sunken tub looked onto the treetop in the courtyard.

In her day job, Ivy often spoke to billionaires and powerful banking executives about wealth and investments and assets. She always told herself it was just numbers, but this was not numbers. Jun Li lived a life beyond anything she had ever conceived.

"I knew you were rich, but I thought you were... Kevin's friend," she said, shell-shocked, as she moved back into the bedroom and onto his private terrace, where he likely ate his breakfast at that teak dining table and read reports on that cozy outdoor lounge. More jungle greenery muted the noise of the outside world, and blossoms perfumed the humid air.

"Technically, Kevin is a consultant on retainer, but I consider him a friend." Jun Li joined her at the rail.

"You were the opportunity, weren't you?" she realized.

"I don't know what you mean."

"The one that made Kevin leave Hong Kong. He said a friend asked him to oversee some investments. That was you, wasn't it? That's why Kevin can afford a house in Point Grey."

Jun Li started to say something and seemed to change his mind before settling on, "My parents invested in several businesses and properties while I was schooling in Vancouver. I managed them when I lived there, but once I moved back to Shanghai and took over from my father, I needed someone I trust to look after things in Canada. Kevin wanted to return home. It was all done legally. I hope you're not suggesting—"

"No. Nothing offside, just..." She touched between

her brows, starting to feel like even more of an idiot for those fantasies she'd had. "He introduced you as his former roommate."

"We did live together. In the Point Grey house," he added after a very brief hesitation. "He was commuting from Surrey. He was sleeping in his car when he had to stay late then be on campus early. I was rattling around in that big house alone."

It wasn't uncommon for parents to buy a house for their child when they were schooling overseas. Most children were lucky to get a studio condo, not a sprawling property worth millions, but that wasn't unheard-of, either.

"Since I rarely visit Vancouver and your government frowns on houses sitting empty in that market, I made the house part of his compensation package." The way Jun Li spoke as though choosing his words carefully told her there was more to the story than Kevin's lab schedule.

"But—" She'd spent way too much time remembering him naked and not enough time looking at him now. She should have already noticed the subtle details like the fact his suit was tailored to his perfect frame at a cost that had to be in the high five figures, maybe six. "I overheard some of Carla's girlfriends talking about the house being a wedding gift, the kind you don't have to return. I thought Kevin bought it for her. You gave it to them, didn't you?"

"Again. All legal," he said crisply. "They already considered it their home, and they want to start a family."

"You gave them a *house* as a wedding gift. A Point

Grey *mansion*." She couldn't help the scoff of laughter. Her voice broke with a creak of hysteria as she added, "I bought them a smoothie bullet."

"I'm sure they'll use your gift every day as well. What point am I missing?" His tone of thick boredom got her back up.

"That there's no mystery as to why you were so adamant we would only have the one night together!" Heat pressed behind her eyes. She was such an *idiot*.

"We were both leaving town," he reminded her stiffly. "You were moving back to a city I dislike. There was no point in trying to date."

"You don't like Vancouver?" Her indignation at his extreme wealth hit a wall.

"Not particularly." His mouth curled. "I have no happy memories there."

"Wow." She dropped back a step, pain emanating from her breastbone as though he'd kicked her there.

He put up a hand. "Let me rephrase that."

"Don't bother. I'm well aware you're not happy about conceiving a baby. That's certainly not going to endear you to the place! Or me. I don't care if I get swarmed by paparazzi. I'm going back to my hotel." Her blood was sizzling with a need for flight as she looked for the bag she'd absently dropped on a lounger. She snatched it up, then remembered. "Give me my phone."

"You're shivering." He waved toward the open doors back into the bedroom. "Let's go inside. Warm up."

"I'm *upset*. I have a right to be, Jun Li!"

"Because I brought you here instead of the hotel? Because I gave Kevin a house? Because you think I'm a snob who doesn't date women in a lower income bracket than my own? You asked me to be your rebound. I didn't take advantage of you," he snapped.

"You said it was okay that the condom broke!" The words came out of her like they were pushed by fire.

His cheeks hollowed, and his nostrils flared as he drew a deep inhale.

"Let's take this inside. I have guards who patrol the grounds." He gathered her in the strength of one arm and guided her inside as though they were dancing, half lifting her so she felt as though her feet barely touched the floor.

She had forgotten he possessed such casual strength. It was unnerving to feel him so close again, surrounding her and awakening her to the feel of his touch. He'd given her such pleasure that night, but she'd been— what? Some final punctuation mark on his last night in a place he had hoped never to see again?

As they entered the bedroom, she tried to brush him off, but he was already turning away to slide the door closed behind them.

"What do you want?" he asked coolly. "An acknowledgment that I should have had myself tested more frequently? You're right. I should have. I was overconfident and you're bearing the consequence of that. Literally."

"At least *try* to sound sorry!"

Emotion flashed in his eyes, quick and searingly bright. It was as if she'd glimpsed the spark of an arc weld or the belly of an incinerator. Something that had the earth-splitting power of lightning, but was gone just as quickly, leaving outlines behind her eyelids while she blinked and his expression became a blank wall.

"Lamenting what should have been isn't going to

solve what is. Sometimes life happens. *Literally.*" He mockingly repeated himself. "And we're forced to make other plans."

"I don't want to make other plans! I was finally starting the life *I* wanted." She tapped between her breasts. "Not the one I was living for some man who doesn't care about me. I landed a good job in a city I *love*—" She hurled that at him.

He only gave an impassive blink, but a muscle in his jaw pulsed, telling her he wasn't as detached as he was trying to appear.

"I was finally going to be near my dad again and I couldn't wait to—to see what other fish were in the sea." She lifted her chin. "I wasn't going to marry the next man I dated. I was going to figure out who I am without a man cluttering up my head and emotions and decisions. I was going to get a *cat*. And learn to windsurf. Now I'm *pregnant* and I can't do any of those things."

He frowned with confusion. "Why can't you get a cat?"

"That's what you heard?" She shook her head in amazement. "Women aren't supposed to clean a litterbox when they're pregnant."

"So the housekeeper will do it." He shrugged. "Problem solved."

She wanted to scream; she really did.

"Problem *not* solved. We're strangers. I'm not going to marry you when we would only wind up divorced and I'll have to take my baby home anyway."

"Our baby." His lips thinned as though he was struggling to hang onto his temper. Jun Li wasn't particularly tall, but she was on the shorter side of average and he had enough height to look down on her. "It's unlikely I will ever consent to the baby living apart from me, so remove that option from your head right now."

"You're saying that if I want to be with my child, I'm stuck with you?" She set her hand against her navel. "No. I refuse to be in a relationship with a man who doesn't love me. Not again." She had worked too hard to crawl out of that vast empty helplessness to fall back into such a void. "You don't want me, otherwise you would have called by now. Did you know I've been trying to reach you?"

The flicker of compunction in his face and the hideously rational way he said, "Ivy," tore a gasp from her throat.

"You *did*." She moved her hand to put pressure over her heart, where it felt stabbed clean through. "You didn't want to see me again. You wouldn't be speaking to me right now if I hadn't come all this way and given you this news. Would you?"

"I was informed you'd left a message." His tone was remote. "On a geographical basis, it didn't seem like a practical relationship to pursue."

"Practical." Was that supposed to spare her feelings?

She squirmed internally, intensely hurt by his ignoring her message. He had been on her mind all this time, even before she'd learned she was pregnant. She had sworn to herself she wouldn't let her heart play tricks and see more interest and caring from a man than was really there, but when her pregnancy had been revealed, she'd been relieved. She'd had a reason to see Jun Li again. To see if they had something.

They had nothing. In fact, everything she had

thought she was building for herself was also not likely to manifest.

"This isn't practical, either." She could hardly see him through the tears of injustice that were gathering in her eyes. She was embarrassed he was able to hurt her so deeply and struck the dampness off her cheeks with impatience. "I won't marry a man who doesn't want anything to do with me. I won't move to a country where I don't know a soul. You can remove *that* option from *your* head. *Right* now."

CHAPTER FOUR

WHAT WAS HE supposed to say? That he had been tempted to fly back to Vancouver, where they could screw their brains out until nothing else mattered? That one night with her had been tripping him up ever since? That he couldn't help thinking these swipes they were taking at each other tonight were the flip side of their sexual chemistry? An expression of something they were refusing to acknowledge?

"This has ceased to be productive." Jun Li moved to yank back the covers on the bed, needing to end this before it turned into something else. "You're tired and—"

"Call me emotional. *I dare you.*" Her throaty warning made him straighten and look at her. Really look at her.

Jun Li had never seen anyone as overwrought as Ivy was right now. Blotchy streaks of red had come up against her bone-white complexion. Her lips were quivering, and the rest of her was trembling like a brittle leaf in the wind. She kept trying to sniffle back tears, but they were leaking down her cheeks in frayed tracks.

If he allowed himself to acknowledge it, he would admit he was stretched to his breaking point as well.

This news had rattled him to his very foundations. And because he was fighting his own existential crisis, he hadn't realized she was in the middle of one herself.

She looked as though she was facing a traumatic event. She was terrified, he realized. She was quite literally fighting for her life, and it set his heart on edge to see it.

"I believed you when you said I was protected. Do you realize that?" She spat it at him, and her bottom lip quivered.

The walls he was using to keep his own emotions at bay felt the impact of her fury. He knew that feeling of believing someone's word and learning later that trust had been misplaced. It was sickening.

"Everything inside me was going wrong. I thought I had the flu. I kept forgetting things. I was three months late and was starting to fear I would be diagnosed with something life-threatening. Because what kind of man would lie to a woman about something like that?"

The punch of accusation in her voice knocked his head back. "I didn't know."

"I didn't know that," she choked. "I sat there in that stupid paper gown and thought, *Here I am again, suckered by a man.* At some point you have to wonder, is it them or me? Was I *that* gullible? Had I slept with a man who gets his kicks running around getting women pregnant all over the world? The only way I could stomach how obtuse I'd been was to believe you didn't know." She threw that at him with a point of her finger. Then her shoulders slumped, and she seemed very small. "Which meant I had to tell you. So you wouldn't do this to anyone else. But you wouldn't even take my call.

You were prepared to call me cab a few hours ago." She flung out an arm. "Now you're trying to force me to *marry* you? Please tell me you can hear how ludicrous you sound."

He ran his hand over his face. He wasn't impervious to the distress she was showing, but one of them had to hold on to control. If he allowed himself to fall into a tailspin like the one she was on…

No. He locked down his emotions with ruthless control.

"I'm glad you went to all this trouble to tell me, Ivy. I am." It was true. And maybe he sounded overly reasonable and patronizing as he held on to this even, factual tone. It was a symptom of his determination to keep a firm grip on all this. "But it sounds as though you knew immediately that you were going to keep the baby. That's exactly how I feel. I want the baby. I want to do what's right. I'm not trying to force you into anything."

"You're trying to force me into your bed!" she cried.

"Because you're exhausted," he snapped, then reined in his temper. "We both need to take a breather while we think this through. We won't talk about this anymore tonight."

He could hear himself being more proprietary than he normally was. The buck stopped with him and he was always the final word on any decision, but he didn't shut down a discussion purely out of convenience. He typically listened and considered other points of view before closing a topic and moving on.

They were both at the end of their ropes, though. It made him do something else he normally wouldn't.

No one liked to be manhandled. He knew that, but Ivy was like a punch-drunk boxer, swaying before his eyes.

He picked her up and felt her stiffen in surprise.

As he rooted his feet, bracing for a fight, she released a whimper and threw her arms around his neck. She buried her face in his throat and, with a convulsive shudder, began to sob so hard, she made his heart lurch.

It took everything he had to stay on his feet. He had intended to put her in the bed, but he sank onto the edge of the mattress with her in his lap, all his control wavering like a house of cards in a hurricane.

He had done this to her. And well over a decade ago, he had felt exactly as sucker punched and overwhelmed as she did right now.

He adjusted her so she was under the open edges of his jacket and tried to warm her. He wasn't particularly affectionate, but instinct had him cradling her and rubbing her back, trying to offer comfort while the hard walls of his chest shook under the force of her anguish.

That old tightness, the one he'd conquered long ago, wrapped around his chest and constricted his breath. He brushed it aside and focused on calming her.

What could he say, though? She wanted him to say he was sorry, but it didn't feel like a truthful statement. He wasn't ready to examine why.

He couldn't promise her the life she had planned out for herself, only fragments of it. Everything had changed for both of them. That was harsh reality, and he was still reeling under that fact himself.

He had to say something. She was crying uncontrollably; her shoulders were racking under the force of it. Her pained, keening noises bruised places inside him.

"We are capable, intelligent adults, Ivy. We'll find a way to make this work."

"How?" she choked out with despair.

He didn't know, but he could make nearly anything work. His degree was in economics, but he had the brain of an engineer. He could rescue billion-dollar mega-projects and work around incompetent officials from foreign governments. Once he had learned that cooking was chemical reaction and sex was biology, he'd never had a problem accomplishing either successfully.

Her lack of confidence in him was an affront, but he hadn't given her much reason to believe she could rely on him, had he?

Don't worry. I've had a vasectomy.

She must have known he would distrust her news. She had planned to have his baby without his support anyway. That humbled him.

But he was offended, too. "You really thought you had to face this alone?"

"I want to," she insisted between her sniffles. "I want to live my life, not someone else's." She must have seen the irony in clinging to him while claiming a desire for independence, because she pressed a space between them and lifted her head.

Her expression was ravaged. His arms instinctually wanted to tighten around her again. Not just for her, but for himself. The constriction in his chest had eased while he held her, but now the magnitude of what they faced loomed over them like a thousand-foot tsunami.

He ruthlessly suppressed the shadows of apprehension it cast over him. He grabbed for normalcy and shifted to set her on the mattress, then rose to remove her shoes.

He set them aside, then draped the blankets across her. He would have turned out the light, but he realized she was fumbling with her dress beneath the sheets.

"Do you want a T-shirt?" He fetched one and waited while she sat up and rocked her hips to wiggle the dress free. He looped the T-shirt over her head, and she pushed her arms into the sleeves.

"Wait," she said when he started to put the dress on the chair.

She did a quick-change act, removing her bra with a release and a flick of the straps down her arms before she fished the beige satin from the neckline of the T-shirt. She handed it to him, then sank onto her back, sliding down and snuggling the covers up to her neck.

"I'm not usually like this." Her eyes were swollen, her voice rasped.

"I know." The day they'd met, there'd been a glow of optimism and conviction in her that had been exciting to witness. She'd been reshaping her life, and the self-assurance she had projected had been the kind only this sort of hit from left field could derail. "Good night."

He leaned down and set his mouth against her own. Soft—it was supposed to be a soft kiss of comfort and good-night.

Which was a lie, he realized as the lightning strike happened, piercing into his belly and setting his blood on fire. He had wanted to see if it was still there, and it was.

Her mouth trembled under his, and her lips moved in welcome, inviting a deeper kiss. He steeled himself to give more than he took, even though he wanted to plunder her. He wanted to immerse them both in that wild excitement that hissed and sparkled behind his eyelids, promising fireworks.

He settled for holding her cheeks and caressing them with his thumbs as he rocked his mouth across hers, stealing and imprinting and lifting his head long before either of them was satisfied.

Damn, that was hard. Which was terrifying. He set his hands in the mattress beside the points of her shoulders. She would consume him if he wasn't careful. There was no avoiding that conflagration, though. Not if he was marrying her.

He had to marry her. Letting her return to Canada so he could become some sort of long-distance father was unthinkable.

At least this way… No. He wouldn't allow the lust pooling in his groin to make rationalizations for him.

He had to marry her for the sake of the baby. That's *all*.

He turned out the light.

"I can't marry someone I don't know," she said into the darkness, sounding despondent. "How are you okay with even suggesting it?"

He didn't know that much about her, either. It concerned him that someone he didn't know could affect him on so many levels—sexually enthralling him and emotionally tying him in knots. She was even destroying his basic autonomy since, married or not, his life would forever be influenced by the connection they now shared.

Even so, he let his weight settle back onto the mattress near her hip, oddly fine with marrying someone he didn't know.

"My mother was sent to work in the country when she was seventeen. Do you know about that policy?"

"When all the students were sent to farms?"

"Yes. She was there for four years. One of her friends—she's my aunt now—talked up my father. She adores him. Most do, once they get to know him. He's the quiet sort who is always thinking. Highly intelligent and determined. My mother wrote to her parents saying he sounded smart and ambitious and kind. It was hard to move around in those days unless you had a good reason, like education or marriage. My mother wanted to return to Shanghai. My father wanted the opportunity of a bigger city. Their parents set it up, and he arrived on their wedding day. Both families were pinning their future on the marriage, but when my mother saw him, she learned he has bowed legs and a crooked spine."

Ivy drew in a sharp breath. "You said—"

"From a nutrition deficiency." He squeezed her arm through the blankets. "It's not genetic. No one else in my family has it. My mother was upset that she hadn't been told, though. She wouldn't have asked for the marriage if she'd known, but as it turns out, he *is* smart and ambitious and kind. They're very happy, but I wouldn't be here—or here—" He waved a hand through the shadows to indicate the house. "And neither would this baby—" He nodded at her middle. "If she had known everything about him before she married him."

"That is actually a very nice bedtime story," Ivy said in a voice thick with emotion.

He had meant it as a reminder to himself that his parents had faced far more dire struggles than he ever had. They had provided him an extremely comfortable life. The least he could do was pay it forward to his own child. It would cost him hardly anything.

Just a wedding ring to a stranger.

A muted bell sounded. "Was that a door chime?" Ivy asked with surprise.

"My PA with your things." He rose. "I'll be right back."

"You look unsure," Jun Li said.

Ivy was confused. She was pregnant, but she was about to have sex with Jun Li for the first time. They were in his hotel suite in Vancouver, an extravagant set of rooms that she poked around like a wary cat, pausing to view the lights on the Lion's Gate bridge through the wide windows before coming back to set her bag near the end of the sofa.

They'd just enjoyed an unhurried dinner on a terrace. Her skin felt sensitized by all the fresh air and sunshine. Her body was loose and relaxed thanks to a glass of wine and an excellent meal. When he'd invited her to his room and languidly kissed her in the elevator, she'd known this was exactly what she wanted.

"Would you rather I drive you home?" He paused in removing his jacket.

"I'm just nervous. I haven't been with anyone besides…" She was saying too much when she was trying to convince Jun Li she was intelligent and mature and self-possessed. She was trying to *be* all those things.

"You've only had one lover?" His dark brows lifted as he meandered toward her.

"How many have you had?" she challenged lightly.

Jun Li pursed his mouth. "Numbers don't matter," he decided and picked up her hand to kiss her palm.

His gaze grew somber as his breath warmed her hand. "But it does make me think a night like this is a more serious undertaking for you than it is for me. Perhaps we should hit pause."

"No, I know. You're leaving first thing. I don't expect to hear from you again. It's okay if you're, um, seizing the moment." She closed one eye.

"Is that what I'm seizing?" His mouth twitched with humor.

Each time she brought that ease to his expression, she felt a thrill of triumph. "If you want to."

"Because you want to get over your ex?" He slanted a shrewd look at her. "Or get back at him?"

"Over. I'm not going to throw you in his face. Ugh, no. I don't intend to speak to him ever again if I can help it." She revealed some of her agitation by rubbing her thumb over his knuckle. "But I was hoping to also… um…pick up a few tips on how this is done."

"Tips," he repeated with bemusement. "On seizing a moment?"

"Yes. Like do I protect my back? Lift with my legs? What's your best advice?"

He barked out a hearty chuckle at the ceiling then brought his gaze back to hers. The warmth and lingering laughter in his eyes made her heart soar.

"Ask for what you want," he suggested in a voice that managed to seduce and reassure her at the same time. "Leave if it doesn't feel right."

The fact he would say such a thing made this feel *so* right.

"I want to stay," she said firmly. "But I don't have a lot of experience. My relationship was mostly long-distance and…" She wrinkled her nose, appalled with herself that she was going to admit this, but she would never see him again. This was the magic of a one-night stand. No smirks or judgy looks to wake up to. What happened in this room stayed here. "I've never really seen the attraction in…" Hitting and quitting? "In a onetime thing. That puts all the pressure on the act itself, and I fear I'm boring in bed."

No laugh. He only tucked a stray lock of her hair behind her ear. "At no time today have I found your company boring. I can't imagine this will be any different." His gaze traced her brow and cheek and lips. "But just so I'm completely clear… What do you mean by boring? Are you saying you've never had an orgasm?"

"Only self-induced."

"Ah." His mouth twitched again at her phrasing. "I think that tells us which one of you was boring in bed. Allow me to show you all my best moves. Let's see if I can enlighten you as to the attraction."

She might have smiled or said something more, but his mouth lowered to skate across hers. It was a light question and an offer. A seal of a deal that asked if she was ready to embark.

She was. A tingle went through her from just that. All he had to do was touch his mouth to hers and she was quaking with excitement, releasing a soft moan.

A rumble of satisfaction resounded in his chest while his mouth opened across hers with more purpose, drugging her with his lack of hurry. He stroked her neck with his fingers as he slanted his head and deepened the kiss by degrees, delving and discovering and devouring her.

She could hardly breathe and set her hands on his

shoulders to ground herself, then immediately splayed her fingers to take in as much of his flexing strength as she could. The nervous part of her wanted him to hurry, and she tried to drag him closer.

He turned with her, pressing her back to the wall and coming with her to press his weight into her. He wove their fingers together as he brought her hands above her head while he continued to kiss her in that lazy, thorough way.

It felt a little dirty and sexy and wicked to be pinned like this. She tested his grip, and his eyes flickered open to meet hers. His mouth lifted slightly as he checked in with her. She didn't want him to stop, though. She drew his bottom lip into her mouth and sucked, letting him know she was enjoying their play.

With a growl, his thick fingers flexed into the tender notches between hers. His hips pressed with more purpose, and he kissed her harder. Desire flared hotter, burning from her middle and licking into her erogenous zones. She quit thinking about anything except the way his deep kiss sent trickles of electric sensations to the ends of her limbs. Her breasts felt so tight they ached, but the pressure of him against her was divine. He held her at his mercy, forcing her to withstand the pleasure he was giving her.

She didn't want to be passive, though. In an instinctive move, she lifted one leg and hooked her calf against his hard buttock, dragging him even closer. He was hard behind his fly. Really hard. With a slouch of his knees and a sweep of one hand, he brushed her skirt to her waist and pressed himself against her aching mound. His open mouth sucked against her neck, and she groaned with gratification.

He released her other wrist and ran both hands all over her, making her buzzing tingles turn to bright heat and snaps of heart-skipping joy. Oh, his touch felt good. She squirmed in ecstasy while that pulsing ache in her loins intensified. She was growing damp and needy for the feel of him there.

She brought his head back and kissed him, holding the sides of his head as she blatantly thrust her tongue into his mouth. She had never had much luck being the aggressor, but he seemed to love it. He groaned and sucked on her tongue and palmed her breast. He began rocking his hips against her, inciting her desire to greater heights. The knot of arousal in her middle tightened, building with promise.

This was what the attraction was. She wanted to hurry to the good part, but she also wanted to stay like this, fondling and playing her tongue against his and savoring the streaks of need that were flooding her loins with anticipation. The build was driving her wild, doubling and redoubling, and he was with her every step of the way.

Now his hand was under the skirt of her dress, stroking her thigh, taking his time when he must know she would *die* if he didn't touch her more intimately.

"Jun Li," she pleaded, dimly aware he would drop to his knees in a moment and give her a *very* flagrant lesson in how gratifying it was to experience an orgasm that was bestowed rather than one she—

"Ivy." The world swiveled. Her eyes opened to darkness.

Her blood was screaming with arousal, her skin damp with perspiration, her body acutely stimulated.

Her hands were filled with his naked skin as he

painted her against the front of his body. His chest mashed her swollen breasts through the thin layer of his cotton T-shirt.

"You're having a nightmare."

No, she wasn't. She was on the brink of orgasm. Practically having a wet dream.

"You're safe," he said, smoothing her hair.

She should have rolled away and let the dark hide her, but she was so inflamed, she stretched herself in a line against him. Her arms slid up to twine around his neck.

If she hadn't felt him stiffening inside his boxers as she moved against him, she wouldn't have opened her mouth on his throat, but she did. And she did. She licked at the soft flesh under his jaw, nibbled at the sandpapery stubble and searched for his mouth while rubbing her breasts against him.

"What—?" His voice garbled a curse as her palm swept across his chest, scraping his beaded nipple. She came back to finger and rub at that tight pebble while her leg climbed to his waist so his growing erection pressed where she was throbbing so agonizingly.

As their mouths fused and his hair sifted between her fingers, his hand clasped her buttock and he thrust against her, fully hard and steely strong. She ground her aching flesh against that thick ridge.

It took only a few pulses of pressure and friction and the libidinous intrusion of his tongue making love to her mouth. The intense golden knot deep in her belly became white hot and suddenly released streaks of joy through her whole body. She moaned, feeling herself break free.

As rolling waves of orgasmic pleasure rocked her,

colored lights flashed behind her clenched eyelids. She broke their kiss to catch ragged breaths between her cries of release.

Everything in Jun Li wanted to drag away the scraps of cotton between them and thrust into her. Was she even awake?

He was. The way she'd rubbed up against him and licked his skin had got him so hard so fast it hurt. Now she was shuddering and making the most erotic noises. His heart was slamming, and his instincts were screaming at him to roll atop her and sensually devour her. He wanted to thrust deep. Claim. Bring her back to explosion and empty himself inside her.

He might have, but she moaned again, this time with tortured realization. She ducked her head and brushed at his arms, trying to roll away.

His muscles reflexively tightened before he overrode his lizard brain and released her. His senses were so heightened, he swore the scent of apricot and vanilla off her skin was pure pheromones. All he could think about was licking every inch of her.

Could she even have sex?

"What just happened?" His voice grated against his own ears, and he thought he heard her sniff in reaction.

"Nothing. A dream. Go back to sleep."

"About who?" She'd said his name, but had she been dreaming of someone else?

He reached out until he found the bumps of her spine. She was curled up like a pangolin.

"I don't want to talk about it," she said in a voice muffled by pillows and blankets. "Don't make me."

Don't make her talk? Or have sex? He wouldn't, but, "Are you okay? Is there any pain? Is the baby all right?"

"Oh my *gawd*. Yes," she hissed with another mortified noise and wriggled farther away on the mattress. "Why are you even here?"

He'd come back after an hour of imparting instructions to find her fast asleep. He'd left her case in the closet, out of the way so she wouldn't trip if she happened to rise in the night, then debated whether to crawl into bed with her.

"I wasn't planning to touch you. I wanted to be here if you woke up confused." Or tried to slip away in the night.

"Well, go sleep somewhere else. Or I will."

He should. He rarely slept with a woman, finding it disturbing. He had enough on his mind without being concerned he was flinging out an arm or snoring loud enough to wake a partner.

As he lay there debating, he heard her shaken breaths relax and even out with slumber.

Must be nice, he thought wryly. She was satisfied and he was far too aroused to drop off. He should go to another room, relieve himself of this erection and get some sleep, but he didn't want to leave her.

And therein lay the reason he should.

He didn't understand this power she had to pull him in and have him casting away his usually inviolable self-discipline.

Although was it really such a surprise when she had come apart with such abandon a few minutes ago? He gave himself a brief squeeze, both tortured and delighted to know she was still capable of such abandonment. Their night in Vancouver had been *hot*.

He relived it often, especially the part where she'd run her hands through his hair while he pleasured her with his mouth. The act always turned him on, but her response—the noises she'd made, the way she'd melted against his tongue and offered herself so unreservedly—had made him wild. When she had shattered, he'd almost lost control himself.

In the aftermath, she'd been so breathless and limp, he'd carried her to the bed like a warrior claiming spoils.

He'd had to spare a moment to dig through his luggage for a condom, though. He had an allergy, so he used nonlatex. He'd been told years before that they weren't as reliable, but he'd never had one break. The one he'd used that night had probably been expired, now he came to think of it. He hadn't bothered to check; he'd been so single-minded about getting back to her.

She'd been delightfully emboldened when he joined her, both of them hurriedly stripping each other between kisses.

"It's okay if I don't come again," she'd whispered against his mouth while they knelt on the bed, kissing and caressing. Her touch across his back while her breasts grazed his chest had made him want to close his eyes and savor the dual sensations. "I just want to feel you inside me."

"Oh, blossom. I can do better than that. This is supposed to be the best sex of your life." The play of his fingers in the dip of her lower back had made her shiver and catch her breath.

"The bar was low. This is already the best ever."

That playfulness amid the passion was unique to him. He'd found it as compelling as the rest and had thrown himself into worshipping her soft skin and pert nipples and quivering stomach, her tender thighs and the honeyed place between.

He squeezed himself again, throbbing at the memory of pressing her onto her back and rising over her. All the play had stopped then because thrusting into her had been all-encompassing. Profound.

If he'd had the discipline, he would have made love to her all night, the act of slowly pumping into her had been so intense and delectable. He wasn't superhuman, however, and it had been all he could do to wait for her.

He hadn't been so mindless that he hadn't felt the condom break when he'd picked up speed in his final strokes, though. He recalled exactly that flash of realization as it was happening. They'd both been on the verge of a powerful, mutual orgasm. It wasn't just his pleasure he would have curtailed, but hers.

He'd let desire override him and gave a last thrust that caused them both to hit their culmination. It had been spectacular. The most intense climax of his life, tearing a shout of gratification from him. The sensation of her wet heat squeezing his naked flesh had taken him to even loftier heights.

Had that moment of ecstasy been worth the consequence? He could rationalize all he wanted that he hadn't believed there could *be* any consequence. He knew his own health was good and hadn't had any concerns about Ivy's. The truth was, however, he could have pulled out and he hadn't. *He* had allowed this pregnancy to happen.

In fact, he'd damned near ensured it. A few minutes

later, when he had told Ivy what had happened, she'd asked if she should visit a pharmacy.

"Don't worry. I've had a vasectomy."

"Really?"

He'd heard the curiosity in her question but had only said, "It's not something I advertise. I'd rather you kept it to yourself."

"Of course."

They'd dozed, and when she'd risen to use the bathroom a while later, he had urged, "Stay the night. I have to leave early, but order room service when you wake. Use the spa."

She did stay but didn't add anything to his bill. When she had rejoined him in bed, he'd asked if he should use another condom.

"What's the point?" she'd asked ruefully.

He'd taken that as license to go without, and this was the result.

He looked across at the shadowed shape of her beneath the covers.

There'd been so many moments when he could have made more sensible choices and hadn't. He would love to blame her for that, but it was all on him. He'd discarded his normal sense of caution and adherence to duty for sex. Really great sex, sure, but at what cost?

It added another layer to his sense of accountability. *They* had had sex, but *he* had made that baby. There was no question that he would take responsibility for both of them.

CHAPTER FIVE

IVY GRADUALLY BECAME aware of Jun Li speaking to a woman in muted tones. Dishes softly clanked. They were on the terrace, she deduced as she crept toward wakefulness. The noises were drifting in with the scent of fresh morning air, coffee and eggs.

She would love coffee, but she was settling for tea these days, usually herbal. She'd kill for a cup of orange pekoe, though.

She stretched and rolled onto her back, aware of a lingering lassitude that made waking in such a comfortable bed pure hedonism. She couldn't remember when she'd last slept so hard and woken this content. Probably the morning after—

Oh no. A ballooning horror gripped her as she recalled what had happened in the middle of the night. Please let it be a dream. *Please.*

It wasn't. She swallowed a groan of chagrin and brought her knees up as she rolled to bury her stinging face in the pillows. She wanted to die. To draw the covers over her head and stay in this bed forever.

She would have if she hadn't needed the bathroom so pressingly.

With a whimper, she lifted her head to ensure no one was around. Damn him, Jun Li had thoughtfully left a silk robe with a cherry blossom print on the foot of the bed.

She snagged it on her way to the bathroom. Why, why, *why* had she thrown herself at him like that? She'd practically attacked him!

In the bathroom, a brand-new toothbrush sat beside the sink along with geranium-scented shampoo, conditioner and body wash.

Ivy used the toothbrush then took the rest into the shower, mostly to put off seeing him. The warm rain from the sunflower head washed the dullness from her brain but none of the ignominy from her conscience. After drying off, she combed out her wet hair and moisturized every inch of her body with a luxurious green tea and lemongrass–scented lotion until she had run out of excuses to avoid him.

Also, she was starving.

Which didn't mean joining him on the terrace was easy. No, it might only be three steps to the table, but it was a mile-long walk of shame.

"Good morning." He wasn't openly smug, but he watched her with a morning-after acknowledgment of intimacy that he hadn't hung around long enough in Vancouver to let her witness.

"Thank you for this," she murmured of the robe, hyperaware that she was naked beneath it.

"More clothes are being delivered. I wanted to let you sleep, but I didn't want you to have to come looking for me amid the crowd."

Crowd? "I have clothes. Don't I? I thought my luggage arrived last night."

"Your things are in the closet, but you'll need a full wardrobe. Twice, I'm told, since maternity wear is its own thing." His attention swept down to where the lapels of the robe exposed her upper chest. "I've been reading about how a woman's body changes during pregnancy. It's remarkable."

Still worried that her orgasm had harmed the baby?

"I packed maternity wear. I didn't wear my dress last night because it kind of gave the game away."

She accepted the plate he uncovered. It held peeled and halved boiled eggs with grilled avocado, cherry tomatoes, a bowl of tropical fruit, a side of subtly spiced noodles and a small banana. She would never get through it all, but she was hungry enough to give it a shot.

"You'll need more than one dress. The delivery is all ready-to-wear, but my mother is looking forward to introducing you to some of her favorite designers."

"You told your mother about the baby?" She nearly bobbled the plate and set it down with a clack. "I was going to tell my father when I got home. She won't post it online, will she?"

"No. I was going to do that as soon as I asked you if there was anyone you needed to notify first. We'll call your father after breakfast." He glanced at his watch. "Before it gets too late there. Is he well? Can he travel within the week?"

"To where?" Her nerveless fingers lost control over her chopsticks and sent a cherry tomato rolling.

"Shanghai." He neatly caught it as it fell off the table. "For our wedding." He popped it into his mouth and chewed. "Next Friday."

"I told you I won't marry you!" Last night began to seem like an even bigger mistake than it obviously was. Had he read it as some sort of capitulation?

"Marriage is the most practical solution."

"For *you*."

He had started to pick up his coffee but set it down again. "I had hoped once you slept on it, you'd see the advantages to you as well." The way his gaze flashed into hers said, *I remember everything.*

The great big lumbering elephant she'd been trying to ignore was suddenly tapping her shoulder with its trunk.

Ivy blushed. Hard.

"Just to be clear, I will never see my child as something that should provide me advantages. Certainly not material ones like a wealthy husband. Marrying up has never been a goal of mine. I won't use my baby to do it."

"I thought when couples fought over money, it was because there wasn't enough. If I were middle-class, would you accept? Are you suggesting I divest of a few zeroes to earn your hand?"

"I'm saying you wouldn't be asking for my hand if I wasn't pregnant." She pinched a bite of mango and ate it.

"I wasn't going to marry anyone. Don't take it personally."

She snorted. "It feels personal when you're asking me to marry you and I know it's the last thing you want. At least tell me why you were avoiding it."

"It simply isn't—wasn't—" he corrected "—something I wanted for myself. I'm already responsible for hundreds of projects, thousands of jobs and billions of dollars. I respect how hard my parents worked to build what I manage today, but I never wanted to put this much responsibility onto my own child. I…" His cheek ticked, and he stole a moment to sip his coffee before admitting, "I had a scare with a fellow student my last year of high school."

"You got someone pregnant?"

His fingertip tapped his cup before he said flatly, "No. But for a short while I believed I had."

Ivy stopped eating and watched his gaze focus on the skies over a distant horizon.

"A fellow student?"

"Yes. My first relationship. First time living alone. I wasn't nearly mature enough to become a father. When she told me, I was terrified. I called home to tell my parents but didn't get a chance. My father's health had taken a downturn. The semester was almost finished, so I said I'd be home soon within a couple of weeks, but I didn't know what I was going to do."

"Was it a false alarm?"

"No. She was pregnant, but it wasn't mine. When I asked her to come to China with me to meet my parents, she confessed there was another man in the picture. He was her manager at the fast food place where she worked after school. He was a few years older, engaged to another woman. He had told her to pretend it was mine because he didn't want it, and look at all the money I had. It was such a mess." He used a light tone that dismissed the whole thing as the hijinks of youth.

Ivy wanted to take his hand and say *Don't do that.* "It was your first love. You must have been crushed."

His face hardened beneath the stubbornly impassive expression he was maintaining. "The not knowing whether it was mine was torture. Lucky me, I had the kind of money to pay for a high-quality paternity test. When we learned I wasn't the father, she went away to stay with relatives."

"Why do I get the feeling you're still wondering if you should have married her anyway?" she asked gently, but with a pang behind her breastbone for the intense young man he must have been.

"She cheated and that's hard to forgive, but she was a child, same as me. That other guy was old enough to know better," he muttered.

"He was her boss."

"That too." His lip curled in disgust. He sat up straighter, giving a small shrug as if divesting himself of the past. "The whole thing left me furious and disillusioned. I had been prepared to cut my education short to become a husband and father. I felt manipulated and realized what a target I had become because of our wealth. How vulnerable I would be if I had a child."

Those sobering words made her hear again *You can't wander. I have guards.* Was that why he was so adamant they marry? He was worried about them?

"My father was still ill, and I was facing the formidable task of taking over from him sooner or later. Of course, my parents have always expected me to marry and have a child someday, but I couldn't see a time when I would be prepared to take on a family when I had so much to shoulder as it was. I couldn't see wanting to put that burden onto my own flesh and blood. When I got to university, I had a student doctor perform the procedure."

She quirked a brow. "I have to ask. Are you sure it was done correctly?"

"Fair," he snorted. "Given my age, he used a technique that was supposed to be reversible, but I did the tests afterward. Every year, for the first while. I only fell down on it the last few years because I've been busy with work and thought... Well, we've seen what happens when we get complacent, haven't we?"

"I'm still surprised." By all of it. "I'm shocked you believed me enough to get tested, given you went through all that."

"You were too upset not to take you seriously," he said soberly. "And I had to know. Please don't mention any of this to my parents, though. I never told them about the scare."

"Of course not. How long had you been in Canada when it happened? You said it was your first time living alone." Had he been sowing the wild oats of a young man away from home for the first time?

"Six, almost seven years."

"Oh. Wow. Most of the foreign students I know didn't come over until they were fifteen or sixteen. You were *ten*?"

"Eleven. When the opportunity came up to send me to Canada, my parents jumped on it. They could barely afford the payments, but they didn't know how long the window would be open. It began as a way for me to learn English, but as their fortunes grew, I was able to help with their early investments there."

"Like Kevin's house?"

"Exactly. Many eggs, many baskets, has always been my father's philosophy. And my time there allowed me to take advantage of a fast track to permanent residency."

So much for dangling that as an incentive to live with her in Canada.

"But you weren't happy there," she recalled from last night.

"No." He dropped his gaze, giving her the impression he was not telling her the whole truth when he said, "I was young to be sent around the world away from my parents. I thought it would be an adventure, but the culture shock was enormous." His cheek ticked as though he was revisiting a difficult memory. "After I was getting As in English, I could have told them I didn't want to go, but I knew how hard they had worked to give me that advantage. My father is in pain every day of his life. My mother spent years away from her own family. Surely I could handle a bit of rain and birthday parties without my cousins if it meant I could provide all of us more options later."

"You were homesick," she realized.

"It lessened over time, but…" He shrugged it off. "I knew Canada would never be my home, so I didn't allow it to feel like one. It was a place where I worked, preparing myself to take over from my father. The day you and I spent together was probably the most carefree I have ever been in that city. I still feel a dereliction of duty over it."

"I can't tell if that's a compliment or a complaint."

"It's a concern. I can't bring myself to complain." His gaze heated, and she blushed.

Last night's passion was suddenly here between them again, but the housekeeper appeared with freshly squeezed juice for Ivy and an apology that she directed at Jun Li.

"Your assistant asks if you have read his text? He says it's urgent."

Jun Li made a face and picked up the buzzing phone he'd been ignoring. He tapped the screen, read, then said, "Hmm. Your father is receiving inquiries from the press. When you didn't answer his calls or texts, he tried to reach you at the hotel. He was told you checked out, but you haven't notified him where you've gone, so he has threatened the hotel manager with a call to the Canadian Embassy if he doesn't hear from you soon." He withdrew Ivy's phone from his shirt pocket. "My bad. I turned it off so it wouldn't wake you."

Ivy stared at her phone as if he was pointing a loaded weapon at her.

"What am I supposed to tell him?"

Jun Li suggested she get dressed first and took her to see the clothes he'd had delivered to the basement.

Ivy came down the stairs to a big, comfortable lounge with an overstuffed sectional that faced a big screen. A wet bar was tucked into a corner on the far side of a pool table.

The top half of one wall was glass that looked onto the bottom of the pool, allowing the sunshine beaming into the water to bounce in and leave patterns on the floor. When she washed her hands at the sink in the powder room, instead of seeing herself in a mirror, she could wave at whoever was swimming.

A child would find that infinitely amusing—and probably wash their hands more often, Ivy thought wryly.

This home was actually a work of art, and she was falling in love with it by the second.

She glanced into a fully stocked gym on her way to the other spare bedroom, which had been filled with racks of clothes. Jun Li was already sifting through the selection.

Ivy normally hated salespeople trying to guess what she might like. It felt especially strange to have Jun Li hold things up to her and replace them on the rack before she could decide one way or another.

"Do you want me to look a certain way?" she asked with indignation.

"No," he said with absent surprise. "Pick whatever you like. I just like shopping. It's my vice. In high school, I didn't go to parties. If I wanted to be around people, I went to the mall."

She wondered if that was why he had insisted they browse the gondola gift shop when they'd been enjoying their stolen day in Vancouver. He had bought her a crystal sun catcher and made a remark about her needing luck to catch any sun if she was moving to Vancouver, but he'd offered it as a housewarming gift anyway.

She had thanked him with a kiss that she still remembered as passionate enough to curl her toes. She had planned to put his gift in the baby's room.

"Try this," he coaxed, snapping her out of her reverie.

It was a flapperesque drop-waisted sleeveless dress with a sailor collar.

"I usually wear clothes that are more classic and conservative." But she was almost always looking for something that could double as work wear, nothing that was purely for the pleasure of looking cute.

She tried it and, as she smoothed the dress down her

hips, instantly felt more comfortable in this changing figure of hers.

"It suits you." The admiration in Jun Li's gaze made her even more conscious of her body. Of the fact she was bustier and had hips and he seemed to think that suited her, too.

Their gazes tangled. The way his gaze dropped to her mouth made her lips part and her breath stutter.

In the dark of his bed, he'd kissed her as though starving for her. His whole body had been taut against hers, his fingers digging into her buttocks as he rocked her world.

She watched the temptation fog his gaze. Her skin tightened. She licked her lips, anticipating the feel of his mouth crushing the tingles from her own.

If he had kissed her right then, demonstrating that he couldn't resist her any more than she could resist him, it would have gone a long way to reassuring her that she hadn't made a complete fool of herself last night.

But just as his hand came up and he looked ready to cup the side of her neck and kiss the daylights out of her, he stepped back and dropped his hand to his side.

"Almeida. Come in. Ivy, this is your stylist. I'll wait upstairs." He disappeared.

Almeida smiled knowingly as she touched a flat iron to Ivy's hair and gave her a few swipes of makeup. Ivy tried to quell a blush that was both unrequited lust and anguished embarrassment that she couldn't hide how she was reacting.

She came back upstairs to find Jun Li holding a meeting with a half dozen faces at the dining room table. He introduced her to everyone. One was his PA from last night, and another was a public relations person who came outside with them and photographed them sitting side by side on a wicker love seat with the lush garden wall as a backdrop.

"I thought we were calling Dad? Why is this happening?" she asked through a gritted-teeth smile.

"For the announcement."

She snapped her head around. "I haven't agreed to anything."

"Not yet," he allowed. "But when you do, the photographs will be ready."

He was back to railroading her. Why? Because he'd seen how weak she was when he had almost kissed her? Or because of the way she'd behaved in the middle of the night?

Her hand curled into a fist beneath his. "You're taking things for granted. Last night didn't mean what you think it did."

He lifted his hand from hers and jerked his head at the photographer. "Leave us."

The photographer scurried away, and Ivy sat there with her face on fire, her flush stoked by fury and hurt and humiliation. A silence pulsed between them.

She could tell he was looking at her, but she refused to look at him. She stared into the stillness of the water.

"What exactly do you think I'm taking for granted?" he asked dangerously.

"That I'm going to marry you just because I—" She couldn't say it. She had to clear a thickness from her throat in order to speak at all. "Last night was just… hormones." She flicked a glance to ensure there weren't any housekeepers or any of the other staff lurking and overhearing. This was humiliating enough. "It's like I have an amplifier inside me. When I'm tired, I'm exhausted. When I'm hungry, I'm famished. I'm trying really hard to be rational over how things are going between us, but I'm fighting tears every second along with an urge to scream. That's how pregnancy affects me. I'm emoting for two. You could have been anyone last night." That was a blatant lie, but it felt like the only way she could save any face.

"Is that right?" He released a jagged, humorless laugh and set his arm behind her on the back of the love seat so he was angled toward her. He touched her chin, urging her to look at him. "Because if you're telling me that pregnancy has made you so amorous you'll wake a man up for sex and come apart before you're even naked, you'd better believe I'm going to be the man in bed beside you."

Her heart hitched and she wanted to pull away, but their stares were locked again, and his thumb was playing across her bottom lip, making it feel swollen and buzzing.

She saw the hungry wolf in him rising, but his nostrils flared, and his expression hardened.

"We'll save it for our wedding night, though. Incentive," he added in a drawl.

Again, she was struck by how easily he could take or leave her while she was ready to fall into his arms. She forced herself to drag forth her own dry chuckle.

"I won't marry you for your money. You think I'm going to marry you for *that*? Good luck."

His hand came back to the side of her face and his head swooped down. His mouth crashed over hers, not painfully, but devastating all the same. His lips swept untamed over hers again and again, exploding her world. He erased her mind of everything but him, exactly as he had from the first time he'd kissed her when they'd stood on a platform three thousand feet in the air.

Her response had nothing to do with her pregnancy. He built her up and tore her down and remade her in a matter of heartbeats. Made her his. Again. Still. Because she'd been his since the first time he'd raked his lips so tenderly across hers, whether she wanted to give herself to him or not.

As he drew away, she realized her hand was clenched around the strength of his wrist. Her lips clung to his, and her eyes felt too heavy to open. Breathing was something other people did because they didn't know how wonderful it was to be smothered by his mouth.

A final touch of his lips to hers that was almost a peck of comfort. His voice was a rumble of masculine strength and suppressed desire.

"Yes, blossom, I do think you'll marry for that."

A wounded gasp left her before she could catch it back. His profile tightened slightly. Compunction? Something else that she couldn't read because she was so angry, her eyes were blurring with unshed tears.

"Because *I* will," he admitted in such a stark, impactful voice he nearly knocked her into the pool with it. "So let's call your father and tell him our happy news."

CHAPTER SIX

THEY CALLED HER father from Jun Li's office, a sparsely furnished space with teak floors and a New Age desk that looked like the metal had poured off the one side to create its own support. A wall of locked glass protected some discreet filing cabinets along with rare books and a few small and likely priceless sculptures.

Despite what he'd said by the pool, Jun Li didn't force the issue in front of her father. He sat beside her and let her do most of the talking.

Her father's eyes welled with happiness at the baby news, and Ivy said she and Jun Li were still discussing how they would proceed. She promised to call him back soon.

As she set the phone aside, she couldn't face the questions in Jun Li's expression. She walked out to the pool, where she kicked off her slippers. She plopped down on the edge to dangle her feet in the water, trying to recalibrate. Trying to think.

But think about what? She knew what Jun Li expected her to do. She knew what her father expected. She knew what the whole world would expect once it was revealed she was carrying Tsai Jun Li's baby. She knew what she would expect of herself if this was a hypothetical situation posed as a parlor game.

Reality was far more complex and arduous.

She was so deep in thought, she only distantly heard Jun Li say, "Do you see anything you like?"

His question didn't make sense. A shadow unexpectedly descended in front of her face. It startled her so badly, she reflexively struck at whatever it was, sending it flying into the pool.

Sparkling droplets flashed as they scattered and rained into the water with soft plinks. Something square and flat landed on the surface and sat there like a boat that was taking on water.

"Apparently not." Jun Li straightened and peeled his shirt up and off, blinding her with his tawny, muscled chest and small dark nipples and abs that were so perfectly defined, they were like stacked blocks of store-bought masculinity.

"What was that?"

"Rings." He opened his belt and peeled himself down to his boxer briefs, stepping out of his slippers.

"Like…diamonds?" She looked with horror into the settling water to see glints of ice and gold sitting on the bottom of the pool. "Why would you stick them in my face like that?"

"Why would you throw them in the pool?" He took a breath and dived in without waiting for her answer. As he skimmed the bottom, his hands swept out a few times before he surfaced to grab the sinking tray.

He swam over to set the tray beside her. It still had a couple of rings stuck into its velvet slots. He poured several more into her hand.

"Is the jeweler still here? What if we don't find them all?" She was so embarrassed.

"Are *we* looking for them?"

"Yes, I'm the spotter. You missed one over there." She pointed to a shimmer of dark green.

He took another breath and made a second tour of the pool's floor while she quietly goggled at the rings she was handling. The man certainly wasn't afraid to be generous. All the stones looked to be at least three or four carats, not that she knew much about such things. There weren't just diamonds, either. There were rubies and emeralds and sapphires. Their shapes ranged from round to square, heart-shaped to marquise, princess to pear. Many were haloed in smaller sparklers that also coated the platinum bands. All were as tasteful as they were extravagant.

Two more trips and she said, "That's all the pockets filled. Should be all of them."

"Good." He hooked his elbow on the ledge beside her thigh. "I'll ask again. Do you see anything you like? We can get something made if you prefer. You don't have to, you know, *throw them away.*"

"I love how you act so accommodating while expecting me to do exactly what you want." She pushed the tray back from the edge of the pool and tucked her palms together between her knees, scowling across the pool.

"Tell me what you think we should do, then. I'm all ears."

She didn't have any idea and he damned well knew it. His story this morning about living away from his parents for so many years had gotten to her. If she hadn't had such a close relationship to her father when her mother had passed, she didn't know how she would have survived.

Then there was the part where the sexual attraction between them seemed to be strong as ever.

I do think you'll marry for that. Because I will.

She heaved an angry sigh. "Wanting to have sex with me and wanting to have a relationship with me are two different things. You didn't call me back. You don't want *me*. It's very hard to commit my life to that."

In the most obscenely effortless show of athletic strength and grace, he levered himself out of the pool and sat next to her in a swoosh of dripping water and gleaming, golden skin.

She swallowed and averted her eyes. "Don't use sex to get your way," she warned. "It's beneath you."

"That's up for debate," he said under his breath, bracing his hands on the ledge next to his splayed thighs. "Tell me about the man you were trying to forget when we made our baby."

"What? No. Why?"

"Because you're comparing me to him. I want to know if it's a fair assessment."

"I'm comparing the situation. You're nothing like him." For starters, sex with Jun Li nearly knocked her off the bed. With Bryant, it had been a lot of fumbling and her trying to be sexy and set a mood and winding up feeling as though she was faking the whole thing.

"He was your only lover besides me. Do I recall that correctly? There's been no one since, if I was the only contender for paternity. What was his name?"

"Our previous relationships don't matter. You said so," she reminded him.

He kept his hard stare pinned on her, refusing to let her dodge or dissemble.

"Bryant," she admitted in a mumble.

"You met at university?"

"High school. He was going into environmental science. I admired his principles."

"Remind me to show you my wind farms."

She rolled her eyes then dropped her gaze to the eggbeater swish of her feet in the water.

"He knew my mother," she admitted. "Kind of. She was his orthodontist. And mine." She automatically showed her teeth since telling people that detail about her mother always prompted a demand she prove it by showing off her perfect smile. "I liked being with someone who had a memory of her, even if it was only that."

"I presumed you'd lost her since you only spoke about your father and said he's remarrying. I'm sorry."

"Thanks. I was sixteen. She was only forty-four. Struck by a car on a crosswalk on a rainy night."

Ivy had thought she had learned to live with her grief until her breakup with Bryant had been all the harder for not having her mother's shoulder to cry on. Then she had wished she could tell her about the surreal day she'd spent with Jun Li. Now she had a pregnancy she couldn't share, and soon there would be a small face with traces of her mother in it. She was missing her more than ever.

"What happened to cause your breakup?" Jun Li's attention sat like a weight on her. She sensed him holding very still as though gripped by a tension he didn't want to reveal.

"Nothing," she said ironically. "Many acts of nothing. Have you ever heard the expression that you only understand your life in reverse? When I look back, I see all the times where I should have cut and run, but at the time I had a vision of where we'd end up so I stuck it out, patiently waiting for that magical day to happen."

"What kind of magic?"

"Marriage. Once we lost Mom, all I wanted was a family that was intact again. I felt like I couldn't be happy again until I had that. It doesn't make sense when I say it out loud, but it's how I felt."

"He didn't want that?"

"No, but I didn't see it. I thought other things were in our way, like education. We were pursuing different programs, so we went to different universities. We actually broke up, but neither of us saw anyone else, and we were always texting and calling. Pretty soon we were flying out to see one another. Except, when I look back, I see that he came to Vancouver to see his family. I was an afterthought." A booty call.

"I expected to start our life together once we got our degrees, but a professor persuaded me to try for an opportunity in Hong Kong. Bryant said I should go for it because he wanted to get his master's and would be away doing field research. Since I was working and he was still in school, I sent him money for things like textbooks and…" She felt like such an idiot. "In my mind, we were making sacrifices up front to ensure we had good careers ahead of us. We were building a strong foundation for our combined future."

"Was he cheating on you?"

"I don't want to sound even more naive than I already was, but I genuinely don't think so. He borders on obsessive about his research. It's fair to say he had a mistress in that regard." She quirked her mouth, dismissing how many hours of editorial work she'd put into his papers. How many times she had double-and triple-checked his data sets. "And I don't think he was consciously using me. He's just a self-involved person. I was a comfortable partner, out of the way, but available when he needed a sounding board or a cheerleader."

She skipped over the part where Bryant had made endless excuses and canceled his trips to come see her in Hong Kong. How she couldn't even count on him to call when he said he would. She was embarrassed by the way she'd clung to a vision that simply hadn't existed.

"I thought it was the nature of commitment that sometimes you have bad times, and you have to stick it out until the better times come around. Then I tried to make the better times happen by taking a transfer to Toronto. It was actually a demotion, but I wanted to be with him. I wanted to start our life together."

"He let you transfer before he told you that it wasn't going to happen? What a jerk."

"He was going away and needed someone to pay the bills for a couple of months, so yeah, that's what he did. When he got back, I finally asked him point-blank if we were ever going to marry. He said he didn't see it happening, so I moved out and started interviewing in Vancouver. I called Kevin while I was visiting Dad, thinking he might have some leads. He invited me to the party, I met you and now we're here."

Bryant's rejection had been four months old when she had met Jun Li. It still felt fresh. She still held deep doubts in her appeal as a woman. In her ability to see what was real in a relationship. In the wisdom of trusting a man to have her best interests at heart.

"How is that situation similar to ours?" Jun Li asked with quiet challenge. "I want to marry you. I want to support you and keep our family intact."

"You want me to arrange my life around yours. For your convenience. You don't know me. You don't want *me*." She set the side of her hand against her breastbone, feeling the knife of that truth deep in her heart.

"You could have had this baby alone and never told me. You didn't."

"Because—"

"Because you were doing what you thought was right for all of us," he said over her. "Which makes you a woman with integrity. If I'm going to marry, surely that's a quality I should want in a wife? You're also intelligent and funny and self-sufficient. I'm sorry that other man made you feel undervalued. I won't do that."

His promise shook things in her. Made cracks and fissures open up for hope to leak out and begin to drug her into believing this would work.

"I won't know if that's true until eight years have passed, though. Will I?" And then, because his sincerity was making emotion gather in her throat and well in her eyes, she waved at her face and said, "See? Everything is exaggerated."

"Including your fears?" he asked gently, cupping her cheek and using his thumb to catch a tear and whisk it away before it rolled down her cheek.

She sniffled, admitting, "Maybe."

He turned away, hesitated, then said, "Incoming," as he presented the tray again.

"Tsk." She looked away, refusing to let him see he was making her smile as he offered the soggy tray of rings. When she looked down at them, the refraction of rainbows dazzled her. "These just make me realize how different we are."

"I'm not trying to buy you, Ivy. I'm saying this is the life our baby is entitled to. That's not a criticism of the life you can offer, but I can offer more. Can we agree that we both want to give our child every possible advantage?"

That was not what he was asking her to agree to. He was asking her to marry a stranger, one who had already upended her life. Now he wanted her to believe he was offering everything she longed for in one go.

Did he realize she wanted a husband who loved her?

Maybe in time they would fall in love, a little voice said inside her.

Oh, Ivy, don't do that to yourself again!

She had a baby to think of, though. A baby entitled to...*this*. A baby entitled to form relationships with both its parents. Jun Li was a man worth knowing, wasn't he? Smart and ambitious. Certainly not *un*kind.

I'm sorry that other man made you feel undervalued. I won't do that.

"This one is by a Vancouver designer." He drew out a true-blue diamond in a triangular cut. It was surrounded by white diamonds that poured down the split band in a swishy curve. "Inspired by the snowy mountains on

Vancouver's North Shore, or so I was told. Perhaps it would help you feel less homesick?"

Eight years with a man she had believed she loved, and he had never once said anything so thoughtful or personal. Or offered a ring.

Before she realized what she was doing, she lifted her hand to see if it fit.

It did. Perfectly. If it had been red, it would have matched the fire that spontaneously ignited in her heart, surrounded by an incandescent glow of hope.

"You'll marry me?"

She made herself look beyond the giddy euphoria of sitting in paradise wearing a priceless piece of art on her finger while a gorgeous, sexy man asked her to spend her life with him.

There was no real debate, though. She had made the choice the moment she'd realized she was pregnant. Her first thought had been that she would have to tell him, and there'd been all those underlying yearnings. *Let him want this baby as much as I do. Let him want us.*

She had been confident she could raise the baby alone, but she didn't want to. She wanted her baby to know its father. *She* wanted to know him.

And there was something bigger at play, too. She didn't believe in destiny in the way of a god preordaining a meeting of souls, but this baby had come about through ridiculously impossible odds. That had to mean her life was supposed to entwine with Jun Li's, didn't it? Was there any sense in resisting the inevitable?

"I will." Her voice was barely a whisper, overwhelmed by the scope and gravity of her promise.

"Good." He gathered her into his lap and kissed her.

Once to seal the deal, then a little longer, until the spark of last night's passion began to flare between them. He hardened against her bottom, and she curled her arm around his neck.

She felt his muscles gather. He was going to rise and carry her into his office to—

He leaped into the pool with her in his arms.

As they plunged into the water, her scream of outrage was caught by his laughing mouth.

CHAPTER SEVEN

JUN LI HAD GOTTEN what he wanted. They were getting married in ten days.

He ought to be pleased. He *was* pleased, but his thoughts were racing with everything that needed to be done. He had worked out in the gym first thing, trying to exercise this restless agitation in him, but his muscles were still tense and he hadn't outrun the nameless thing chasing him.

It had a name, he reminded himself scathingly. He just didn't want to acknowledge it.

He wanted to call it sexual frustration because Ivy had gone to bed before him and he'd made himself sleep elsewhere. He'd woken early and hard, thoughts swirling with how her sexual responses were "amplified."

He ached for her, had done for months. It was all the more acute now that she was under his roof, but he had gone without sex before and hadn't suffered this sensation of dogs snapping at his heels.

He knew what the real problem was, but he wanted to be strong and capable and reliable. Fully in control of everything around him and within him. Admitting he was prone to depression when things got too big for him to handle was demoralizing. This shouldn't be too big. Ivy was doing the real work. All he had to do was keep her warm, dry and fed.

He'd been fine for years without medication. He resented even having to think about taking it again, but of course this massive life change had the power to knock him off balance. He was as prone to self-delusion as anyone else, but he wasn't stupid. This was the sort of thing that *should* make a man pause and take stock. That's what his body was telling him.

Easier said than done, and he would cut out his own tongue before he said aloud to Ivy that the prospect of marrying and having a child was threatening to depress him.

He glanced across at her. Apparently, he'd turned into one of those lechers who couldn't take his eyes off a woman's chest, because he noted *again* the way her top showcased her cleavage. That baby really was amplifying everything.

But they'd had a spat on the flight from Singapore and he wasn't sure if she was speaking to him yet. He'd been busy taking calls and organizing things and said, "My mother needs a guest list from you as soon as possible."

"For the banquet? It's just my father's fiancée and her daughters. The names I gave you."

They had agreed the ceremony would be an intimate civil affair with only their parents in attendance, but the banquet would be more lavish.

"What about friends? What about your family in Hong Kong? No one wants to come?"

"Well, of course they'd love to come, but they can't

drop everything and book a flight to China at a moment's notice. For a weekend. It's something they have to save for." She gave him a look that called him a wealthy, out-of-touch knot head. "They'll visit me later, after the baby comes."

"They don't have to save. My travel office will make all their arrangements. I have a block of rooms set aside at the hotel. Once they're on the list, you only need to give them the link. They'll have three nights with all their meals and travel covered. Invite as many people as you want."

She snorted. "That's very generous, but I'm not going to hand out an all-expenses-paid trip to everyone I know. How many people are *you* inviting?"

"Mother's list has three hundred."

Ivy had glared at him for a full minute before she had pulled out a small tablet and plugged in some earbuds to shut him out while she, presumably, curated a list of her closest two or three hundred friends and family.

"Are you feeling all right?" Jun Li asked. "You've been quiet." Still angry?

She drew in a breath and sat straighter, seeming to become aware they were in the car winding through a neighborhood in Quinpu District.

"Just thinking. There's a lot to process."

"The wedding?" he guessed.

"Yes. I don't know what I expected, but…" She sighed and waved it off. "Turning down that job bothers me more. I would have had to take maternity leave in a few months anyway, and I haven't really burned a bridge. I'll always be able to find work if I want it. Executive recruiters are still sending me leads," she said with a flick of her hand to where her phone was tucked into her handbag. "I have savings. But it bothers me that I won't have an income. It feels very retro to become dependent on my husband."

She was reluctant to let a man govern her life again. He understood that and had a small desire to punch her old boyfriend in the throat for treating her so poorly, since it left her with very little faith in him.

"I'll hire you when you're ready to work again," he promised.

"I don't want a job by nepotism."

"You just said headhunters are still after you. That suggests you have qualifications that would benefit my organization."

"I guess." Her mouth crinkled in a reluctant smile. She turned her attention out the window as the car slowed at a pair of gates. "This is where my family will stay?"

"If you approve, yes." He scratched his upper lip. She was going to be mad again, but he would wait until she had seen inside before starting that fight.

Many of the houses in this area were Western-style mansions, but this one was very modern and sleek, almost looking as though colored children's blocks had been assembled in a haphazard but pleasing way. A staff of eight greeted them as they entered.

The butler introduced each one, adding to Ivy, "Once your guests arrive, we'll have four more."

"Oh. Um, I'm sure my family will be very comfortable. Thank you."

They dispersed, and Jun Li watched her as she moved from the spacious foyer to an airy lounge. It was decorated in a tasteful and elegant color palette of soothing grays with gentle pops of dusty blue and muted gold. The wall was a unique half circle that showcased as much of the serene river view as possible.

"What a beautiful home," she said with awe.

"My mother has a talent for finding exceptional properties."

"She certainly does." She moved onto the veranda to admire the garden before they toured the rest. "It seems bigger than they need. Although, I guess your parents will be here for some dinners with them," she mused as she took in the dining room that sat twenty-four. "But five bedrooms?"

Each had its own bath, and there was accommodation for four in the pool house, plus a small flat for the butler over the garage. Rooms were also set aside for a nanny next to a potential nursery. All of it was decorated in clean, uncluttered lines that still managed to look warm and elegant.

"It's beautiful, but if it's super expensive—"

"It's not," he assured her, waving her into the master bedroom. Like the rest of the house, it was a soothing space with recessed lighting and had a killer view of the river.

"Dad's going to feel like a king in here."

"Um…" Time to come clean, especially since a maid ducked out of the closet, bowed and said she would finish unpacking later.

"Unpacking?" Ivy frowned and moved into the closet. Her modest belongings from Vancouver hung alongside some of the outfits she'd chosen in Singapore yesterday. Now that her designer had her size and a sense of her taste, the selection had been filled out. Parcels and bags were stacked at the back, and the price tags still hung from many of the garments.

"I thought this was a rental for my family." Exactly as he had expected, she sounded royally peeved.

"It's for you. If you approve, I'll tell Mother to finalize the paperwork."

"You're sticking me in a house here? What about all that talk about raising our baby together? What about—"

"Oh, hell. No. Ivy." He caught her flailing hand. "Until the wedding," he stressed.

"Then you'll move in here with me?" She tugged her hand free and folded her arms, looking very apprehensive.

"Okay, I thought this would be a fun surprise." He rubbed his jaw, trying not to laugh.

"It's not," she assured him stridently. "Tell me exactly what is happening. I won't spend a lifetime guessing what you're thinking and being wrong. Been there. Hated it."

He sobered and ran his tongue over his teeth. "This is too far from the city for us to live here full-time. Once we have the wedding out of the way, my mother will show you some properties in the city. That's a bigger decision, so we'll take our time. The penthouse will be perfectly comfortable until we're ready to make that leap."

That mollified her a little. "So this *is* just a rental for the wedding?"

"No." He braced himself for another pithy reaction. "I can't take you to Vancouver and collect you from your father's home, so I'm buying you one here."

"You're buying this house as a *staging* area? You really do have too much money." She shook her head.

"It's not just for the wedding. I asked Mother to find something that would make a nice retreat when we have a free weekend. A place for you to put up your overseas friends when they visit."

"Oh. Like a cottage at the lake."

"Exactly."

"I'm being sarcastic, Jun Li!" Her fists punched the air by her hips. "Any family cottage I've ever been to has had secondhand bunk beds in it, not original art and live-in staff."

"If you don't want them, fire them." He had reached the limit of his patience and walked out of the closet. "This is yours to do with however you see fit."

"Don't be ridiculous." She came flying out behind him and glared at the incomparable view. "It's not *really* mine? Because I don't know what the foreign ownership implications are. I don't have the means to pay the staff. You realize that, don't you?"

The way she flung that at him made him realize something far more important—how far apart they were in understanding one another.

"Ivy. When I said I wanted to take responsibility for you and our baby, I meant that I would ensure the safety and security of both of you. That I will use every possible tool at my disposal."

She folded her arms defensively and let her weight fall onto her back foot. "Okay. What does that mean?"

"It means this house will be yours. Outright. The funds for upkeep will be spelled out in our marriage contract along with a budget for all your staff. It will specify your living allowance, your share in the corporation and the terms of settlement should we divorce. I'm going to discuss all that with my father after I leave here. You'll have time to review and weigh in, but I suggest you hire a lawyer to review it as well."

"That's not going to endear me to your family, is it? How angry are they that I've turned up pregnant this way, forcing you to marry someone they've never even met?" She bit her lip and said in a smaller voice, "I've been terrified to ask that."

"They're so thrilled it makes me feel like a jerk that I was planning not to marry or give them a grandchild. You'll see." He moved to take her by the shoulders and dipped his chin to look her in the eye. "Now, so you won't have any other surprises, I'll also tell you I've asked my mother's assistant to set up interviews for a mirror of her own team for you. Once I'm married, we'll both be in demand as guests and hosts. You'll need an assistant, a social secretary, you already have a stylist and you'll probably want a personal shopper."

"That's not you?" she asked weakly.

He smiled. "You also need a midwife and nutritionist for the next while, and a nanny once the baby is born. Mother's decorator can help with the nurseries and any other changes you wish to make to our homes."

"That's… I mean…" Her hands came to his forearms as if she felt dizzy.

He squeezed her shoulders and tore off the rest of the bandage.

"You'll also have your own driver and bodyguards. Unfortunately, we all need them. It's the price of our success. As for the household staff, we have an interfamily agent who manages all that. If you need to make changes, your assistant will set that up. And—"

"There's more?" she squeaked. "Please stop."

"You'll have your own bank account once we're married, but use this credit card if you need anything immediately." He withdrew two from his shirt pocket, read them and replaced his own, then offered hers.

She swallowed as she looked at it. "This is one of those 'invitation only' kind. Limitless. I saw one in Hong Kong once. How did you get one with my name on it? So fast?"

She was so cute. "It has a concierge service. I made a call, and it was waiting when we landed. There's a new phone around here, too. It should be programmed with my direct line. I'll find it and check it before I go. If you don't have any objections to this house, I'll tell Mother to go ahead with the paperwork?"

"My objections are all of the 'Are you of sound mind?' variety," she said faintly.

"Very sound. But you're looking wan. Take the afternoon to rest before I bring my parents by later. Let the staff spoil you."

"You really have to go?" She swayed slightly toward him. Her eyes were wide with uncertain invitation as she met his gaze.

It would be so easy to walk her back to the bed and lose himself in passion. So easy. Probably even healthy.

But with so much of his life fraying and peeling off in its own directions, he had to maintain a firm grip over everything, most especially himself. Just thinking about blowing off his afternoon caused the itch of angst and tension to rise in him.

He was hovering at the entrance to an unhealthy spiral and would have to make time amid the rest of his busy day to visit his doctor for a prescription. It was frustrating and lowering, especially for a man with perfectionist tendencies. It was the best thing he could do for both of them in the long run, though.

"I do have to leave." But he couldn't make himself walk away without one kiss, one *taste*...

He cupped her face so he wouldn't touch her anywhere else. And he tried to keep it to a teasing, tender kiss of parting, but her mouth flowered open beneath his. Her tongue swept across his bottom lip in explicit desire.

He instantly hardened, nearly overcome by sudden, raw sexuality. He took complete possession of her mouth, made love to her with his tongue. He wanted to strip them both naked and plunge into her like this, again and again until they exploded. Not a sensual seduction like she deserved, but animalistic mating that left them panting and sweaty and sated.

He jerked his head back, unsettled by how tenuous his grip on his control was. The less he showed, the less he would have. This had to stop here.

She was trembling, eyelids fluttering open, breath short.

When he dropped his hands and stepped back from her, she bit the lips he'd left swollen and shiny.

"What's wrong?" She sounded uncertain. Hurt.

He bit back a curse at how untenable this was and grasped for the first rationale that came to him. "I have to be able to look your father in the eye."

"My father doesn't own my sexuality." Her brows crashed together in annoyance.

"I still think it would be best to wait until the wedding." He needed time to get himself back on track.

She snorted. "My father knows how babies are made. He slept with Mom before they married."

"And how did *her* father feel about that?" he countered dryly.

"My grandfather was never told." She spoke snippily, then seemed to realize that wasn't a point that worked in her favor. She waved dismissively. "Their situation was different. My grandmother wasn't angry they slept together. She was mad they married without permission. She wanted Mom to marry someone else."

"In Canada?"

"In Hong Kong. She took Mom to visit relatives and meet him, but while Mom was out with her cousins, she met Dad. Grandma said it was just lust." Ivy pressed her mouth into a line of consternation.

That small show of disquiet in her made the floor feel soggy beneath him. Was she worrying they didn't even have that, because he wasn't throwing her onto the bed and ravishing her? He wanted to. It was taking everything in him not to reach for her, but he was also aware it would weaken the dam holding all the emotional junk he'd bottled up out of self-preservation. He was protecting her and their combined future as much as himself.

"What happened?" He had completely lost the plot, far too aware that she was withdrawing mentally and physically, hugging herself and stepping back from him.

"Grandma tried to break them up by taking Mom home. Dad followed and married her on the sly. Grandma said he only married her to immigrate." She moved to the window. "But they loved each other," she said with quiet conviction.

And that was what Ivy wanted for *her* marriage. That's why she had been quiet and blue and solemn all day. She was seeking reassurance in passion and turning away when he didn't offer it.

A slab of concrete settled over his chest as he realized he had cheated her of something he didn't know he could ever provide. He cared about the people close to him and expected he would come to cherish her the way he did the rest of his family, but she wanted the grand, romantic love that pursued someone across continents and defied parents and couldn't be resisted because it had to be.

He pushed his hands into his pants pockets. Swallowed an acrid taste of failure.

"Your father must be sympathizing with his mother-in-law at this moment, worried about *my* motives. I need to do this right, Ivy." It was the least he could do.

"Sure. Fine. Do what you have to, and I'll wait here like a good girl. Ignore that," she commanded, immediately throwing up a hand. "I'm freaking out. Staff, Jun Li? A *house*? I appreciate everything you're doing, but how am I supposed to react to any of this? I was excited when I heard my new job came with a *title*."

He relaxed a little. "You'll get used to it."

As he hovered one more second, he realized he wanted to draw her into an embrace and kiss her to reassure them both. It bothered him to leave her with this discord between them.

"Do you want me to tell the butler you're lying down?" He took a step toward the door.

"Thank you." She nodded, mouth pouted in a way that made walking away hurt like hell.

"Jun Li."

His heart tripped as he turned back. His breath caught as he took in one of the loveliest women he'd ever seen in his life. Her hair was loose around her face, and her chin came to that adorably obstinate point. Her dress hugged her shoulders and cut low across the swells of her breasts then billowed loosely to flutter around her pretty knees. The dress's mossy-green color made her skin look like honey illuminated by sunshine.

"You know what I'm getting you as a wedding gift, don't you?"

"A baby?"

"A smoothie bullet."

It took him a moment, then he recalled that was what she'd got Kevin while he'd given his old friend a house. For some reason, that very lame joke had him grinning all day.

"Your blood pressure is up a little," the midwife said the morning of the wedding. "Not much and this is a big day. I'm not worried, but we'll keep an eye on it." She made a note.

The days had flown by in a flurry of meetings and interviews, fittings and meals with friends and relatives from both sides, all visiting from around the globe. Everyone was very happy for them, and several cooed quiet asides to Ivy about how lucky she was.

She was. She might have no time alone with her husband-to-be, but that didn't mean he wasn't ironing wrinkles from her days before she even saw them. They texted frequently, and at one point he sent her a link for a nine-hundred-watt stainless steel blender.

Says it's also good for baby food?

She had bought it with her own credit card, despite its extravagant price tag, and had it sent to his penthouse with a note.

Make some congee. Let me know.

I'll use it every day, he promised in a text.

Such flirts they were.

But despite learning the names of his cousins and hearing stories of his childhood, she still felt as though she was marrying blindly. Any reservations she dared whisper had been refuted by whomever she voiced them to. He was Tsai Jun Li. He was rich, gorgeous, doting and had fired one of his executives when it was revealed the man had made some derogatory remarks about Ivy carrying Jun Li's baby before the wedding had happened.

Did she not realize she was the envy of every single woman in the *world*?

She had so much more with Jun Li than she'd had with Bryant. Did it matter that they weren't in love? It would come in time. Wouldn't it?

She had run out of time to change her mind if she believed it wouldn't. She was dressed in a demure red cheongsam for the ceremony. She was so nervous, she thought she would shake the petals right off her bouquet of wine-red roses before Jun Li arrived to collect her.

There was a stir below, and she came to the top of the stairs as he entered the foyer. He wore an embroidered red Tang jacket over black trousers. He was so wickedly handsome, her knees threatened to give out.

His penetrating gaze swept up and found her. He stilled as though she was something that stole his breath. She thought his throat might have flexed with a swallow.

Some of her relatives had threatened to perform playful traditions, saying they would make him earn their surrender of her, but Jun Li only had to hold out his hand. Everyone went silent as Ivy came down the stairs as though in a spell. He linked their fingers and held their clasped hands to his chest.

"Are you ready?" he asked.

"Yes," she said breathlessly.

The trip to the government office was solemn. Their parents stood by as they spoke their vows. Ivy could hardly get hers out, she was so overcome by the power of their promises to one another.

Jun Li squeezed her hand as he spoke, as if he were trying to press each word into her skin and blood and bones. When his mouth touched hers in a brief kiss, her qualms faded away. Surely something that felt this right *was* right?

From there, they went to the home of Jun Li's parents, a beautiful beaux arts villa in the Bund. They performed a tea ceremony to serve their parents. Jun Li's mother, Mo Chou, gave Ivy a stunning gold necklace made of links shaped like ivy leaves. Some were solid, some hollow, giving it an airy, delicate look. It had a matching bracelet and earrings and was so pretty, Ivy said sincerely, "I'll treasure this always."

She was already wearing a gold hair ornament that had been worn by her mother and grandmother for their own weddings. Her father had brought it along with some rare coins and jade carvings that he had collected over the years for exactly this occasion, so he could gift them to her new husband's parents.

After a light meal, they went to the hotel, where she and Jun Li were shown into a lavish top-floor suite. Ivy's stylist had taken over one bedroom, where she had organized all Ivy's outfits for the banquet.

She helped Ivy into an elaborate qipao with a long silk train. It was embroidered down one side with gold threads and colorful flowers. Jun Li was waiting for her when she emerged. He had changed into a different red wedding tunic with embroidery similar to hers.

Moments later, when they entered the ballroom, the wave of excitement off the five hundred guests nearly felled her.

They visited every table while the guests ate, each requiring introductions and toasts. It took hours, and they disappeared several times to change. Each time, Ivy discovered Jun Li had gifted her more jewelry and he switched to a jacket that matched her own gown.

When she put on a traditional Western wedding dress and wore a necklace of diamonds, he changed into a white tuxedo. Her dark pink gown was a foil for rubies of an intense magenta color while he wore a burgundy-colored vest over a black shirt. She switched to a mermaid-style gown in buttercup yellow, sunny sapphires falling like petals over her collarbone while he appeared in a mandarin-collared jacket of muted saffron.

Finally, after the speeches were finished, Ivy put on a sleeveless cocktail dress in midnight-blue velvet. A necklace and earrings appeared that matched her engagement ring of blue and white diamonds.

"You look incredible. Edible," Jun Li told her. He dipped his head to press a kiss to the point of her bare shoulder.

Each time they'd entered the elevator, he'd complimented her. Each time, she had thanked him profusely for the jewelry.

This time she could only smile weakly. Her feet ached and her cheeks were sore from forcing herself to smile. Her voice hurt from talking, and she still had to get through sending everyone off with their wedding favors.

"Are you okay?" he asked, giving her elbow a squeeze.

"Just tired. But I can stay in bed all day tomorrow if I want to."

"That was my plan."

A blush hit her cheeks, and she looked down to hide it.

She was nervous about making love again but glad to hear some enthusiasm from him. Despite the passion that had overwhelmed her in Singapore, he'd been adamant about keeping their affection to a few tame kisses. They'd constantly been surrounded by friends and relatives, barely able to exchange private words, let alone more, but it bothered her that he hadn't even tried. The desire seemed to be all on her side, not so much on his.

"Ladies and gentlemen, our groom has arranged a special treat for you," a voice announced as they reappeared.

The ceiling opened to reveal the night sky. While everyone murmured with surprise, the first testing streak of fireworks appeared like a shooting star. Music began to play, and the colorful explosions were perfectly synchronized to the booms in the music. Everyone cheered with enjoyment.

Ivy stood in Jun Li's arms, head tilted up to watch. It was beautiful, but the roof seemed to be closing in before the show was over. Jun Li's arm tightened around her, making her feel as though he was cutting off her air because none was entering her lungs.

"Ivy!" His voice was a million miles away.

CHAPTER EIGHT

IVY WILTED IN his arms, head lolling, scaring the hell out of him.

As she crumpled, Jun Li caught her behind the legs and cradled her to his chest while he scanned for one of the physicians in attendance. As people began lowering their attention from the sky and releasing murmurs of alarm, his uncle on his mother's side—a general practitioner—hurried toward him.

"She saw her midwife this morning. She said the checkup was fine," Jun Li told him.

His uncle motioned to the dais. A screen had been set up behind the podium to provide a backdrop for the speakers. It afforded them a little privacy as Jun Li lowered Ivy onto the carpeted floor behind it.

Her eyes were already fluttering open in disoriented alarm. "What—?"

"Let him take your pulse," he told her as she instinctively tried to pull away from his uncle's hold on her wrist.

His uncle asked whether there was bleeding or cramping, questions that put a knot of sick terror in the pit of Jun Li's gut even after she dismissed them.

"No, I'm fine. I haven't eaten since this afternoon," she admitted with chagrin.

"We had food in the room." Jun Li had been snacking each time they changed and had presumed Ivy was doing the same.

"I didn't want to risk staining any of the gowns."

"They're just clothes," he muttered, but while he'd been shrugging on a new jacket, she'd been sitting to have her hair restyled and her makeup retouched.

"The midwife told me to stay hydrated, but we had so many people to meet," she continued with apology. "I didn't want to excuse myself every five minutes. Honestly, I'm fine. All the running around this week has caught up to me, that's all. Now I'm making a scene and I feel like a fool. Please let me up."

His uncle helped her sit but watched her closely. "Dizzy?"

"Mortally embarrassed."

A waiter was hovering with a phone. He asked Jun Li if an ambulance was needed.

Jun Li sent him for a rehydration drink. "Something with protein," he added, then crouched beside Ivy. "You should have told me you weren't feeling well."

"I've gone without eating and drinking before when I've been traveling or had work deadlines. I've never fainted."

"Your baby is using all of your resources now," his uncle scolded. "You have to take better care of yourself."

"I will," Ivy promised.

"*I* will," Jun Li swore.

"Can we please go back out there? Before everyone

thinks this is more serious than it is? Oh, Dad, I'm fine," she said, looking past Jun Li.

He stepped out of the way so she could reassure her father.

The music was finishing up with a finale of explosions, but the cheering had stopped. The air of concern was palpable. Jun Li moved to the podium and waited for the last notes of the music to fade before he spoke.

"Ivy is feeling the strain of the day," he told the crowd. "We are honored and grateful that you took this time to be with us today, but we'll be leaving shortly—"

The crowd gave an audible sigh of relief and beamed, clapping as Ivy came out from behind the screen to join him.

"I'm fine," she insisted and showed him the milky drink she was sipping. "I'd like to stay and see everyone off."

Her color was better, but Jun Li had a chair brought for her to sit in while their families gathered around them and guests filed by to say their good nights. No one lingered, and Ivy's soon-to-be stepsisters did most of the work in handing out the gift bags. They were shaped like sedan chairs and held handmade candies, oranges, red chopsticks engraved with his and Ivy's names, gold pendants with the double happiness symbol, and other keepsakes.

"I thought you might want one of these," Kevin said at Jun Li's elbow.

Jun Li dragged his watchful eye off Ivy to see Kevin was offering a glass of scotch.

"Thank you." Despite the many toasts in their honor today, Jun Li hadn't imbibed. He typically avoided alcohol since it was a depressant, but he accepted the drink, appreciating the stimulating bite as he sipped. "And thank you for interrupting your honeymoon to be with us today."

"We wouldn't have missed it. You two should join us in Bora Bora for a few days. Ivy could use the R and R. You too?"

Kevin was the only other person Jun Li had ever told about his long ago pregnancy debacle. He understood the pressures Jun Li had put upon himself from an early age and the load he carried today. He knew how Jun Li's drive to succeed had a downside. Any sort of failure hit him like a northbound bus.

Kevin's new wife, Carla, was chatting with Ivy. The crowd had thinned, and everyone else was occupied in pockets of conversation. Jun Li stepped away from the line to speak more privately with Kevin.

"I saw she was looking tired, but she said she was fine. I should have listened to my gut." Jun Li was furious with himself.

"That tracks. For Ivy, I mean," Kevin said with a dry chuckle, holding up a hand. "Your instincts remain infamously sharp, and I'm surprised you ignored them. But when I worked with her in Hong Kong, I saw very quickly that she was the kind of person other people feed a sob story to so she would do their work for them. She reminds me of my sister. Doesn't know how to set limits and say no."

Like when a man asked her to come to his hotel room? Or pressured her into marriage? Jun Li's heart fishtailed in his chest.

"You'll be good for her. You're notoriously self-sufficient. Nothing like that vampire of needs who had her throwing away a promotion in Hong Kong so he could throw *her* away. What an idiot," Kevin scoffed. "His loss was supposed to be my gain. That's why I introduced you two at our engagement party. I wanted to find a place for Ivy in my office. Thanks, by the way, for stealing her away and killing that masterful plan."

Jun Li had a flash of where he would be right now if Kevin had made that clear to him. Ivy would have been off-limits and none of this would have happened. He took a deep sip of his scotch to burn away the uncomfortable dryness that arrived in the back of his throat.

"When I saw her again a few weeks ago, I was planning to feel her out on working for me, but she asked whether you'd be coming to our wedding. She was wearing the guiltiest, most painfully casual look I've ever pretended to believe. Have you been seeing her this whole time?"

Jun Li licked his lips. "Not exactly."

"Hmm." The noise was neither pleased nor dismayed.

That shouldn't bother him, but Kevin was his closest friend. "Look, you know why I've avoided serious relationships. I felt stretched too thin as it was."

His instincts had been correct there, too. He had feared the responsibility of a wife and child would put him into a depression, and the sense of not being enough had been closing in on him for days.

"I know." Kevin gave the back of his shoulder an affectionate slap. "Ivy might remind me of my sister, but you are like a brother to me." They had never spoken frankly about why Jun Li had opened his home to Kevin even though he had felt alone for so long by then, he had come to believe he preferred it. "I want you to be happy, Jun Li. I believe Ivy could make you happy. If you let her."

His response ought to have been, *I am happy.* It was his wedding day. But he didn't know what happiness *was*. It was hard for Jun Li to say he was even content. He experienced brief moments of satisfaction over accomplishments, which was what he'd been feeling until Ivy had fainted.

He was filled with self-criticism at not having predicted her faint. He'd been distracted, ruminating over her reaction when he had mentioned staying in bed all day. The thought of making love to her was the only thing keeping him sane through this demanding week. Once they were married, she would be *his*. He couldn't wait to make it so.

She'd looked conflicted, though.

He wasn't about to force himself on her, especially when she was passing out from low blood sugar and exhaustion.

Ivy looked over then. Her smile faltered as she met whatever severity his thoughts were putting into his expression. After a disconcerted blink, she offered a warm smile to Kevin. Kevin nodded at Jun Li and went across to wish her well.

Someone else came up to him, and Jun Li threw himself back into thanking their departing guests while privately continuing to brood.

Ivy was still feeling sheepish over her faint when she and Jun Li entered his penthouse a short distance from the hotel. Bridal shyness accosted her. After a week when they'd begun to feel more like business partners than romantic ones, she was ready to explore a deeper, more intimate connection, but she was ridiculously self-conscious about making love again.

Everything had changed since their first time. *She* had. Their relationship had. In Vancouver she'd felt more like his equal, muscle car and five-star hotel room notwithstanding. She had known that she wouldn't see him again, so the emotional stakes had been minimized.

Now their lives were irrevocably tied. Whatever happened between them tonight would carry over into the next day and the next for the rest of their lives.

What if it wasn't like it had been in Vancouver? What if the passion was only on her side and she went off like a firecracker the way she had in Singapore, making a fool of herself?

Jun Li had been watching her like a hawk since her faint, and not in a good way. She felt as though a wall had come down between them, and she wasn't sure what to do about it.

Aside from his butler, the place was deserted. As soon as the man pointed out the refreshments he'd left for them, Jun Li dismissed him.

Ivy sank onto the sofa, trying to read her husband as he filled a bowl with soup and brought it to her.

"Are you angry with me?" she asked as she accepted the soup.

"I'm angry with myself. I could see you were tired." He sat next to her and pointed at her foot then patted his thigh.

She carefully shifted her position and set her shod feet in his lap then sipped the fragrant ginger-scented broth while he unbuckled her shoes and eased them away. He dropped them, then rubbed through the blue silk of her hose where the straps had left small indents across the tops of her feet.

"Why are you wearing shoes that are too small?"

"My feet are swollen from being on them all day."

He sighed. "I expect you to tell me when I'm asking too much of you." His grip shifted, gently crushing her arch so the tension released.

It made for a confusing contrast of dull pain and sharp relief. Of feeling like she was being punished but doted on at the same time. She bit back a groan.

"I kept thinking it was only a little bit longer—" she started to say.

"Isn't that what you thought with that other man?" He gently bent her toes back and forth. "That you only had to put up with his disregard a little longer?"

"That was different," she protested, practically shuddering as the flex and relaxation in her feet caused her whole body to melt.

"I promised I wouldn't ignore your needs. I'll be more careful with you from now on, blossom, but I need your help. I'm not a mind reader." He gave her foot another firm squeeze.

She couldn't help her moan of pleasure-pain. Her eyelids fluttered closed.

"That feels so good," she sighed.

"Finish your soup." He kept rubbing her feet while she sipped. He rolled her ankles and massaged up her calves. By the time she had drained her bowl and she set it aside, she was a puddle of flesh.

"Do you want me to run you a bath?"

"That sounds nice." Her shoulders and upper chest had been dusted with pearlescent glitter for this dress. She was dying to wash it away and lose these false eyelashes along with the rest of her makeup.

Jun Li went down the hall. She walked shoeless to the table, where she prepared a plate of finger foods they could enjoy in the tub.

When she caught up to him, he was lighting floating candles in the water-filled bowls that stood on the three stairs leading up to the tub. Bubble bath was beginning to froth in the water, releasing a calming aroma of lavender.

"You are hungry," he said wryly as he took the plate from her and set it on a shelf within reach of the tub.

"It's for both of us." She turned her back to him so he could open her zipper.

The silence that greeted her remark had her lifting her gaze to the mirror.

His profile had become very remote as he slowly slid the zip down. The freedom to draw a deeper breath was profound, but even though it was warm in here, she shivered and defensively clasped the gown to her front.

"You're not planning to join me?" Why did that hurt *so much*?

"You're tired. There's no rush," he said, very offhand, as if he didn't care one way or another if they ever made love again. It drove a fresh spike of agony through her.

Ivy had spent the last week counting down the minutes until they would be together again, when she could discover if they still had, at the very least, the passion that had made this baby they had married for.

Throat aching, she moved to the sink and peeled off her lashes, then began to pull the decorative pins from her hair. It caused her dress to slump to her hips.

Jun Li was turned away, closing the taps on the bath. Ivy hurried to wriggle free of her dress and toss it over the back of a wooden chair. She took up the silk robe that had been artfully draped there and started to shrug it on before Jun Li saw what she was wearing.

The room was nothing but mirrors, though. He turned his head, caught her reflection from the corner of his eye and did a swift double take, swinging around and swearing under his breath.

"What?" Her heart leaped into her throat, but she acted as casual as possible as she started to close the robe over the underwear she'd chosen for his pleasure. Heaven knows, it wasn't for her comfort.

At the last second, however, a prickle of defiance stopped her from belting the robe. She turned to the mirror and held it open, cocking her head as she regarded herself.

"I chose blue to go with the dress. It's pretty with the necklace, isn't it?" The strapless bra was more of a bustier with blue satin cups and a white lace overlay that hugged her ribs. Below it, she wore blue satin cheekies with a white lace garter belt. It held up the blue hose that looked closer to black in this low light.

"You should have seen it with the shoes." She went up on her toes, noting that he was paying *very* close attention and looked rather feral as shadows appeared in his hollow cheeks.

A pulse of triumph scattered butterflies of danger within her.

She dropped back to flat feet and said, "But there's no rush. Is there?"

It was a challenge, absolutely. Probably not a wise one.

When she would have belted the robe, he appeared behind her like some sort of avenging angel and tangled his hands with hers, so she was captured in the circle of his arms. Trapped, but not crushed. Pinned by the reflection of his fierce gaze meeting hers in the glass.

"I was trying to be considerate," he growled.

"I'll tell you if I'm not up for sex."

"Will you?"

It was a dig at her driving herself into a faint earlier.

"Yes," she said petulantly.

As if to test her, he tugged the belt free and opened the robe himself, exposing her to the mirror and taking another long look over her shoulder.

The naked desire in his face made warmth run into all her erogenous zones. She shifted restlessly and became aware of his hardness against her backside. She flashed him a wary look, and he quirked a brow.

"Will you tell me if you *are*?" he asked. "Up for sex?" His voice seemed to have dropped several octaves so it reverberated from within his chest against her back.

"This underwear is a bit of a neon sign, isn't it?" she tried to joke, but she was very aware that he was still drinking her in with the most ravenous, lustful look on his face. It was both heartening and exciting but made her wonder what she had started.

"I think I'd like to hear it," he said softly, fingertips trailing across the naked skin of her midriff before he traced his thumb beneath one breast. "To be absolutely sure."

"I want to," she whispered, distracted by the sharp ache that came into her breasts. They were already swollen and tight. His light caress made her nipples sting and chafe against the satin cups.

"You want what? To be touched?" His thumb climbed higher and higher while his other hand brushed aside her hair. "Kissed?" He opened his mouth against her nape.

Her knees went soft. "Yes. Both. Everything."

"Oh, be careful what you invite, blossom." His teeth lightly scraped against the side of her neck, making her scalp tighten while she reflexively slouched into him. Her breast fell into his palm, and he gave her nipple a light pinch through the cup.

It was enough to make a sob pang in her throat, more alarm at the threat of pain than the real thing, but her reaction was quick and instinctive.

He started to jerk his hand away, but she covered it to keep it there.

"They're really sensitive," she said. "Just be gentle."

"Are they?" His touch drew patterns on the swells above the edge of the cup while his lips nibbled at her earlobe, heavy with the dangling blue diamond she was wearing. "I won't suck your nipples, then. I'll only taste and blow on them."

He blew softly against her damp earlobe. She gasped at the sensation, half-drunk with passion from a few words of a sensual promise. She tried to turn, but he didn't let her.

"Are you hurt? Do you want to stop?" His smile flashed.

"You know I don't."

"What then?"

"Keep going. Touch me. Show me what *you* want," she dared, meeting his gaze in the mirror.

"I want all of you." He held her stare while his hand went down from her breast, down her center, down, down until he cupped her mound. "I want this." He pressed his touch over her, possessively claiming her. "I want to feel you melt and hear you scream my name."

She was shaking with want, throbbing beneath the pressure of his hand.

"Open your legs," he commanded softly. "Let me touch you."

She did. He shifted his touch so his fingertips stole down the front of her cheekies. It was blatant, both of them watching as his flattened fingers petted down her sensitive flesh. The garter belt framed his caress as he rocked his hand inside the satin. Her eyelids fluttered.

"Are you breathing, blossom? I don't want you to faint again," he teased.

She was gasping with anticipation. Aching and needy. Biting her lip as he took his time tracing into the furrow of her folds, intensifying her sensations. A rumbling noise of satisfaction tickled her ear as his touch moved freely in the moisture gathered there.

"I've wanted you for months." His mouth swept her neck again. "Since that night. It's all I've thought about. Feeling you shaking and digging your nails into me again."

Was she? One of her hands was up around his neck, the other gripped his upper arm through his sleeve. He still wore his shirt and pants, the crispness of the fabric a further stimulation through the layer of silk against her back.

"Let me watch you come apart." His touch began to roll and dip and slide against the small knot of nerves that were already dancing waves of escalating pleasure through her. "Move with me. Show me how to make it good."

She couldn't resist his command. Her hips began to rock. She ground her bottom against his hardness while he played his touch inside the satin and lace. His cheeks grew flushed with excitement as he watched them. As she saw what her pleasure was doing to him, hers increased, making their sexual play that much more erotic.

Her excitement reached breaking point. Climax swept up and over her. She called out his name and shattered in his arms.

CHAPTER NINE

FOR THE SECOND time tonight, Jun Li picked up Ivy.

This time she wasn't a dead weight in his arms. She was weak with postorgasmic lethargy and coiled her arms around his neck, offering her mouth. He spared a moment to ravage her, holding back nothing since she met his kiss with equal abandonment. Her mouth opened unreservedly beneath his. Her tongue brushed against his while she moaned and pressed the back of his head, urging him to kiss her harder.

He was so aroused, he could have taken her to the floor, but he wasn't consummating their marriage on the hard tiles of a bathroom. He dragged his head up and strode to the bedroom, where he set her on his bed. He began yanking at his clothes.

"Don't take that off," he ordered when she flicked at a clasp against the top of her hose.

"You *do* like what I'm wearing." She smoothed her hand over one knee and arranged herself more provocatively, weight propped on an elbow. She hooked her other thumb in the top of her underpants. "These don't come off unless I release the garter straps." She crooked her knee up and popped the second clasp.

"Let me do it, then." His guttural voice didn't sound like his own. He was sinking into a barbaric one-track head space that originated nowhere near his head. It was the abandonment of control he'd been avoiding, and it took everything in him to keep himself this side of civilized.

He rolled her over, nearly dying at the way the underside of her plump cheeks was outlined in blue satin and white lace. He wanted to bite those tender, buttercream-colored swells.

"I'm going to give you a special allowance to spend exclusively on lingerie," he informed her as he blindly kicked away his trousers. "I should have written it into our contract as a marital requirement."

She propped herself on her elbows and gave him a sultry look over her shoulder, kicking one foot. "You realize how much power you're giving me? If I dent the car or burn the cookies, I'll buy a thong before I tell you."

"Dent all my cars." He was naked and so aroused, he was shaking.

He braced one knee on the bed to survey the lissome shape that had dominated his fantasy life for months. Finally, he could touch her again. He did, running his hand over the silk that hugged her calf until he arrived at the back of her thigh. He caressed all the naked skin he could find, running his fingers beneath the tension of the straps and the lace of her underwear, making her squirm and lift her plump cheek into his touch.

He wanted to cover her and have her like this. In a thousand ways. Kiss and lick and thrust and claim.

He could. He had a lifetime to explore all the ways they could drive each other mad. It was mind-blowing.

He kissed her shoulders and discovered the lace that hugged her ribs had a dozen hooks closing it. He nuzzled her spine as he released them one by one, enjoying the way she flexed and writhed and caught her breath.

"I want to eat you alive. Every inch." He ran his mouth over her naked back as he fully exposed it, up to her nape, where she seemed particularly sensitive, and back down her spine to where it dipped into her lower back.

"Quit teasing. I'm dying," she moaned.

He laughed but saw she was still supporting herself on her arms as though to keep her weight off her breasts. He flicked open the clasps at the backs of her thighs and rolled her face up, dragging the bra from where it had fallen between them and throwing it away.

"Sore?" he asked as he grazed a knuckle along the side of one breast.

"A little. It feels good to be out of that." She gave a luxurious stretch.

Damn, she was beautiful. Most of her wore a fading summer tan, but her naked breasts were a subtle gold with light brown nipples, pert as toffee candies. He wanted to suck each one into his mouth, savor and play and make her melt, but he remembered his promise and only anointed one with his tongue then blew softly.

Her legs pinched together as though she was trying to protect herself from the intensity of sensations. He set his thigh across them, teasing himself with the feel of the hose and a stray garter buckle digging into the inside of his leg.

Her breath hitched as he used his weight to control her. He glanced into her eyes to see if she was uncom-

fortable with his light dominance and saw excitement
glowing there. A charge of power and sexual thrill went
through him.

Oh yes. She enjoyed a little constriction, didn't she?
It was absolutely his pleasure to deliver it.

He shifted atop her, pinning her wrists beside her
head while holding his weight off her chest with his
elbows. His legs closed on the outsides of hers and he
held her trapped and still, though she tried to arch up
into him.

"Careful, blossom." He nibbled his lips against hers
and kissed her chin before lifting a little so he could
admire her quivering breasts again. "These are mine
now. I won't let them get hurt."

"Is that mine?" Her thighs twitched, stimulating his
throbbing length where he had nestled it in the valley
above the tops of her hose where her legs were pressed
together.

"All yours." He pulsed his hips, teasing both of them
with a small stab against the satin protecting her plump,
tender flesh. The satin that covered her mound, radiant
with the heat of her desire, caressed his swollen tip and
nearly turned him inside out.

"I'm claiming the rest of what's mine first," he said
with possessive intent. He licked into the small hollow
at the base of her throat and kissed across her upper
chest. He nuzzled and blew softly and tantalized her
nipples until she was moaning beneath him, hips trying to rock and wrists turning in his grasp.

"I'm ready," she gasped. "You don't have to…"

"Oh, I do." He rose onto his splayed knees, keeping
her legs trapped between his own.

She was a vision of sensuality, hair spilling around her, arms weak against the covers, breasts hitching and stomach quivering. The scorching way she looked him over, gaze arrowing downward until she fixated on his erection, nearly burned his skin from his bones. She licked her lips, and he nearly lost it on the spot.

He had wanted to take his time nudging the scrap of lace down to expose her a centimeter at a time, teasing both of them. He didn't have that kind of discipline left. He shifted off her and dragged her underwear away, taking a legging of hose with it.

She opened her legs and held up her arms invitingly, but he had to—*had to*—taste her. He slid down the bed and curled his arm around her thigh, taking soft bites of her smooth skin while she threaded her fingers into his hair and gave a ragged cry at the first press of his mouth against her hot, sweet core.

He could have lingered there forever, but she was more than ready to take him, and he was so drunk on the essence of her, he rose over her again.

No condom, he realized as the reflexive thought flitted into his mind. She was his and he was hers, nothing between them but the heat of their passion.

He pressed into her. Her soft flesh briefly resisted, then he was enveloped by paradise. Swallowed. Engulfed. Her legs closed around his waist, and her arms looped around his neck.

It took everything in him to keep a leash on himself. To be gentle. To thrust with measured power when he wanted to lose himself in wild, unfettered abandonment. He wanted to imprint himself on her for all time.

That's how it had been before. The urge was even stronger now. She was his and he wanted her to know it. *His.*

If anything, his enforced restraint made the act even more intense. He was shaking with effort, his entire body one live nerve that was being stroked by her soft hands and hugged by her strong thighs. Her gasping breaths were painting his shoulder and her heat, her incredible heat, was bathing him in more pleasure than he'd ever known.

"Deeper," she gasped. "Don't stop, Jun Li. Don't stop. Keep going—" Her cries of culmination struck his ears and stripped him of his last vestige of control.

He straightened his arms and threw back his head, pressing into her one final time as he gave himself up to her.

Ivy woke a few hours later, eyes clogged with the makeup she hadn't removed. She slipped from the weight of Jun Li's arm, feeling very languid and lovely. She was still wearing the garter belt, and the dangling straps titillated her as she walked to the bathroom. She let it drop to the tiles as she entered.

The tub water had gone cold, but most of the candles were still burning. She left the lights off, flicked the knob to release the water, then brushed her teeth. She rubbed cleansing cream all over her face before starting the shower.

As she stood with her face turned up to the stream, rinsing away cream and makeup in one go, Jun Li asked in a rumbling voice, "Need help in there?"

"Always," she invited and skimmed the water out of her eyes.

She turned to face him as he entered the huge glass cubicle. The candlelight picked up glints on his jaw and amid the shadows of hair on his chest.

"You're covered in the sparkles I was wearing." She tried to brush them away with her damp hand, but it didn't work.

"I believe that's the magic of sex within the sanctity of marriage." His hair was rumpled, his eyelids heavy with satisfaction. "Let's hope it never wears off."

She chuckled throatily as he dragged her close and kissed her.

They began to soap one another and he grew steely between them, but just when she thought things were going to turn very magical, he stilled. His hand had been on her abdomen but lifted away while he stared intently at her belly button.

"I'm starting to show, I know." Her hand had no hope of hiding it, but she covered her navel anyway.

"I was too distracted by the sexy underwear to notice earlier."

"The dress designer was going crazy trying to downplay it."

"Why?" He gave her a perplexed look.

"Well, it's not very sexy, is it?"

"I assure you this curviness suits you. You're sexier than ever." He brought his slippery hands up to gently cup her breasts. In the golden glow of the steam-filtered candlelight, his expression was very somber. "It makes me realize the baby is real, though."

She choked on a disbelieving laugh. "The paternity report didn't clue you in?"

"I gave it to my parents without reading it," he said

with a distracted shrug. "I had all the proof I needed. Rationally." He waved at his own head, then his tongue touched his bottom lip, and his expression grew introspective.

The shadows of reservations lingering behind his eyes worried her.

"Are you…" She hesitated, fearful of the answer. "Are you happy about the baby?"

"I'm still in shock," he said with candor. "Concerned about both of you. I'm constantly thinking about everything that needs to be done before the baby arrives." He absently circled his palm in the soapy bubbles at her hip. "I have no idea what sort of father I'll make, which is the kind of uncertainty and lack of confidence I hate most. I prefer to tackle things that are only a matter of reading a few books to master. There's no way to know or prepare for what we face."

It wasn't the effusive joy she had hoped for, but it was honest and gave her some insight into his thoughts at least.

"Are you?" he asked. "Happy?"

She nodded helplessly, smile wobbling with emotion. "From the first minute, even though I was terrified and knew you would be furious."

"Confused," he corrected.

"I assumed I would have to do it on my own, which was scary, but I always wanted to be a mother. I was glad I was pregnant by you. I didn't regret anything about our night together so I couldn't regret that it resulted in a baby." She bit her lip, hesitating before she admitted, "I was glad it gave me an excuse to see you again. I wanted to."

A subtle flinch tightened his expression.

"I wanted to see you, too," he said, but she could tell it was hard for him to reveal that. "But I wasn't planning any sort of future with anyone. I didn't want to lead you on. This..." He waved at the steam around them. "Marrying for practical reasons... I'm confident I can meet your needs and give you a good life, but I'm not sure I can be everything you want. That concerns me."

"You mean...love?"

"Yes."

Her arms seemed to tremble all the way to her fingertips. In these last hours, she had begun to believe something wonderful was around the corner. Now it slipped out of sight.

She wanted to say *Why did you marry me, then?* But she could turn that question on herself, and the answer was because she was falling for him.

"You don't have to be anything but who you are." She spoke bravely, trying to convince both of them. "A marriage isn't a project with deliverables and milestones and once it's commissioned, it runs like clockwork. It's something we'll build over time."

His mouth relaxed. "Am I going to have to learn more about what you do for a living so I can liken our marriage to analyzing compliance?"

"You do not want our marriage to be anything like my work," she assured him. "I make a career of being a wet blanket. I say, 'You can't do that or you'll risk a lawsuit.' Then people tell me to leave the room because I've ruined their party. And something tells me you know that." She pinched at his belly, determined to return to a lighter mood and a sense of accord. "All the top guns I've ever known have ducked into the men's room when they've seen me coming."

"Because plausible deniability is a very useful thing to possess." His smile flashed.

"Well, you're missing out on valuable information. For instance, I happen to know you're not supposed to talk about work on your wedding night. There are other things you're legally required to do."

"Legally?" he repeated. "Educate me. I don't want to overlook a single directive."

She wanted to make a joke about being unable to deny the plausible evidence that was hard against her slippery belly, but their gazes tangled, and such giddy happiness arrived, she couldn't speak.

He cupped her damp cheek and kissed her, tender and profound at once, erasing all other thoughts in her mind except the desire to touch and taste and steep herself in the pleasure they gave one another.

She wound up taking hold of his steely length, smoothing her hands over him in the rain of the warm water, saying, "Let me show you."

She drew him with her as she backed up and sat on the bench. Then she took him in her mouth, making him hiss and brace a hand on the glass. As steam gathered around them, she stroked the iron strength of his thighs and caressed his buttocks and reveled in completely dismantling him.

Afterward, he took her back to bed and did the same to her. Twice.

They both passed out then, sleeping late, but woke to make love again. It went on like that for the whole of the following day, both of them immersing themselves in one another. It was tender and playful and sexy, and it was a long time before Ivy feared again that she might not get everything she needed from this marriage.

Jun Li had had a handful of long-term relationships. Aside from taking a date to company-sponsored charity galas, he had mostly kept his romantic life separate from work. Because of that, he expected Ivy's presence at his business dinners to distract him and divide his attention.

On the contrary—she proved to be a surprising asset at the mixers and networking events they began to attend together. She slid effortlessly between the small talk of social niceties and the meaty business discussions that were often held in multiple languages.

In fact, when they were flying back to Singapore after breaking ground on a port project, she said, "If I heard correctly that some of the project is financed with cryptocurrency, I'd double-check your financing contracts on how that's to be reported. The EU has been updating their regulations. You don't want to fall into noncompliance. The fines are huge."

He did, caught a potential oversight that would have put them grossly over budget if they'd been fined for it and replaced a less competent officer with one who had Ivy's proactive attitude and attention to detail.

When they visited Hong Kong, she introduced him to the president of the bank where she had earned a reputation for being conscientious and scrupulously honest, once recommending the termination of a trader who had arrogantly tried to avoid her audits. She had rescued the bank from the jaws of a damaging scandal, and the president still bemoaned the fact she'd transferred back to Canada rather than take the promotion he'd offered her.

"Thank you for making a point of introducing us," Jun Li said when they were back at his villa in the Peak. "He's an invaluable connection. There's a certain snobbery when it comes to old money versus new." And occasional suspicions over how new money had been made. "Now he knows I'm legitimate."

"Yes, I know. That's why I did it."

Her smile bordered on smug, but the sly way she slanted it at him caused a hard pulse inside him. Her face was rounder these days, her skin wearing the glow the pregnancy books talked about. Her breasts and backside were something men sneaked glances at, himself included. From behind, she didn't even look pregnant, just sumptuously curvy.

"Are we keeping track?" she asked as she used her hands to frame the small pot filling out her front. "This evening it was unanimous that the way I'm carrying indicates a boy."

"We could ask the doctor." He averted his gaze and shrugged out of his jacket, throwing it over the back of a nearby chair.

"Where's the fun in that?"

Where was the fun in any of it, he almost asked, but bit back what would sound very cruel. The more obvious her pregnancy became, however, the less he could deny his impending fatherhood. He didn't want to, not really. It was just that when he let himself contemplate how much more his life would change than it already had, his sense of control eroded to the point he was only grasping grains of sand. Everything else was slipping through his fingers.

It didn't matter that Ivy was fitting into his life so seamlessly. A baby would be different. No matter how much he read, he didn't feel prepared. In fact, he was beginning to think reading about it fed the dark clouds that danced around his periphery, threatening to close in on him.

"Can you please?" She turned her back on him and held up her hair.

He unclasped her necklace and opened the zip on her dress.

"I'm going to miss this," she said as he impulsively placed a kiss on the spot where her neck met her shoulder.

"What?"

"You. Traveling with you and…being husband and wife." He'd left her alone for a night or two here and there, but she'd accompanied him on his longer trips throughout Asia. She was starting her third trimester, though. Her midwife had advised this be her last flight of nonessential travel. "It's felt like a honeymoon."

"Now I feel really guilty that we've put off taking one until after the baby comes."

"That's not why I said it. I wanted you to know that I like being with you." Her smile was offset. Self-conscious. The way she searched his eyes made his chest tighten.

He was going to miss her, too. That's what he should have said. He wasn't letting himself think about how he would feel, though. He'd been leaning on old, not very healthy habits of pressing negative feelings deep into his subconscious rather than dealing with them.

"You're tired, though." He saw it in the way she stole catnaps every chance she got. "It's time you began to take it easy."

She made a noise of reluctant agreement, then tilted another look up at him. It held the sort of invitation that made his blood heat.

"I'm not *too* tired."

Good, because his appetite for her never seemed to abate. Nor hers for him, which was intensely gratifying. She tended to be on top these days since it was more comfortable for her. No matter how they made love, he was transported to a euphoria that left him spent and satiated. Even the feel of her damp skin against his in the aftermath, when her hair tickled his jaw and he was afraid to move because he didn't want to wake her, was deeply satisfying.

She nudged him in the side, then drew in a startled breath even as he realized her arm was across his waist. She hadn't nudged him. The baby had.

"Did you feel that?" she asked with a sleepy laugh and tried to bring his hand to her bump. "Our little gymnast woke me up."

"Mmm. No wonder you're so tired, building us a gold medalist." His heart was clogging his throat. He extricated himself and left the bed. "Try to go back to sleep. I'm going to get a little work done."

She made a noise of disappointment but drew a pillow into the space he'd occupied and sighed, dropping back to sleep in an instant.

While he berated himself. This was ridiculous. He should not be this unsettled by something so natural. He wanted to crawl straight back into bed beside her, but there was something grimly familiar about the looming emptiness of leaving her behind once they returned home. It made him wary of allowing himself to become too attached to her presence next to him as he slept.

He told himself it was better that he return to his mostly solitary life before he couldn't face it without feeling like a limb had been amputated, but that was exactly how it felt. From the moment he installed her in his penthouse in Shanghai and left for New York, the pit of his gut became heavy with dread. He moved through his days as though walking through gelatin.

He hadn't started his medication. That was the problem. It had some unpleasant side effects, so he had done what he had scolded Ivy for doing. He had put up with a few more days of feeling worked up and overloaded with apprehension and self-doubt, suffered a little longer and a little longer, hoping it would go away.

Once the wedding had been behind them, his symptoms had evened out into something he thought he could handle, but he was missing the hell out of her now.

He was a grown man, far beyond the age where he should be suffering terminal homesickness and missing a wife he'd only had for ten weeks.

He didn't want to feel this tearing need to be in two places. It was impossible. Painful. It wasn't as though his responsibilities away from her were unimportant. Given the proposed expansion into aeronautics, there was only so much he could delegate. Much of the decision making rested on him.

This sense of dependence on her was an additional stressor. This was why he hadn't wanted a wife and child. They were people he had to worry about, but also people he had to worry about being *without*.

Wrapped around all this was the knowledge that he wouldn't feel this resentment and irritation, wouldn't be brooding this hard when he ought to be paying attention in a meeting, if he had started taking his damned pills when they were prescribed to him.

"Sir." His assistant tapped his shoulder and showed him his phone with an incoming call from Ivy. He had tried her earlier, before this presentation, but her assistant had said she was lying down.

"I have to take this," he said, rising and swiping to accept the call as he left the boardroom.

"I'm sorry I missed you earlier," she said, sounding tired. "I feel silly for calling, but I promised I would tell you if I wasn't feeling well. I don't."

"What's wrong? Have you called the midwife?"

"She's here now. She said my blood pressure is up a bit, which is weird because I was reading a book, not doing anything strenuous. She's not *worried* worried, but she wants me to go to the clinic for a few tests as a precaution. I have a headache, too. I think I picked up a bug. I don't mean to worry you. I just wanted you to know."

"Do you want me to come home?"

"No. I'm sure it's fine. I just wanted you to know."

"Ivy." Everything in him had gone very still. "What do you need from me right now? Be honest."

There was such a long pause, he almost spoke her name again to be sure the call hadn't dropped. Then he heard her ask, very quietly, "Will you please come home?"

His heart flipped over in his chest, and his mouth went dry.

"I will," he said unsteadily, instantly repeating to himself the lies she had served him. He was sure it was fine. "I'll text once I'm in the air. You text as soon as you have news."

"I feel like I'm making a fuss over nothing. You really don't mind?"

"I really don't." In one way, he was glad for the excuse to go to her, but it was the worst possible reason. Asking for him was killing her, he could tell. She would only do it if, deep down, she truly felt something was wrong. "I'll see you soon."

"Okay. Thank you." She sounded subdued, not like herself at all.

He ended the call and reentered the board room long enough to excuse himself from the rest of the week's meetings and presentations. He could see the faces twisting with annoyance over the delay, but he turned his back on it, discovering he cared very little what they thought of his departure.

Two hours later he was in his private jet, reaching cruising altitude. He texted Ivy to let her know.

She texted back.

They think it's preeclampsia.

He looked up the term, read for fifteen minutes, then went to his stateroom and cracked the childproof cap on his prescription.

CHAPTER TEN

BED REST.

It could be worse—that was what Ivy kept telling herself. It was a mild case of preeclampsia, so she wasn't hospitalized, but she was only allowed to move from her bed to the sofa or a lounger on the terrace. She had to lie on her side and drink a million glasses of water and give samples to the midwife so often, she felt like a pincushion. She was scheduled for an ultrasound every week and had to wear a fetal heart rate monitor at different times to reassure everyone that things were not escalating.

Two weeks in, so far so good, but Ivy had to work at not stressing out over what "escalating" would mean: early delivery. They were already talking about inducing labor at thirty-four weeks. She had crossed into thirty today. Every minute was a slightly better chance for their baby, so she was doing everything she could to buy them that time.

Which meant four more weeks of watching mindless sitcoms and reading all the romance novels she had saved to her e-reader over the last several years. She'd been trying to find time to conquer her digital to-be-read pile, but it was hard to concentrate. Every day her father offered to leap on a plane, but for what purpose? So he could pace the house restlessly the way her husband was doing? Setting her nerves on edge?

It wouldn't be so bad if she could occupy herself with continuing to shop for nursery items, but she didn't want to tempt fate.

Maybe Jun Li felt the same. She wouldn't know because he didn't want to talk about the baby. Or even *to* the baby. Yesterday, he had caught her singing to her bump. She had asked him if he wanted to join in or tell the baby what a silly mom it had.

He had stiffened and dismissed the suggestion very quickly, saying he had a call to return. When she had asked him about work later, he said, "What call? Oh. It was fine."

There hadn't been a call. She was sure of it. Why would he lie? In so many ways, he was the height of attentiveness, but there was this *wall* between them, one that had arrived with her diagnosis. When she had been traveling with him, she'd thought they were falling in love. Now, she wondered if he felt anything toward her at all.

Brooding, she told him she was going to nap.

He came up a little while later to check on her, found her awake and reading, so he fetched his laptop.

"Just go to work," she blurted, unable to deal with his mixed signals any longer.

"I am working," he claimed, but he set aside the laptop and rose from the chair to look out the window.

He wasn't working effectively or efficiently or even literally now that she'd spoken to him. She could tell he was agitated. He wasn't sleeping any better than she was, and she saw him chew an antacid several times a day.

"I'm glad you aren't traveling, but you could at least go in to your office. It's only a couple of hours back if you need to come home. I'll move to the penthouse if you want."

"The midwife and clinic are closer to this house. You need to be here, and I'm managing well enough working remotely. Quit trying to solve a problem that doesn't exist."

"I *am* a problem that exists, and I feel guilty about it," she muttered, plumping the pillow beneath her cheek.

"Why? Did you do something to make this happen?"

"No." She hated when he logicked her out of a perfectly good sulk. "But there's nothing that either of us can do. Your hovering doesn't change anything, so you should go to work."

"Ivy." He came to stand over her, hands hooked on his hips. "I am a grown man who makes his own decisions about whether to go to work or hover over his wife. If you want me to work in the other room, say so and I will."

"I want you to tell me you're angry. Or that you begrudge that I got pregnant. Tell me you regret sleeping with me."

He tucked his chin. "Is that how *you* feel?"

"No." Her heart thunked as she realized she had started a far more sobering conversation than she had meant to. She couldn't look at him, but she had to know. "I keep thinking you must resent me, though. I'm just this lump that lies around making demands."

"I feel none of those things. I'm concerned for both of you and angry with my inability to help, but I regret nothing." He sank onto the edge of the bed. "I know that relying on me is hard for you, but I hope you know me well enough by now to believe I would hire someone to fetch your socks if I didn't want to do it for you."

She couldn't help a small "pfft" of laughter, because it was such an arrogantly truthful statement. She did know that much about him, but not a lot more. That was what was bothering her. She didn't know what he was thinking or feeling.

"What is this really about, hmm?" He rubbed her arm. "I can see you're miserable and frightened. I can't fix that. I can't even tell you not to feel those things. They're warranted. All I can do is be here so you know you're not alone."

Why did he have to be so freaking *perfect*? If she had had doubts about whether she was falling for her husband, they incinerated as her heart practically exploded with love for him. It was so powerful, her eyes stung with the force of the emotion. She had to bite her lips together to keep them from quivering.

"You play your cards so close to your chest." She caught his hand, needing to touch her lips to his knuckles, needing to give this thing happening inside her a small outlet. "I'm never sure how you feel." *How do you feel about* me?

She was too frightened of the answer to ask it aloud. It had been a lot easier to feel confident about how he regarded her when she had felt more like a partner in this marriage. When her own feelings had merely been developing, not filling her to brimming. When she'd been able to *show* him—

"Do you want sex?" she asked with dawning realization.

"What?" He pulled his hand away. "Where did that come from?"

"You're so edgy. Is it because we can't make love? We could get creative. Figure something out." She wanted—needed—to feel close to him.

"You're determined to have a fight today, aren't you?" He spoke with indignant wonder. "I'm offended that you think I would ask my sick wife, who is barely moving so she can keep our child alive, to perform sexual favors. There is a perfectly good shower in there if I feel a need for an orgasm."

"So I'm just a plumbing device?"

"Now you're being horrible. We're not talking about this." He rose.

"I need to know how you feel, Jun Li!" Frustrated tears arrived to wet her lashes. "You think I can't sense you pulling away? You're doing it right now. We were so happy when I was traveling with you. Weren't we?" Maybe she was deluding herself.

"This is a stressful and difficult time. Of course neither of us is happy."

Another nonanswer that quashed her confidence in his feelings toward her.

"I was afraid to marry you because I thought the baby was all we had between us," she reminded him. "But if that's true, what happens if…if…"

"No." He used the sternest tone she'd ever heard from him.

Fractures were working their way across her heart, though, spreading outward, making her entire being ache with anguish. She sniffed back the tears pooling in her sinuses.

"Stop. Ivy, no. Shh. Stop thinking that." He slid onto the bed and gathered her in gentle arms. Held her. Enveloped her. "Don't go there, blossom." His voice softened as he crushed her to his chest. "Stay here. Stay right here with me. We're all okay right now. Hmm?"

His hands stroked over her from crown to tailbone, grounding her and reassuring her as she fought back the wraiths and demons that were trying to steal her faith that her long-held dream of a family would come true.

"I'm really scared," she admitted, cold to the marrow of her bones.

"I know." His arms tightened. "I can't allow myself to fear, though. I can't let you see any doubt in me. If I'm turning away, it's because I don't want you to see anything but strength in me. And belief in our best outcome."

"Oh, Jun Li." Oddly, she felt a compulsion to reassure *him*. She curled herself closer, so the bump of their baby was nestled securely between them.

His touch faltered briefly before he continued petting her hair.

She tilted her head back to see up into his face. "You're doing it again." Dejected, she shifted back an inch so her bump wasn't touching him.

He made a noise of reluctance before he admitted, "I feel guilty. I don't regret sleeping with you. Never. But I feel responsible for what you're going through."

"You shouldn't. It's no one's fault." She had already run through the gamut with the doctor. This was one of those complications that could strike any pregnancy.

He rolled away for a tissue and handed it to her. As she used it to mop beneath her eyes, he sat up with his back to her. Doing it *again*.

She sighed.

"I know," he said, voice not quite even. He kept his back to her, rubbing his hands restlessly on his thighs. "There's something I've been keeping from you. I want to tell you, but it's difficult to talk about."

Her heart clunked. A chill froze her motionless. "What?" Her heart began to pound so hard she worried it was bad for the baby.

"I'm taking an antidepressant."

It was so far from anything she had expected—her mind had gone straight to divorce, cheating, terminal illness—she didn't know what to say.

"I had no idea," she stammered. "I mean, you've never left a bottle around or anything."

"I only started taking them again since…" He glanced over his shoulder and nodded at how she was lying on the bed. "I didn't like hiding it, but I didn't want you to think getting married and becoming a father has made me depressed."

"Has it?"

She watched his profile wince. "Kind of."

She stifled her gasp of hurt but felt the tendons in her neck flex.

"This is why I didn't want to tell you." He shifted so he was angled to face her. "I'm not sure I'm capable of the kind of happiness you want me to feel, Ivy.

I'm wired to worry about what will cause *un*happiness. Once I start down that road, it's all I see. Heaviness and darkness. When I'm in control of my life, those shadows fade."

"But I showed up and you couldn't control this."

"Exactly. I got through our wedding without medication and thought I would be able to handle starting our life together without falling back on it."

Got through? She had to swallow another knot of agony forming in her throat. A sensible part of her understood this wasn't about her, but it still hurt to think of herself as something he *endured*.

"But when this complication happened…" For one brief second, torment flashed across his expression. His anguish was so tangible, it made her feel small for thinking he wasn't as deeply invested in this pregnancy as she was.

He smoothed his expression, and his mouth quirked. "If I'm on the pills, I worry the appropriate amount. The darkness is there, but at the edges. It doesn't take over. Maybe I'm still worrying a little more than necessary, which is why I'm hovering." He rubbed the backs of his knuckles on her upper arm. "But if I wasn't taking the pills, I would risk a far more serious depression and be no use to you at all."

His hand went back to his thigh as he regarded her. The wall was up again, but she saw it for the defense mechanism it was.

She reached to cover his hand. "And you knew what was happening because…"

"I've been here before." He nodded.

"In Vancouver." All the pieces were coming together.

"Yes. That's why Kevin came to live with me." He caught her fingers in a warm grip, but his mouth flattened.

"It's okay. I'm not judging you. Tell me as much or as little as you want."

After a moment, he pressed her hand under his, sandwiching it against his hard thigh.

"I'd been living alone for years and didn't really have any friends. I didn't understand that depression made the idea of making friends feel like too much work, like no one would want to be my friend. I came out of class one day and there was a flyer on my windshield about mental health. It said, 'Are you suffering from?' and had a list. I ticked every box." He snorted, but there was no humor in it.

"There were numbers for counseling and meeting times for group therapy. I was standing there thinking I should do something, but already knew I probably wouldn't. Classic symptom," he said in a rueful aside. "Then Kevin came up to me. His car was parked next to mine, and I was so embarrassed to be caught with that thing in my hand."

"You shouldn't be." She squeezed his thigh and slithered closer.

"I know. But he must have seen how guilty I looked. He said he answered phones at the counseling office if I ever wanted to talk. He called me 'one of the quiet ones,' the ones he worried about. I didn't even realize he was in two of my classes, I was that checked out of the world around me. But while I was standing there feeling like a tool, I noticed he had pillows and blankets in his back seat. He said he stayed late to help at the group sessions, then had morning classes, so he slept in his car half the week. I had never invited anyone into my house, but I said I had a room he could sleep in if he wanted to. He followed me home and stuck around for two years."

"And helped you?"

"He did. Not because he'd taken training sessions on mental health support, but because he was a friend. He went with me to the doctor and asked about my life and dragged me to the beach and cooked so I ate properly. None of it was a silver bullet, but it added up over time until I was much healthier."

She wanted to ask if the pregnancy scare in high school had started it. That might explain why he seemed to be holding back on bonding with the baby. And her.

I'm not sure I'm capable of the kind of happiness you want me to feel.

"You never told your parents about any of it?"

"You do know me." He cradled her jaw and ran his thumb across her cheek. "You have the softest skin," he noted absently. "I want my lips against some part of your body every minute of every day. I want to kiss you and make love to you and, yes, I am definitely missing that, blossom. But…" He sighed and moved his hand to her hip, shifting his gaze to the headboard. "These pills have side effects. Insomnia, heartburn, muscle tension, dry eyes. Erectile dysfunction. That's another reason I put off starting them," he said wryly.

"Oh. So you can't…?"

"I can. But it's not as… Let's talk about that when it's relevant," he dismissed. "Most of the side effects will settle down after a while, and hopefully our lives will, too. Then I can wean off the pills and my little issues won't matter."

They weren't little, but at least they weren't as dire as she'd feared.

"Thank you for telling me all this." She squeezed his thigh again. "It helps to know what's going on for you. I'm sorry I pressured you to talk about something so private."

"You're my wife. Keeping it from you bothered me. I don't want secrets between us." He leaned down to kiss her.

It was sweet and soft and tender and made all her love glow like a dawn sun inside her.

When they broke apart, she had to say it. *Had to.* It had been building for so long, and now he'd opened himself up, letting her see his most vulnerable inner self.

"I love you."

A light flared in his eyes before his expression shuttered, hiding it. Denying it?

She quickly closed her eyes, ignoring the way his rebuff sheared off a layer of her heart. "It's okay if you don't want to say it back, but I couldn't keep it in any longer."

"Ivy." He spoke in a shaken voice and set his hand on the side of her neck, where her pulse probably throbbed against the heel of his palm hard enough to alarm him.

"Honestly." She brought his palm to her mouth. "It's okay. I just needed you to know. No secrets." Her smile was unsteady as she peeked at him.

He didn't smile back. His brow was tortured. "Blossom, I don't know if I'm capable of that sort of love." His tone was laden with those painful words—*no secrets*.

Her heart gave a wounded cry, but she understood him better now. "I know."

She was trying to ease his tension by letting him know she didn't blame him, but he flinched and the lines of agitation in his face deepened.

The anguished silence between them might have dragged out for hours, but the butler texted to say the midwife had arrived.

"The other woman in my life," Ivy said with a weak smile. She was actually grateful to have her. The woman had become a close friend. She was the kindest, most thorough and confidence-inspiring person in the world.

Jun Li smiled faintly and went downstairs to bring her up to Ivy.

CHAPTER ELEVEN

"IT MAKES ME wonder if this baby is all we have."

All the pills in the world couldn't drown out Ivy's vulnerable words.

Jun Li heard them on repeat in his head, along with, *"I love you. I couldn't keep it in any longer."*

She had humbled him with that. With the fact she had felt so deeply about him for a while and kept it to herself. She humbled him every day as she took every smidge of the doctor's and midwife's advice to heart, accepted treatment from his mother's acupuncturist and choked down Chinese medicine once the specialist okayed her to supplement with it.

She was quietly fighting with everything in her to give their baby its best chance.

Because she feared the baby was all they had between them.

That wasn't true at all, but his damned dark brain kept dredging up those same fears he hadn't let her voice. If they didn't have the baby, he would be devastated. More than he could articulate. So would she, and there was no way he could protect her from that sort of pain. The threat of it was turning him inward to brood.

And he was bottling everything so he wouldn't spill any on Ivy and scare the hell out of her. His medication could only do so much. He would need the sort of tranquilizer that dropped a bull elephant to really do the job.

Somehow her acceptance of his limitations where love was concerned kept stabbing through all his best efforts to numb his emotions, though. He couldn't help wondering if he was fighting on two different fronts. Maybe he was still trying to protect himself after that youthful offering of his heart had turned so painful.

For years, he had lumped all that dark time in Canada together as one bleak episode that he had firmly put behind him. Where was the use in picking apart those years to find which scars belonged to which injuries? That could crack the urn where he was keeping all his suppressed emotions.

He was compelled to do something tangible for Ivy, though. Something that demonstrated he did care for her, more than he knew how to express.

That's what had brought him to his parents' home in the Bund today.

"Jun Li," his father greeted him with mild surprise as he joined Jun Li in the office that was dusted daily but otherwise no longer saw much use. "Ivy?" he asked with concern.

"As well as we can expect. Her blood pressure has been coming up in the last week. They gave her medication the other day to help the baby's lungs develop. We're hoping she lasts to thirty-six weeks, but it's likely they'll have to induce labor soon."

His father made a noise of concern, but they were interrupted briefly as tea was brought in. His father invited him to sit, and they settled into the comfortable chairs, poured tea and took a few moments to appreciate it.

"You want to discuss a restructure with the company?" his father prompted.

"I do." A cleaving sensation pried in his chest. Jun Li felt disloyal and ungrateful even bringing this up, but when he looked into the future, he saw Ivy and their baby first, not the company. "I'd like to cancel the expansion. And sell off all but the core infrastructure division."

His father's brows went up. After a moment, he brought his tea to his lips and sipped.

"Something will fail otherwise. *I* will." Jun Li abandoned his cup and rose to pace. "It galls me to say I can't do it all. I know you built and managed all this while supporting a wife and child, but I can already tell that something will suffer if I don't narrow my focus. Ivy and the baby will suffer. I've been forced to delegate more while Ivy has been so ill, but that's not sustainable. The expansion would be a feather in our cap, but I find myself asking, How much is enough? How does it provide more security than we currently have? Isn't it more prudent to do fewer things well than many things poorly?"

Jun Li looked out to the Huangpu River, waiting for his father's response. There were knots of self-reproach in his stomach, but his father was never one to speak without considering his words. It took a few minutes.

"You seem to be crediting me with building an empire by myself. I had your mother. Your aunts and uncles. I had *you*. Would we have anything in Canada if you hadn't driven those investments? You're a strong leader, Jun Li. Ambitious and capable. The way you've stepped into my shoes makes me very proud, but I never ran this alone the way you do. I supported the expansion because it was what you wanted. I will always stand behind you. You're my son."

The back of Jun Li's throat grew tight, partly from his father's willingness to support his decision, which was a relief, but more from the sentiment in them. They weren't a family that used the word *love* openly, but when his father said, "You're my son," that's what he was saying. *I love you.* Jun Li heard it clear as a gong that reverberated in his ears.

For a few seconds, all he could think was that he had said the same to Ivy more than once. *You're my wife.* It was a different type of love to his father's for him, but that's what it was. Deep, enduring love.

"Your cousin would like a more prominent role," his father mused. "Perhaps rather than sell off those divisions, move them under a different banner and give her the role of president. Keep it in the family, at least."

"That's a good idea." Jun Li came back and retook his seat, mind quickly seeing the potential. They discussed it further, then he called Ivy. "I'd like to run up to Beijing to see my cousin. Will you be all right without me for a few more hours?"

For a moment, Ivy couldn't speak. When she drew a breath, it broke slightly. He heard it.

"You're crying." His voice gentled. "I'll leave now and come straight home."

"No. I was just speaking to Dad," she admitted.

"You're homesick? Did you tell him to come? I'll arrange it."

"He's going to call my assistant." She wasn't homesick. That was the problem. She had realized the place she thought of as home was wherever her husband happened to be. Jun Li had become her world.

It made her realize she had not become the woman she had aspired to be when she had had her affair with him. For a brief time, she'd been self-possessed and capable of creating happiness for herself, not relying on a man to provide it to her. She had promised herself she wouldn't fall for a man who didn't love her, but she had. She was both desolate and deliriously happy.

The worst part was, Jun Li deserved her love. He was considerate and respectful, and when she reached for him in the night, he took her hand and kissed her knuckles, silently reassuring her that she wasn't alone in the dark.

She was trying to understand how detached and untethered he must have felt all those years, suffering in silence, alone in a country that wasn't home. He'd been betrayed at a young age, too. She didn't want to pressure him to feel things that didn't come naturally, but she couldn't deny that she was hurting right now. She needed a little time to put herself back together before he came home.

"I'm fine," she lied. "Just wishing the aspirin was doing a better job with my headache. The midwife is coming soon. I'll ask her if I can take anything else. Then I'll have a nap and won't even notice you're not home yet."

"All right. Text me if anything changes."

"I will."

"Ivy—" He cut himself off.

"Yes?"

There was a lengthy silence where she heard her own pulse in her ears.

"I'll tell you when I get home," he said in a voice she'd never heard. It was tender and strong and wedged itself against her heart. "I'll be back before you go to bed."

"Is that supposed to be funny?" she asked with mock ire.

He gave a dry chuckle.

Another silence fell between them, one that acknowledged the distance between them. She wanted to say *Come home*. Not because she was scared or lonely or feeling less than one hundred percent. She was all those things, but she wanted to be with him. *I need you.*

Don't be that person, she admonished herself.

"The midwife is here," she said as the butler appeared at the door. "Travel safe. I love you."

"I'll see you soon."

Me too. That was what he should have said. *I love you, too.*

His heart was swelling like a balloon. A thousand thoughts and words had filled his throat, none of which did justice to the intensity of what he was experiencing. He had swallowed it back, wanting to get it right. He might not be the most romantic man in the world, but he thought the first time he opened his heart to his wife, he ought to do it in person.

He ended the call, and the glow that her voice had

instilled in him continued to warm him as he continued with his day.

Four hours later, he shook his cousin's hand. She was smiling broadly, excited for the prospect of new responsibilities. He wanted to caution her to be careful what she asked for, but he was feeling too lighthearted. He was more optimistic than he'd been in a long time.

He was considering the best way to tell Ivy. He couldn't claim he had done this entirely for her. It was for himself and his own sanity, but also for *them*. For their growing family.

Deep down, he hoped she would see it as the grand gesture a man made when he wanted the woman he loved to know how deep his feelings ran. He wanted her to know that she was his priority. His everything.

He said his goodbye to his cousin and turned to the door as his assistant rushed in from ordering the helicopter. His face was pale, his voice urgent. He thrust out his phone.

"Sir. A message about your wife. She's had a seizure. The ambulance is on its way to the house."

CHAPTER TWELVE

"IT WAS VERY SUDDEN," the midwife told him as she escorted him to the maternity ward. "I put the fetal heart rate monitor on her in the afternoon and came back a few hours later to check it. The baby was not in distress, but her blood pressure had gone up. I said we should go to the hospital as a precaution. She wanted to call you, but before she could pick up the phone… Thankfully, she was on the bed and didn't fall. They delivered by surgery and it went well. She's in critical care. Your son is doing very well."

She took him into a nursery, where most of the babies were in open cradles, but she led him to the impossibly small, black-haired infant wearing only a diaper as he sprawled on his back in an enclosed unit.

"He's breathing on his own but getting a little oxygen as a precaution. He doesn't have much body fat, so we're keeping him warm. Those wires are monitors, again for precaution. Would you like to touch him?"

Jun Li was numb from the anxiety of his travel here and felt split in half as he washed his hands. Mentally, he was racing through the corridors in search of Ivy. He'd nearly had a stroke when he got the news about her seizure. He wouldn't be able to breathe properly until he'd seen her and reassured himself she was all right.

The other half of him was here, taking in a miracle that put tears of gratitude in his eyes. How had he been afraid of what it meant to be a father? He knew exactly what he needed to do. He had to reassure his son that he was here. That all would be well.

As he reached through the aperture, his hand shook. It looked ridiculous, like the meaty paw of a giant as he ever so gently let it come to rest on his son's warm, bare belly, careful not to dislodge the stub of his umbilical cord. His new, thin skin was softer even than Ivy's cheek.

As Jun Li touched him, the boy's limbs seemed to fold in like a flower to clutch at his hand. It was reflexes—Jun Li knew that in his rational mind. In his heart, it was the yearning of a child to be held safely by its parent.

I'm here. I will always protect you, he silently promised.

He leaned his free arm on the top of the warming unit and rested his forehead on his wrist, breathing against the glass as he gazed on his son. He had Ivy's mouth, as if he needed anything more to imprint himself on the center of Jun Li's heart. The rise and fall of his tiny belly against his palm was timed to the heavy drum of Jun Li's heart in his chest.

This baby shouldn't have even happened. The forces that had come together to make him were impossible odds, yet here he was. He was a gift from a benevolent god. The link that had pulled Ivy's life into his own, joining them forever. He was so grateful for that. So grateful.

"Does he have a name?" the midwife asked gently.

He and Ivy had discussed several, but he refused to make that decision without her.

I have to find your mother. I'll be back. I love you.

Jun Li left a piece of his heart in the enclosure as he withdrew his hand and straightened.

"I need to see my wife."

"Blossom. My heart, my sunshine, my soul. Come back to me. You know I need you."

Ivy smiled in her sleep, not wanting to wake, because in her dream Jun Li was finally saying the things she had longed to hear.

"Destiny brought us together, Ivy. Fate. That is not something you can sleep through."

"I know you can hear me. You're smiling. Don't you want to see our son? Open your eyes."

Her hand was lifted, which somehow dragged her the final distance out of her heavy sleep and forced her to blink her eyes open.

Jun Li held her knuckles against his mouth. His expression shone with such emotion, such love, her vision immediately blurred with tears.

"I want you to stop scaring years off my life. Do you think you can do that?" he asked with gentle humor. "Because I want as much time as possible with you."

"Is—" She moved her free hand to her empty belly, discovered she was wearing an IV wire on that hand. She was in a hospital. "Did you say son?"

"Yes. He's small but strong and fierce and beautiful.

A quiet little fighter, like his mother. Do you know how much I love you, Ivy?"

"No." *Yes.* She could see it gleaming in his eyes. It went into her like a force that scattered light and joy within her, making her feel so special and precious, she wanted to close her eyes against it. It was almost too much to bear, being loved this hard by this man.

"I should have been here." His regret was palpable.

"You're here now." She really should have paid attention to the fact he had always been there in the ways that counted. She swallowed the knot that formed in her throat.

"I'll be here more." He released her hand to lower the rail. He hitched his hip onto the bed beside her, then took up her hand again. "When I left to see my father, I was only thinking of how much you were doing for me—having our baby no matter what it cost you. How could I ever match that? I wanted to show you how much you matter."

"What did you do?" she asked with a trace of apprehension.

"Nothing drastic. I canceled the aeronautics expansion and restructured so my cousin will take a large chunk of responsibility off my plate."

"Oh, is that all," she said with a bewildered laugh.

"I wanted you to know how much you and our son mean to me. Then I wasn't here when you needed me. It will be a long time before I forgive myself for that."

"I don't remember any of it," she assured him. "I'm guessing you wouldn't have been able to do anything. I needed a doctor." She gently palpated her belly through the bandages, discovering the tender spots. Her head was spinning as she tried to absorb all he was saying. "But… Jun Li, I don't need gestures. I mean, I love that you'll have more time with us, but words are enough. I know you wouldn't say them unless they were true."

"They are true, but they're not enough." He gave his head a solemn shake. "I love you in ways that are so new, so complex, I didn't know what I was feeling. I fought examining it." He caressed her cheek with the backs of his fingers. "As if I could avoid the potential for pain if I didn't acknowledge how much you meant to me. But these last hours… The thought of losing you is beyond what I can bear, Ivy. I love you with all my heart." He leaned forward and kissed her in a soft benediction. A seal of the words scrolled across their hearts.

"I love you, too," she said when he lifted his head. She set her hand against his unshaven cheek. His eyes were deeply set and bruised with lack of sleep. Lines of stress were scored next to his mouth. He was still preposterously beautiful. "I would like to circle back to this and kiss you a few thousand more times, but… Can I see our son first?"

Six weeks later, Ivy was about to rise and take Li Qiang back to his room when Jun Li came into their darkened bedroom.

"You're home." She hadn't expected him until tomorrow afternoon.

"We finished early." He spoke quietly as he came to steal Li Qiang. "And I missed you. Both of you," he whispered and kissed the baby. "Were you taking him back to bed? I'll do it."

Ivy snuggled under the covers, drowsy since it was after midnight, but listening on the baby monitor as Jun Li briefly spoke to the nanny and settled their son with tender words for the boy.

When he came back, he dragged off his tie and shirt, throwing all his clothes to the floor as he undressed for bed. He'd been in Beijing for three days, finalizing the restructuring.

Ivy had stayed home because she had had a doctor's appointment and a million other things to organize. They had spoken daily, mostly about Li Qiang and the various details for their upcoming travel and move. With Jun Li's cousin taking over most of the operations based here in Shanghai, she and Jun Li were spending Christmas with Ivy's father, who had put off his wedding until she could attend. Afterward, they would decamp to Singapore, where Jun Li would be closer to the port construction and other projects he would oversee for the next few years.

Ivy had agreed to chair the committee that organized the annual strategy meeting there. It was a good way to get to know more about the company and see where she might fit at some future point. She had also reached out to some of her contacts asking if there was work she might do piecemeal. She wasn't in a hurry to go back to work, especially not full-time, but she wanted to keep her hand in.

Jun Li lifted the blankets and slid in, gathering her to his naked body.

"Oh," she said with disappointment.

"I only want a kiss," he said, drawing back. They had fooled around a little in the last few weeks but hadn't made love since she'd been put on bed rest three months ago.

"No, um, I bought something. I should have changed into it while you were putting Li Qiang down. I didn't think of it until I realized what I was wearing."

"Something?" he prompted.

"Something better than a nursing nightgown and sleep bra. Something I was going to put on when we got to Vancouver, to see if I could improve your opinion of my hometown." She lightly pinched his flat stomach, and he caught her hand.

"Describe it." He brought her hand to his mouth and scraped his teeth against the heel of her palm. "In detail."

"I should start with the price, because it was outrageous considering what little I got."

"Less is more. Everyone knows that. Expense approved. Keep talking."

"There's no garter belt. I hope that doesn't upset you. I got the kind of stockings that stay up on their own so I could keep them on... Mmm."

He rolled her beneath him as he covered her mouth, kissing her hungrily.

Oh, it felt good to feel his weight, his skin, his *hardness*. She scraped her nails lightly against his buttocks, and he groaned and nibbled at her chin.

"Color?" he asked against her throat.

"Purple. I got the size wrong and the bra cup is too small."

"An understandable mistake to make." He gathered her breast, gently massaging through the layers of cotton she wore. "You're forgiven."

"The panties are barely a fig leaf on a satin thread."

"Maybe better suited to tangling around your wrists?" He caught her hands and swept them under the pillow.

A streak of excitement hit her belly, thrilling and hot.

"Tell me there are slippers with a four-inch heel and feathery pom-poms on the toe."

"I'll buy some," she assured him. "There's a sheer nightgown that goes over it. It's *very* short."

"Good, because this one is too long and has to come off." He gathered a handful and started to tug it up.

She wiggled to help, and he flung it away while she wrestled herself free of her bra and plain cotton underpants.

"There is one more thing we have to talk about," she said as their naked bodies brushed deliciously against one another's.

"If you tell me there's some sort of elbow-length gloves, I may not last to finish what we're starting. I have really missed this, blossom. Really. *Really.*"

She could tell. She smiled into the dark and opened her legs so he nestled his erection against her soft, damp folds. She draped her arms around his shoulders and caressed the back of his neck.

"I made a decision without your input," she informed him. And she was aware he could make his own decisions without her having a say, but she hoped he agreed with hers. "I asked the doctor to give me an IUD. I know you said you would have another vasectomy and didn't want to put me through another pregnancy, but I don't want to close the door on having another baby. Not yet."

"Your body, your choice," he said promptly. Then

kissed her. "I wasn't ready to close that door, either. Thank you for leaving it open for both of us."

"For all we know, it's wide-open." She twined her legs up to his waist. "Does birth control even work for us?"

"I guess we'll see."

"I guess we will."

EPILOGUE

"PLEASE, MAMA?" LI QIANG placed a hand on her knee and tilted his head appealingly. "I really want a sleepover."

He had only learned the word three seconds ago, but he was deeply sincere and, unbeknownst to him, breaking his parents' hearts by appearing so willing to have a night apart from them.

"I think we'll play until bedtime, then go back to our hotel." Ivy stroked his hair to cushion the blow. "You and Mimi have time to finish your puzzle." She nodded at the giant floor puzzle Li Qiang was assembling with Kevin and Carla's daughter.

Mimi had been conceived on the couple's honeymoon and had been born only a few months after Li Qiang. The pair got on like a house on fire.

"But why?" He turned to his father and tilted his head. "Bàba, please?"

Why was Li Qiang's favorite word these days, but that wasn't what made Carla and Kevin bite back grins. Li Qiang, their late talker, had spent a full three years pointing and grunting and only using a handful of words. As a preemie, certain delays were to be expected, but the speech therapist had said he was also probably confused.

Initially, Ivy and Jun Li had made the decision that Ivy would read to him in English while Jun Li read the stories in Mandarin. They spoke to each other in whichever language the words came to them but decided to focus strictly on Mandarin until he started to speak.

The day Ivy had picked up a Mandarin book, Li Qiang had said clear as day, in English, "That one is Bàba's. I get *Goodnight Moon*."

From then on, he had been speaking nonstop. The funny part was, he spoke to Ivy in English and Jun Li in Mandarin. Her father always greeted Li Qiang in Cantonese over the tablet, so now that was "their talk."

Kevin was highly amused by it and had tried to confuse Li Qiang by throwing out the little Hokkien he knew. The joke was on him—that was the nanny's first language, and Li Qiang knew more than Kevin did.

"Come." Jun Li invited Li Qiang into his lap. "What happens if you need us in the night? We don't want to be so far away." To the adults, Jun Li added, "I've never understood the North American obsession with sleepovers."

Kevin barked out a laugh. "This from the man who let me sleep over for two years?"

"It was your home," Jun Li corrected with a small frown of annoyance. "We were roommates."

"Well, my home is your home, and we'll always have a bed for you here. You can all stay the night. How's that?" Kevin asked. "We could do calculus homework like old times."

"Tempting," Jun Li said dryly and looked to Ivy.

"The children are playing so nicely," she pointed out.

Jun Li put Li Qiang onto his feet and said, "We will all have a sleepover, then."

Li Qiang and Mimi ran back to their puzzle, giddy with excitement.

"The appeal of sleepovers," Kevin said as though explaining it to a simpleton, "is that you get your child out of your bed for a night so you can make another one."

"I'll take that under advisement," Jun Li said blandly while Ivy looked into her soda water with lime.

They were ahead of the curve on that one. A month ago, after much discussion, she'd had her device removed. She'd fallen pregnant laughably fast, so they'd booked this trip. Hopefully there wouldn't be any complications this time around, but they were putting a plan in place in case she was put on bed rest again and were getting all their overseas visiting done early.

Some hours later, when Ivy was spooned into her husband's body, replete from their lovemaking, she sensed a lingering tension that wasn't allowing him to fall asleep.

"He's across the hall," she murmured. "Go check on him if it will make you feel better."

"I just want to hear him if he calls out."

Just then, little feet padded up to the door and the latch rattled. "Mama?"

Jun Li rose before she could and stepped into his boxers while she sat up to pull on her nightgown. He unlocked the door and picked up Li Qiang.

"What's wrong? Bad dream?"

"I missed you."

"You did? Well, it's a good thing we're here, then."

He closed the door and brought their son to bed. "Your feet are freezing. You missed putting them on me, didn't you?"

There was some giggling and wiggling as they all made themselves comfortable.

Jun Li reached across their son to set his hand on her hip. "*Now* I can sleep," he said around a big yawn.

Ivy smiled in the dark. "I love you, you know."

"I love you, too."

"And me," Li Qiang said.

"And you too."

Life wasn't perfect. Both she and Jun Li knew that. He was off his medication, but he might need it again sometime. Her pregnancy could be difficult, and any of their parents could suffer a downturn in health.

That's why they had agreed that when a moment was as blissfully perfect as this one, they had to acknowledge and treasure it.

"Thank you for what we have," she said, searching out his face in the dark so she could caress his cheek. "I'm really happy right now."

"Me too, blossom." He kissed the inside of her wrist. "Me too."

* * * * *

HIS
BILLION-DOLLAR
TAKEOVER
TEMPTATION

EMMY GRAYSON

MILLS & BOON

Mom and Dad
Hubby
Little Man and Kels-Kels
Baby Boy
My editors, Charlotte and Flo
Mama P
Ted, Jo-Jo and Kit-Kat
Shark Bait and Juddy
Thursday Night Critique Kitty Writing Group
Mama Steph and Ash
Austin, Long, Flory, Young, Schrock and Banner
Lakeland Ladies
The women who shared and trusted me with
their stories of heartbreak, loss and hope

Thank you. I made it because of you.

CHAPTER ONE

THE TOWERS AND high-rises of New York City glittered against the backdrop of a darkening summer sky. Adrian Cabrera raised his glass of Merlot to his lips and took a long drink, soaking in the sight of the metropolis from the second-floor balcony in the crowded Grand Ballroom of the Kingsworth Hotel.

The view was a preferred distraction from the vapid comments coming from the woman plastered against his side. Jackie—if he recalled correctly from her hurried introduction when she had appeared behind him—had wasted no time attempting to seduce him.

"Cabrera," she purred. "Such a sexy last name."

"A proud last name," he countered, making no attempt to keep the irritation out of his voice. "Traced back four generations to an ancestor who planted the first grapevines at the base of the Sierra Nevada in Spain."

"Like the Sierra Mountains in California?"

Adrian gritted his teeth. "The Sierra Nevada is a mountain range in southern Spain."

"A winery at the foot of a mountain." Jackie giggled. "How thrilling!"

Yes, being at the helm of Spain's most successful winery and a member of the ultra-wealthy Cabrera clan *was* thrilling. But he doubted his over-eager lady-friend would understand the excitement of a business acquisition, the anticipation of tasting a new wine that was the result of years of hard work…

No, all she cared about was a night spent with the mysterious Adrian Cabrera and perhaps a few weeks being jetted around the world on one of the family's private planes.

He risked a glance down. A skintight orange gown enhanced Jackie's slender figure, including the generous amount of cleavage that threatened to burst free at any second. Dark curls fell in an artfully arranged waterfall over her shoulder, accentuating sharp cheekbones and a large, blindingly white smile any model would envy.

But, other than the vaguest stirring of a physical response to her amply displayed breasts, he felt nothing. After years of entertaining himself with models, politicians, business leaders and actresses, he was very selective in his choice of bedmate. Married women and overly attentive ladies who wore their greed on their sleeves topped his off-limits list.

"I'd love to know more about your winery." She smiled again and pressed her breasts flush against him.

The move jostled his arm. Ruby-red wine sloshed out of his glass onto the white cuff of his dress shirt. His mild irritation flared into icy displeasure.

"Oh, no! I'm so sorry…" Her voice trailed off as their eyes met. "Um… I'll just let you get cleaned up."

She scuttled down the length of the balcony and hurried down the stairs. He watched as she reached the ballroom floor and disappeared into a sea of evening gowns and tuxedos.

A glance down at his shirt made him sigh. He had plenty of dress shirts in his closet upstairs in the Roosevelt Penthouse Suite. It would only take ten minutes to change and rejoin the party. But the deviation to his routine annoyed him. He always spent the first half-hour of a wine release alone, surveying whatever grand room his event planner had booked and savoring the success that had brought him to this moment.

From evaluating the mineral levels in the soils of the vineyards to collaborating with his head of marketing on the international campaigns that had taken Cabrera Wine to the top of the industry, each wine release marked the end of a long, demanding journey.

As a Cabrera, he could have asked for much more by way of reward. All he wanted was thirty minutes to himself.

She's gone. Focus on the party. Don't let her ruin your night.

Tiffany chandeliers cast a sparkle over the golden ceiling as partygoers milled about the ballroom. Waiters expertly danced in and out of the guests with silver trays full of culinary treats like brie-stuffed mini burgers and pork chop bites with a tangy orange barbeque sauce.

Adrian's blood had curdled when Cabrera Wine's event planner, Calandra Smythe, had read the menu to him. Did Americans have to put barbeque sauce on everything?

Yesterday's final tasting had altered his view somewhat, when he'd been forced to admit that the unique recipes brought out the velvety flavors of the Merlot. And the surprisingly tasty offerings had been a hit with both his American and international clients.

Down below, he watched Calandra flit through the crowd, her eagle eyes seeking out every tiny imperfection with laser precision. From relighting candles to adjusting the angle of the tall vases overflowing with Spanish bluebells and white carnations, she had everything under control. As always.

He'd started to turn back to the arched window, to pull the curtain aside and take just a moment longer to enjoy the sight of the skyline, when he caught sight of a woman gliding in and out of the hordes of people. Her confident, graceful movements, coupled with the tumble of blonde hair cascading over her shoulders, piqued his interest. Elegant, yes, but something about her seemed out of place compared to the stiff-necked men and women milling about.

The crowd broke for a moment. He could see her below him, illuminated by the golden light of the chandeliers and the glow of the hundreds of candles that lit the ballroom. Her head snapped up and their gazes collided, caught and held.

The distance between them didn't diminish the sudden heat in his blood. Who was she? And why, after months of no one catching his interest, was he suddenly so drawn to this random stranger?

The woman looked away and the crowd surged once more. His eyes narrowed. He wasn't used to women turning away from him. Between the handsome looks he'd inherited from his father, his family's fortune and his fondness for ensuring his romantic partners left his bed feeling completely sated, he never had to seek out female companionship. It always came to him.

A grin tugged at the corner of his mouth. It would be a novelty to pursue a woman who had dismissed him with a glance. Perhaps novelty was just what he needed.

"Are you hiding, brother dear?"

Adrian rolled his eyes and turned his attention from the ballroom to Alejandro. His younger brother walked down the length of the carpeted balcony, his broad shoulders barely contained within the tailored sleeves of his tuxedo. While both of them sported the dark hair and chiseled features of the Cabrera family line, Alejandro's stockier build had led many a tailor to curse when designing his suits.

But his rugged appearance served him well as head of Cabrera Shipping. Alejandro never shied away from hopping on one of the freighters that crossed the Atlantic and working alongside the deckhands as they braved rough seas to deliver cargo around the globe.

"I'm not hiding. Just taking a break from the crowds," Adrian retorted as he turned his back on the party and moved toward the window. He drew the curtain aside to gaze out into the night.

Alejandro joined him. "I saw Jackie Harold rush downstairs. You're supposed to seduce the women, not frighten them off."

Adrian ignored his brother's jibe and swirled the remaining wine in his glass. "The Cabrera Merlot is a success."

The teasing smile disappeared from Alejandro's face as he clapped Adrian on the back. "It is. Congratulations, brother."

For a moment they stood side by side, surveying the impressive layout of New York. While Adrian's heart would always rest in Spain, his jaunts to America provided a brief respite from his chaotic life in his home country.

Cabrera Wine had grown from a small operation just outside of Granada into a respected international brand under Adrian's guidance. The resulting success came with a price—specifically the demand of time. Between meetings with the heads of marketing, business and accounting and trips to the various vineyards and wineries scattered across Europe, his schedule left little time for pleasure.

He shrugged off his musings. The success of Cabrera Wine would always take precedence. He'd made that choice eleven years ago and hadn't looked back since.

"How's Antonio?"

Alejandro chuckled. "Baby brother is celebrating the success of his most recent launch with a model in the Caribbean."

Despite Antonio's wild youth, the youngest Cabrera brother had surprised everyone by assuming control of a small real estate firm attached to the family's name. Antonio's opening of a luxury hotel in the French Riviera marked his third consecutive success since he had taken over three years ago.

Pride swelled in Adrian's chest. Nothing could diminish the success he and his brothers had achieved.

"Madre is worried, of course, but she still acts like he's five, not almost thirty years old."

The mention of their mother momentarily overrode Adrian's pleasure and crushed it under the old, familiar sense of anger. He squelched it and focused his attention back on the crowd beneath them, where energy and laughter pulsed through the ballroom.

He'd achieved this on his own. Other than the occasional visit, his *madre* had no place in his life.

"Antonio can take care of himself," he said.

Alejandro picked up on the thread of warning in Adrian's voice and swiftly changed the subject. "Are you coming back down?"

"I am. Although first I'm going to enjoy the rest of my drink. Alone."

Alejandro held up his hands. "I'm going. While you savor your solitude, I'll see if I can track down a suitable companion for you to celebrate with," he threw over his shoulder.

Adrian ignored the jape. Yes, his brother was right. He hadn't been tempted by anyone since the day he and his last lover had amicably parted ways. The release of the Merlot had consumed his every waking hour, even his dreams. He'd had no time for sex. And, with the aging of the Tempranillo almost complete, the next year would demand even more of his time.

But, while he preferred relationships with agreed upon terms, perhaps one night of passion was just what he needed.

Not with a woman like Jackie, he added mentally. *A woman who was intelligent, savvy and sophisticated.*

"Mr. Cabrera?"

The husky feminine voice slid over his senses and sent a flash of heat over his skin. He took another deliberate sip of his wine before turning his attention to the second woman who had invaded his space this evening.

Her.

The blonde woman he'd locked eyes with before Alejandro's arrival now stood before him. The neckline of her dark blue gown plunged down in a V to the silver ribbon wrapped around her slender waist. From there the dress flowed into a long, billowing skirt that reminded Adrian of the waters of the Mediterranean before a storm.

His eyes drifted back up to her face in a slow, deliberate perusal. Lush silver-blonde curls enhanced her delicate features. Violet eyes stared back at him, and her caramel-colored lips were set in a firm line.

"Yes," he finally responded, his voice cool, showing that, despite the unusually intense effect she was having on him, he was still in control.

She stepped forward and held out her hand, bare except for a simple silver band on her wrist. Adrian grasped her fingers, pleasantly surprised by her firm grip.

"My name is Everleigh Bradford. Congratulations on your Merlot. It's exquisite."

"Thank you." He arched a brow. "While your compliments are appreciated, was it necessary for you to ignore the 'Balcony Closed' sign and invade my privacy?"

Everleigh's chin came up and her eyes flashed with stubborn fire. "Yes."

Intriguing… There were plenty of men who would have cringed at the slightest hint of his disapproval. But not this woman. She stood her ground, shoulders thrown back, lips now set in a determined line.

"You're a busy man, Mr. Cabrera. I need to speak with you on an urgent matter. I'm sorry for breaking the rules, but it was necessary for me to have a moment alone with you."

Her honesty was refreshing. A night with someone as bold and beautiful as Everleigh would more than make up for his past few months of celibacy.

He infused his smile with sensuality as he raked his

gaze up and down her slim form once more, this time letting his appreciation for her body show. "I would greatly enjoy a moment alone with you."

Everleigh's cheeks flushed pink. The blush caught Adrian unawares. Was she an innocent or just playing a role? Much as it would disappoint him, she wouldn't be the first to go to such lengths to catch his attention.

"This has nothing to do with sex, Mr. Cabrera."

"Adrian."

Her lips parted. "I... Excuse me?"

"Please call me Adrian."

Those beautifully shaded violet eyes narrowed. "This is a business discussion, Mr. Cabrera. First names are for friends and family."

"We could become friends, Everleigh."

What was wrong with him? He never teased a woman like this. He complimented, touched, seduced... But with this woman he just couldn't help himself.

Perhaps it was the blush. Yes, that had to be it. The delicate coloring that even now crept down her throat toward the rising slopes of her breasts...

"We will never be friends, *Mr.* Cabrera," Everleigh snapped. "I'm here to discuss your proposed purchase of Fox Vineyards."

Desire fled, replaced by the cold calculation Adrian wielded in every business meeting. "Then let's talk."

He watched as his quick change of personality threw her off balance. She glanced out over the ballroom, her chest rising and falling with a deep breath. He waited, never taking his eyes off her. It was a tactic that had served him well and caused many a nervous business partner to blurt out something they wished they hadn't.

At last she turned back to him and speared him with an angry gaze. "You're trying to bully my terminally ill father into selling the vineyards and the winery that have been in our family for generations to your international conglomerate. I want you to stop all communications with my father and allow me to step into his role."

He finished off the last of his Merlot while he processed her words. He'd met with Richard Bradford on several occasions as they'd negotiated the sale of Fox Vineyards to Cabrera Wine. The older man had been thinner the last time they'd met, but Adrian had chalked it up to the hectic lifestyle of owning a winery.

While Fox Vineyards only maintained one location in upstate New York, their wines had grown in popularity these last two years. Adrian had made it known that he wanted to expand Cabrera Wine into the States, so when Richard's attorney had contacted him about selling Fox it had been a welcome proposal. Not once had Richard mentioned any illness or a spoiled daughter wanting to take over the business.

It didn't matter. Adrian wasn't about to turn down the opportunity just to appease this brassy young woman. The fact that he hadn't made the connection between her last name and Richard signaled that he was too distracted. Better to put as much distance between Everleigh and himself as possible.

"Just so I'm clear, Miss Bradford, you believe I've intimidated your father into selling Fox Vineyards?"

"Yes." For a moment her eyes glittered.

Dear God, please don't let her cry.

Adrian had zero interest in comforting a bawling woman in full view of hundreds of guests.

"I see. Have you spoken with your father about how he and I came to be doing business together?"

Everleigh's hands curled into fists. "He refuses to talk about it. All he'll say is, 'I had no choice.' You may be a successful businessman, and well-respected in some circles, but I also know you're ruthless. I will not have you run my family out of our own vineyard."

Adrian set his glass on a small end table, his movements slow and deliberate. The simple action kept him from displaying the wrath that was rapidly boiling to the surface. He was a determined businessman who went after what he wanted, but he wasn't heartless. The accusations this upstart American was leveling at him—and on the night of his own party—angered him as nothing had in a long time.

"Miss Bradford, I could have you arrested for slander."

Everleigh's jaw dropped. "Are you denying that you're—?"

"Threatening a man well-respected in the wine community? Yes, I deny it because it isn't true."

He leaned in, expecting her to back up, but she didn't. No, she just jutted that stubborn chin up another notch until her lips were just a breath away. A mad desire gripped him to haul her against him and kiss her senseless until she apologized.

No. He would never kiss a woman who disrespected him like this.

"Never accuse me again of something I haven't done, Everleigh Bradford. Tonight, I'll walk away and leave you with the embarrassment of knowing you were wrong. Next time, I will not be so generous."

CHAPTER TWO

EVERLEIGH STARED AT the retreating back of Adrian Cabrera, hands clenched tight, nails digging into her palms.

Take a deep breath, girl.

The man was an infuriating beast. None of the stories she'd heard about him had prepared her for their encounter. His seductive manner had put her on her guard. She didn't need an attraction to her mortal enemy muddying the waters.

And *him*.

She'd seen plenty of pictures online when she'd done her research. Dark brown hair, combed back away from his forehead in a whimsical style that belied his often stern expression and the tense set of his broad shoulders. Strong, square jaw with a small cleft in his chin. Chiseled cheekbones, thick brows over piercing blue eyes and full lips that, in all the photographs, rarely seemed to curve up in a smile.

So when he'd smiled at her she'd been completely unprepared for the rush of heat that had pooled between her thighs.

Maybe she did need to get out and date more. She hadn't had such a strong reaction to…well, *anyone*.

She uncurled her fingers and with slow, measured steps moved to the balcony railing. Her confidence waned as she took in the opulence spread out below. She'd never been surrounded by such luxury. How could a girl from upstate New York possibly take on a man who'd been raised with a silver spoon in his mouth?

There had to be over eight hundred people below. Guests sporting Cartier diamond bracelets and Rolex watches while they sipped Cabrera Merlot from crystal wineglasses.

The band now assembling on the stage at the front of the ballroom had been at the top of the U.S. music charts for the past three weeks. God only knew how much it had cost to have them perform in the Grand Ballroom instead of a stadium that could seat tens of thousands.

The Cabrera family obviously had more money than they knew what to do with.

So why had Adrian Cabrera targeted Fox Vineyards?

Her family's business had been a part of her life ever since she could remember. When her mother had finally succumbed to cancer in her senior year of high school, Fox had been her saving grace. The winery had filled the hole her mother's death had carved out of her heart. She'd thrown herself into every job imaginable: maintenance, being a cellar hand, running the tasting room. Achieving a marketing position there after college, followed by her promotion to Director of Marketing two years ago, had taken her ever closer to one day inheriting the role of director from her father.

Her stomach knotted. But her dad had yanked all her hard work—nearly a decade of it—out from under her when he'd agreed to sell to a spoiled rich boy without even talking to her. The only thing he'd said, after her constant badgering, was that she needed more in her life than Fox Vineyards.

Sure, managing the marketing for Fox left little time for a social life. But, contrary to her dad's beliefs, she still enjoyed her fair share of dates with some very attractive men.

Unfortunately, Adrian Cabrera was in an entirely different class of man than she normally dealt with. When she'd first spied him on the balcony he'd looked like a monarch surveying his kingdom. She'd seen plenty of pictures of him when she'd researched him after her father's revelation of the pending sale to Cabrera Wine. But in person strength radiated from every feature—from the confident thrust of his chin to the hardness in his eyes.

And the photographs hadn't done justice to his confident sensuality.

His black tuxedo had obviously been customized for his subtly muscular build. Despite the inches her French heels added to her height, he'd towered above her when he'd leaned in, those blue eyes cold and determined. And yet, moments before her hasty outburst, his eyes had simmered with a sensual fire. Just the memory of that look sent a shot of heat through her veins…

Don't go there, Ev.

She resisted a waiter with a tray full of wineglasses and grabbed a glass of water from a nearby buffet table. The icy liquid cooled some of her unexpected ardor and brought her back to her senses.

Yes, it had been nearly a year since she and her last boyfriend had broken up. But she didn't do one-night flings with strangers—and certainly not with the bastard who was intent on stripping her father of everything he held dear.

The last time she'd seen her dad rose in her mind. Once a slender but still formidable man, with iron-gray hair and a sharp wit, he'd been reduced by leukemia to a gaunt, hollow shadow of who he'd used to be. He'd been at the window of his study, his T-shirt hanging loosely off his shoulders.

She'd already known he had cancer—she had been at the doctor's appointment and had felt the world tilt beneath her feet when the doctor had announced the diagnosis. But yesterday morning, seeing his skin the color of ash and his once vibrant eyes now listless, reality had crashed in.

Richard Bradford was dying.

The band struck up the beginnings of a classic song, yanking her out of her memories and back into the ballroom. Her dad still refused to tell her why he'd decided to sell to Adrian Cabrera, but that wouldn't stop her. She might have jumped the gun with her accusations, and mucked up her first meeting with the conceited jackass, but she hadn't donned her tallest heels and put on twice the make-up she normally wore for nothing.

With a deep breath, and a squaring of her shoulders, she walked down the length of the balcony and descended the elegantly carpeted staircase to the ballroom floor.

Adrian pulled another glass of Merlot off one of the passing silver trays. What he really wanted was a shot of whiskey after that encounter with Everleigh Bradford.

He risked a subtle glance up at the balcony. The infuriating woman had disappeared. If she had any sense, she'd be walking toward the elevator and would never darken his door again. He wouldn't punish Richard Bradford for his quick-tempered daughter's actions, but he would certainly have a word with him.

His blood boiled as her accusations whirled in his head. Yes, he was a shrewd businessman, but he would never force a fellow vineyard owner into selling if he didn't want to.

What the hell had Richard Bradford told Everleigh? Why would he lie about their deal?

He had just taken another drink when the pesky woman reappeared at the edge of the room. He leaned against the wall and watched as she smoothed the skirts of her dress before advancing into the crowd, her head twisting every now and then.

Looking for him.

He smirked, despite feeling an odd pang of disappointment. She was just like all the others who pursued him— not because they wanted him, but because they wanted something from him.

Just another Nicole.

His one attempt at a relationship had gone down in

flames not six months after it had started. He hadn't been a fan of relationships even before Nicole. Her machinations and her epic performance the night he'd broken things off had cemented his bachelor status for life.

Down below, Everleigh paused and greeted a couple seated at one of the round tables. The man said something to her and she threw her head back and laughed, those blonde tresses dancing with a life of their own. Seeing her like this, carefree and without baseless accusations falling from those sumptuous lips, chased away the memory of Nicole's scheming smile and sparked his desire.

His eyes roamed over Everleigh's heart-shaped face. Compared to many of the women here tonight she wore minimal make-up. She was beautiful, but naturally so. Rather than simpering and throwing around a seductive pout, she laughed and hugged and smiled. She had obviously come here tonight on a mission, but in this moment, unaware that she was being watched, he saw a glimpse of a woman who could seduce just by being herself.

It was intoxicating.

Perhaps he should speak with her.

At the very least, he wanted to satisfy his curiosity about why she had decided to invade his party and risk his wrath.

And maybe, if they could resolve that little matter, she would agree to spend a night in his bed…

Everleigh ran into several familiar faces as she navigated the crowd in her search for Adrian. Neil Mikaelsen, the head sommelier of a popular New York restaurant. Alesha and Ben Gaiman, owners of a well-known winery in Missouri.

The wine industry spanned continents, but it was still a tight-knit family. Too bad Adrian Cabrera couldn't see how being respectful and even friendly was not only good business practice but also led to decades-long friendships with people who knew the challenges and hardships of operating a winery.

The few people she'd spoken with about him had described his success in glowing terms. The man himself? Not so much. Aloof, cold and distant had been common adjectives.

She looked around the ballroom once more, but didn't see him. The blasted man had to be six and a half feet tall. How hard could it be to spot him?

She had just congratulated Cora and Cole Owens on their daughter's recent marriage when she passed by the dessert buffet. The table, draped in burgundy silk and lit with gold votives, offered up treats like gourmet chocolates infused with caramel and raspberry, chocolate soufflé bites, and an elevated crystal tray stacked high with cookies dusted with powdered sugar—*polvorones*, according to a black sign with gold cursive.

Beneath it, in small print, was a note.

My abuela *would bake up a batch of* polvorones *in her tiny kitchen every weekend. We include a dish of "dust cookies" at every Cabrera Wine event to honor her memory.*

The signature at the bottom, written in a bold script, read *"Adrian Cabrera."*

Surprise filtered through the adrenaline that still pulsed through her. She hadn't thought of the man as sentimental.

Curious, she picked up a cookie and bit into it.

Oh, heavens.

Bursts of cinnamon and chocolate filled her mouth as the delicate treat melted on her tongue. Her senses quivered at the rich taste. Not that she had any experience with sex, but if she had, she'd bet these cookies would give lovemaking a run for its money.

"Delicious, aren't they?"

Her eyes flew open. Adrian Cabrera stood in front of her, shoulders thrown back and hands casually resting in his pockets.

Everleigh swallowed quickly, her mouth drying out under the intense scrutiny of his hooded gaze.

"Um...yes." She smiled slightly. "Possibly the best cookie I've ever tasted." She gestured toward the sign. "And I think this is great. To honor your grandmother like that."

Something dark flickered in his eyes, but disappeared too quickly for her to discern what it was.

"You were looking for me."

"Mind your manners, Everleigh."

Dad's voice echoed in her mind. She mentally forced herself to relax and not point out that it was polite to thank someone when they gave you a compliment.

"Was I?"

"Yes."

Arrogant jerk. She bit down on her tongue. Her first inclination was to cut this sexy but maddening man down to size, but she wouldn't let her temper get the better of her again. This second chance to speak to him was a blessing, and not one to be taken lightly.

"I want to apologize for my harsh words," she forced out.

He tilted his head, his eyes narrowing. "Really?"

She clenched her hands together and looked down. "I'm not normally so rude. Dad's health has..." A lump rose in her throat and she swallowed hard. Now was not the time for tears, and Adrian Cabrera did not seem like the type of man who would tolerate weakness. "I reacted hastily and made some horrible accusations."

Silence stretched between them. She looked back up and maintained eye contact. She might have forced out an apology, but she wouldn't give him the satisfaction of letting him intimidate her.

For what seemed like forever, but was probably only ten seconds or so, they stared at each other. The energy between them changed, nearly causing her to totter back on her heels. The strength of the attraction that crackled between them was like lightning. Carnal thoughts rose in her mind, accompanied by vivid images of his bronze skin pressed against her body as they rolled across a bed, tangled in the sheets.

Her cheeks grew hot. One hand flew up to her face before she could stop it, as if she could hide her response.

Judging by the slow smile spreading across his face, he knew exactly what was going through her mind.

The band finished their song to a round of hearty applause. A beat later they struck up another tune. The sultry notes of the slow song floated on the air as the ballroom lights dimmed.

"Dance with me."

Her mouth dropped open. "What?"

"We're at a party. It's a practical invitation."

"As I previously stated, Mr. Cabrera, I'm here to discuss business. I have no interest in pleasure of any kind."

His eyes darkened. "That's too bad."

Oh, no. That damned heat spread down her neck, into her chest and then lower. Her heart kicked into high gear and drummed a frantic beat against her ribs. She'd experienced desire before, but never like this.

"Mr. Cabrera, I—"

"No, Miss Bradford," he said, his voice low and husky.

She knew it was to prevent eavesdroppers from listening in, but that didn't stop the fluttering sensation spreading from her stomach to her fingertips.

"I'm celebrating a momentous achievement. You crashed my party. You insulted me. I'm a busy man, with hundreds of guests who would like to speak with me tonight." He took a step closer, his gaze pinning her to the spot. "So you may dance with me, and we will discuss business, or you may schedule an appointment with my secretary." The corner of his mouth tilted up. Confidence and power were rolling off him in waves. "I leave tomorrow for Spain and will be back in five weeks. The day Fox becomes a part of Cabrera, in fact."

He had her, and they both knew it.

"Fine," she ground out. "Let's dance."

Ignoring the satisfaction in his eyes, she accepted his outstretched hand. His fingers curled over hers and she sucked in a deep breath. Her gaze met his and she saw it— the same unexpected raw desire.

This is not a good idea.

Never had someone just holding her hand inspired the type of lust that now pulsed beneath her skin as he guided her toward the dance floor. Her heart thudded as if she was a teenager going to prom.

Relax. Relax and breathe.

She was a grown woman in a crowded ballroom, dancing with a man and discussing business. There was absolutely no need to be acting like a love-struck fool.

He turned and placed one hand on her bare back.

She arched forward, feeling his fingers like flames against her skin.

How could she relax when she had just walked straight into the lion's den?

CHAPTER THREE

EVERLEIGH FIT PERFECTLY in Adrian's arms. Her body, lithe and fit beneath the shimmering folds of her gown, pressed fully up against his as he swung them into a turn. The feel of her skin beneath his touch, hot and silky, aroused him like nothing had in a very long time.

"You dance well, *señorita*."

"Thank you."

That delicate blush reappeared, staining her cheeks the color of rose petals. Would the rest of her body glow with the same golden-pink hue after they made love?

He blinked. *Made love?* Where had that thought come from? He enjoyed *sex* and, judging by the enthusiastic responses of past lovers, he was very good at it. However, he had never "made love" to a woman because he never had fallen, and nor would he ever fall, in love. Even the affection he'd felt toward Nicole had been at such a minor level that when he'd tossed her out he'd been angrier at himself for being duped by her charade than he had at losing the woman herself.

Besides, Everleigh might be beautiful and intriguing, but until they sorted out this mess about the sale of Fox Vineyards he had no business pursuing her.

A single tear suddenly appeared and clung to her lashes. The sight created an uncomfortable feeling in his chest. Tears—as he'd found out on numerous occasions—were often a ruse. Yet the genuine sadness in Everleigh's eyes inspired in him a protectiveness that was foreign to his seasoned perspective.

"I'm sorry to hear about Richard's illness," Adrian said, making a guess as to the reason for her sorrow.

And he meant it. While Fox Vineyards was a small winery, Richard Bradford maintained an excellent reputation in the wine community.

She nodded once, confirming his suspicions. "It's difficult to see him go through this."

"I'm sorry."

He knew that loss all too well. Abuela Sofia's unexpected death just before his tenth birthday had left a gaping hole. The wizened, silver-haired woman who had steadfastly remained in the cottage at the edge of the family estate until her death had been the one constant in his tumultuous childhood. Unlike his father, who had always been traveling, or his mother and her lack of interest in his existence.

His time with Abuela had been simple, uncomplicated and steadfast. She'd been the one person he'd trusted himself to love unconditionally, just as she had loved him.

Everleigh drew in a shuddering breath. "Thank you. I assumed you knew. Then again, Dad isn't telling a lot of people."

"It's not easy losing someone you love. My *abuela* passed away in her sleep."

The words escaped before Adrian could stop them. Honoring Sofia Cabrera by sharing her chocolate *polvorones* at his release parties was the closest he came to sharing personal details of any kind.

Everleigh's hand slid up to his shoulder. She gave him a gentle, reassuring squeeze. "Those cookies are truly incredible. She must have been an amazing woman for you to honor her like that."

"She was."

Everleigh smiled again, but this one was tinged with the kindred pain of losing a loved one.

Between anger, desire and sorrow, he'd experienced a full scale of deep emotions in the past thirty minutes. He didn't like it. It was time to return to familiar ground.

"Back to business. What do you want to know?"

Blinking away her tears, Everleigh smoothed her face into the mask of a skilled businesswoman. Adrian's admiration ratcheted up a notch.

"Why do you want to purchase Fox Vineyards?"

"Cabrera Wine is growing quickly. We maintain multiple vineyards in Spain, three in France and two in Sweden. We have yet to break into the United States market."

Her lips thinned. "I see."

The current of growing irritation in her voice could not be missed.

"Is a business not allowed to grow and expand?" he asked.

"Of course it is. But why purchase Fox? I love it, but it's small. You clearly have the money necessary to buy your own land and build a much bigger winery."

"We do. Billions of it."

Her cheeks reddened again, but this time a deeper color that spread down her neck and toward the valley of her breasts. How could anger look so sexy?

"The question stands, Mr. Cabrera. Why purchase Fox?"

"Your vineyards produce some of the finest grapes for Riesling and Pinot Noir. Your port has won numerous accolades. Why would I waste time and resources replicating what is already a well-established operation almost guaranteed to grow with the right investment?"

"Operation?" Her fingers curled in his grasp. "Fox Vineyards is more than just an 'operation.' It's a family."

"A family?" he repeated. "Miss Bradford, that's a quaint notion. But holding on to a winery that's dying in its current format because it has a 'family' atmosphere is not good business. That's why Fox is failing."

"Fox is not failing!" Everleigh snapped.

Several dancers turned to look at them.

Adrian leaned down, putting his lips almost to her ear.

"Unless you want to become the talk of the party, I suggest you lower your voice."

She stiffened in his arms and focused on some point over his shoulder. They swayed to the music for a good thirty seconds before she spoke again.

"Fox is not failing," she repeated, her voice a monotone. "We've had some struggles, but struggle does not equal failure."

"You haven't released a new wine in six months. Your father told me that at least half of your equipment needs to be replaced and that profits have dwindled. Your winery has an excellent reputation, but it cannot exist on good recommendations when it's hemorrhaging funds."

"I can fix it," she insisted.

"I'm sorry. I don't know why your father has decided to sell instead of pass control of the winery to you. That's a conversation you'll have to have with him."

The blood drained from Everleigh's face. "What did you say?"

"Your father contacted me six weeks ago. He asked if I wanted to buy Fox Vineyards."

Betrayal sucked the energy from Everleigh's limbs. Had Adrian not been cradling her in a dancer's embrace she might very well have collapsed onto the floor.

How could her dad have done this? He knew what Fox meant to her—knew that she wanted to take over. At least before she'd thought Adrian had pressured him, backed him into a corner somehow. But for him to have contacted Adrian...

"Miss Bradford?"

Adrian's voice echoed in her mind as if he were at the end of a long tunnel. She'd known Fox wasn't doing great, but could it truly be in such dire straits?

Even as she looked up at Adrian, hoping to see some glint

of artifice in his eyes, she saw nothing but truth and concern. It made a horrible kind of sense. Her dad's increased worries about the company's finances… His scheduling meetings for when she was busy with another project… His refusal to tell her why he had decided to sell…

Each puzzle piece that fell into place felt like a shot to the heart.

"It seems I owe you another apology, Mr. Cabrera," she managed to force out. "When my father said he had no choice but to sell, and refused to tell me more, I assumed you had pressured him into selling." The music stopped and she stepped out of his arms. She needed to get out of here. *Now.* "Thank you for the information, and the dance. Enjoy the rest of your party."

With a quick nod of her head, she turned and walked as quickly as she could through the crowded dance floor toward the elevator. Blood pounded in her ears, drowning out the band and the conversations swirling around her. Each step felt as if someone else was taking it…as if she wasn't in control of her own body.

How could her dad have done this to her? The question jackhammered its way around her head.

How could he have sold Fox Vineyards without talking to her first? Did he really think so little of her?

A sob rose in her throat but she squelched it. She would not break down in front of all these people—and certainly not in front of Adrian Cabrera.

She reached the elevator just as the doors opened. She stepped in and pressed the button for the third floor.

A sixth sense made her look up. Adrian was striding toward the elevator, his long legs eating up the distance. His face was blank—a handsome façade concealing his thoughts.

Did he want to discuss the sale? Make her understand why her dad selling Fox was better than her taking over? He might not be the manipulative capitalist she had assumed him to be, but he was still arrogant, spoiled and cold. If his comments about a family business versus an "operation" were anything to go by, he would turn Fox into a hollow shell of what it currently was, all for the sake of profit.

She pressed the button to close the doors. Surprise cracked Adrian's aloof mask, followed swiftly by anger. She saw him quicken his pace, but the doors slid shut before he could reach her.

A tiny smile tweaked her lips as the elevator descended. It was childish to close the door in his face, but also immensely satisfying.

The ache from earlier returned and squeezed her heart tight. Disappointment, fear and betrayal warred for control as she scrunched her eyes tight.

The one thing she had held on to after her dad's diagnosis had been that she would be able to continue the family legacy with Fox Vineyards—maybe even one day pass it down to her children. The dream of honoring her parents through Fox, of staying in the place that had brought her so much joy, had kept her going on even the darkest days.

Now that dream was gone. Her dad was dying, leaving her just like her mom had, and she was powerless to save him. Her entire world was slipping through her fingers and there was nothing she could do to stop it.

The next morning

"Mr. Cabrera, I cannot give out another guest's hotel room number."

Adrian planted his hands on the marble counter and leaned forward. The front desk attendant, a small wisp of a girl with oversize black-framed glasses that dominated her paper-white face, didn't move an inch.

"This is urgent."

"If it's an emergency, I can dial the police."

His fingers curled. When had everyone become so impudent?

"It's not that urgent," he ground out.

"If it's not that urgent, then I can't be expected to break protocol and put the safety of a guest at risk."

Alejandro walked up to him, his hair messed and his eyes sleepy. Unlike Adrian, in his pressed pants and buttoned-up shirt, Alejandro sported jeans and a wrinkled gray shirt that barely stretched across his chest.

Alejandro flashed a smile at the clerk. "Is my brother bothering you, Leia?"

Of *course* Alejandro would know the names of the hotel staff. He made friends wherever he went.

Leia narrowed her eyes. "Yes. He's asking me to break security protocol. Unless a guest has told us that their room number can be given out, I'm not authorized to share that information. With *anybody*," she added with a glare in Adrian's direction.

Alejandro turned to Adrian. "Why not just have Leia call the room?"

"Because I want the room number."

Alejandro grinned. "Because you know that if Leia calls up there and tells whoever it is that you want to speak with them they'll tell you to go to hell and hang up."

"I don't recall asking for your assistance, *hermano*."

Alejandro leaned up against the counter and yawned. "This wouldn't happen to be about the second woman you chased off last night, would it?"

Adrian pulled his phone out of his pocket and looked down at the screen. He didn't need Alejandro seeing how deeply Everleigh Bradford had worked her way under his skin.

When she'd closed the elevator doors in his face, fury had sent him back to the party. He'd channeled that energy into making the rounds, speaking with guests, sampling the hors d'oeuvres and delivering a brief speech on the Cabrera Merlot to thunderous applause.

Halfway through the evening he'd grabbed a *polvorone*. The sweet taste of sugar and butter mixed with decadent chocolate had conjured up a look of pure pleasure on Everleigh's face when she'd eaten a cookie.

The memory of her candidness and her passion for Fox Vineyards had started to chip away at his anger, until he'd been left with a hollow sensation that had dogged him the rest of the evening. Even when Alejandro had introduced him to a stunning nurse practitioner, whose ebony legs had been displayed to perfection in a champagne-colored cocktail dress, his mind hadn't been able to let go of the sight of Everleigh walking toward the elevator, shoulders thrown back defiantly even as defeat had radiated from her body.

That image was the reason he had woken up in bed alone and come to the lobby to track her down. He didn't owe Everleigh an explanation. The sale between Cabrera and Fox would move ahead, as Richard wanted.

But he could at least check on her before he flew back to Spain.

"If you're looking for that woman, she checked out this morning."

Adrian spun around and pinned Alejandro with a steely gaze. "How do you know?"

Alejandro grinned wolfishly. "I escorted a young woman to her taxi this morning. Around seven or so."

"Seven?"

Alejandro shrugged. "It was a good night. But as we were…ahem…saying goodbye, I saw your blonde friend walking out with her suitcase."

Ten minutes later Adrian was back in his room packing up his clothes, when his cell rang.

"Good morning, sir," said his personal assistant, Eli. "I trust the party went well?"

"Very," Adrian responded shortly.

Everleigh's face, pale and yet strong, still filled his mind. He rubbed his hand across his forehead. Why could he not focus?

"Good. I have the itinerary for your trip to Spain. You'll land at—"

"Eli, change of plan."

A brief pause, and then "Yes, sir."

"Get me on the first plane to Rochester, New York, out of La Guardia—first class—and then a rental car."

"Yes, sir. What should I tell your father about the meeting with the Granada tourism board?"

"I'll follow up with him when I arrive later this week. Tell him I have some unfinished business with Fox Vineyards."

CHAPTER FOUR

EVERLEIGH URGED HER HORSE to go faster, savoring the rush of hot adrenaline and its contrast to the cool wind rushing by. The thick clouds grew darker. At any moment the skies would open and douse the landscape with rain.

But Everleigh didn't care.

"Faster, Paris!"

Paris obliged and quickened her pace, thundering up the hill so fast the trees passed by in a blur. Half a mile away a long driveway curved up and over the velvet green hills and led to the front door of the farmhouse she called home.

She grabbed the reins and eased Paris back from her gallop until they achieved a slow, easy walk. Paris's ears drew back and she snorted.

"Did I slow you down too soon?" Everleigh asked with an affectionate pat on Paris's damp neck.

The growing blackness of the sky mirrored her resurfacing anger. Her fingers tightened on the reins as the disastrous confrontation she'd had with her father that morning rose up in her mind.

"You did *what*?"

Her dad had almost shouted when she'd cornered him in the library this morning. He hadn't even let her talk.

"What I do with Fox is none of your concern. Stay out of it!" he'd snapped, before he'd turned and left the room, slamming the door behind him.

A minute later she'd heard his car accelerate down the drive, leaving her alone in the house, with its once comforting walls pressing in on her like a prison.

Her dad had never spoken to her like that before. They'd always been partners. Or at least she'd thought they had.

Sadness tugged at her heart, but she shoved it away. Anger was easier.

Dad might think the discussion was closed, but she wouldn't let go so easily. She'd fight tooth and nail to keep Fox in the family, where it belonged. Keeping it out of the hands of a man as smug and entitled as Adrian Cabrera would merely be an added bonus.

The thought of her newfound nemesis conjured memories of the previous night. The feel of his body against hers as they'd danced...the woodsy scent that had clung to her dress...

Stop! She didn't need an unwanted attraction muddying the waters.

Paris's ears perked up. A second later a low rumble of thunder rolled across the countryside.

Everleigh sighed. "Time to go home."

She reached the driveway and nudged Paris into a brisk canter. Another rumble broke through the air—but not thunder. This one was steady and low, like the purr of an engine.

Her shoulders tensed. Maybe her dad was already back.

She glanced behind her, then did a doubletake. A black Porsche, sleek and elegant, raced up the drive. Behind the wheel sat Adrian Cabrera.

Everleigh uttered a word that would have made her mother cringe. What the hell was he doing here?

Adrian pulled alongside her, keeping pace with Paris, and rolled the window down.

"Miss Bradford."

"Mr. Cabrera." She inwardly winced at the rudeness in her voice. It wasn't fair to focus her anger on Adrian. By all accounts her dad was the one behind this whole mess. Knowing this, however, didn't dispel her antagonism.

Adrian was still a snobby elitist who had been born with a silver spoon in his mouth. Plus, this ride had been her time to gather her thoughts, to relax before attempting to talk to her dad again. How the hell was she supposed to calm down with Adrian's dark gaze piercing through the armor she'd spent all morning piecing back together after their erotic dance?

"Are you lost?" she asked.

His lips quirked. "I came to see you."

Shock rendered her speechless, followed by a warmth that spread from her chest to her limbs and left her feeling a little lightheaded.

She blurted out the first thing that came to mind. "Why?"

"And your father."

Her eyes narrowed. *Of course.* "To tell him you'll be canceling your purchase of Fox since there's another interested buyer?"

A scowl marred his chiseled features. "Forget it, Miss Bradford. You do not want to come between me and something I want."

Before she could retort, a loud bang rent the air and sent Paris skittering several paces to the left. Adrian slammed on the brakes as Everleigh pulled Paris to a halt, her heart pounding in her chest. She looked up, but no rain fell.

A string of fiery Spanish drew her attention back to the Porsche and the rapidly deflating front tire.

Everleigh couldn't stop herself. She threw her head back and laughed.

Adrian glared at Everleigh as she doubled over on top of her horse. Her mirth brought a rosy glow to her cheeks. The wind caught her hair and tossed it in wild blonde disarray. The stubborn woman was laughing at him, and he couldn't stop staring at her.

Today she sported blue jeans and a threadbare violet

sweater with the sleeves rolled up to her elbows. Barely a hint of make-up, no jewelry, no bewitching gown…

She was beautiful. And even though the flat tire was a nuisance he could have done without he enjoyed the result—seeing her uninhibited and happy.

Her laughter trailed off and she had the grace to look a little contrite. "Sorry…"

"Judging by the glint in your eye, *señorita*, you're not the least bit sorry."

Her grin returned, and the smile punched him hard in the chest with an emotion he didn't care to examine.

"You have to admit a Porsche isn't the best vehicle for a trip into rural New York."

He conceded her point with a shrug. "I didn't realize how far Fox Vineyards was from the city of Rochester."

The smile disappeared as her violet eyes sharpened. "Then perhaps it isn't a good fit for your empire."

Adrian sighed. Always the winery. He could appreciate a professional with an unwavering focus on business. But with Everleigh, he very much wanted to mix business with pleasure.

"I think—"

An earth-shattering clap of thunder cut him off. Everleigh's horse whinnied frantically.

"The storm's almost here!" Everleigh shouted over the rising shriek of the wind.

She guided her horse next to a tree, so the thick trunk would block some of the gusts that barreled over the hills. Another burst of thunder released the rain the clouds had been holding on to.

He rolled the window up and stepped out into the storm.

"What are you doing?" Everleigh yelled as he moved under the tree with her. "Stay inside, where it's dry."

"I'm not going to stay dry while you get drenched," he snapped back.

"I'm going to ride back to the house. I don't recommend waiting out the storm under a tree—but do what you want. Doesn't matter to me."

"Or I could ride back with you."

Her mouth dropped open. "What?"

"Who knows how long this could last?" He raised his voice to combat the growing intensity of the tempest. "I'd prefer to wait until it dies down to change the tire. I know you despise me, but surely not enough to leave me stranded out here?"

A second passed, then two. Indecision was written all across her face.

He took a gamble and turned back to the car. "Never mind. I'll—"

"Oh, for heaven's sake. Come on."

He suppressed a triumphant grin as he hit the lock button and walked back to her. She scooted forward in the saddle, her face set in a stony mask. He put his foot in the stirrup and pulled himself up. The lack of space and the rain-slicked leather saddle made him slide flush against her back.

Dios mío... The curves of her backside were pressed against him. Desire flared—more intense than last night, more primal. He hardened in an instant. He tried to keep his lurid thoughts at bay, so the evidence of his want didn't make her uncomfortable. But, damn, it was difficult.

Especially when she shifted in the saddle and her body rubbed against him...

"Hold on."

Before he could reply she uttered a command to the horse and they were off. His arms slipped around her slender waist. She stiffened, but he didn't let go. The flat tire had been embarrassing enough; he wasn't going to fall off a horse in front of the proud Miss Bradford, too.

Despite the storm's fury, Everleigh guided her horse with

skill. Even when lightning lit the darkened landscape and thunder roared overhead she stayed focused. If he hadn't admired her before, her control of a situation that many women of his acquaintance would have shied away from made her even more attractive.

Damn it.

The trees lining the drive provided little shelter from the rain. The wind sent sheets of water sideways and drenched them both. His hands rested on her stomach, and he felt the heat of her skin seeping through her soaked sweater.

"Almost there!" Everleigh shouted over her shoulder.

The house appeared, hazy at first and then sharpening as they drew closer.

Everleigh Bradford's beloved home—a rambling farmhouse with a wraparound porch—was the exact opposite of his palatial estate in Granada. What would it be like inside? Bright colors? Lots of plants and cozy nooks?

Everleigh intrigued him. And the possibility of taking her to bed was becoming more enticing by the minute. Maybe her attitude toward him would thaw once she heard from Richard why he was selling. He knew she found him attractive. The way her body had curved into his on the dance floor, the sparkle of attraction in her eyes, had told him plenty about how she felt about him—at least physically. Once the conversation with her father was out of the way they would spend the night together, have incredible sex, and then he'd be off to Spain first thing in the morning.

He just needed to get her out of his system and regain control.

Everleigh guided the horse around the house to the back. They galloped past a stone patio, a covered pool, and numerous maple trees fighting to stand upright against the wind. A large red barn came into view, with yellow light spilling out through the doors onto the lawn. Everleigh tugged on the reins and the horse slowed as it entered the barn.

They'd barely stopped before Everleigh had dismounted and hurried back to close the doors. Adrian climbed down, but before he could say anything she disappeared into one of the stalls.

One of many, he noticed as he glanced around. The barn looked almost brand-new, with rows of empty stalls, a clean concrete floor and lights fashioned to look like antique lanterns hanging from the rafters. The faint scent of hay wrapped around him as the rain drummed a furious beat on the roof.

Everleigh walked back into the main aisle with a thick blanket and a towel draped over her arm. She ignored him and began toweling off the horse's neck, cooing soft words of endearment.

"What's her name?"

Her shoulders tensed as his voice broke the silence between them. "Paris."

"An interesting choice." He leaned against one of the stall doors.

"She's an interesting girl." Everleigh removed the saddle and tossed the blanket over Paris's back. "My mother spent her senior year of college in Paris. We were supposed to go there together the summer after I graduated high school, but she passed away that spring. I like having something that reminds me of her."

"Why not just go yourself?"

She shrugged. "I will. Someday."

He glanced around at the empty barn. "Where are the rest of the horses?"

"Paris is the only one we've ever had."

She crouched down to wipe off Paris's legs, and the back of her sweater rode up to reveal a pale expanse of skin. The sight heated his blood.

"Then why so large a barn?"

She finished drying Paris off and led her into a nearby stall. With her back to him, he could indulge in a thorough perusal of her legs, displayed to sensual perfection in her wet blue jeans.

Once she'd locked the door, she turned and faced him, sadness pulling her lips down into a frown. "We planned on rescuing more—abused horses, old ones in danger of being put down... When we expanded the winery, we built a special events barn on the other side of the vine-yards. We were going to use the calmer horses for horse-back rides and the ones who couldn't be ridden would get to live out their lives here and add a little atmosphere to the place."

Adrian crossed his arms over his chest. "A good idea. And still possible with Cabrera."

Her eyes narrowed as her hands came up to rest on her hips.

"Also possible if I were to take over the vineyard."

"Possible, yes. But not probable," Adrian shot back. "I have experience in multiple aspects of business—not just marketing—and a team of professionals and a fortune at my fingertips that could take Fox to new heights."

Everleigh squared her shoulders and took a step forward, closing the gap between them to less than a foot. The sweater clung to her, hugging the curves of her breasts. With her hair hanging in damp curls around her face and fire snapping in her eyes, she reminded him of a feisty kitten caught in a storm.

"Oh, I'm sure... Cabrera sells glitz and glamor and sex. Oh, and occasionally wine."

Adrian arched a brow. The kitten had even sharper claws than he'd realized.

"Sex and wine go hand in hand. Have you not enjoyed that combination before?" Even as he uttered the words, he felt his stomach harden. He didn't care for the idea of her in another man's bed.

Two spots of red appeared in Everleigh's cheeks. "What I've *enjoyed* is watching the hard work my friends and family have put into this vineyard come to fruition in a glass of wine bursting with flavor." Another step forward. "What I've *enjoyed* is getting out into the vineyards and pruning the vines we've cared for."

Another step brought her so close he could see flecks of gold in the violet of her eyes and feel the heat radiating off her body.

"When was the last time you worked in your own vineyards? Talked to one of your employees? When was the last time you did anything but party like the pampered playboy you are?"

Every muscle in Adrian's body tensed. He'd let his libido run the show for the past twenty-four hours, but no more.

"You, Miss Bradford," he replied, with a thread of steel in his tone, "are one of the most arrogant, rude young women I've ever met."

Her mouth dropped open. "Me? Arrogant?"

He leaned down until his lips were just a breath away from hers. "You crash my party, then close an elevator door in my face. When I make a very long and unplanned trip to sort out this mess with your father, you almost leave me stranded in a storm. And then you yell at me for wanting to ensure Fox Vineyards continues instead of collapsing in on itself. Lest you forget, your father reached out to *me*, not the other way around. Perhaps you should direct some of your anger toward him."

He'd barely spoken the last words when the rain suddenly abated, becoming a soft patter. Quietness settled over the barn.

Everleigh blinked, and some of the fight dissolved from her eyes. "I just…"

She started to turn away, but Adrian put a hand on her arm. The heat of her skin warmed him once more. His breath caught in his throat at how quickly and fiercely his desire flared.

"You just what?"

"You're right."

The words were spoken so softly he almost didn't hear them.

"I still don't think you're the right person to lead Fox." A regretful laugh escaped her lips. "But it's easier to be angry at you than at my father. You're not at fault. I'm sorry."

Her words of apology froze him in place. As a child he'd craved an apology from his mother, a reason as to why she'd rejected him. But even years later, when she'd made a few feeble attempts to connect with him again, she'd never once explained her actions or apologized. The couple of times he'd tried to initiate a conversation she'd just teared up and walked away.

Everleigh looked down at his hand on her arm and then up at Adrian, uncertainty in her eyes. His fingers curled around her elbow and he tugged her closer. She obliged, her lips parting as her gaze settled on his mouth.

"Mr. Cabrera…"

Never had his last name sounded so sexy. The harsh words hanging in the air dissolved under the heat of the unbridled lust swirling between them. He leaned down, the uncontrollable need to taste her overwhelming his good sense.

"Everleigh!"

A sudden shout from outside the barn broke the spell. Everleigh blinked and took a step back, just before the barn doors swung open and Richard Bradford rushed in.

CHAPTER FIVE

HER DAD RUSHED into the barn and threw his arms around Everleigh. Her eyes sought out Adrian over her father's shoulder. Whatever desire she'd seen there had gone, replaced by an impenetrable shield of aloofness.

Had she really been about to kiss Adrian Cabrera?

What must he think of her? Especially after she'd once again lost control of her temper and behaved in a manner most definitely *not* becoming in an aspiring winery owner.

She closed her eyes against the shame. Adrian's accusation had hit home with painful accuracy. She *was* displacing her anger and focusing it on him. In moments like these, when she let her emotions control her tongue instead of common sense, she feared that perhaps her father had made the right choice after all.

Her dad released her and she opened her eyes as he held her at arm's length, his gaze scanning her. "Are you all right? Are you hurt?"

"Dad, I'm fine. What's wrong?"

He blew out a breath and released his grip on her shoulders. "I turned around when I saw how bad the storm was getting. I didn't like how we left things this morning, and when I saw the abandoned car in the driveway and the house empty…" His voice trailed off as he focused on the man looming behind her. "Mr. Cabrera?"

Adrian stepped up next to Everleigh and executed a short bow of his head. "*Sí.* It's good to see you again, Mr. Bradford."

Her dad's eyes narrowed. "What are you doing in here with my daughter?"

"Dad!" Embarrassment heated her face. "I was riding

Paris when he pulled up in the driveway and got a flat tire, so I brought him home."

Her dad had the grace to look abashed. "Of course. My apologies, Mr. Cabrera. I know you wouldn't... That is to say..."

Adrian Cabrera waved his flustered comments aside. "No apology needed. If I had a daughter as beautiful as yours I would have the same protective instinct."

He probably threw out compliments left and right to woo actresses and models into his bed. But that didn't stop the electric tingling in her limbs. The men she'd dated before had never called her beautiful. The few times they had complimented her they'd used words like "hot" and, on one memorable occasion, "so doable."

Her dad cleared his throat. "Would you like to join us inside the house? I'm shorter than you, but I'm sure we can find some dry clothes for you to change into."

Adrian Cabrera's smile flashed white in her peripheral vision. "Excellent. And then perhaps we can talk. All three of us."

Her dad's lips thinned. "All three of us?"

"Yes."

Adrian didn't elaborate. He just maintained that smile that appeared friendly on the surface but carried an edge that said he would accept nothing less than what he wanted.

"Fine."

Her dad's voice had lost some of its politeness. He returned Adrian's smile, his teeth bared like a cornered dog.

"Twenty minutes in the library, then. All three of us."

Everleigh resisted the urge to roll her eyes at their battle of wills and merely murmured her consent before slipping out through the door. Sunbeams broke through the holes in the clouds hanging overhead, illuminating the raindrops clinging like tiny diamonds to the leaves of the trees. The thunder let out one last, distant grumble that was quickly overridden by the sweet trill of a bluebird.

The storm had only wreaked its havoc for twenty minutes or so. So why, Everleigh asked herself as she hurried up the steps of the back porch, did it feel like so much had changed during that short period of time?

She yanked open the screen door. The hinges shrieked in protest at her rough treatment. She paused, breathed in deeply, and stepped inside.

The kitchen greeted her with its cheery yellow warmth. The floorboards uttered their usual comforting creak as she fetched a glass of lemonade from the fridge. The sweet liquid brought a welcome respite from the humidity left behind by the storm. Unfortunately, it did little to calm the heat still churning in her veins.

Dear God, the man hadn't even kissed her and she could barely stand up.

As much as she loved her romance books, she'd always rolled her eyes when she'd read about the heroine's knees growing weak. But, given that she'd nearly sagged against Adrian Cabrera in the barn as her head had spun from the intensity of her yearning, apparently her favorite authors had based their writing on fact.

She gulped down the rest of the lemonade and escaped upstairs before her dad and Adrian walked in. She banished the memory of how strong and protective Adrian had felt against her back, of how nice his arms had felt wrapped around her waist, by hopping into the shower and cranking up the hot water until it nearly scalded her.

After throwing on a pair of jeans and another sweater she dried her hair, and was about to head back downstairs when she caught a glimpse of herself in the mirror of her vanity table. Dark half-moons stood out under her eyes against the pallor of her skin. Her lips were equally pale and colorless.

With a groan, she grabbed a tube of lip gloss and swiped on a caramel color. It didn't completely take away the zombie look, but it gave her enough of a confidence-boost to face whatever awaited her downstairs.

They were both already in the library, where a fire was crackling in the hearth. Adrian sat in a comfy chair, dressed in sweatpants and a hoodie. He clearly did not care for the casual clothing; he sat stiff and straight, despite the plush cushions of the chair that invited him to relax.

Her dad paced by the fire, his hands behind his back.

"Ah, Everleigh." Dad's voice shook even as he forced a smile. "Please, sit. Tea and muffins from the Fox Creek Bakery."

Everleigh grabbed one of the muffins and plopped into the matching chair across from Adrian. She bit into the muffin, savoring the flavors of fresh blueberries and rich butter that melted on her tongue.

She glanced over to see Adrian staring at her. His gaze was unreadable, his face a mask of granite. "Would you like a muffin?" she asked with an arch of her brow.

"No, thank you."

He looked away. The man certainly knew how to flip from seductive billionaire to cold-hearted executive in the blink of eye.

"All right." Her dad stopped pacing and stood in front of the fire. Tension radiated from his body.

Against the backlight of the fire, there was no hiding the way his clothes hung off his body. Everleigh swallowed hard and looked away. Some days she could pretend he was recovering from an illness, or that he'd just lost weight. But on days like today there was no denying that Richard Bradford's clock was running out of time.

"Everleigh, I'm so sorry."

The despair in her father's voice dragged her eyes back to him.

"I shouldn't have gone to Cabrera Wine without first consulting you. I know you've always had your heart set on running Fox. I wanted to give you that legacy, and I know... I know you would have done me proud."

He walked over and knelt before her, clasping her hands in his. Hot tears filled her eyes. She brushed them away with the back of her hand even as one escaped and trailed down her cheek.

Adrian Cabrera cleared his throat and stood. "Perhaps I should leave. This seems like a private matter."

Her dad leaned forward, kissed her forehead and stood. "It is, but it also involves you. Everleigh deserves to know the reason why I'm selling to Cabrera Wine. And, as you pointed out, if you're to lead the business we all need to be on the same page."

Everleigh frowned. "You're still going to sell?"

Her dad sighed and ran a hand through his hair. "Yes. Not because I want to, Everleigh. Because I *have* to."

Her heart started to pound against her chest. "What?"

Her dad turned away and looked back at the fire.

Her fear ratcheted up another notch. "What aren't you telling me?"

He finally looked back at her, and she barely resisted the urge to shrink back in her chair. His skin had gone gray, as if every drop of energy had been leeched from his body. His shoulders curled in and he gripped the edge of the mantle.

"Everleigh, the winery is bankrupt. If I don't sell to Cabrera next month we'll have to shut down."

Adrian watched Everleigh as her father's words sank in. She stared at him for a moment, the color slowly draining from her skin. Then she drew a shaky hand through her hair.

He'd known about Fox's troubles ever since Richard had reached out—had known last night, when Everleigh had confronted him at the party. But it hadn't been his place to tell her.

He'd eased his discomfort by telling himself that Richard had withheld the information from his daughter because he didn't trust her, because she wouldn't be able to handle the change in the family's finances. But, no. It had all been because a father hadn't wanted to hurt his daughter.

Everleigh sank back into her chair as she rubbed her forehead. "How did this happen?" she asked finally.

Respect stirred in Adrian's chest. A quiver laced her voice, but other than that she appeared calm...focused.

Richard scrubbed a hand over his face, defeat deepening wrinkles. "Little by little," he finally ground out. "I was too focused on what was going on with my illness. I ignored the warning signs. Broken equipment that set production back... Not having enough inventory to cover orders for the last rosé..."

"But you said the equipment had been fixed," Everleigh broke in, a frown etched into her forehead. "And what happened with the rosé last fall? The reviews, the pre-orders, social media...everything was so positive."

A weary smile tugged at Richard's lips. "I know. Because you're great at your job. The rosé sold *too* well."

That gave Adrian pause. Everleigh worked for Fox? He'd been impressed by the winery's branding, and their social media presence rivaled Cabrera's. But the idea that he might still have to deal with Miss Bradford after this sale was over was not a positive one. The possibility of a night with her disappeared in a flash and left him burning with suppressed need. He'd dated an employee once. One disaster was more than enough.

"I didn't hire the best inventory manager and I wasn't paying attention," Richard said to Everleigh, bringing Adrian's attention back to the conversation. "By the time I realized we didn't have enough to cover orders it was too late. I had to issue a lot of refunds and pass on business to other wineries."

Everleigh sat forward in her chair, her lips parted and her face pale. Adrian had taken a step toward her before he'd even realized what he was doing. He changed direction and walked over to one of the windows, shoving his hands deep into his pockets.

"How did I not know about any of this?" Everleigh's voice trembled.

Adrian kept his gaze trained on the green sloping fields of the countryside.

"Because I kept you and the rest of the staff in the dark. I kept thinking I could make it work…that the next thing would be what was needed to turn Fox around. But that didn't happen and it's led…" He sucked in a shuddering breath. "Led to the winery being on the verge of bankruptcy."

Silence reigned, broken only by the crackling of the logs in the fireplace. Adrian regretted requesting this little meeting. In a moment of irritation he had suggested it as punishment for the way Richard had handled this situation. But now, as he turned just in time to see the play of emotions across Everleigh's stunned face, he felt like a bastard.

His mother might have shut him out of her life after losing the baby, but she'd still ensured that he was raised in luxury. While Everleigh might not live with the same extravagance, she nonetheless enjoyed a comfortable life. What would it be like for her to find out in the blink of an eye that everything she'd had was gone?

"But surely there must be something we can do," she protested. "We have a new wine this summer, two in the fall, and we have weddings booked for the new venue starting in October. Dad, we—"

"Fox will continue as a sub-brand of Cabrera," Adrian interjected.

That and paying off the mortgage on Richard's home were the two things the older man had stood firm on. To Adrian, paying the mortgage was inconsequential. The compromise to change the labeling to *Cabrera Wine Presents Fox Vineyards* still rankled. Selling up should be just that—selling a company, not sharing new billing.

Still, the bottom line was worth it.

"So I'm sure you'll still have your job as Director of Marketing," Richard told his daughter. "It's not just about you and me. It's about our employees—all the families who depend on us—and the other businesses we work with in Fox Creek. The debts are so... They're astronomical. If I don't sell, we'll have to declare bankruptcy and we'll lose the vineyard. This way we still have some choice."

"All employees will be retained at their current salary," said Adrian. "Including you, Miss Bradford," he added, even though a warning bell clanged in his mind. "I didn't realize you were behind Fox's marketing, but you'll be a valuable asset."

Everleigh murmured a thank-you, but he could see that, unlike Richard, she wasn't done. No, gears were turning in that beautiful blonde head of hers, and she was scheming to solve her father's predicament. She didn't strike him as the kind of woman to shrink away from a challenge, even one as seemingly insurmountable as this.

Everleigh whirled and pinned him with her sharp gaze. "What's in this for you, Mr. Cabrera? Why pay so much money for a winery that's financially unstable?"

The woman should have been a lawyer, with her fearless ability to fire questions at him.

"Like I told you last night, Fox is small, but it's an established and well-respected brand. Quality wines. A presence in the United States. It will give me an opportunity to expand Cabrera Wine, plus give me well-trained employees loyal to the company. All things I wouldn't have if I started

fresh. An infusion of cash and the strength of an international brand can elevate Fox to an entirely new status."

"Speaking of which," Richard said as he stood, "the sale
will be announced at a party here at Fox in five weeks, as
well as who Mr. Cabrera names as director. I'd like for you
to collaborate with Cabrera Wine's marketing team in the
meantime, to ensure a smooth transition."

Everleigh's gaze swung between Adrian and Richard.
Something flared in her eyes—the briefest flash of cun-
ning and determination.

"Why don't I accompany Mr. Cabrera to Spain? If I'm
going to continue as Director of Marketing for Fox under
the Cabrera name, I should meet his marketing team and
learn more about the brand in person."

Oh, she had boldness—Adrian would give her that.
Their eyes met and he could almost feel the resolve burning through her.

Richard Bradford's eyes narrowed. "Why?"

"Like you just said—to ensure a smooth transition. We
might be moving forward as Fox, but I'll need to collaborate with our parent company." Her lips curved in a devil-
ish smile. "Mr. Cabrera himself said I'd be a valuable asset.
Might as well put myself to work as quickly as I can."

Judging by the creases in Richard's forehead, he knew
his daughter was up to something. But, like Adrian, he
didn't know what, and the argument she presented was a
logical one.

Richard glanced at Adrian. "Mr. Cabrera, I know this
would be imposing on your hospitality—"

"Not at all," Adrian interrupted smoothly. "I meant what
I said about Everleigh's talents. She can join me tomorrow
on my plane back to Spain and she can stay at my family's
home just outside Granada."

He took pleasure in the surprise that widened her eyes.

"That's not necessary," she said. "I can fly commercial and I can get a hotel."

"If we're going to be one big, happy family moving forward, then I insist you enjoy the amenities and perks that come with being a part of Cabrera Wine. Unless there's something holding you back?" He flashed her a challenging smile.

Stubbornness tightened her mouth. Her shoulders straightened. "No."

A litany of curses rushed through his head as his groin hardened. Knowing she was off-limits as a future employee of Cabrera Wine made him want her even more.

"Excellent. We leave first thing in the morning."

Adrian turned and left the room before Everleigh or her father could utter an objection. This fascination with her—this desire to poke and prod and tease—concerned him. It opened the door to emotions he had kept locked away for decades.

Allowing himself to experience anything more than physical attraction was an invitation to play with fire.

Yet the possibility of getting burned had never felt so enticing.

CHAPTER SIX

EVERLEIGH WALKED BY the library later that night, just in time to see her dad pour himself exactly four ounces of Fox's Riesling and sink into the depths of one of the comfy chairs. Part of her hesitated about going to Spain, knowing his prognosis. But when she'd mentioned her hesitation he'd dismissed it, saying, "Not only will this be good for Fox's future, but you need to *live*, Everleigh."

She leaned against the doorframe and smiled at the sight of him curled up in front of the fire, feeling a nostalgic warmth settling in her chest. When her mom had been alive, her mom and her dad had spent countless nights in front of the fireplace. She'd always wondered as a child why sometimes they closed and locked the doors, although as an adult she had a pretty good idea what they'd been up to. Their love for each other had only grown stronger with every passing day.

Her throat squeezed. Eleven years...

Numerous friends and acquaintances had told her that the pain would fade over time. But on nights like these, when she could almost swear her mother's rose perfume lingered in the air, the pain was just as fresh as the day her mom had grasped her and her dad's hands one last time in the hospital and breathed her last.

Even in the dim light of the flickering flames Everleigh could see her father's fingers curl around the stem of the wineglass. Tension tightened her neck. Was that old craving to guzzle the entire contents rearing its ugly head?

After her mom's death he had spent countless hours locked in this library. First it had been wine, then port, and then whiskey. He'd spent weeks in an alcohol-induced haze, signing the papers his manager Bobby had brought him and sleeping in his chair.

He'd once told her he had no memory of seeing Everleigh during those weeks. Hardly anything had penetrated the hazy existence he'd created for himself, save for his own grief. He'd left his seventeen-year-old daughter to navigate the loss of her mother alone. Some days she'd felt abandoned. Other days had been fraught with anger and grief. But most of them had just been empty. The winery had filled the gap left by both her parents.

It had been two months after her mom's funeral when he'd stumbled into his office, looking for a bottle of wine, and found Everleigh at his desk, having worked herself so hard that she'd fallen asleep. Then he'd changed.

As he'd told her the following morning—the first time he'd actually been sober since the funeral—the sight of his daughter, so thin and pale, sleeping with her head on a stack of marketing plans, had shocked him back into sobriety.

To this day, no matter what she'd said, he hadn't been convinced that the winery had saved her. But the frenetic pace of staking trellises, trimming and mulching out in the vineyards, working until closing time in the tasting room—all of it had saved her from facing the reality of a dead mother and an alcoholic father.

Her dad's fingers shook now, and he set the wineglass down. Everleigh stepped back into the hall and walked away. The past was the past. She and Dad had repaired their relationship over the years, had grown close again.

Although, she admitted to herself as her feet guided her to the oak door at the back of the kitchen, never as close as they'd been before her mom's illness. She suspected part of that was guilt on his part. And she'd never fully opened up to him, or to any another person, again. The only constant in all the mess—the one thing that had been there for

her—had been Fox Vineyards. It had become her identity...
something few people seemed to understand.

The door opened noiselessly, revealing a set of stairs that
curled under the house. She flipped a switch and lanterns
came on above the steps. She descended into the wine cellar, trailing her fingers along the rough brick as she took
a deep, cleansing breath that eased some of the pain of
the past.

The cellar lay before her—racks upon racks of wine
bottles, gleaming beneath the lights. Some of them were
covered in dust and at least fifty years old, others brand-
new and polished to a shine.

She ran her fingers down the length of a bottle of rosé,
feeling the smooth glass soothe some of the raging emotions
that pulsed in her chest. The cozy space had been comforting her ever since she was a child when, on one particularly
stormy afternoon, when the lightning had frightened her,
her mom had packed a picnic basket and they'd lunched
between the racks on a checkered blanket.

And today she desperately needed comfort. Tomorrow
she'd leave America for the first time in her life. Not on
the trip to Paris she'd put off every year since her mom's
death, and not for a tour of German vineyards like she and
Dad had talked about, but to fight for the one thing she had
left in the world.

Going to Spain was the right move.

With Dad stepping down after the sale, Fox would need
a leader. And, as much as she'd hate it, she'd use this time
with Adrian Cabrera to demonstrate how she would be an
ideal candidate to move up from marketing to being director of Fox.

The thought of having to work under Adrian at Cabrera
Wine made her grind her teeth. But it would be better than
losing the family's winery completely...living next to the
vineyard she'd been raised in and watching it shift from

being a laid-back, country winery into a glitzy destination for Adrian's wealthy friends. Perhaps, sometime down the road, she could even establish herself enough to buy the winery back…

A lump rose in her throat. She'd spent countless hours down here in the dark coolness—sometimes studying for her bachelor's degree, other times reading, or thumbing through family photos. The history that pulsed through the brick walls, the comforting glow of the lanterns…all had been a balm for her broken heart.

Her dad hadn't intended to abandon her after her mom's death. She knew that now. But back then she'd been cast adrift, left to deal with her own grief as she buried one parent and watched the other turn into a wraith.

In her moments of crisis the juicy burst of a grape in her mouth had brought her a fleeting moment of joy. The dark warmth of the cellar had cradled her while she'd cried. The challenge of creating a campaign to drum up business for their new tasting room had sparked her love of marketing. Every day the winery had provided something new— something to keep her going forward instead of following in her father's footsteps.

She'd lost her mom.

Now her dad was trying to sugarcoat his condition, but she knew he had less than a year left.

The winery was all she had that she could count on.

And it was slipping out of her hands, no matter how tightly she tried to hold on.

The door to the cellar stairs uttered a groan as it opened. She quelled her irritation at being disturbed.

"I'm down here, Dad."

"Your father went to bed."

Adrian's voice slid down her spine, dark and sultry. Just the sound of his husky tones had her heart thumping against her chest so hard it made her lightheaded.

"Mr. Cabrera." She stayed where was, eyes fixed on a rack of Merlot, shoulders thrown back in defiance of the erotic sensations the damn man ignited. "This is my family's *private* cellar."

"Your father invited me to take a look around."

Of course he had.

"Have I intruded on a private moment?"

She whirled around, angry words on the tip of her tongue. They died as Adrian stepped out of the shadows. Dressed in dark blue jeans and a black T-shirt that hugged his muscular chest, he oozed sexuality. Stubble dusted his granite jaw.

What would it be like to feel the scrape of that rough hair against her skin? Feel it against her neck as he trailed kisses down to her breasts, her stomach, and even lower still to her thighs…?

Dear God, Everleigh, get a grip.

Her gaze snapped up to his. Those piercing eyes were fixed on her, the blue of his irises glowing hot, as if he could see her every lurid thought.

"Yes," she forced out, her voice breathy. "I wanted some time alone before we leave in the morning."

"You say that as if you're never coming back."

The sensual thoughts disappeared as grief tightened her chest. When she did come back it would be the day before Fox would officially be announced as being part of Cabrera Wine. She'd be coming back, but it wouldn't be the same.

"The house and grounds will always be yours," Adrian said, once again reading her mind. "The mortgage is being paid off as part of the sale."

"How generous." Everleigh winced at the snide undertone in her words. "Truly," she added softly. "You didn't have to agree to that."

The cellar seemed to shrink around them as Adrian

stepped closer. The vise around her heart tightened. But this time it was something far more seductive and dangerous than grief.

Desire.

Whoever said the road to hell was paved with good intentions had obviously not been around someone as devastatingly attractive as Adrian Cabrera. No, it was paved with lust, and seduction, and a desperate want for something more than just a casual relationship or a quick fling.

"I'm glad it makes you happy."

He stopped in front of her, his well-built body towering over her. Rather than feeling afraid, or intimidated, she wanted to lean in, press her cheek against his chest and listen to the steady rhythm of his heart while he held her and told her everything would be okay.

Their dance had lingered on her mind during the entire drive home, creeping into her dreams where the night had ended with Adrian slipping off her dress and kissing his way over her naked body instead of her closing an elevator door in his face.

She wanted him so much it scared her.

But no matter how attractive she found him, no matter how much she wanted him to show her the pleasure sex could bring, she couldn't give in. Sex would be fleeting. Relationships ended. People left.

And each time she lost someone she lost another piece of her already broken heart.

She stepped back—out of his reach and out of danger. "If we're leaving at six in the morning, I should get to bed."

She started to brush past him, trying to keep as much distance between them as possible. His hand wrapped around her wrist, the heat of his grasp scorching her skin.

"I'm just trying to help, Everleigh."

The softness in his voice was ten times worse than the

hard tones of the suave billionaire who seduced with a single glance.

Tears pricked her eyes. "I don't want your help. I want…"

"What?" Adrian prodded when she fell silent.

She lifted her head and looked him in the eye. Words faltered in her throat, and the yearning to confess her deepest heartache warred with her not wanting to look like an emotional fool in front of the man who held her future in his hands.

"Nothing."

She'd known Adrian for a mere day. Dumping her vulnerabilities on one of the world's richest men was definitely not the way to convince him to sell to her or put her in a leadership position.

Adrian released her wrist and she sucked in a breath. A second later his palm cupped her cheek. Before she could stop herself she'd leaned into the caress as a breathy sigh escaped her lips. How could one simple touch be so soothing and yet spark so much want inside her?

His eyes flashed hot in the dim light. Before she could say anything, he lowered his head and captured her mouth with his.

Oh, my.

The desire she'd experienced before paled in comparison with the white-hot flames licking her body now, as Adrian's kiss rushed through her. Firm lips pressed against hers… His arms wrapped around her—thank goodness, because she was about to melt to the floor.

No previous kiss could even be described as a real kiss anymore. All the chaste pecks and several very dissatisfying attempts at making out faded as Adrian's tongue teased the seam of her lips. She gasped and arched against him, wantonly pressing her feverish body against him.

Each sensuous stroke of his tongue, the tightening of his arms around her waist, the throbbing need growing between her thighs—all of it took her to new heights. The hard press of his erection against her belly emboldened her. She tangled her fingers in his thick hair and moaned. She wanted him closer, naked, inside her—oh, dear God, please, inside her...

"Everleigh... *Dios mío.*"

The ragged edge in his voice spurred her on. She brazenly pressed her hips against his, thrilled at how he grew even *harder*. He fisted one hand in her hair as he continued to shatter her reality with his incredible kisses. His other hand drifted down, fingers blazing a hot trail down her neck, over her collarbone, then lower still.

Sensation exploded in blazing stars as he cupped her breast. No one had ever touched her like this—so intimately, and yet with such tenderness it brought tears to her eyes.

"Adrian..."

She breathed his name, ready for the next step, ready to rip his shirt off and run her hands over his bare chest. Maybe, if her confidence continued, she'd even let her hands drift lower to the button on his jeans and—

He released her and stepped back. The loss of the support of his body sent her stumbling against a wine rack. The bottles clinked and swayed, but thankfully none of them tumbled to the floor.

"Are you all right?"

She looked up. Adrian reached out a hand to steady her, but when he saw that she'd caught her balance he took a step back. His hair was disheveled, his shirt wrinkled and mussed. But there was nothing in his face to indicate that he had practically made love to her in one phenomenal, mind-blowing kiss.

"Everleigh?"

She jerked and dragged her gaze from his lips up to his

eyes. His cold eyes. No heat, no desire. Just chips of blue ice, regarding her with detachment.

"Um…yes, I'm—I'm fine," she stammered as she tried to pull the reins on her racing thoughts.

What the hell had just happened?

Had she imagined their kiss?

"I'm sorry," he said.

Dread curled around her heart and twisted viciously. "For what?"

No, please don't say it.

"For kissing you." He slid his hands into his jeans pockets. "That was inappropriate. I'm going to be your boss."

Shock rendered her speechless. Had that just been a normal occurrence for him? To kiss a woman and then just stop—shut it off as if he had flipped a damn switch? Or had she done something wrong? She was a virgin, sure, but he'd responded with such intensity…

"I…" She swallowed hard and focused on the last thing he'd said. "I agree. Entirely inappropriate. Thank you for putting a stop to it before we did something we'd both regret."

His eyes stayed trained on hers, hard and unreadable. A part of her had hoped he might disagree, or say that, while it wasn't a good idea, he wanted her as much as she wanted him.

But no. Nothing. Nothing but horrible, humiliating silence.

Embarrassment stung her cheeks and swept downwards, engulfing her body in a wave of shame that made her want to sink into the floor.

She should have pushed him away. She should have slapped him. Anything but respond like a virgin desperate for the slightest display of affection.

She pasted a small smile to her face. "Six a.m. Sleep well, Mr. Cabrera."

Before he could respond, she turned and walked up the stairs. Each step was precise, measured, designed to show him she could be just as unaffected as him.

She wouldn't let him see the mortification that nipped at her heels, nor the entirely unreasonable yet deep hurt that had broken off another piece of her heart.

CHAPTER SEVEN

ADRIAN KEPT HIS EYES trained on his laptop, with the distant hum of his private jet's engines providing familiar and comforting background noise. Emails had piled up in his inbox over the last twenty-four hours—everything from a list of upcoming events from Calandra to an unsolicited horoscope whose subject line gleefully announced that he was about to find the love of his life if he'd just "click now" to read more.

His gaze flickered to the partition that separated the areas of the plane and provided a bit of privacy for the two couches in the back. He'd spent countless hours catching a quick nap there, in between trips to and from wineries and events. And now a golden-haired distraction slumbered peacefully on one of those same couches, unaware of the havoc she'd wreaked in his world over the past thirty-six hours.

When he'd gotten up to stretch his legs, he'd noticed that she'd fallen asleep on her side, her face turned away from him. That had left him with an all too enticing view of the curves of her hips and backside. His libido had conjured up images of her, of his hands gripping her waist as he claimed her body...

Maldición.

He shouldn't have gone to the cellar last night. He'd stopped by the study to say goodnight to Richard and, before he'd been able to stop himself, had asked after Everleigh. Then his feet had moved of their own accord to the cellar door and carried him down the stairs right into the arms of temptation.

After their kiss he'd stood, feet rooted to the floor, and

listened to Everleigh's footsteps fade overheard. The desire to go after her, to finish what they'd started, had burned so hotly it had scared him.

The one and only time he'd allowed himself to go further than a few weeks of physical pleasure, disaster had ensued.

He'd enjoyed working with Nicole—had appreciated her insight into public relations. But when she'd sashayed by him on the beach at the company retreat, clad in a bright red bikini and flashing him a sweet smile tinged with se-duction, she'd caught his interest.

He'd broken his rule about dating co-workers and bought her a drink.

She'd suggested dinner at a local restaurant.

One thing had led to another and he'd awoken the next morning after a rigorous night of sex to a note on her pillow.

Last night was fun. Find me if you want a repeat.
—Nicole

The thrill of doing the chasing, instead of being chased, and finding a woman who knew wine, enjoyed sex and talked with *him* instead of fawning over his money, had been a novelty. So much so that he'd helped her secure a job at a new company so they could continue to date.

The few women he'd been with before had been trans-parent in their greed and their interest in his fame, not him.

Nicole had seemed different.

At first.

But he hadn't missed the sudden gleam in her eye when she'd first laid eyes on Casa de Cabrera. The razor-sharp comments she made behind her former co-workers' backs when she'd stopped by his office. He'd ignored those early warning signs, swayed by the adoring way she looked at him, the chemistry between them in bed and, most of all, the temptation of caring about someone and having them care in return.

It was sickening to think of how he'd succumbed to his own weakness.

The cracks that had lurked beneath the surface of their seemingly idyllic relationship had widened into enormous fissures over time. He'd been in lust with the *idea* of Nicole, the possibility she had offered. Love had never been part of the equation, but there had been some affection... trust. Things that he could now admit he'd craved since his mother had shut him out of her life.

Nicole had taken the seed of faith he'd given her and ground it into dust under her too-tall leather heels.

Every relationship he'd had since then had been strategic—physically pleasurable, with an interesting companion, but no strings attached. The few times one of his partners had tried to initiate something more he'd ended it, swiftly and at times ruthlessly.

They knew the rules.

The same rules he'd bent by following Everleigh home.

The same rules he'd flat-out broken last night, when he'd succumbed not only to physical desire but to a need to comfort the woman who was making his life a living hell. The woman now sleeping as if they *hadn't* shared a kiss that threatened to unhinge him for the first time in years, with her delectable body, sun-kissed skin and violet eyes that seduced him with a single feisty glance.

But he would not succumb. The temptations Everleigh offered weren't worth the risk. He would make use of her knowledge of the Fox brand and its marketing over the next few weeks. And then, after the celebration at Fox, announcing the sale and the expansion of Cabrera Wine into the United States, he'd jet off to Rome or Tokyo or even Sydney.

As far away from Everleigh Bradford as possible.

* * *

Everleigh woke with a start. She rolled onto her back, blinking the sleep from her eyes. A white leather couch, identical to the one she'd fallen asleep on, ran the length of the wall across the aisle from her. A low rumble trembled beneath her. Somewhere behind her a deep voice was firing off a string of words in Spanish.

That's right. She was on Adrian Cabrera's private plane, on her way to Granada, Spain.

As much as she hated having fallen asleep and placed herself in a vulnerable position, the nap had refreshed her. Thankfully, the nightmares that sometimes plagued her had held back.

She'd tried to sleep last night, but had tossed and turned, with unfulfilled lust waging a war with common sense and shame. Finally she'd pulled on sweatpants and ventured into the vineyards around midnight, where she'd sat down on the grass and cried as she said goodbye.

The vineyards would still be there when she got back. But Fox as she knew it would be gone forever.

When her cries had softened into shuddering breaths, and acceptance had settled into her bones, she'd lain back and looked up. The stars she'd looked at so many times over the years had twinkled down at her against the smooth blackness of a country night sky. Hopelessness had drifted away as resolution had settled once more into her bones.

She might not be able to own Fox, but she could still lead. She just needed to show Adrian Cabrera what she was capable of.

Now, she sat up and smoothed her hair. In an attempt to portray herself as a consummate professional, she'd taken pains with her appearance this morning. Her alarm had blared at four a.m., rousing her from the depths of a dream in which Adrian was slowly removing every stitch of clothing from her body. The warmth of his skin had felt so achingly real that she'd hopped straight into an ice-cold shower as soon as she'd rolled out of bed.

Apparently being rejected by one of the most handsome men she'd ever met hadn't been enough to discourage her suddenly awakened libido.

Ninety minutes later she'd dried and straightened her hair, applied just enough make-up to show she'd put in the effort, and donned a white long-sleeved blouse and tucked it into silky violet trousers. She'd stepped out onto the porch at six on the dot, laptop case in one hand, purse slung over her shoulder and a single suitcase at her feet.

Adrian, damn him, had already been parked out front in his car, dressed in a black suit and sporting a bored expression. He'd glanced down at his wristwatch and then, without a single word, had strode forward, grabbed her suitcase, tossed it in the trunk and opened the passenger door for her.

She'd followed his lead and kept silent for the twenty-five-minute drive to a private airfield on the other side of Fox Creek.

The sight of the Cabrera private plane, in all its sleek elegance, with its espresso-colored hardwood floors and white leather furniture, had been an excellent reminder of just how different they really were. And just how far she'd have to go to impress this man to get what she wanted.

She'd managed to keep herself busy the first couple of hours on the plane, researching Cabrera's brand and taking notes on all she needed to accomplish in the next five weeks. But somewhere over the Atlantic the research, the early wake-up and the overall stress of the past two days had propelled her to the little lounge at the back of the plane, where she'd curled up on one of the couches and fallen asleep.

She stood, smoothed the wrinkles from her pants, and walked out from behind the partition that separated the couches from the executive space of the plane. Four plush chairs arranged around a table dominated one side. The other side played host to two overstuffed plush chairs, one of which was occupied by Adrian.

Golden light filtered through one of the windows and lit up Adrian's face as he spoke on the phone. Her breath caught. His teeth flashed white against his golden skin as a smile spread across his lips, genuine and so handsome it made her chest tighten.

His eyes landed on her and the warmth disappeared so fast she nearly took a step back.

"Adiós." He hung up and stared at her with a blank gaze.

Everleigh sat down across from him. Despite the several feet between them, distance did nothing to tamp down her racing pulse or quell the fluttering in her belly. The cold mask he wore now couldn't hide his masculine beauty, the striking planes of his face and the strength in his jaw. She knew now what his skin felt like to the touch…rough and hot.

Stop. She didn't want to hope that something might come of their acquaintance, whether it be a night of passion or something more. She couldn't handle another disappointment. Not now, when her entire world was spinning so quickly she could barely catch her breath.

"Where are we?"

Adrian glanced out the window. "Two hours from Spain."

"I didn't realize I'd slept that long."

He returned his gaze to his laptop. "It was an early morning. I trust you slept well?"

"I did. Thank you."

Silence descended, filled only by the distant roar of the plane's engines. She glanced around, taking in the splendor and mentally trying to tally up how much something like this must cost.

"What's the first thing you'll do if you get Fox?" she asked.

Adrian looked up, one brow arched. "You mean when."

She gritted her teeth. "Yes, *when*."

"Is this a trick question?"

"No. I'm curious."

And she was. The thought of Fox passing into someone else's hands hurt like a punch to the stomach, but she needed to face reality.

He closed his laptop and regarded her with a hooded gaze. "Increase salaries. Replace equipment. Expand distribution. Ensure efforts like your event venue and horse sanctuary continue."

She blinked in surprise, warmth filling her chest. "The horses? Really?"

"It's an excellent marketing tool to draw in more guests."

The cozy feeling disappeared. Of course Adrian would see the horses as nothing more than a means to an end.

"Sounds like a lot to accomplish in a short amount of time."

"If you're not up to the task, Miss Bradford, Cabrera Wine can provide you with a generous severance package and a recommendation that will land you any job you want."

Panic flared, along with a healthy dose of anger—a common emotion around this infuriating man.

"No, Mr. Cabrera. I'm more than up to the task. I was merely going to point out that with my father stepping down after the sale you're going to need someone to lead Fox. And not just lead, but take it through the major changes you're suggesting."

A cold smile spread across his face. "Ah... The real reason why you're here on this plane."

"What?"

"You didn't come to ensure a smooth transition." He leaned forward, his eyes hard. "You came because you want something from me. What happens if I say no?" He didn't wait for her to answer, just continued on. "Will you actually do your job? Or will you try to make the sale fail?"

Everleigh stood, stalked to the back of the plane where she'd left her bag, and grabbed it. Each step she took back toward Adrian upped her wrath, until she almost trembled from not giving in and lashing out.

She pulled out her laptop, opened the document she'd been working on, and set her computer in front of Adrian. "Yes, I want you to consider me for the position of director of Fox. But I also spent two hours researching your brand and developing a campaign to announce the sale of Fox to Cabrera." It took every ounce of control she had to keep her volume low and her voice steady. "I'm not going to sabotage the winery and all the people who work for it just because my family no longer has control over it."

Adrian stood and the plane seemed to shrink. It was no longer spacious and welcoming, but too small as he filled the space. Today he was back in his customary outfit of black suit pants and a dress shirt buttoned neatly at the throat and wrists. A navy tie emphasized the blue of his eyes that she knew could turn from ice-cold shards to fiery seduction in the span of a heartbeat.

They blazed now with a fire that moved the heat of her anger lower into her belly, where it settled, traitorously, between her thighs, and sparked an altogether different kind of heat. She sucked in a shuddering breath. His eyes flickered down to her chest, and then her hips, before coming back up to her face.

Was he remembering their kiss in the cellar? The way they'd fit so perfectly against each other? The way his arms had tightened around her?

The feel of his strength and the evidence of his arousal had made images of them naked, his body pressed against hers as he slid inside her, light up her imagination…

"I've known women who would do just that."

His blunt words brought her erotic thoughts to a screeching halt. In that moment she hated him. Hated that he would even entertain the thought that she could be like the women he'd known, hated the attraction raging like wildfire through her veins, hated how her world was once again being tossed into turmoil.

She leaned in, taking pleasure in the surprised look in his eyes. Adrian Cabrera wasn't used to being challenged. "If you think I'm that petty, you can go to hell."

With that parting remark she grabbed her computer and moved back behind the partition. The idea that she would purposely torpedo Fox violated not only her professional ethics but her personal sense of responsibility to all the people who worked for her family, who had helped give them the success and comfort she'd enjoyed all her life.

Not that her display of anger had helped her chances of getting the director position...

Doubt flickered in her mind. She hadn't even lasted five minutes around Adrian without losing her temper. How could she possibly work under him, even if it meant staying at Fox?

But, really, did Adrian think she would be that conniving? How horrible to live in a world where you constantly suspected the people around you of having ulterior motives.

She put that disquieting thought, and any bit of sympathy and desire for him, out of her head and stared out the window of the plane.

CHAPTER EIGHT

TIME FLEW BY, and before she knew it the shimmering turquoise waters of the Atlantic gave way to the white sandy beaches of Spain's coast. Sailboats dotted the ocean, looking like little toys bobbing on the surface of the water. Beyond the water lay Motril, a modest-sized town perched on the edge of the sea.

She swallowed past the lump in her throat. Her dad had planned on joining her and her mom in Paris for her graduation trip, and surprising her mom with a two-week tour of all the major wineries of France, followed by England, Spain, Switzerland, Italy...

All that had been dashed away with three words from a doctor in the hospital to her mom, the day after she'd collapsed, which had ripped Everleigh's fairy-tale upbringing to shreds.

"You have cancer."

The sight of the tears in her dad's eyes yesterday when he'd finally told her the truth about the winery had thrust her back to the day of her mom's funeral. It had been a sunny day, and the brightness had taunted them as they'd stood side by side, clutching each other's hands as if they'd drown without each other.

Before her dad had disappeared into a wine bottle.

She'd never blamed him for his actions, but what if he had been there for her? Would Fox still have become the focus of her world?

More than one man she'd dated since college had accused her of putting the winery before them. One had even snapped, as he'd stalked out the door, "You'll never find someone who'll put up with your obsession."

Obsession. She could still hear the ugliness in his tone. The idea that Fox was an obsession, instead of a passion, a place to hide from the world, had dug its claws into her and never fully let go.

Which was why, she reminded herself now, letting go of the possibility of owning Fox was a big step. One she should be proud of.

The flight attendant walked into the main cabin, her ebony hair curled to perfection and a perky smile on her face. She nodded to Adrian, who had hardly looked up from his laptop the entire flight, and stopped in front of Everleigh.

"We will be landing in just a few moments, Señorita Bradford," she said in a musical voice. She leaned down and, before Everleigh could protest, buckled her seatbelt for her. "Please remain seated until we taxi in. I hope you had a pleasant flight."

"Yes, th-thank you," Everleigh managed to stutter.

Adrian didn't even glance up, his eyes focused on the screen.

What had he been like as a child? Had he always been so serious? Or had something turned him from a happy boy into the intense, brooding beast he was today?

The plane touched down and within minutes Adrian had ushered her outside into the warm Spanish sunshine, onto the runway, and immediately into a stylish black limo without saying a word.

Patience.

They'd gotten off to a bad start, but she still had five weeks. A little over a month to wow him with her marketing skills and show him just how valuable she'd be as director.

Unlike the private jet, Everleigh had been in limos before. So she managed not to act like a girl from the country as she took in the full mini bar and polished custom wood trimming.

"Casa de Cabrera is half an hour from here, just outside of Granada," Adrian said as the limo merged into traffic. "Once we arrive, our butler Diego will show you to your rooms."

"Rooms?" Everleigh repeated. "As in plural?"

Adrian nodded briefly. "You'll have a suite with a bedroom, a sitting room, a balcony and a private bathroom. Dinner is at seven-thirty in the main dining room, or you can dine in your own rooms if you prefer."

Everleigh acknowledged his comment with a nod, and focused her attention once more on the view outside the window.

The city of Granada was stunning. Medieval-style buildings meshed with modern construction, creating a beautiful blend of past and present. Each side street they passed overflowed with plant life, from large purple flowers that tumbled over brick walls to trees dripping with oranges that begged to be plucked.

As they left the city and continued on toward the mountains, she spied the beige-tinted walls of the famed Alhambra palace and fortress, sprawled across a hilltop, partially obscured by a dense elm forest.

Maybe she would find a day or two to escape into the city and soak up the culture of the city.

Or at the very least escape the powerful presence of the man seated across from her who, despite her best intentions, continued to dominate her thoughts.

Adrian hit "Send" on his latest email before his eyes flickered to Everleigh. Her fury at his suggestion that she would sabotage the sale had seemed genuine. But the emotions clouding his normally excellent judgment made him even more suspicious.

Truth be told, she would be a good candidate to lead Fox. Her knowledge of the winery, her experience in branding and marketing, her relationships with the employees, would all help with the transition, and they might even retain Fox's current clientele if a familiar face led the way.

But a decision of that magnitude required more than a one-minute pitch from a woman who had quite a temper on her. Although since their latest argument on the plane she'd been quiet. Her gaze had remained fixed out the window almost the entire drive. However, with each passing mile he'd noticed some of the tension easing from her shoulders. And the joy in her expression when she'd seen the flowering fields had unsettled him.

He looked out his own window and surveyed the fields. When had he last looked at the beauty of his home? So much of the time he was focused on his computer, on a call with his chief financial officer, on anything but the world right in front of him.

It reminded him of that last morning he'd sat with his *abuela* on her front porch, sipping tea and watching the sun rise. Funny how he could remember those details so clearly—the crisp scent of mint tea, the faint buzzing of bumblebees. She'd encouraged him to try talking to his mother once more. He'd brushed her comments aside.

That was when she'd asked him the question that still haunted him twenty-six years later.

"When will you trust yourself to love?"

The next morning his parents had come into his room—something they hadn't done in years. His mother had kept her eyes trained on the floor. His father, with a hitch in his normally steady voice, had shared the fact that Abuela had passed away in her sleep.

The one relationship that had never failed Adrian—the one love that had never demanded anything—had been gone in the blink of an eye, leaving behind a sorrowful pain more intense than anything he'd ever known.

He shoved away the sharp sting of old memories and

turned his attention back to his laptop. He'd found happiness of a sort in the surge of adrenaline he experienced with every accomplishment for Cabrera Wine, in the pride he took in seeing Alejandro and Antonio prosper.

They'd never been close as children, but as they'd each tackled their own endeavors in the Cabrera empire the bond between the three had grown and strengthened. They were colleagues, friends, united in the common pursuit of success.

The limo turned a corner and Casa de Cabrera appeared—a stunning mansion sprawled across fifteen thousand square feet. Stone stairs swept up to a wide flagstone path that led to two-story wrought-iron doors. Arched windows glinted in the sunlight, hinting at the luxurious rooms inside. A fountain splashed in the middle of the circular drive. Flowerbeds full of bright magenta blooms served as an elegant contrast to the sandstone-colored walls and reddish-brown roof tiles.

A small red convertible caught his eye. His chest tightened. Why had Madre not accompanied Padre to Paris? Trying to avoid both Everleigh *and* his mother while trying to get caught up on work was going to be a challenge he didn't need right now.

Out of the corner of his eye, he saw Everleigh's mouth drop open. He bit back a smile. "Welcome."

She turned to him, her eyes wide. "This is your home?"

"Yes."

A small frown creased her forehead. "Do you ever get lost?"

"Not since I was eight."

His attempt at humor didn't faze her. If anything, she seemed to withdraw into herself, her expression growing pensive. He'd got used to Everleigh's spark, her confidence and wit. He didn't like this change.

But you don't need to like it, he reminded himself. *Use*

her knowledge and expertise. Deliver her back to New York. Complete the purchase of Fox and move on.

The limo pulled up to the stairs. His driver, Miguel, hopped out and opened the passenger door before Everleigh could unbuckle her seatbelt.

"I hope you enjoy your stay with us, *señorita*."

Adrian missed whatever it was Everleigh murmured back to Miguel, but he caught her subdued tone. It shouldn't bother him.

But it did.

Diego, the family's long-time butler, opened the front doors. The only two clues to the recent celebration of his sixty-fifth birthday were the slight tinge of silver at his temples and the crinkles at the corners of his eyes. The man had barely aged since Adrian was a toddler.

"Welcome, *señorita*," Diego said with a slight bow and a gentle smile. "Señor Adrian has said you will be joining us for a few weeks. We're delighted to have you."

His words brought a small smile to Everleigh's lips. "That's very kind of you. I know this was arranged last-minute. I'm sorry if I've put you out."

"Nonsense," Diego replied. "Señor Adrian tells me this is your first trip to Spain. We must make it memorable. But first, I imagine you'd like to rest?"

"That would be lovely."

Diego picked up the suitcase Miguel had brought in from the limo and disappeared up the north staircase.

Everleigh turned to Adrian and, again, the faintest wisp of a smile crossed her face. "Thank you."

Her simple words surprised him. Rarely had a woman thanked him for something without having a hidden agenda behind her gratitude.

The smile disappeared. She turned and started to follow Diego.

"You're welcome, Everleigh," he finally forced out.

He saw her shoulders tense, saw her hesitate, but then she quickened her pace and disappeared up the stairs. Leaving him alone in the marble entryway of his family's home. The house he'd grown up in, lived in practically his whole life when he wasn't traveling.

He turned in a circle, ignoring the family portrait that featured him, his brothers and his parents, seated on a white bench outside the house.

A lie on canvas.

That day had been terribly hot, with the sun beating down as the artist had taken far too long to capture the scene. Adrian had stood next to his mother, his hand resting listlessly on her shoulder. The artist had painted him with a small, innocent smile on his round face, instead of the daggers Adrian had given him for forcing him into such close proximity with his mother.

His eyes traveled over the hallway, from the rosewood table topped with a crystal vase to the marble sculpture posed in front of a two-story mirror. What had Everleigh seen when she'd first laid eyes on Casa de Cabrera? Had she been impressed? Or had the sight confirmed her accusations that his world of glamor was unsuitable for Fox?

His hands curled into fists as he stalked down the hall into his study. This questioning of his own ability as a businessman and leader in the wine industry was unacceptable. He analyzed, yes, and self-critiqued, and looked for ways to improve. But he never questioned himself like this—never had before that headstrong woman had crashed his party and upset his world.

He hadn't thought about Abuela, Nicole or the pain of his childhood this much in a very long time, and he could place the blame of reliving the past squarely on Everleigh's shoulders.

CHAPTER NINE

EVERLEIGH WAITED UNTIL Diego closed the door before letting her shoulders sag. She fell back on the feather bed, sinking into a plush silver comforter.

The opulence surrounding her was almost too much to take in. The sleigh bed was the comfiest thing she'd ever laid on. A watercolor painting of the Alhambra palace she'd seen on the drive in hung above the headboard. Luxurious button-tufted armchairs were arranged in front of a large bank of windows that led out onto a balcony, where there was a view of the nearby snowcapped peaks of the Sierra Nevada Mountains, stretched tall against a periwinkle-blue sky.

She got to her feet and walked outside to breathe in the crisp, clean mountain air. The sight of the house had unnerved her. The private jet, the limo, the mountainside mansion—all of it reminded her that not only was she no longer in New York, but she was moving in an entirely different kind of society.

Tears stung her eyes. Her mom would have loved all of it. The scenery, the adventure of traveling, the challenge of talking to a man like Adrian... She'd had a gift for making even the most curmudgeonly soul smile.

Everleigh gripped the railing. God, she wished he'd never kissed her. Although it didn't matter how strong their attraction was—they were too different. She was a country girl. He was a sophisticated international billionaire. She wanted love, a husband and a family she could share the farmhouse and Fox Vineyards with. He wanted status, fortune and the occasional tryst. All she'd get from him would be a night, maybe two, and then he'd move on.

A gentle wind teased her hair and drew her back to the moment. The bed called for her to crawl under the covers and sink into a blissful sleep. But just beyond the gorgeous gardens she spied a familiar sight: row upon row of vines.

Her feet moved of their own accord and took her out of the guest room, down the stairs and out through a pair of doors at the back of the main hall. She stepped into a lush backyard, thick grass cushioning her steps as she bypassed flowering trees and bushes. A wrought-iron gate sat in the wall surrounding the gardens, separating the cultured landscape from the rambling beauty of the vineyards.

She lifted the latch and walked into the fields.

A deep breath brought the welcome scents of foliage and moist soil, and she felt the stress melting away and leaving her more relaxed than she had been in days. She slipped off her sandals and savored the softness of the earth underneath her feet. *Heaven.*

She walked over to one of the vine stakes and bent down for a closer look. The trunks of the vines were healthy, thick, and covered in bright green leaves. A couple bunches of tiny grapes hung from the vines. In another month or two the grapes would mature and be ready for harvest.

"Buenos días."

Everleigh whirled around to see an older woman standing a few feet behind her. Thick brown hair tumbled over one shoulder, with delicate strands of silver weaving through the tresses. The sharp angles of her jaw and strong, pronounced cheekbones were offset by a kind smile that made Everleigh feel at ease.

"Uh…*buenos días,*" Everleigh replied.

The woman's smile widened. She was dressed in jeans with dirt-stained knees, a black shirt and gardening gloves. A straw hat hung from one hand, while the other clutched a pair of pruning shears.

"You are a guest of Casa de Cabrera?" the woman asked, her voice husky and tinged with a lilting Spanish accent.

"Sort of," Everleigh replied with a laugh. "I'm here on business for a few weeks. Mr. Cabrera was kind enough to give me a place to stay."

"Mr. Cabrera has good taste in who he chooses to do business with."

Everleigh flushed hot at the implication behind the woman's words. "Oh, no. No, I'm just here to help with the transition of a purchase he's making." Everleigh tugged on the end of her ponytail, suddenly self-conscious. "I didn't catch your name…?"

"Isabella."

"It's nice to meet you, Isabella. I'm Everleigh." Everleigh gestured to the vineyards. "Have you worked here long?"

"Oh, yes, many years. I am prejudiced, but I think it's the most beautiful winery in Spain."

Everleigh smiled. "I've only seen this one, but I'd have to agree. The flowers along the main drive are out of a fairy-tale."

Isabella cocked her head slightly. "So you like it here?"

"Very much. Whoever designed all this had an eye for detail."

A twinkle appeared in Isabella's eye. "I agree. It was nice to meet you, Everleigh."

She bowed her head in Everleigh's direction and then continued on, deeper into the vineyards.

Adrian might make her feel about as welcome as the plague, but at least there were some people at Casa de Cabrera who were pleasant and welcoming…

Adrian looked up as his mother walked into his study. His shoulders tightened as his chest filled with the resentment he often felt around Isabella Cabrera.

Had it really been thirty-three years since she'd come

back from the hospital? The memory of her getting out of the car, with dark circles under her eyes and lines of sorrow etched into the skin around her mouth, and turning away from him as he ran to her with arms outstretched was burned into his mind forever. That and the sight of the empty baby carrier in the backseat.

He never would have guessed that that one moment would lead to years of Isabella barely being able to stand to look at him, let alone try to be his mother.

In the blink of an eye, he shut off the emotions that seethed beneath the surface. Stoicism was his only means of surviving being around his mother.

"Been digging in the gardens, have we?" he asked, with a glance at her dirt-stained jeans.

"Just checking the vines for the new Cabernet Sauvignon." Isabella walked over to the decanter of ice water Diego had brought in and poured herself a tall glass. "And meeting your new American friend."

He paused, detesting the slight uptick in his heartbeat at the mention of Everleigh. "Oh?"

"Lovely young woman."

Isabella casually sipped her water, but Adrian knew that tone. She had latched on to something, and now she was on the hunt for information.

"She is."

Isabella waltzed over to a green armchair and sat, still trying to look casual and failing miserably. He felt her eyes on him as he walked back to his desk. He sat and turned his attention to his computer. She was up to something, but he was damned if he would give in and ask her what.

The chair squeaked as she stood and meandered over to his desk. "I hear we're taking her family's winery."

His fingers paused over the keyboard, frustration tightening his jaw. "Is that what she told you?"

"No, your father told me."

He took a deep breath, followed by another, as he forced his muscles to relax. To him, Javier Cabrera was more of a business associate than a father. As a father he'd been distant, focused on growing the Cabrera empire. As a mentor and member of Cabrera Wine's executive board he was exceptional—a seasoned professional with a brilliant mind who never hesitated to give his sons advice and guidance.

"Did he also tell you that Everleigh's father is the one who reached out to me? Or that without Cabrera purchasing Fox the winery would most likely go under?"

"He mentioned that, yes."

"And that I offered to keep all employees on?"

Isabella perched on the edge of the desk. "Yes. It just seems very sad."

"So the poor, pampered heiress is now left a pauper?" Adrian snapped. "Except that I'm paying top dollar for Fox, I've left her and her father the house and land, and I've added a twenty-five percent increase to the salaries of everyone who chooses to stay." He stood, feeling that familiar irritation crawling underneath his skin. "I even agreed to Bradford's terms that Fox be a sub-brand of Cabrera. A *sub-brand*. I've been more than generous. And, if that weren't enough, I'm keeping Everleigh on as head of marketing and even considering promoting her to director of Fox. She has no grounds for any complaints."

Triumph flashed in Isabella's gaze. Adrian resisted the urge to squirm. He had a sinking feeling he had somehow revealed something his mother had been searching for, although for the life of him he couldn't imagine what.

"Did you ask her what she wanted?" she asked.

"Of course."

Did you?

Everleigh had certainly made her intentions clear from the beginning, but had he truly asked her what she wanted?

"I like her, Adrian."

He rolled his eyes. His mother's endorsement of anyone's character meant nothing to him. In fact, it should serve as a warning to stay away from Everleigh.

"Just because you like someone it doesn't mean I'm going to alter a business deal. I'm considering Everleigh for the position of director. But I will not make a decision on something this important without considering other candidates."

Isabella hopped off the desk. "I did not ask you to."

Uh-huh.

"Why not take her to dinner? If you're going to do business together, you could at least be a good host and show her Granada."

Considering how the last time they were alone he'd nearly ravished Everleigh against a cellar wall, dinner with her was the last thing he needed.

"I'm busy."

To his surprise, Isabella didn't push. She walked around the desk and planted a kiss on the top of his head. As much as he tried to maintain his neutrality, the motherly gesture produced in him a longing he hadn't felt in years. He jerked away before he could stop himself.

Isabella reared back as if she'd been slapped. He saw the flash of pain across her face, and in that moment he hated her for it. She had been the one to inflict years of heartache on him. And now she just expected his forgiveness...?

In all the years she'd been trying to worm her way back into his life she'd never once apologized for the hell she'd put her three-year-old son through. One day his mother had gone to the hospital, happy and devoted and ready to bring home a baby—a sister Adrian had envisioned sharing his toys with. The next Isabella had come out of the hospital empty-handed, a hollow shell of her former self who could barely look at him.

She'd no longer dried his tears when he had a nightmare.

There had been no more afternoons spent splashing in the pool. His mother had disappeared into her room, and whenever Adrian had asked for her Abuela had been the only one to respond to his cries. It had finally sunk in a year later, when she'd come back once more from the hospital, with a baby boy in her arms she couldn't stop smiling at, that she no longer loved him.

"Just remember," Isabella called over her shoulder as she walked to the door. "I didn't raise you to hide from something that scares you."

"You didn't raise me at all."

The cruel words hung in the air between them. Isabella paused, her shoulders slumping. He waited. Would she finally say something?

She walked out, closing the door softly behind her. Running, as she always did.

She'd started to show an interest in him again around the time of Abuela's death. She'd played with his emotions, reeled him in with meaningless gestures and made a small part of him hope they could reconcile.

But when he'd tried to talk to her about the past she'd always run away with her tail between her legs, dashing his hopes repeatedly, until he'd just stopped hoping and started throwing his walls up again. The lack of emotion had been a welcome respite from the constant up and down—the torture of ceding control again and again, only to be faced with more pain. Never an apology, never an explanation.

He'd never figured out what his mother's end game was. Assuaging her own guilt? It clearly wasn't making amends for the trauma she'd inflicted on her oldest child. And the one time he'd broached the subject with his father, he'd merely said it wasn't his story to tell.

Adrian sat back in his chair and rubbed the bridge of his nose. As tense as their relationship was, he didn't enjoy hurting his mother. But her accusation that he was scared of Everleigh had been a slap in the face. The emotions he'd been feeling for her were coming too fast. Most likely rooted in a combination of lack of sex and the novelty of Everleigh compared with the women he normally dated.

Fresh off a rigorous year of preparing for the launch of the Merlot, and not experiencing any female companionship, it was only understandable that he'd had an extreme reaction.

An extreme reaction that included daydreaming of Everleigh…of swiping the papers off his desk and laying her, naked, on the smooth surface so he could…

Stop!

He just needed to keep his desires at bay until the sale was done and he could get her out of his house and back to the United States.

Yet what his mother had said about connecting with Everleigh in a strictly professional way made sense. At the very least Everleigh would be a part of Fox. If he chose her for director of Fox Vineyards they would need to have a good working relationship.

After their disagreement on the plane he wondered if, given her resentment, she'd contribute her best efforts to Fox's success. Having resentful employees was never a good business practice. Perhaps behaving in a more conciliatory manner would be in his best interests.

Before he questioned himself again, he stood and stalked out through the door, up the stairs and down the hall to her room. He knocked once.

"Just a minute!"

The smile disappeared from Everleigh's face as soon as she opened the door. She'd changed into black yoga pants that hugged her legs and a light blue T-shirt with the Fox Vineyards logo emblazoned across her chest. Had he ever found a woman in such casual wear sexy?

"Oh. Hello."

He arched one brow. "You were expecting someone else?"

"No." She leaned against the doorframe and crossed her arms, the move making her breasts shift under her shirt. "Just not you."

"Then perhaps this isn't the best time to invite you to dinner."

Those violet eyes widened in astonishment. He liked it that he'd thrown her off balance—a fair trade for her surprising him on the plane, when she'd leaned so close he'd been able to feel the warmth of her body and smell the exotic perfume clinging to her skin. He'd tasted her mouth, but what would the rest of her taste like? Would she arch and sigh as he kissed her breasts, or bury her hands in his hair and demand satisfaction as he licked the soft folds between her thighs?

"Dinner?"

Her one-word question pulled him back from the brink.

"A meal usually taken in the evening. Sometimes people eat it together."

"Uh-huh." A frown wrinkled her nose. "Why are you asking me to dinner?"

"The party to announce the sale of Fox to Cabrera is just over a month away. You're here to review marketing, branding, and possibly to become the new director of Fox. We have a lot to discuss." He glanced down at his watch. "It's four-thirty now. We'll leave at seven."

He turned and left before Everleigh could say another word. If she wanted a say, she'd show up. If she didn't, then he would make the necessary decisions without her.

Either way, he was going to be taking a very cold shower tonight.

CHAPTER TEN

EVERLEIGH STRUGGLED TO contain her awe as she took in the courtyard of the restaurant. Round tables were artfully scattered amongst the flowering almond trees, their tops dressed with flickering candles and small bouquets of red roses. Water fell from a three-tiered fountain in the middle of the square—a pleasant melody against the backdrop of sultry instrumental music and the hum of conversation.

She'd been frantically eyeing the dresses she'd stuffed in her suitcase when Isabella had arrived with two evening gowns. It had been disconcerting to realize the woman who had made her feel so at ease in the garden was Adrian's mother.

"Fortunately, we are the same size," Isabella had said as she'd blazed into the room with a bright smile and hung the dresses up, bowling over Everleigh's discomfort with her cheery energy. "I thought you might want more variety to choose from."

A tactful way of saying she'd guessed that Everleigh hadn't brought anything formal enough for the restaurant Adrian was taking her to.

Gratitude had overridden her embarrassment, and the dress she'd settled on—a silvery gray with a silky halter top and a sparkling skirt that fell in soft waves to her sandaled feet—made her feel glamorous. She'd taken pleasure in the slightest widening of Adrian's eyes when she'd walked out through the front door at five minutes to seven. He hadn't complimented her, and this was most certainly not a date—as she'd reminded herself at least twenty times. But the confidence-boost from being on an equal footing had quieted her nerves.

Now Adrian sat across from her, his eyes coolly surveying his surroundings.

Tonight he'd donned another suit, obviously custom-tailored by the way it followed the lines of his solid, muscular frame. Everything from his lapels to his shoes was black, save for a burgundy tie. The dark colors made him look even more forbidding and formidable.

As much as she hated to admit it, Adrian knew the wine industry. The questions he'd shot at her, about everything from their competitors in the States to the strategy behind their latest marketing campaign, had revealed a sharp mind and a resolve to be number one in a very competitive business. And the conversation had turned out to be surprisingly enjoyable.

Whenever she'd talked about Fox Vineyards with the previous men she'd dated their eyes had glazed over and they'd responded with the occasional grunt. Adrian not only engaged with her, but he paid attention, his eyes never leaving her face as she talked.

The intimacy of his unwavering focus both shocked and thrilled her. She felt emotionally bare—naked to his intense scrutiny as she answered his questions—but she didn't want to stop. It was exhilarating to be listened to and heard for what felt like the first time in years.

But, despite the surprising sensuality threading its way through their discussion, she managed to reply with detail and diplomacy. Adrian wasn't just making pleasant small talk. No, he was testing her.

"What are your thoughts on the party?" he asked.

She took another deep sip of wine and looked out over the courtyard, trying to achieve the same aloofness he'd conveyed all evening. Did he not feel the electric tug of attraction between them? Or was he just ignoring it?

"In terms of...?"

"It will be an event that will set the tone for Fox moving forward under the Cabrera name. It's not just about the customers, but the employees, too."

He speared her with that dark gaze that sent sensual shivers up and down her spine.

"How would you accomplish that?"

Before she could answer their waiter reappeared, giving her a much-needed moment to think.

"Have you decided on your entrées?" the waiter asked.

Adrian glanced up and said something to him in Spanish. The waiter bowed his head, collected the menus and disappeared.

"I ordered for us," Adrian said in reply to her quizzical look as he raised his wineglass to his lips.

Irritation rippled over her skin. "Typically, a guest gets a say in what she's going to eat when dining out."

"Yes. But when I already know what's best, why waste time?"

The man was insufferable. But now, she reminded herself as she bit down on her tongue, was not the time to take him to task over his rudeness. Not when she was essentially being interviewed for the position of director.

"I would say collaboration," she said.

Adrian arched that irksome brow. Never had she seen someone convey so much emotion with an eyebrow.

"Collaboration?" he repeated.

"Yes. My thought for the party. Unity, teamwork, partnership—whatever you want to call it." Her mind raced ahead of her, all the puzzle pieces falling into place as she envisioned the event. "Invite employees and our biggest clients, the owners of restaurants, grocery chains, et cetera. Create a social media build-up the week before the party. Publish joint statements from my father, myself, you...the new director." She shot him a look, but his face remained passive. "Feature both Cabrera and Fox wines and use the event to announce the next new wine for Fox—the first official release after Fox becomes part of Cabrera."

Pride burned bright in her chest. There were so many details that had to be worked out, but it was an excellent beginning. It was the perfect blend of what Fox Vineyards was and what they could be moving forward.

"Hmm…"

She bit down even harder on her tongue. *Hmm? That was it?*

"It has potential," he said.

"Potential?"

"Yes, potential."

Their waiter reappeared before her temper got the better of her. He set a steaming bowl of paella in front of her. Shrimp, mussels and chicken topped a bed of onions, tomatoes, green peas, bell peppers and rice, all of it covered in an olive oil sauce mixed with parsley, lemon juice and garlic.

She picked up her fork and took a bite. The hearty flavor of the shrimp with the crisp, sweet freshness of the peppers hit her tongue. She closed her eyes and let out a small moan. "This is heaven."

She opened her eyes and nearly choked. Adrian's gaze was fixed on her lips, and his eyes were blazing with a heat that sent her heart thundering. She swallowed hard and reached for her water glass to cool the lustful fire burning its way across her skin.

"Um…good choice."

Adrian blinked and the expression was gone.

How did he do that? Suppress any emotion as if it was nothing while her own were wildly out of control?

Before she could ruminate on that concerning thought, the strains of a guitar came over the courtyard. Three musicians had set up by the fountain. A woman in a red dress with a rose perched in her black curls stepped up to a microphone and began speaking in Spanish.

"A local Spanish band," Adrian explained. "They perform around Granada. She's encouraging the audience to embrace the spring weather and dance."

The singer smiled coyly, issued a command to her band and dove into a sultry but lively tune. Several guests stood and began to dance in the space around the fountain.

Everleigh smiled. No matter what happened in the weeks to come, she would savor this memory of couples dancing across the stone patio beneath a blanket of stars.

Adrian's phone rang. He glanced down at the screen and frowned. "My apologies. I must take this."

Before she could comment, he stood and moved away, his phone pressed to his ear. Did the man ever stop working? He hadn't relaxed since the moment she'd met him.

A young man with a confident smile flashing white under his beard approached her. *"Me concedes este baile?"*

Everleigh smiled back. *"No comprende."*

"Would you dance with me?"

She paused. Would it be rude to dance with another man when Adrian was treating her to this incredible dinner? But, he'd had made it clear this was a business dinner and, that steamy kiss in the cellar aside, he had no interest in anything other than using her expertise and knowledge to ensure a smooth transition.

"I'd love to."

The man led her out to where the other couples danced and swept her into a lively version of what she assumed was a tango. He led her around the courtyard, occasionally twirling her out, only to bring her back against him, his hand resting on her lower back as he smiled.

She smiled back, focusing on enjoying the man's skillful mastery of the dance and how well he led her into each turn before expertly moving them in a circle around the fountain. Gradually all thoughts of Adrian disappeared as the music filled her veins and the novelty of the moment chased away her tension.

Out of the corner of her eye she caught movement behind one of the trees. She turned her head and met Adrian's furious gaze. She stumbled.

Her dancing partner caught her as the song finished with a flourish. "You are all right?" he asked as the diners burst into applause.

"Yes." Everleigh forced a smile to her face even as her heart thudded wildly. "Thank you for the dance. I just... I saw someone, and it startled me."

Before he could ask more questions, she squeezed his hand, thanked him again, and walked back to her table. She kept her pace slow and measured, but inside her stomach was twisted up in knots.

She sat down and forced herself to take a drink of water as Adrian approached, his movements like a predator stalking its prey.

"Have fun?"

The ice in his words froze her blood. "Yes, I did. Did you get your business taken care of?"

"Yes."

He snapped the word out with such ferocity she leaned back. "Are you all right?"

He stared at her for what felt like forever before he sat down in his chair.

"I stepped away for two minutes—three at the most. I came back and you were cavorting with another man."

His statement cut deep. "What is wrong with me dancing while you took a business call? You've made it clear on more than one occasion that there's nothing between us but a professional relationship. You stepped away to conduct some business, so I decided to dance with a charming man."

His eyes narrowed. "He wanted more than just a dance, Everleigh. Don't be naïve."

She wanted to punch him in the mouth, but that would certainly ruin any chance she had of securing the director's position. So she did the next best thing she could as her anger surged into fury.

"This conversation and this dinner are over. Goodnight, Mr. Cabrera."

She stood, grabbed the silver clutch Isabella had loaned her, and walked away. She'd made a commitment to work on her temper. A good business leader didn't surrender to her emotions. But, *damn*, it was hard to walk away without tossing the remnants of her wine in his arrogant, holier-than-thou face.

Everleigh forced herself to take measured steps toward an arch carved into the wall of the courtyard. She stepped into a quaint street, each side lined by rows of orange trees. A terrace of little shops sat on the other side of the cobblestones, with displays of pottery, jewelry and clothing in their windows. Fortunately, the shops appeared to be closed for the night, leaving her alone to contemplate this latest insult.

Defeat settled heavy on her shoulders as she walked over to a wall surrounding one of the groups of orange trees. She sank down onto the cold stone and closed her eyes.

Even if she'd kept a lid on her temper she'd no doubt offended Adrian to the point where he would consider removing her from Fox. Why bother keeping on an employee who seemed to do nothing but set him off? Would working at Fox even be enjoyable if she and Adrian did nothing but spar every time they were in close proximity to each other?

But why had her dancing upset him? Logic told her that he was jealous—a thought that gave her an unwelcome thrill. However, given how far he'd gone to keep at her arm's

length since their interlude in the cellar, him being jealous
didn't make sense. He made decisions without emotion,
with only facts and statistics to guide him.

So what the hell had set him off tonight?

Her hair prickled on the back of her neck as awareness
skipped across her skin, hot and electric. She looked up to
see a man standing in the archway.

Even with his face in shadow, she knew him in an instant.

Adrian.

CHAPTER ELEVEN

ADRIAN TOOK A cautious step forward, keeping a watchful gaze on Everleigh. She stared back at him, her eyes unreadable, her body tense as if she would flee at any moment.

He'd screwed up. Everleigh's proposal for the party had impressed him more than anything he'd heard from his own marketing team in a long time. His employees followed his lead; they focused on numbers and statistics. Everleigh had responded in less than a minute with an idea that wasn't just smart but personalized. She was excellent at her job and, judging by her ready answers to every one of his other questions, she had the background to serve as an excellent director of Fox.

But when he'd come back to see her in the arms of that man, jealousy and rage had burned through him like a wildfire. Even discovering the texts on Nicole's phone between her and her lover hadn't inspired an ounce of the possessiveness he'd felt as he'd watched another man's hands move over Everleigh's body. It should have been *his* hands cradling her hips, *his* fingers gliding up and down the curve of her back as she arched against him.

Why was he so drawn to this woman? He'd spent most of his life making informed decisions, using common sense like armor against the unstable emotions that so many of his fellow businessmen fell prey to. He didn't let feelings get the better of him. He'd been enticed by Nicole, had entertained something more than just a physical attraction, but even then he'd kept a certain distance between them.

Yet just the sight of Everleigh casually dancing with someone had made him want to hunt the man down and wring his neck. Dangerous thoughts that he hadn't seemed able to control no matter how hard he tried.

Now he stood here in this empty street, angry all over again because Everleigh had walked away from him. Because she had broken through his resolve to stay away from her.

"What do you want?" she asked, each deep breath making her chest rise and fall, giving him a glimpse of the swells of her breasts beneath her silky top.

"For you to come back inside."

She looked away and muttered something under her breath.

"What?"

"Nothing."

She bit down on her lower lip, the action reigniting his banked lust.

"Thank you for the invitation, but I don't think us spending any more time together tonight is a good idea. I'll find a ride back to the house."

She started down the street, her hips swinging back and forth under the dress. The slit parted, revealing the warm ivory of her thigh.

Adrian caught up to her in three strides and blocked her path. He should let her go. But some unexplained madness drove him on.

"How? You don't speak a word of Spanish, you have no idea what a taxi costs in Granada, and I'm guessing you don't have any euros."

Everleigh gritted her teeth, as if trying to control her temper. "I memorized the address of your mansion and I have a credit card."

She tried to brush past him, but he stepped in front of her. Even though she was on the tall side, the top of her head barely came up to his chin. What if she came across a mugger, or worse, as she stumbled around Granada at night?

"I have no doubt you could find your own way back. But it's after dark, you're in a new city and you're upset. Don't be a fool."

She blew out another breath and ran a hand through her hair, making those enticing golden curls kiss the tops of her shoulders.

"I don't get it. One minute you kiss me like you own me, then you tell me it's business only, and then you turn into an alpha ass because I have the audacity to dance with someone while you're on the phone. And now you're concerned for my safety." She looked up at him, her eyes flashing in the dim light of the streetlamps before she refocused on the ground. "You frustrate me, and you anger me, and you're sexy as hell and it's driving me crazy."

Each word hit him with the force of a freight train, sinking into his veins and fanning the banked coals of his desire into a raging inferno. He moved in front of her once more. She either didn't notice or didn't care. She stayed where she was, hands on her hips, eyes trained on the ground. The intoxicating passion radiating off her in hot waves enticed him like nothing ever had.

A soft moan escaped her and she lifted her tearstained face, her eyes meeting his. "Why won't you just leave me alone?"

"Because I can't."

And with that pronouncement Adrian surrendered to temptation once more and kissed her.

The world slowed to a crawl. He tasted the wine on her lips, felt her surprise. She froze. And then she came alive. Her arms encircled his neck as she pressed her body flush against his. He groaned, the memory of how good she felt against him spurring him on as his hands tightened on her waist. The heat of her skin seeped through the silk of her top. He fisted his hands in the material so he didn't pull the dress off in the middle of a public street.

Her lips firmed under his as she returned the kiss. She moaned, and the sound increased the desire that pumped through his blood to a fever pitch so intense it almost hurt. He moved his hand up and cradled her face, pulling her even tighter against him so he could feel her…any part of her that he could.

"Everleigh…" he whispered against her mouth.

The sound of him saying her name seemed to feed her lust. She pressed her hips against his and he groaned again. God, he wanted her. He wanted to see her naked, feel her surround him with her wet heat and hear her cry out as she came undone in his arms. He wanted to see her wake up, to watch a satisfied smile stretch across her face before she kissed him and let him savor her body again and again.

Before he could question himself, and before common sense could stop him, he dragged his mouth away from hers and kissed his way down her neck, over her chest and down. His hands cupped her full breasts, bringing them to his lips as her head dropped back in submission. One tug and one of her breasts was bare to his gaze. He bent down and placed the lightest kiss on its rosy peak, his groin tightening as her nipple pebbled under his lips. He sucked her into his mouth as her fingers dug into his hair, her hips bucking against his as she whispered his name and moaned.

Then the restaurant's band struck up another tune, the fast-paced melody carrying over the walls of the courtyard. Everleigh's hands slid down to his chest and suddenly pushed him back. His eyes flew open to see her staring at him, her mouth slightly agape, her hair falling in messy waves around her flushed face. She frantically pulled her top up before her fingers drifted up toward her lips, swollen and red from kissing.

A burst of raucous laughter sounded behind them. Adrian looked over his shoulder to see a trio of young men walking down the street, their boisterous singing an indication that they were well on their way to being drunk.

When he turned back Everleigh was halfway down the street. She glanced back at him once, eyes wide, chest heaving, lips still swollen. And then she disappeared around the corner.

He stood, rooted to the spot by the remnants of his desire and the volatile tide of emotions their kissing had let loose.

What the hell had just happened? He hadn't been able to keep his hands off her. Never had desire and emotion combined in such a heady concoction that he'd seriously contemplated pushing Everleigh up against the nearest wall and burying himself inside her.

Slowly, breath by breath, he calmed his racing pulse. He continued on down the street and stepped onto the main road outside the restaurant in time to see Everleigh getting into a cab. Casa de Cabrera was well known in Granada. The cab driver would see her back to his home safely.

An hour later his limo pulled up in front of Casa de Cabrera.

Diego met him at the front door. "Did you have an enjoyable evening, *señor*?"

"Yes, thank you." He glanced at the stairs. "Is Miss Bradford in her room?"

"Sí, señor."

Diego, ever the professional butler, didn't even blink an eye. The man had a better poker face than Adrian.

"She arrived thirty minutes ago."

"Thank you."

He went to his study and, once the door was closed, yanked his tie off with a curse. What the hell was going on? Where had his iron control disappeared to? Above all, why was he so attracted to a woman he couldn't spend more than five minutes with without arguing?

He needed time. Space. No more conversations with Everleigh.

He'd arrange for her to meet and work with his marketing team. He'd screen candidates for the position of director, although the chances of finding someone better than her were unlikely. But that was a conundrum he'd deal with at a later date.

From now on he'd be dealing with Everleigh Bradford from a distance. For both their sakes.

CHAPTER TWELVE

EVERLEIGH WOKE WITH a gasp. Her arm flailed out and knocked into the juice glass perched on the patio table. It fell onto the balcony with a crash, the glass shattering across the pavestones. Her chest rose and fell as she sucked in a breath. She ran shaking fingers through her hair.

It was just a nightmare.

Knowing that didn't slow her thundering pulse or wipe away the sorrow squeezing her lungs so tight she could barely breathe.

Ten years later and it was still so vivid—the horrid memory of her mother on that hospital bed, her frame almost skeletal beneath the stark white sheets, whispering, "I love you," her words weak and raspy. Everleigh had smoothed the hair back from her mother's face and forced a smile to her own as she'd promised that they'd spend Christmas in Paris.

Not five minutes later her mother's hand had gone limp. And the shrill, unending beep of the heart monitor sometimes echoed in her mind—the soundtrack of the worst day of her life.

A knock on the door startled her out of her morbid musings. Diego had probably heard the glass break.

"I'm fine, Diego," she called over her shoulder.

The door opened and a second later clicked shut. The butler had been so kind to her these past two days, bringing her food in her room since she'd holed up there to avoid Adrian as much as possible and recover from the jet lag that had overcome her with a vengeance.

A cowardly move on her part, but also effective. She'd accomplished quite a bit during her self-imposed exile.

She'd also had multiple video calls with her dad. Just being able to see him had eased some of her worry. The impending sale of the winery and knowing that his employees would be safe had taken quite a bit of stress off his plate. That was evident in his voice and the glimmer of energy in his eyes. It was a positive in what seemed to be an endless cycle of bad news.

But, lovely as her brief sabbatical had been, Adrian had set up a meeting between her and his marketing team for tomorrow. She hated to leave the haven of her room, but she knew the longer she hid, the more difficult it would be for her to rejoin the world. Her chances of being named director were probably slim to none by now, and she certainly wouldn't win herself any points by playing hermit.

Doubt whispered in her ear. If a forbidden kiss with her new boss sent her into hiding, was she even capable of leading? No matter how hot the kiss had been, and no matter how incredible Adrian's rock-hard body had felt against hers, she should have pulled herself together, acted like an adult and put their interlude out of her mind.

Easier said than done when the taste of him still lingered on her lips… He'd left his mark on her—from the woodsy scent she couldn't get rid of, no matter how many times she showered, to the lustful heat that had sunk its roots deep into her heart.

She closed her laptop as the footsteps behind her grew louder. "Diego, there's really no need…"

She turned in the chair and felt the words die on her lips. Adrian stood in the doorway, dressed in dark jeans and a black cable-knit sweater, the sleeves rolled up to his elbows. Stubble shadowed his jaw and his hair was tousled, as if someone had been running their fingers through it.

Just like she had two nights ago, when she'd nearly given up her virginity in a side street.

"Are you all right?" he asked.

She swallowed hard. "Yes. Fine."

He glanced down at the glass shards scattered across the balcony. "Do you make a habit of smashing glasses?"

"No."

Despite the distance from her chair to the doorway, he loomed over her...an overwhelming presence that sent a shiver down her spine. She tossed aside the blanket draped across her lap and stood. A sharp pain stabbed the bottom of her foot and she fell back into the chair with a hiss.

Adrian uttered something in Spanish and rushed over. "Little fool!"

"You know I can hear you, right?"

He ignored her as he took her bare foot in his hands, wrapping his fingers around her ankle with the utmost care. A stinging throb warred with the warmth of his grasp.

"Let go."

"There's a piece of glass stuck in your foot. Wait here."

As much as she wanted to argue, she stayed seated, biting her bottom lip to offset some of the pain pulsing in her foot. He disappeared into the bedroom and reemerged with bandages and a wet cloth in one hand and ointment in the other.

"Are you always this prepared?" she asked through gritted teeth.

"I own a winery that hosts parties. Sometimes they get raucous. The housekeeping staff keep necessities in all of our guestrooms." He knelt before her and took her foot in his hand once more. "Stay still."

He cradled her foot and slowly pulled out the piece of glass. The initial removal sent an electrifying sting up her leg. Her fingers tightened on the arms of her chair, but she didn't let out a peep. Adrian placed the offending glass on the table and started to wash the wound.

"I fell asleep in my chair...jet lag," she said.

"And then what?" he asked.

She struggled to keep her face impassive. "What do you mean?"

"Something startled you?"

"Just an accident, that's all." She wasn't about to share the intimate details of her nightmares with him.

"Don't play games with me, Everleigh."

"I'm not the one who plays games."

He sighed and set the cloth aside. "I overreacted. To you dancing. I'm sorry." He dabbed ointment on the cut.

Stubbornness demanded that she refuse his almost apology. But logic overruled. "Well...thank you."

He nodded, his eyes trained on her foot as he wrapped it in gauze. The sight of his tan fingers against her skin made her thighs clench. If he noticed her reaction, he ignored it. He tossed the glass in a nearby waste basket and went back inside, reappearing a moment later with a broom and dustpan.

He made quick work of sweeping up the mess before sitting down at the patio table opposite her. His eyes zeroed in on her, pinning her in place with the dark intensity that made her think very sensual thoughts.

"What were you dreaming about?"

Everleigh rolled her eyes. "You're like a dog with a bone."

"Tenacious? Yes. You're hiding something from me."

"I'm not hiding anything."

Adrian's eyes softened, and the abrupt change threw her off-balance. He reached across the table and before she could jerk back he grabbed her hand, his thumb rubbing slow circles on her palm.

She swallowed hard against the sudden ache in her chest. This was the Adrian she had glimpsed on their ride in the rain...the man who'd refused to wait inside his car while she was outside in the storm.

But was this the real Adrian? Or was he merely being

kind to her to ensure she followed through on her work instead of making trouble?

"Talk to me," he said.

Those words broke through the strong wall she'd built around her heart. She'd never felt the urge to share her innermost thoughts, even with the men she'd dated. If they had zero interest in Fox, her greatest passion, why would they care about anything else that mattered to her?

But here, now, she wanted nothing more than to talk to Adrian.

She looked out over the gardens and the vineyards that stretched beyond. As soon as she talked she'd be opening a door. A door that would be extremely difficult to close. Was it worth it?

A hawk soared in the distance, its wings dark against the bright blue sky. Keeping her eyes trained on the bird, she started to speak.

"My life before my mom's cancer was incredible. I grew up in a beautiful farmhouse... I had two parents who loved me. It was perfect." A hard lump lodged in her throat. "Until it wasn't."

She withdrew her hand, hating the loss of his warmth and comfort, and stood. Distance would make her confession easier. Ignoring the pain in her foot, she hobbled to the edge of the balcony.

"When my mother got her diagnosis it didn't seem real at first. Plus, you hear so many success stories—people beating it and going on to live even more amazing lives." Her voice broke. "Except she didn't. She died in the hospital right before my high school graduation. I still dream about my last night with her." She swallowed hard past the lump. "My father didn't handle her death well. The first couple of months after she died I was by myself. Fox was all I had. It became my lifeline. Eventually my father and I got back to a good place, but it was never quite the same."

Her eyes fell upon the rows of grapevines, and the familiar sight calmed some of the ache in her chest.

"Fox is real. Physical. I can reach out and touch it. It's always been there. My mom's death, my dad's diagnosis, the guys I dated who didn't understand why I loved the winery so much…everything's always changing. Fox is the one thing that has never changed." She closed her eyes as that ever-persistent sense of loss crept over her—a darkness she couldn't escape. "Now it's going to. No matter what my role is at Fox, it'll never be the same."

A chair scraped against the pavestones. She opened her eyes and turned around just as Adrian stopped in front of her. The smell of cedar curled around her. The fragrance catapulted her back to their kisses, to how beautiful and sexy and safe she'd felt in his arms.

Don't go there.

Just because he was being nice right now, it didn't mean jumping into bed with him was the right thing to do. She'd waited years for the right man—for her Prince Charming. Adrian might have the wealth and status of a prince, but "charming" was not the first adjective that came to mind. Brooding, perhaps, or sensually forbidding…

"I know the sale is the right thing for the winery." She looked up at him. "For the people who work for us. I've accepted that. But knowing that my dad is doing the right thing isn't enough to take away the pain."

Adrian stared at her for a long moment. She resisted squirming under his inquisitive gaze. Then something in the air changed between them. Made her forget all the reasons why she shouldn't go there. Maybe it was her dark musings, or that horrid sense of loss, but she felt the charge between them even more acutely, felt their attraction all the way to her core.

She didn't know whether he moved first or she did. But suddenly he was just a breath away. And then they were kissing, her hands on his face, his arms wrapped around her body as if he couldn't bear to let her go. His lips moved over hers and coaxed from them a gasp, which he took advantage of to slide his tongue along her lower lip.

"Adrian…"

His lips left hers to trail kisses over her cheek and down her neck. Her fingers tangled in his hair, clutching tighter as he placed a soft kiss on the tops of her breasts swelling above her neckline.

"Yes," she moaned. "Please, Adrian."

He pulled back and clutched her face in his hands, his eyes glittering with passion. "*Dios mío, novia.* What are you doing to me?"

She stood on tiptoe and placed a soft, teasing kiss on his lips. "Exactly what you're doing to me."

A growl rumbled in his chest as he pulled her back against him. And if she had thought his first two kisses passionate, they didn't compare to the carnal assault he now leveled on her body. His hands drifted over her, skillfully caressing her in places no other man had touched.

He lifted her off her feet, spun her around and pressed her against the wall. Her legs instinctively went around his waist, pressing her most intimate place flush against his hardness. A gasp escaped her at the sheer, sensual pleasure. Never had she felt such desire…such raw, aching need.

Her hips moved of their own accord, arching against him as he rained kisses down on her jaw, her neck, her chest. When she ground herself even harder against him, he captured her wrists in his grip and pinned them above her head.

"Are you trying to make me embarrass myself?" he demanded, his voice raw.

She stared at him for a moment, lust robbing her of the ability to think. But then realization hit and she couldn't help herself; she laughed. To think that she, an inexperienced country girl, could bring someone like Adrian Cabrera to the edge. It was empowering and, oh, so delightful…

"What?"

The glower on his handsome features made her smile. "I don't know what I'm doing, Adrian. I just want you."

The words were out before she could snatch them back. She saw the instant he comprehended what she meant.

"You've never been with a man?"

She squirmed under his penetrating gaze. "Could you put me down?"

"No, this is actually quite a good position for getting the information I want."

He leaned down and nipped her collarbone, sending another shock of desire through her.

"Answer my question."

"Fine. I'm a virgin."

Slowly he released his hold on her wrists and gently set her on her feet. Did the idea of bedding a virgin really displease him that much? Embarrassed, she tried to scuttle to the side, but his arms flew up and he pressed his hands against the wall, caging her in.

"Don't run from me now, Everleigh."

She stared at him. The shame she'd felt in the wine cellar back home crept over her once more. "I'm not running. Had I realized you didn't care for women of my inexperience, I wouldn't have kissed you back."

Before she could escape he captured her lips again, his tongue teasing hers, his teeth grazing her lower lip. The distance he kept between their bodies heightened the tension coiling inside her, tighter and tighter, until she was sure she was going to explode.

Finally he released her and rested his forehead against hers, his breathing ragged. "It surprised me, that's all. If you haven't noticed, the knowledge has not changed my wants."

Her eyes drifted down below his belt. Oh, no, his desire had not ebbed in the slightest.

"Why me?"

His question caught her off-guard. "What?"

"You're twenty-eight years old. You're a stunningly beautiful woman and you've been in relationships before." He leaned in, his eyes glittering, the sun creating a halo around his hair that made him seem like a dark angel. "Why me?"

She started to answer and then faltered. There wasn't just one reason. The pull she felt toward Adrian, the emotions he stirred inside her, were unlike anything she'd experienced before. Everything she'd ever wanted—the passion, the raw desire, the intoxicating man she couldn't get out of her mind—was right in front of her.

"Because you make me *feel*, Adrian."

And, dear God, she wanted to feel something other than loss, other than heartbreak. She wanted, for just one day, not to be reminded of her mom's death, of her dad's illness, of everything that was about to change in her world. Whether or not this moment with Adrian was just that—a brief moment in time—the need to feel him against her, to feel him inside her, burned so hot she could barely catch her breath.

She sucked in a deep breath and met his gaze head-on. "Take me to bed."

CHAPTER THIRTEEN

ADRIAN STARED AT HER for so long, the daring that had seized her started to retreat. Then she looked up and swallowed at the naked desire glittering in his eyes.

"Are you sure?" he said.

The harsh raggedness in his voice sent shivers of pleasure down her spine. He wanted her—truly wanted her.

Boldness pushed her up onto her toes as she wound her arms around his neck and pressed a kiss as light as butterfly wings to his granite jaw. "Please..."

He scooped her up in his arms in one powerful motion that left her breathless. She curled into him, keeping her arms around his neck, and laid her head against his chest as he carried her inside. The thump of his heartbeat against her cheek brought a smile to her face and an unexpected rush of longing.

She leaned up to press a kiss against the pulse visibly pounding at the base of his throat. Another growl emanated from Adrian's chest as his arms tightened around her. Thrilled that she had such a visible effect on him, she flicked her tongue against his skin.

"If you keep teasing me, this will be over far too quickly."

Feminine satisfaction flooded her veins as he set her gently on the bed. His eyes flared as he raked her body with a gaze that threatened to burn the clothes right off her body. He kneeled on the bed, his tall, muscular frame looming over her, before leaning down and capturing her lips once more in a kiss that shook the ground beneath her.

His hand settled on her belly, the pads of his fingers burning her skin and sending hot trails of liquid heat to the junction of her thighs. She wanted to melt into him, to tear off her sundress and slide, naked, down his body until he filled her. Wicked, wicked thoughts…but she wanted, *needed*, to feel all of him.

The speed of their kissing slowed, mellowed, but they did not cool. The sensual pace and his deliberate caresses—a brush of lips, a nip of teeth, a teasing tongue—made her squirm against him. He traced lazy circles up her waist, teasing the skin beneath her breasts.

A whimper escaped and he chuckled in response. She pulled back and was about to issue a demand when he cupped one breast. The pressure, the intimacy, made her knees weak. He gently squeezed, caressing her flesh with long, gentle strokes even as he continued to kiss her sense-less. When he tugged on her nipple she arched, writhed as her blood boiled and she sagged against him.

Before she could utter another word he released her. In the span of a heartbeat he slid the zipper of her dress down and pulled it up over her head. Cool air danced on her skin, drawing her nipples into hard points. A moment later he drew one of those hard buds into his mouth and sucked, making a line of fire blaze from her breast straight to the apex of her thighs.

"Adrian!"

He released her, trailing his lips across her skin and covering her other breast with gentle kisses. He didn't stop kissing her as he masterfully divested her of her panties, so quickly she didn't even have time to be embarrassed by her nudity, leaving her bare beneath his gaze.

Seconds passed as he took her in. She fisted her hands in the sheets, trying not to cover herself. Finally, after what seemed like hours, he uttered one word that made her feel like a goddess.

"Beautiful."

He stood, stripped himself of his clothing and reached

into the nightstand. He pulled out a condom and she watched in fascination as he rolled it onto his thick length.

Dear God.

She'd felt his desire before, but the sight of him erect made her wonder just how someone of his size would fit.

He rejoined her on the bed, the sunlight streaming in from the balcony windows casting shadows over the tendrils of dark hair curving over his muscular chest. He pressed a kiss to her forehead, then her eyelids, then her cheeks, and finally to her lips in a caress so sweet she thought her heart would burst from the tenderness of it all.

When he lay on top of her, his naked heat covering her from head to toe, she squirmed beneath him. His hardness settled in the cradle of her thighs and she arched her body, begging for release.

"Everleigh?"

Her eyes met his and she paused at the seriousness reflected in the dark depths.

"I want you. But I need to know that you're sure. Once you give me this, there's no going back."

Tears pricked her eyes as her heart sang.

Adrian started to push up, away from her, but she snaked her arms around his neck and kissed him with all the passion she could pour into a single touch. "Please don't stop."

He guided himself inside her, the initial sensation foreign. He pressed soft kisses on her face and neck as her body stiffened against the sharp pain.

She gritted her teeth. "I don't like that."

"I know, *querida*. And I don't want to cause you pain. Do you want me to stop?"

She paused. Already the pain was subsiding. Some of that warmth lingered just beneath the surface. And as she shifted beneath him, getting used to the sensation of him being inside her, the desire slowly returned.

"No. Just…be gentle."

He pressed the sweetest, softest kiss on the tip of her nose. "I can do gentle."

Slowly he withdrew, and then pressed back inside her, each thrust accompanied with a feather-light kiss to her jaw or a soft caress on her breast. And with each thrust her desire grew along with her confidence. Gradually she started to meet his thrusts, her hips moving in sync with his. His breathing grew erratic, his eyes hotter as they moved together. She wrapped her arms around him, savoring each touch, each movement, as a heat built inside her unlike anything she could have imagined.

And then she came apart in his arms, her cries matching his as beautiful pleasure filled her and carried her over the top.

She didn't know how long she lay there, sated and drowsy, but at some point the bed dipped as Adrian got up. The sensation of something warm on her thighs a moment later made her open her eyes. Adrian knelt between her legs, gently cleansing her skin with a wet towel.

"You don't have to do that."

Embarrassment made her reach for the sheets—anything to cover her—but Adrian captured her hand and brought it to his lips. The gentle kiss he pressed to the inside of her palm touched her heart and threatened to pull her under.

"Let me do this for you."

When he'd finished, he tossed the towel into the bathroom and lay back down, pulling the sheet over both of them. She curled up against his chest, soaking in the heat radiating off his incredible body. Her eyes drifted shut and she slowly descended into sleep, with the soundtrack of Adrian's heartbeat playing against the palm of her hand.

The soft trill of a bird drew Everleigh out of the most relaxing sleep she'd had in ages. She smiled, her eyes still closed, as she stretched under the covers. Her hand reached

out, seeking the warmth of Adrian's body. Her fingers settled on a cool sheet.

Her eyes snapped open and her head swung around.

Aside from a slight indentation in the sheets, and the
lingering scent of cedar on the pillow, there was no sign
that Adrian had even been there.

She didn't know how long she stared at the empty space.

Her decision to sleep with Adrian had been one that,
in the heat of moment, had seemed so right. Every touch,
every kiss…seeing the flare in his eyes when he'd looked
at her, feeling him move inside her…all of it had surpassed
every expectation and drawn her into a web of emotion that
had ensnared her body, heart and soul.

She'd fully embraced every feeling, even though Adrian
had made it clear so many times how he felt about relationships. So this shouldn't hurt. She shouldn't feel abandoned,
adrift, embarrassed.

But she did. She felt all of that and more.

Because it hadn't just been the incredible, mind-blowing
sex. It had also been the tenderness when he'd taken care
of her afterwards…the way he'd cradled her in his arms as
she'd fallen asleep. For a moment she'd thought that maybe
their time together had meant something more to him.

She pulled the sheets up over her nakedness and rolled
away from the spot where Adrian had lain just hours ago.
No matter what she'd thought, she'd obviously been wrong.

CHAPTER FOURTEEN

ADRIAN STARED AT his laptop a couple of days later, his anger ratcheting up a notch every time he reread Calandra's email.

My apologies for the short notice, but I've accepted a job with Harrison Industries. I will be unable to attend or co-ordinate the Fox party in two weeks. I have attached my notes for the event. Best wishes.

He closed the screen of his laptop. Never in a hundred years would he have pictured Calandra being the type to quit with such short notice and just a brief apology—let alone before a major event.

But his head of marketing, Jade, and her team were building a great campaign. Everleigh had only been with them for two days, and already Jade was praising her work. They would assume some of the responsibilities for planning the party. Calandra had an assistant who could probably handle most of the other details, and there were other employees he could call on.

But the massive change caused by Calandra's message did not bode well.

Although, come to think of it, Calandra had not been at peak performance since the night of the wine release party in New York. A typo in a client email…entering a meeting two minutes before it started as opposed to her customary ten… Little things, but he should have paid more attention.

Something had obviously been wrong, and he'd let his damned attraction for Everleigh distract him to the point where he'd lost one of his most valued employees. He could reach out, offer her more money, more time off—whatever she wanted. But the ring of finality in her email told him she would turn him down.

An ache built in his temples. He leaned back in his chair, his eyes falling on the row of awards displayed on the far wall. The sight of the gold and silver plaques, each one a testament to the success of his company, anchored him. And he clung to that anchor to keep himself from falling even deeper into the mire he'd created for himself.

When he'd given in to his desire and claimed the gift Everleigh had offered him his desire had woven together with a fierce need to protect, to keep her from anyone else who might even dare to look at her.

Mine.

That mantra had played over and over in his head until he'd woken, hours later, with his arms wrapped around her slender body. The sight of her bare skin, glowing golden-red under the rays of the afternoon sun, had aroused him once more and made his hands tighten possessively on her hips.

Possession. Protectiveness. Need. Emotions he hadn't experienced in...*ever*.

The languid warmth had disappeared under a crushing cold wave of reality. It hadn't just been sex. No, it had been something much more.

Which was why he'd eased himself out of bed, dressed quickly and disappeared.

It was also why he had avoided her these past couple of days as he'd pondered how he could possibly name her director after he'd compromised them both.

Until this morning, when he'd passed his director of human resources in the hall and an answer had come to him. He'd sent Everleigh a professional, carefully worded email, telling her to report to his office in Cabrera Wine's main building in downtown Granada. The less personal the setting, the better...

"Mr. Cabrera?"

He turned and his breath caught. Everleigh stood framed in the doorway, her lush hair tumbling down over her shoulders. A scarlet skirt followed the curve of her hips and flared out around her knees. Her sleeveless black top, loose and tucked into her waistband, did little to curb his imagination from filling in the blanks of what was hidden beneath.

His eyes snapped back up to her face, to see irritation evident in her narrowed gaze.

"You summoned me?"

He suppressed a smile. He knew she'd been working on curbing that temper of hers, but when it did slip through it sent a bolt of desire straight to his groin.

And it wasn't just about the sex—although that had certainly exceeded even his wildest expectations.

No, it was *her*. The passion that motivated her actions, her pursuits and dreams. It aroused him, enticed him, like nothing ever had.

No.

The more he thought of her like that—the more he looked beneath the surface of her incredible body—the more he risked the inevitable hurt that came with opening up to someone. Yes, sneaking out of her bed had been cowardly. But staying and risking getting caught up in something that would end in pain hadn't been worth it. He'd done the best thing for both of them.

"I did," he said.

As she walked toward him a blankness descended over her face. It threw him. He'd anticipated anger, that he'd left her bed without a word. But this was unexpected and, as much as he didn't like it, it bothered him. Had their night together had such little impact?

"My event planner just quit. No notice."

Everleigh sat in the chair before his desk and crossed

one leg over the other. Her skirt rode up, exposing a knee and the barest glimpse of her thigh. If she were any other woman he'd suspect her of deliberately taunting him. But the gaze she leveled at him was disappointingly professional.

"The one I met in New York?"

"Yes. Calandra." He handed Everleigh his laptop and kept his eyes off her legs. "Very unlike her. She's worked for me for years. I never would have expected this."

"It does seem odd. But people are complicated. What are you going to do?"

There. The tiniest undercurrent of anger. She wasn't impervious to what had happened between them. But instead of satisfaction, he felt regret and that damned longing cut through him. He should have stayed...should have ensured she was all right. He had been her first and, so far, only lover.

The thought of any other man touching her made his fingers curl into fists.

"I can manage almost all of it," he said. "Calandra kept good notes and confirmed everything before she quit." He leaned back and steepled his fingers. "But the next event she was supposed to oversee was the Fox party. She has a good assistant. Between her, some other employees, and by bringing the marketing team into the mix, I can make sure the event will go smoothly. Which is why I've 'summoned' you." He paused. He knew he was doing the right thing. "I won't be overseeing the hiring of the new director for Fox."

Surprise widened her eyes. "You won't?"

"No. Given recent events, I feel I'm not able to provide an unbiased review."

The blank façade dropped from her face and a rosy pink hue dusted her cheeks. He knew what she was thinking—could see the memory of him pressing her into the silk sheets as her wet warmth clenched around him reflected in the darkening of her eyes, her parted lips.

"Even if that night hadn't occurred, Everleigh, given the way we met, and everything that's happened since, I cannot be the person to choose the new director of Fox. My HR department, led by Benny Alonso, will be conducting interviews in two weeks. I've already told him you will most likely be applying for the position."

"So... I still have a chance?"

"Yes." He breathed in deeply. "Everleigh, you're good at your job. Fox's marketing is excellent, and so is your knowledge of the wine industry. You're a great candidate. But I cannot be the one to make that decision. If it ever got out that we'd had a previous...encounter it could hurt both of us."

She stared at him for a long moment and then nodded. "I understand. Thank you."

Perfect. She'd accepted his reasoning without question—hadn't given in to theatrics or thrown something at his head. But he could still sense anger and hurt lurking beneath the surface.

Words rose up in his throat. She'd confided some of her deepest secrets to him. Perhaps sharing his own sordid experience would help explain why he'd left her bed, why there would never be anything between them aside from the memory of an incredible night. Was that why he felt so compelled to unburden himself? To tell her his secrets in return?

"I learned the hard way that having a relationship with a coworker always ends badly. Nicole was an employee in our public relations department when my father handed me the reins of Cabrera Wine and told me to make it grow. I knew her only professionally, but she caught my attention on a company retreat to Italy. The façade she presented hooked me."

Years later and it wasn't the loss of Nicole that still ate at him. No, it was the shame of being duped—the anger of letting his guard down and giving even a modicum of control to a woman who had ruthlessly used him as a means to an end.

"It was eleven years ago. We dated for six months. She moved to another company, so we could see each other without breaking the no fraternization policy. The first two or three months were enjoyable. She was from a wealthy family, but she told me she didn't want to be just another spoiled rich girl."

Everleigh sat quietly, her eyes trained on him. He resisted the urge to shift, to scoot his chair back, further away from those violet eyes that saw far too much.

"One day her phone started beeping incessantly while she was in the shower." To this day he didn't know how, but he'd known. "I checked it. She'd been carrying on an affair with a former colleague of mine almost the entire time."

Everleigh's hand flew up to her mouth. "Oh, Adrian. I'm so sorry."

"Don't be." The words came out harsher than he'd intended, but he didn't want pity. Didn't deserve it. Not after the fool he'd been. "I can forgive myself those first few months. But I shouldn't have been so taken in. I should have ended it."

He stopped short of telling her the last thing Nicole had done in an attempt to keep him on the hook. The pain and anger at how ruthlessly she'd acted, how hard she'd tried to manipulate him in one last desperate act, still pulsed inside him, raw and ugly.

"Adrian, I don't know anyone who hasn't made mistakes when it comes to a relationship," she tried. "Even me."

Her defense and her compassion touched him. But it didn't matter. Compassion couldn't erase the years of damage that had been done.

He'd accepted that falling into that relationship with Nicole had just been a Band-Aid for the bigger issue—the hole left by years of firstly abandonment, and then the confusion and heartache his mother had wrought. He didn't just avoid relationships to protect himself. No, he protected others from falling for a man who by all appearances was the epitome of success, but who outside of his career was nothing more than a damaged, hollow shell.

The hand on his shoulder made him start. He looked up to see Everleigh looking down at him with such mercy in her eyes it churned his stomach. He didn't deserve any of it.

"Adrian—"

"Don't." He stood, making her drop her hand from his shoulder, and moved away. Distance. He needed distance from the temptation she offered with her kind heart and passionate soul.

"Nicole manipulated me. I will never put someone else through that hell. I've shared this with you to explain why I won't be a part of the hiring process." He turned and caught her gaze with his, needing her to understand. "And why we can never have more than one night."

Seconds ticked by. He saw her jaw work as if she wanted to say something, a myriad of emotions flashing across her beautiful face. And then she took a step back. Relief clashed with regret. He wanted her. But he'd already taken too much from her, with nothing to offer in return. Everleigh was a forever kind of girl. And forever was something he could never give any woman.

"I understand." She smoothed the wrinkles from her skirt. "Thank you for sharing, Adrian. Just remember—everyone makes mistakes, including you. You shouldn't have to keep paying for it."

She started to walk away. His heart clenched. He wanted her to stay. How many times had a woman walked away from him? His mother, so many times over the years. Nicole, when she'd stalked down the driveway in a flight of fury.

But there were no tears from Everleigh. No, there was grace and compassion—an offering so tempting he barely restrained himself from reaching out and grasping her gift as if it was a life-preserver that would pull him out of the emotionless prison he'd created for himself.

She paused, one hand on the doorframe, and turned to look back at him. "I imagine it's pointless stating this now, but I did not give up my virginity to secure that job."

Maldición. "Everleigh, I never thought that. Not once."

A wistful smile appeared. "Thank you."

With that she turned and slipped out of the room.

He wanted to follow her, sweep her into his arms, take her home and carry her up the stairs to his room, where he would lay her naked across his bed and take her to new heights of passion until she was crying out his name. He wanted to feel not just her body beneath his but the emotions she inspired…warmth and protectiveness and affection.

But he sat, hands curled into fists, until the sound of her footsteps had faded.

CHAPTER FIFTEEN

EVERLEIGH PAUSED IN the hallway outside Adrian's office a few days later, her heart hammering like a jackhammer. The last time she'd stood here she'd been vacillating between anger at his silence in the days since they'd made love and shame that it bothered her so much. Emotions that had been tempered by their interaction and which had vanished altogether when Adrian had shared why he was turning the decision about Fox's director over to a hiring panel.

As much as she wanted him to name her director, he was right. If someone found out that they'd slept together, and that he'd been behind her promotion, her career in the wine industry would be ruined. The fact that he'd even considered her reputation in all this had left her with a dangerously warm feeling in her belly.

Then there'd been his confession about Nicole. Just thinking about it made her chest hurt. The more he'd shared, the more the puzzle pieces had fallen into place. She physically ached for the young man who had just wanted to be loved for who he was, for the years he'd been punishing himself by never allowing another woman into his life.

The more she came to know him, the greater was the challenge in keeping her feelings at bay. Still, she'd made the effort to do just that.

The last few days had passed in a hazy blur. As much as she'd initially detested the idea of working with another team, she'd actually enjoyed collaborating with Cabrera Wine's marketing department. Led by Jade, a no-nonsense director with a dry sense of humor, the team had show-

ered her with compliments while also providing suggestions and feedback that had given her a boost she hadn't
felt in years.

New ideas were flowing as if a dam had been opened,
and the work she was putting in was some of the best
she'd ever produced. And with her busy schedule she'd
thought she'd succeeded in keeping her thoughts off
Adrian.

Except whenever he dropped in to discuss the upcoming party with the marketing team and their eyes met, restrained passion snapping in the air with such electricity
she couldn't believe no one else felt the heat. Or at night
when she awoke, damp and gasping, from another dream
that seemed so real she could still feel Adrian's lips lingering on her skin even as her hands clutched the cool empty
sheets beside her.

It wasn't just the memories of their ardent night that
kept him in her mind. It was seeing him greet the recep-
tionist by name and ask about her recently married son. It
was watching him hold an umbrella over an elderly man
outside the office one rainy afternoon while his designer
suit got soaked.

Most of all, it was the pain he'd trusted her with that afternoon. How had she ever thought him cold and unfeeling?
Beneath the billionaire's mask he was an incredible man
who, while powerful and sometimes downright arrogant,
was also intelligent, kind, and just as passionate about his
career as she was about hers.

Now she stood outside his door, heart fluttering and
knees weak. Adrian had sent her another frustratingly brief
email, asking to see her in his office as soon as possible.
Her mind raced with possibilities. Did he want to talk about
her work? The sale? Or was he, too, still consumed with
illicit memories of their night together?

"*Buenos días*, Señorita Bradford."

Everleigh whirled around to see Isabella Cabrera smiling at her.

"Oh, good morning." Everleigh barely caught herself from bringing her hands up to her cheeks. Nothing like having the mother of the man she'd slept with catching her daydreaming about him.

Isabella held up a small paper bag. Sporting a green silk pantsuit and with her dark hair twisted into an elegant chignon, she looked as if she'd just stepped out of the pages of a fashion magazine.

"I imagine my son is very busy, but I was in town and I wanted to surprise him." She leaned in with a conspiring twinkle in her eyes. "He's always had a sweet tooth. When he was little, I used to take him to a bakery off the Plaza Nueva and get him *leche fritas* for breakfast."

Everleigh smiled, imagining a dark-haired boy staring wide-eyed at the treats inside the bakery. Something tugged low in her stomach. What would Adrian be like as a father...?

"That sounds like a wonderful memory."

A shadow passed over Isabella's face. "It is." She glanced down at the bag, her previous enthusiasm gone. "I... I was not a good mother for many years."

"I have a hard time believing that."

Isabella shook her head. "The child I had after Adrian—a little girl—died during delivery."

Everleigh sucked in a breath. "Oh, Isabella... I'm so sorry."

"The loss...it took a toll on me." Isabella tapped a finger on her forehead. "Emotionally and mentally. It was a topic not discussed as openly as it is today. And then, when I got pregnant with Alejandro, I was so terrified I was going to lose him I sequestered myself in my room. Once he was born, I clung to him his entire first year." A deep sigh escaped her lips. "By the time I clawed my way out Antonio had been born. Before I knew it years had passed, and I realized I had lost my first son."

The older woman's frank admission had stunned Everleigh into silence.

"I'm sorry," Isabella said with a forced smile. "I should not have shared such personal details—"

"No," Everleigh rushed to reassure her. "My father and I went through a difficult period after my mother died. It took us a while to repair our relationship."

"I am glad you were able to. Unfortunately, Adrian and I have not had the success you and your father did." She rubbed a spot on her temple. "Probably because I haven't been able to bring myself to talk to him about it."

"Why not try?"

"I need to. I'm trying to work up to it, to explain…" Isabella's eyes fell to the floor, her voice becoming so soft Everleigh could barely hear her. "But after so many years, how could he possibly forgive me?"

The grief in Isabella's words soaked into Everleigh's bones. Not just grief for the lost years between mother and son, but for yet another reason as to why Adrian held himself back, kept his emotions at bay. She would, too, if she'd experienced the repeated pain he had.

"Buenos días."

Everleigh and Isabella both turned to see him standing in the doorway of his office, his handsome face frozen into a granite mask.

"Buenos días, mi hijo." Isabella recovered more quickly than Everleigh, and held out the bakery bag with a smile. *"Leches fritas* with extra cinnamon. I was out shopping and wanted to surprise you."

Adrian took the bag and pecked Isabella on the cheek, the gesture brief and almost businesslike. *"Gracias."*

Isabella blinked, longing evident in the lines around her eyes. "Well… Have a good day."

Adrian turned to Everleigh as Isabella disappeared down the hall, his face blank. "Good morning."

"Good morning." Everleigh nodded toward the bag. "That was very thoughtful."

He shrugged. "I suppose."

He turned and walked back into his office without another word, leaving the door open behind him. She took a tentative step inside. Should she say something about what Isabella had shared with her? No, she decided as she closed the door behind her. As much as she wanted to see a reconciliation between mother and son, it was Isabella's choice.

She looked around the office. Last time she'd been so focused on him and their conversation that she hadn't really noticed the environment Adrian ruled his empire from. The room mirrored the man. Black marble flooring, a cluster of sleek silver chairs around a coffee table and a desk in front of floor-to-ceiling windows that overlooked Granada. The outer walls of the Alhambra stood tall and proud in the distance.

He gestured for her to take a seat. She knew if she had any sense at all, she'd maintain the same level of indifference Adrian was displaying and keep things professional.

"Jade says your work has been exemplary."

"Thank you."

He scrubbed a hand over his chiseled chin and she realized that, for the first time since she'd met him, Adrian was uncomfortable.

"What's wrong?" she asked.

His eyes flew to her face and he stared at her for a long moment. She barely resisted the urge to squirm under that dark blue-eyed gaze that heated her blood.

"There are several Fox Vineyards partners who share your concerns about an international brand buying the winery."

"Who?"

"The entire town of Fox Creek, for starters." He drummed his fingers on the desk. "The mayor, the chamber of commerce, several other wineries in the area… They're all afraid we're going to try and turn the area into New York City."

Everleigh suppressed a smile. "Not surprising. We like our small-town way of life."

He frowned again, his jaw tightening. "Cabrera Wine is not going to change that."

"But how do they *know* that, Adrian?" She waved her hand around the office. "This place looks like a spread from *GQ*. I told you before: Cabrera Wine is glamorous. Your brand represents luxury—jet-setting around the world in a private plane while sipping a hundred-dollar bottle of wine. Fox Vineyards is sipping a glass of rosé in your backyard while the sun sets. You have to understand why some people are nervous about this takeover."

"Sale," he ground out.

She rolled her eyes. "Sale, takeover, buyout—whatever you want to call it. Unless you allay their fears, you're going to have problems."

He sat back, irritation evident in the tense set of his shoulders. "So how do I fix it?" he asked finally.

She leaned back in her own chair, unable to contain a Cheshire cat's grin from spreading across her face. "Are you, the great Adrian Cabrera, asking for my help?"

Judging by the darkening glower on his too-handsome face, he was doing precisely that.

"You have to say please, Adrian."

His fingers curled around a pen, his grip so tight she half expected it to break in two.

"Por favor, señorita."

The words rippled over her skin and sent a delicious shiver down her spine. She swallowed hard, praying he hadn't seen her visceral reaction to the seductive sound of his native language.

With a casual smile meant to conceal the dangerous effect he still wielded over her heart and body, she stood.

"Then let's get started."

CHAPTER SIXTEEN

EVERLEIGH SET HER PHONE down with a relieved sigh and leaned back in her chair.

"Good work."

She looked up as Adrian handed her a glass of water. "Thank you."

Their fingers brushed and the electric spark that had become so familiar to her arced between them. By unspoken mutual agreement, they ignored it.

The office that had seemed so spacious three days ago had shrunk with every hour they'd spent together. She'd spent most of her time keeping her eyes on her screen and off his tan muscled arms when he rolled up the sleeves of his dress shirt. But as the true depth of the situation for Cabrera Wine had been revealed—including a threat from the president of the Fox Creek Chamber of Commerce to withdraw support for Fox Vineyards—she'd become focused on the task at hand.

She took a long drink, the cool water soothing her throat. She'd been glued to her phone and her computer all weekend, soothing ruffled feathers, uttering reassurances... Over two dozen more invitations had been issued for the party. Hopefully meeting Adrian in person and hearing how Fox would continue would ensure a peaceful transition—not just for the winery but for the town, too.

A quick glance at the clock revealed that it was past eight o'clock. She'd adapted quickly to Granada time, but working nonstop had drained her.

Adrian sat down across from her. She averted her eyes. Having finished putting out several of the largest fires had the unfortunate side effect of giving her time to bring her attention back to how devastatingly attractive he was.

How was it possible for a man to look so sexy in something as simple as black pants and a dark green dress shirt? He'd left the top button undone, giving her the barest glimpse of the skin at the base of his throat. Had she kissed him there as they'd made love? Those minutes had been a pleasurable rush of silky caresses, hot skin and burning kisses as he'd moved inside her.

She took another drink of water, hoping to squelch the lust burning through her. She'd enjoyed working alongside him, brainstorming and laying out a plan for the future of Fox Vineyards. They'd ordered lunch in every day, discussing discounts at the winery's event space for local businesses over Spanish delicacies like gazpacho and fried green peppers. The plan they'd eventually crafted had been so well done, it had left her with an incredible sense of pride.

Hard to believe that just recently she had felt like giving up control of the winery. It would have been like cutting off her own arm. But, seeing her dad grow more and more relaxed on their nightly conference calls, and seeing a future for Fox Vineyards she'd never thought possible, it had become clear to her that the sale was the best thing for the winery.

She closed her eyes and let her head fall back against the chair. "Thank you," she said again.

"For what?"

The surprise in his voice was evident. She opened her eyes to see curiosity flicker across his sculpted face.

"I can see how this sale will help Fox Vineyards prosper. There's a part of me that will always be sad that things didn't go as I planned. But," she added with a smile, "I haven't enjoyed my work this much in years."

"It's I who should be thanking you," Adrian replied.

"We could have sold a lot of wine without you, but I doubt we'd have had the support we have now because of you."

His compliment sent a cozy warmth spiraling through her and deepened her smile. "That means a lot."

Adrian stood, turning his back on her to move to the windows. Her contentment dimmed a little. What would it be like if he opened up, took a risk and allowed himself to feel as she had these past few weeks? Would he still be the billionaire who broke hearts and eschewed commitment? Or would he find happiness in a relationship with someone he could trust? Someone like her?

She shook her head and stood up too. Her eyes landed on the Alhambra. The last rays of the setting sun illuminated the reddish hue of the outer walls of the fortress. "It's so beautiful. Someone mentioned the gardens are incredible."

A heartbeat later Adrian turned to her. "Let's go."

She blinked. "What?"

"To the gardens."

"But it's eight-thirty at night. Aren't they closed?"

"They offer night tours. And even if they didn't, my mother sits on the board and my father donates an obscene amount of money every year."

She should say no. Common sense demanded that she decline, go back to Casa de Cabrera and crawl into bed. That would be a much smarter option than exploring a romantic garden at night with the only man she'd ever slept with.

"I'd love to."

Thirty minutes later Adrian escorted Everleigh through the gardens adjacent to the historic palace. Ancient cypress trees spread their branches out against the backdrop of a darkening sky, where stars were blinking between the leaves like little diamonds. The look of wonder on her face as she gazed around made the late-evening sojourn more than worth the trip.

"It's beautiful," she breathed.

"*Sí.* I once knew the Alhambra like the back of my hand." Adrian felt Everleigh's inquisitive gaze land on him. "Abuela Sofia brought me up here nearly every day one summer."

"Was that the summer your mom lost the baby?"

His head snapped around, the cozy feeling of nostalgia disappearing under a splash of ice-cold reality. "How do you know about that?"

Instead of shrinking from his frigid tone, Everleigh held his gaze. "Your mother told me."

"She what…?" Old wounds rose up, ugly and pulsing with pain.

"The day she brought the *leches fritas* to your office."

For a moment he couldn't breathe. Black spots clouded his vision. He turned away from Everleigh before he yelled at her. She didn't deserve his wrath. How many times had he wanted to talk to his mother about how she'd abandoned him in his younger years—first after the loss of his sister and then when she'd focused all her attention on Alejandro and Antonio? He'd never blamed his brothers; they'd been babies. And his father had been distant ever since Adrian could remember. But his father had never dangled love and adoration in his face and then snatched it away in the blink of an eye.

"She's been trying to buy her way back into my life for a long time," he finally grated out.

"I don't think that's what she's trying to do."

Slowly he turned to face her. "Then what *is* she doing?"

"Your mother shows love with gifts. She brought me a dress for that dinner you and I had."

Pinkness tinged her cheeks. He knew she was thinking of their kiss in the street afterward, just like he was.

"I call that bribery."

Everleigh laid a hand on his arm. He froze, wanting to shrug off the comfort she offered and yet not wanting to lose her touch.

"People show love in different ways. I don't want to break your mother's confidence, but she feels guilty over whatever happened between you two."

He counted to five, forcing his muscles to relax as he regained control. "When I was three years old my mother became pregnant. With a little girl. The last three months of the pregnancy were hard. She went into the hospital and I thought she was coming back with my sister. She came back alone."

Before Everleigh could spout words of condolence, he turned away again and walked over to a myrtle hedge, his eyes fixated on the fountains that sent arcs of water up into the air before splashing down into the pond.

This had been one of his favorite places as a child. The soothing sound of the fountains had eased some of his pain as he'd sat on the walkway and watched the water for hours. How ironic that his place of refuge should now play host to him confessing his deepest pain.

He didn't have to. Everleigh wouldn't push. But he needed her to understand—needed her to hear his side, not just his mother's version.

"The loss of her child sent my mother into depression. For months she just lay in bed. I can't imagine what that loss did to her. But…" His throat grew thick. "I'd been happy. I thought our family was going to grow. And instead I lost both my mother and my sister. My mother acted like she could barely stand to be around me. I was three and she just…left."

The fountains continued to play their relaxing melody, the joyful sound a stark contrast to the thunderous cloud of emotions building in his chest.

"Abuela became my caregiver. She helped ease a lot of the pain. When my mother became pregnant with Alejandro she remained on bedrest until she gave birth. I would go into her room in the mornings, kiss her on the cheek, and then spend the rest of my day with Abuela."

He didn't stop to see if Everleigh was still listening. He looked up at the covered mezzanine on the other side of the courtyard, where the stone archways were lit up like jewels by the last fingers of sunlight clinging to the horizon.

"Alejandro was born. Then, soon after, she was pregnant with Antonio and again on bedrest. Aside from my morning kiss on the cheek and the occasional meal, I hardly saw my mother for years. She only started paying attention to me after Abuela died. By that time I barely had any idea who she was."

Silence reigned behind him.

He shoved his hands in his pockets, his throat growing tight. "Maybe that's why I made excuses during my time with Nicole. I just wanted…"

The words wouldn't come out. Even though he'd admitted it to himself, the thought of saying out loud what he had truly been seeking made him feel so cowardly, so weak and desperate.

"To be loved?" Everleigh whispered.

The words hit him so hard he could barely breathe. Invisible fingers squeezed his chest, tightening around his lungs as the truth lingered in the air.

"Nicole didn't just play me. She lied to me. When I broke things off and she was begging me to reconsider she told me she was pregnant."

He could still feel the curl of his lip over his teeth, feel that hard rock settle in the pit of his stomach as years of suppressed fury had taken hold of him and he'd ordered her out of his room, out of the house, and out of his life.

"My mother lost a daughter. I lost my mother. To hear a woman throw around something so valuable, so important as a child, as a way to manipulate me…" His nails dug into his palms. "I saw in her face almost immediately that it was a lie. I hated her. In that moment I hated her so much. I'd allowed myself to feel just the slightest bit of affection for her, and all it led to was pain."

He'd wanted—needed—to grab something, to break it and watch it shatter into a thousand pieces. And he'd despised that feeling…knowing he wasn't in control.

"Adrian."

The sound of his name on Everleigh's lips slid over him—a soothing balm to his pain. He breathed in deeply, the perfume of bougainvillea flowers and Everleigh's scent filling him and easing his fury enough that he was able to rein himself in.

Slowly, he turned. Everleigh stood right behind him, her beautiful face lit by the garden lights. Her lips were parted, her eyes shining with unshed tears.

"Don't cry for me. It was a long time ago."

"That doesn't mean it doesn't still hurt. Sometimes I'll see something, hear something that reminds me of my mother's death, or my father burying himself in his grief. It still smarts."

It made Adrian furious even to think about seventeen-year-old Everleigh alone, heartbroken and scared. Richard might have made amends for his past behavior, but it didn't stop the rush of anger. Why did parents have to cause their children so much pain?

Before he could respond, Everleigh stepped forward and slid her arms around his waist. He froze, even though his body responded, desire and a fierce need coursing through him at her touch.

Bit by bit, he relaxed. He settled a hand on her back. The warmth of her skin seeped through the material of her dress. His fingers started to move of their own accord, drifting up and down in a light caress.

Everleigh looked up at him. Their eyes locked and the night ground to a shuddering halt. He wanted to lay her down beneath the branches of the cypress trees, kiss her naked skin as he undressed her and savor the sounds of her desire, the moans and sighs that had whispered through his mind and tortured him ever since he'd claimed her body as his own.

It wasn't just pleasure he craved, though. Sex with Everleigh had been more than physical enjoyment. With her, he'd felt alive, and the emotions she'd brought out in him had taken their lovemaking to new heights he'd never enjoyed with any of his past bedmates.

He'd told her everything—laid bare every secret he had to hide—and still Everleigh stayed. What would it be like to fully give in to the need pulsing through him, drawing his heart closer and closer to the woman he held in his arms?

A camera flashed, the light making them blink and break their eye contact. Everleigh stepped back, her hand flying up to shield her face, and Adrian uttered a curse.

"Sorry!" an older man called from across the courtyard.

His wife chastised him about looking like a tourist as she pushed him down the walkway and into another part of the garden.

Suddenly Adrian felt the night which just a moment ago had cradled the two of them in an intimate embrace press in on him. The allure of opening up to Everleigh, of trying something new, was gone. Fear sank its hooks into him so deep he couldn't shake loose.

"It's getting late."

Everleigh glanced down at her watch. "It is."

She looked up at him, eyes wide and uncertain.

"We should go."

Not the words he wanted to say. But he couldn't do it. Even if he could overcome his past, he'd spent eleven years turning himself into the opposite of the kind of man Everleigh deserved. As much as he wanted her, he would never cause her the type of pain that had been inflicted on him.

Everleigh deserved warmth, affection, love. Everything he couldn't give her and never would.

CHAPTER SEVENTEEN

FOUR DAYS LATER, Everleigh walked into the soaring front hall of Casa de Cabrera, exhaustion tugging at her body. Her interview with Adrian's HR panel had taken over an hour and a half. She'd answered each question confidently. They hadn't thrown anything surprising at her. But, once she'd shaken the hands of all the committee members, thanked them for their time and walked out of the conference room, the motivation that had energized her had abruptly disappeared.

The last three weeks—the uncertainty, the rollercoaster of emotions that had taken her to extraordinary highs and horrific lows—had all hit her at once.

Halting steps carried her up the stairs and to her suite. She walked into her bedroom, dropped her purse on the floor and collapsed on the bed. The last week had been a blur of working with Jade and her team during the day on marketing campaigns for Fox after the sale was announced and spending her evenings reviewing every piece of information on Fox and the North American wine industry she could get her hands on.

The few times she'd seen Adrian they'd exchanged polite greetings, but nothing more. There'd been no glimpse of the raw sorrow she'd seen in the Alhambra gardens, just a bold billionaire who commanded respect by walking into a room.

Every time she saw him—every time that tantalizing cedar scent summoned memories of being wrapped in his muscular arms—she'd barely stopped herself from reaching out and touching him.

He'd made it clear that one night was all they'd have, and

she'd accepted that. But it didn't stop the flood of emotions he'd released with his caresses, his attention, and—whether he wanted to admit it or not—the trust he'd placed in her when he'd shared his painful past.

She sat up and buried her face in her hands. As much as she wanted to deny it, she was falling for Adrian Cabrera. And acknowledging it left her at a crossroads. One road led to the safety she'd come to crave over the past ten years—firm ground, built by things like Fox Vineyards, that at least until recently had been invincible. Another was a twisted path that led to God knew what. Happiness? A future with the family she'd always wanted yet hadn't quite believed could be hers?

Would Adrian entertain the possibility of a relationship with her if he knew how much she was coming to care for him?

Or was she just setting herself up for more heartache?

She pushed herself off the bed and shed the burgundy business suit Isabella had lent her for the interview. Isabella had shared the fact that she'd invited Adrian to lunch, and that she was finally going to talk to him. That tidbit of information had sent Everleigh on another emotional rollercoaster ride. Would talking with Isabella heal some of Adrian's old wounds? Help him realize that loving someone didn't always have to end in pain?

The white cotton sundress she'd bought this last weekend in Granada whispered over her skin as she pulled it on, the feel of the soft fabric soothing her inner turmoil with its gentle touch. She released a pent-up breath and walked to the door of her balcony, soaking in the view of the majestic mountains stretched tall against the sky.

Even if Adrian felt something for her beyond casual desire, a literal ocean separated them. Granada was beautiful—an oasis in the midst of so much turmoil. But Fox

Vineyards was still her home. How could they make a relationship work with thousands of miles between them?

With a frustrated sigh she turned, grabbed a pair of sandals and walked out of her room. Once more she navigated her way through the palatial home, out through the patio doors and across the manicured lawn to the gate that led out into the vineyard. The one place in Spain where she truly felt at home.

Home.

Tears pricked her eyes. She missed her father. He'd looked good last night when they'd spoken, his face fuller. Their conversation had been the best they'd had since she'd run off to New York City. In one week they'd be reunited, when she and Adrian returned for the party. And then, regardless of whether she was named director or not, she wouldn't leave her dad's side again. Not until...

The aching sense of loss she'd tried to keep at bay since sleeping with Adrian returned with a vengeance, creating a lump in her throat so thick she could barely gasp for breath. How could she be falling in love, be thinking about her future, when her father was dying?

A strong breeze blew through the vineyard and stirred the leaves. The landscape darkened and a coolness chased away the late spring heat. She looked up in time to see large clouds the color of slate move over the tops of the mountains.

"A storm's coming."

She froze. That voice—so deep, so husky, so *familiar*—wrapped around her and cradled her with such warmth it brought tears to her eyes. How cruel was it that she'd only had one night with him? Just one night to touch him, to feel him move inside her with such tenderness as he stared into her eyes, seeing and accepting every part of her?

She swallowed hard, stuffing her emotions as far down as they'd go, and turned to face Adrian.

* * *

Everleigh was trying to keep her face neutral. But Adrian didn't miss the flatness in her eyes, the slight strain about her lips.

"It's beautiful," she said softly.

His eyes drifted to the clouds, billowing into thunderheads over the mountain peaks, then moved back to her.

Clad in a white sundress and silver sandals, her golden hair falling in waves past her shoulders and her violet eyes focused on him, she looked like a Greek goddess. The material hugged the slope of her breast and teased him with the sight of her long legs. Legs he desperately wanted to be wrapped around him as he sheathed himself inside her...

She crossed her arms over her middle, as if comforting herself against whatever darkness had invaded.

"Are you okay? Is it your father?" he asked.

She nodded. "He actually looks well. He's in New York right now. I know he's not going to get better, but..." Her voice trailed off and she ran her hands through her hair. "I can't help but imagine that something's different."

So Richard hadn't told her about the clinical trial.

"Maybe he's just feeling better."

A small smile tugged at her lips. "Yeah. I should probably just be glad he's doing well."

The day after they'd slept together Adrian had called Dr. Nathaniel Pratt, a world-renowned hematologist based in New York. The doctor had been the guest speaker at a fundraiser Adrian had attended in London—the brains behind a clinical trial with late-stage chronic leukemia patients, during which all his patients had gone into remission or seen a reduction in cancer cells. Two more phone calls and a seven-figure donation to Dr. Pratt's research later, Richard had been on a plane from Fox Creek to New York to become a participant in Dr. Pratt's trial.

In between profuse thank-yous that had made Adrian

uncomfortable, Richard had issued one stipulation about accepting Adrian's offer.

"Don't tell Everleigh. Not until I know if there's a chance."

It hurt Adrian now, to see her continue to worry about her father. He wanted to be the one to comfort her, to reassure her that there was hope as he smoothed the lines of worry from her face. He never wanted to let another man touch her—wanted to have Everleigh always be his and his alone.

All things that should terrify him.

These past few days of living under the same roof as Everleigh had been sheer hell—even worse than after they'd first slept together. He'd managed to avoid her at work, leaving for his office as the sun was rising and not returning until the dark of night crept over the city streets.

Home, however, was a different matter. He avoided the guest wing of the house, but he could still hear her laughter echoing down the hallway, smell her sweet floral scent on the air. The commitment he'd made that night in the gardens, to let her go and keep himself safe, was no match for the need that had planted its roots deep in his heart.

He blinked. He was staring at her, but he couldn't help himself. After the long hours, the distance he'd struggled to maintain, he drank in the sight of her.

That delicate pink rose in her cheeks again and set off a spark of desire that burned through him with wicked intensity. He wanted to follow that blush with his lips, down her neck to the swells of her breasts, over her stomach and down to her thighs. He would bring her to the edge of reason, kissing her as he tasted her sweet body until she was sobbing his name.

"How did the interview go?" He managed to keep his voice professional.

"Well, I think. It took over an hour. I felt confident walking out." She frowned. "Didn't your mother say the two of you were grabbing lunch in town?"

"We rescheduled for tomorrow."

Another risk he was about to take. Isabella had stopped by his office and asked if they could have a talk over lunch.

"A long overdue talk," she'd said, her voice raw.

He was finally being presented with the one thing he'd craved for years. Even though he'd shut himself off emotionally, the little boy buried beneath the pain still ached for an explanation. For love. Everleigh had finally made him admit that.

He'd agreed to lunch with a casual "yes." But inside his feelings had raged like a stormy sea. And that, coupled with his obsessive thoughts of Everleigh, had led to him texting Isabella and asking if they could postpone until tomorrow.

It was downright cowardly. But he'd waited thirty-three years for his mother. She could wait one day while he pulled himself together and mentally prepared himself.

Except he wasn't preparing himself at all. He'd seen Everleigh walk out into the vineyard, had watched her from his balcony, his chest tightening at the mere sight of her. The chaos inside him had snapped his resolve in half. His feet had moved of their own accord and brought him to her side.

Any sense of control he had was gone. Surprisingly, he didn't care anymore. He just wanted Everleigh.

She smiled slightly. "She loaned me a suit. She also splashed a bit of Cabrera champagne into my orange juice this morning. For luck."

"Have you been officially converted to Cabrera Wine, then?"

She rolled her eyes, but her smile grew. "I still love Fox, and all the smaller local vineyards. But, as much as I hate to say it, I judged too quickly. Cabrera is much more than I gave it credit for."

"Not just glamor and sex?"

She grimaced. "I was pretty harsh, wasn't I? I'm sorry. You've built something great here, Adrian. You should be proud."

Something tugged at him. Everleigh *admired* him. Not his fortune, not his family's status, not his reputation in bed, but *him*. What he'd secretly craved in his younger years, what he'd been searching for with Nicole, was now sitting right in front of him. Despite the losses she'd experienced, Everleigh had never once strayed from being the fierce yet kind-hearted woman she'd proved herself to be time and time again.

He reached out before he could stop himself and stroked a finger down her cheek. Her eyes drifted shut as a soft sigh escaped her lips.

A distant rumble broke the spell. The clouds grew blacker and a flash of light illuminated the darkening vineyard.

Everleigh stepped back, no doubt remembering the last time they had been interrupted. When, instead of accepting the gift she'd offered him, he'd done what his mother had done for years. He'd run away.

"Time to go inside."

She started to turn away, but Adrian caught her hand, threading his fingers through hers. Just the feel of her hand in his made his breath quicken, and every nerve in his body ignited, thrilling at this slightest touch.

"Do you trust me?" he asked.

Everleigh met his gaze, a small smile playing about her lips. "I do."

He changed direction and led her down the hill toward a thick grove of trees. They'd just reached the edge when the rain started. Adrian tightened his grip on her hand and quickened his pace as rain drenched them in seconds.

"Where are we going?"

Adrian squeezed her hand. "Trust me."

A moment later they rounded another small hill. A cozy little cottage sat there, tucked in a copse of evergreen trees. Adrian opened the door and pulled Everleigh inside the darkened interior.

"What is this place?" Everleigh's voice was hushed as she took in the cobblestone fireplace, vaulted ceiling and blue beaded chandelier. "It looks like a fairy tale."

"It was my *abuela*'s cottage. After my parents married, and my father built Casa de Cabrera, they offered Abuela her own suite in the house. Instead, she asked for this cottage. It used to be the gamekeeper's house."

She smiled. "So this is where you made *polvorones* for the first time?"

"Yes. Once she passed away my father had it redecorated as a guest house." He nodded to the watercolors gracing the walls. "Abuela loved painting. My father kept every single one."

"It's beautiful."

As she spoke a shiver racked Everleigh's slender frame. Adrian grabbed a fluffy blanket off the back of a chair and wrapped it around her shoulders. "Give me a moment and I'll build a fire."

Within minutes, flames crawled over the logs in the grate and warmed the air. Adrian turned to see Everleigh crossing the room, two steaming mugs in her hands. She passed one to him.

"Hot tea."

Everleigh sat in one of the chairs. The blanket rode up, revealing bare legs and feet. Adrian's fingers tightened on the mug.

Everleigh glanced down and shifted under the blanket. "Sorry. My clothes were pretty damp."

Hunger rose up and lashed at the tenuous grip he was keeping on his lust. But he didn't want to go to her like an animal in heat. He wanted to seduce her, to tease and ease her into all the pleasure he could offer.

Hard to do when just the sight of a bare ankle made him hard…

Everleigh took a sip of her tea. "So, what do you think?"

I think I want to start by kissing your bare shoulders before I trail my lips down your back.

"About…?"

"Your mother wanting to talk."

He breathed in deeply. His first inclination was to brush her question aside, but he didn't want to keep running…to hide. He'd accused his mother of doing that over the years. But had he been any better?

"Surprised. Suspicious." He shrugged, the casual gesture at total odds with the turmoil inside him. "I suspect I have you to thank."

"She would have come around eventually."

Before he could stop it his hand came up and he slid his fingers into the wet silk of her hair. Again and again life had smacked Everleigh down. And again and again she'd stood back up, determined to move forward, forgiving her father, choosing to see the positive in the sale of the winery. She amazed him.

"Are you warmed up?"

That shy smile teased him again. "I'm feeling much better, thank you. My feet are still a little chilled, but…"

Her voice trailed off as he set his tea down. She didn't protest when he wrapped his hand around one of her legs and gently drew it out from under the blanket. His fingers pressed firmly against her skin as he massaged her, up and down, his eyes focused on the expressions flitting across her face. Pleasure, contentment, desire.

Each flicker of her lashes, each soft sigh that passed her lips, hardened him until his control shattered. He leaned down and pressed a kiss to her calf. She watched him, her breath coming in short gasps, as he trailed his lips up, closer to her knee. Anticipation built in him as he imagined peeling the blanket off her and baring her naked body to his gaze.

But before he could act, she stood.

And then she shrugged the blanket off her shoulders.

CHAPTER EIGHTEEN

EVERLEIGH LET THE blanket fall off her shoulders, feeling her vulnerability warring with her need for Adrian. Cool air kissed her skin, pebbling her nipples into hard points. She resisted the urge to hide herself, to shield her naked body from his heated stare.

He stood in one smooth motion. He raked her with his gaze, his eyes dark with a desire so intense it scorched her soul and ratcheted up the pulsing heat between her legs.

At last he stood within arm's reach. "Do you trust me?"

His voice came out harsh, ragged. Slowly she nodded.

"Turn around."

With hesitating steps, she turned away from him. His scent lingered on the air, woodsy and masculine. She wanted to reach out behind her, to reassure herself that he was still there and she wasn't making a complete and utter fool of herself.

The first touch of his lips on the back of her neck electrified her nerves. She gasped and arched. "Adrian…"

His hands settled on her waist, his fingers possessive as they pressed against her bare flesh. His lips trailed over her neck and continued down her spine, each kiss as light as butterfly wings.

"So beautiful…"

His hands drifted up to her waist and cupped her breasts. She leaned into him, felt his chest hard against her back. Another kiss on the side of her neck made her squirm against him. Her skin tightened with pleasure. Never had she felt so empowered as a woman, with the evidence of how much Adrian wanted her pressed hard against her.

Slowly he turned her around. He leaned down and kissed

her, his lips hard and possessive, almost as if he were branding her. She embraced every touch, every graze of his hands on her body, as she sank into the liquid heat that engulfed her in a flood of desire.

Adrian's lips trailed over her jaw and then, before she could take a breath, moved down to her breast. She cried out as he captured her nipple in his mouth, the sight of his dark head at her breast making her heart hammer so hard against her chest she was sure it would burst out of her.

When he'd applied the same loving attention to both breasts he knelt before her, kissing the swell of her stomach. And then, before she could stop him, he placed his mouth on her most intimate place. The flick of his tongue on her core made her scream. If his hands hadn't been clamped on her hips like a vise, she would have fallen to her knees.

"Adrian, I can't...please..."

He chuckled, the sound vibrating against her most sensitive skin. "Sit down, *novia*."

She sat, her legs trembling, heat lashing through her. Before she could even begin to recover her sense, Adrian placed his hands on her knees, separated her legs and kissed the inside of her thigh. As the world burned around her, and white-hot desire coursed through her veins, he once more placed his mouth on her.

Each kiss, each sensual caress of his tongue, shattered her inhibitions as she submitted to his seduction. He slid a finger inside her and gently stroked. Somewhere inside her something burned, brighter and brighter, until she arched beneath him and cried out, pleasure shimmering through her as she finally found her release.

Dimly she felt Adrian's arms wrap around her, cradle her against his chest. His lips grazed her forehead and she allowed him to lay her down on the thick rug in front of the fire. She opened her eyes and smiled at him, content and sated. He sat next to her, his eyes focused on hers, deep and dark and hungry.

"That was…"

A confident grin curved his lips. "That was…?"

She stretched, enjoying the way his gaze zeroed in on her naked breasts. "Amazing. Incredible. Better than all the books and the movies."

He stared at her for a moment before throwing his head back and laughing. "I'm glad I exceeded your expectations."

She propped herself up on her elbows and raked an equally frank gaze over his still clothed body. "I'm naked and you're not."

His smile turned challenging, his eyes growing darker. "What are you going to do about that?"

Boldness propelled her up onto her knees. She reached out, undoing his buttons one at a time, her fingers grazing over the bronze skin she uncovered. She kissed his muscular chest, reveled in the groan her touch elicited. Her hands drifted slower, across the hardness straining against his pants.

"You should take those off…"

He stood and in a couple swift movements shed the rest of his clothes, standing before her in his stunning naked glory. All of him was hard muscle and sculpted strength, lightly dusted with dark hair.

She wrapped her fingers around his arousal, hard and silky to the touch.

His breath hissed out. "Do you know what you're doing to me, *novia*?"

"Seducing you?"

She ran her tongue along his length. He grew harder, his fingers tangling in her hair as a string of fiery Spanish words burst from his lips.

Before she could continue he was on the ground in front

of her, gently but firmly pushing her back. "If you don't stop, I'm going to embarrass myself."

The thought that she could bring him to the edge of losing control—a man who'd been with plenty of women far more experienced than she—was a very pleasurable one.

She relaxed back into the soft embrace of the plush rug beneath her. The fire backlit Adrian's incredible body, the flames casting a golden haze over his sculpted chest and muscular arms as he braced himself above her. Slowly, ever so slowly, he lowered himself until his naked flesh pressed flush against hers. She gasped and arched against him, aching to feel him inside her once more. Her fingers ran up his thighs, over his hips and across his back, savoring the heat of his skin.

"Adrian…"

He captured her lips in a kiss that rocked her world. His tongue slipped inside her mouth and rubbed against hers, the intimacy of the act bringing tears to her eyes. One of his hands drifted up and cupped her breast. He slid a finger over one taut nipple. Bolts of lightning shot along her veins.

How was it possible for any experience to top what they'd shared the first time? Yet the pleasure suffusing her body now was even more intense, even more erotic than before.

Adrian broke their kiss. He reached into his pants and pulled out a condom. He pulled it on and before she could say a word leaned down and captured her nipple between his lips. He drew it deeper into the warm, wet heat of his mouth, consuming her. She tangled her fingers in his air and pulled him closer. With one last suck he lifted his head, gave her the most wicked, powerful grin, and then lowered his head to her other breast.

Moments later, when he had her writhing beneath him, he trailed his kisses over her belly and down to her thighs. Before she could utter a protest, he'd lowered his mouth onto her molten core again, his tongue exploring the most sacred part of her body once more.

She arched up off the floor with a cry. As he kissed and licked and nibbled, he danced his hands over her body, weaving intricate patterns on her belly, her thighs, her breasts, with his fingertips.

The fire inside her built, growing stronger and stronger until she could no longer hold back. She cried out as release swept over her.

Before she could fully recover Adrian moved up her body and slid his thick, hard length inside her. Her fingernails sank into his back as she wrapped her legs around his waist. Adrian's eyes widened as he groaned and sank even further inside her.

"Adrian!"

"Everleigh… *Dios mío*, Everleigh."

Each stroke lifted her higher, brought them closer, and their gazes met, clashed, burning with need and some unspoken emotion that fanned the lust between them into a scorching heat so hot Everleigh was sure she'd burst into flames.

Harder, faster… Their breaths mingled and her heart pounded in her chest as she felt the muscles in his back shift with each powerful thrust. Every movement, every time their bodies joined, stoked not only her desire but the love that had been growing inside her since she'd met him.

Time paused—and then her nerves exploded with sensation. She cried out his name, over and over again, sobbing as the most exquisite pleasure rushed through her body, leaving her trembling and weak. Adrian followed a moment later, shuddering as he slid inside her one last time.

She didn't know how long they lay together on the rug, arms and legs wrapped around each other. She only knew that, no matter where her future took her, she would remember this moment as long as she lived…remember the feel of his skin beneath her hand, the slowing pulse of his heartbeat, the scent of sex and cedar lingering on the air as the fire crackled behind them.

The moment she accepted that she was in love with Adrian Cabrera.

After he'd cleaned up, he came back and pulled the blanket over them. She curled against his body, savoring the heat of his skin and the warmth of his arms around her. The rain continued to drum a steady but soft beat on the roof.

"I like this rainstorm better than the last one we got caught in."

His chuckle reverberated in his chest. "Me too."

Her eyes drifted shut and she surrendered to the sleepiness calling to her.

As she snuggled against him, she dimly heard him whisper her name. "Yes?"

A pause, and then a kiss on her forehead.

"Nothing. Go to sleep."

A shrill ring cut through the pleasant fog of sleep. Everleigh opened her eyes just as Adrian rolled away from her, his absence creating a cool chill against her bare back.

"*Sí?*"

She smiled at the grumpiness in his voice. Perhaps she could ease his frustration when he got off the phone...

"*Qué? Cuando?*"

The urgency in his tone made her sit up, alarm chasing away her drowsiness.

Adrian sat on the edge of the couch, tension etched in the tautness of his muscles, the rigid set of his neck. "*Estaré ahí.*"

He hung up, and for a dreadful moment silence stretched between them. She got up and reached out a tentative hand, touched his shoulder. He flinched and stood, keeping his back to her.

"Adrian...what happened?"

Another long stretch of stillness, filled only by the wild pounding of her heart and the blood rushing in her ears.

At last Adrian turned. She drew back, clutching the sheet to her bare chest. This was not the man who had just made love to her. Gone was the gentle curve of his lips, the softness in his gaze. No, this man's face was a mask of dark fury. Lightning flashed in his eyes as his jaw tightened, so hard it might have been carved from granite.

"My mother. She's had an accident."

CHAPTER NINETEEN

EVERLEIGH SAT IN the hospital corridor, her head against the wall and her eyes closed, as she listened to the sounds around her. The squeaky wheel of a medicine cart, the slapping of nurses' shoes on the floor, the distant cry of someone who had just been given news that changed their life in an instant.

Amazing how after ten years, and even across an ocean, the sounds of a hospital were still the same.

She opened her eyes and glanced down at her watch.

Adrian had gotten dressed and disappeared out through the door of the cottage before she'd had a chance to get her bearings. By the time she'd pulled on her dress and made it up to the main house Adrian had already left. She'd gotten the name of the hospital from Diego, pulled up directions and driven here as quickly as she could.

Anxiety rippled through her. She'd texted Adrian once she'd reached the hospital but had received no reply. What if Isabella had permanent injuries, or worse? She knew life could be cruel, but this... After so long, Adrian and his mother were on the verge of reconciliation. What if that possibility was on the verge of being yanked away?

The pain of losing a parent was something she wouldn't wish on her worst enemy, and certainly not on the man she loved.

If their time together in the cottage hadn't cemented it, being confronted with the potential loss of another person in life had given her the courage to finally admit the truth to herself. She was deeply, hopelessly in love with Adrian.

As if her thoughts had summoned him, he walked into

the waiting room. His eyes settled on her and she barely resisted flinching at the coldness in them that threatened to freeze her in place.

Limbs shaking, she stood and walked over to him. "Your mother…is she…?"

He placed a hand at the small of her back and guided her down the hall into a small chapel. Wooden pews sat in neat little rows in front of an altar and a stained-glass window. The dim light cast shadows over Adrian's face, lending even more menace to his countenance.

"She's in surgery. Another driver hit her on her way home from Granada. She has a broken wrist, a concussion, and some cuts from broken glass. But she'll survive."

Relief left Everleigh's knees weak. She started to move forward, to hug Adrian and offer him comfort, but then she stopped. Obviously something was still horribly wrong.

"I'm very glad for that," she said softly. "But what are you not telling me?"

He stared at her, his gaze moving over her face and her body with laser-like precision. But unlike a few hours ago, when her body had responded with fire and desire, his current perusal left her feeling cold.

"I've arranged for you to fly back to the States tomorrow."

For a moment she couldn't speak. "Why?" she gasped finally, inwardly cursing the weakness in her own voice.

"We've had our fun, Everleigh, but it's over. Your work with the Cabrera Wine marketing team is complete. And I received an email after I finished with the doctor. The HR panel is going to offer you the position of director of Fox. You have what you wanted. You can go home."

Hot tears pricked her eyes. There was no joy in finding out that she'd gotten the job. "Is that what you think? That I just wanted to be director? That everything that happened between us…that it wasn't real?"

He shrugged. "It doesn't matter. Whatever it was, it's done."

The cold cruelness in his tone didn't match the Adrian she'd come to know and love over the past month. No, this wasn't like him at all.

"Adrian... I don't understand why..."

He held up a hand. "I thought I could do this, Everleigh. Let you in. Let my mother in. But I was wrong."

The last four words delivered a blow to her heart so forceful she took a step back. "Why?" she croaked.

"I learned a long time ago that when you care about someone you give them power over you. Power to hurt you, to control you." He gestured at the room around them. "My mother, Nicole... I'm not going through it again. I can't."

Her mouth dropped open. "So...you're going to throw away a reconciliation with your mother and a...a future with me because you don't want to risk getting hurt?"

He took a step forward, his eyes hardening into icy shards. "Yes."

It was another blow to her heart. She wasn't worth the risk.

"You loved your *abuela*," she said.

"I did. She was the one constant in my childhood. But I still gave her power by loving her and being loved by her. And when she died..."

His voice faltered and she saw the sorrow in his eyes, saw the little boy who had experienced too much loss. But before she could say a word his mask slid back in place.

"When she died, so did my ability to love anyone else."

Oh, Adrian.

She grabbed onto the back of a pew before she fell to her knees. She wanted to reach out, to hug him and tell him all the reasons she loved him, to comfort this man who clung to the familiarity of past pain.

"You were raised with two parents who loved you." A

vein in his neck started to throb. "You have a father who still loves you. You have no idea what my life has been like."

"Then *tell* me!" She nearly shouted, desperate to keep him from pulling away from her and the life he'd been on the verge of embracing. "You don't have to go through this alone, Adrian. You don't have to let those events control you for the rest of your life. You showed *me* that!"

He froze. "What do you mean?"

"The winery. The sale." Her words came out in a rush as she tried to make him understand. "I focused so hard on Fox Vineyards that I lost myself. Fox became my identity and I couldn't see anything else. But the more time I spent with you…the more I saw how much better Fox could be with your help…how much more I could be if I didn't spend every waking moment focused on it…"

Her voice dropped, trembled, and she decided to take the leap.

"Adrian, I got the courage to not only become myself, but to risk falling in love with you." She took a step forward. "It's messy, and complicated, and I might get hurt, but loving you is worth all of that."

Adrian didn't move—didn't even blink. It was as if he'd turned to stone.

"Say something," she begged.

He looked back at her and something flashed deep in his eyes…something that gave her the tiniest bit of hope.

And then it was gone.

"What's done is done." He glanced down at his phone as the screen lit up. "She's coming out of surgery. Thank you for the past few weeks, Miss Bradford. I look forward to seeing your work as director of Fox Vineyards."

With that, he brushed past her and walked out of the chapel without a backward glance.

A cry burst from her chest, the sound amplified in the

tiny chapel, and she collapsed into the pew, sobs racking her body as she bent over and wrapped her arms around herself.

He didn't even realize that he'd done what his mother had done all those years ago. Turned away from someone who loved him because he couldn't see past his own hurt. His rejection had taken the fragile pieces of her heart and ground them into dust.

Everleigh dropped her head forward and placed her forehead against the back of the pew, the coolness of the wood a welcome balm to her feverish skin. He had told her repeatedly that he had no interest in a long-term relationship, in anything beyond a few pleasurable encounters. *She* was the one who'd gone and turned it into something more, who'd started to believe that the warmth she'd glimpsed had been something deeper than desire.

How ironic that just when she'd found the courage to look beyond Fox Vineyards for happiness she was being handed the job of director—the closest she would get to her dream of leading her family's business. Just in time to have a future with the man she'd fallen in love with yanked away.

She didn't know how long she stayed in the chapel. But by the time she left the hospital stars were peeking out from the storm clouds that chased the sunset beyond the horizon.

Her last night in Spain.

Tomorrow she'd be going home to her dad, to her new job.

But tonight she would grieve. She would grieve for the life that could have been, the love that could have brought her a happiness she'd never thought possible.

And then she would do what Adrian couldn't.

She would move on.

CHAPTER TWENTY

Bam! Bam! Bam! Adrian buried his face in his pillow. The pounding on his door continued, rousing him from the blessed blackness of sleep.

"Detener!" he commanded.

He opened his eyes and immediately shut them against the blinding pain of morning sunlight. The glass of brandy on top of the wine he'd drunk last night had been a grave mistake.

The intensity of the knocking grew.

"Dios mío, stop!"

"Only if you open up, big brother."

Adrian cursed. *What time was it?* He groped for his phone and managed to peel his eyes open enough to see the time on the screen.

"Noon?" he muttered to himself. When was the last time he had slept until noon?

"Thirty seconds more, Adrian, and I knock down the damned door!" Alejandro called.

"You do and I'll toss you over the balcony!" Adrian hollered back.

The action cost him as a headache split the middle of his forehead with a crushing sting. He somehow pushed himself out of bed, stumbled over to the door, unlocked it and pulled it open.

"What do you want?"

"I want to know what the hell's going on," Alejandro retorted as he barged in. His eyes landed on the half-filled brandy bottle. "Did you seriously drink all that brandy on top of wine?"

Adrian shielded his eyes and leaned heavily against the door. "Maybe."

"At least pick a quality brandy if you're going to drink yourself to death."

"I assume you're here for a reason?" Adrian growled as he brushed past his brother and moved into the bathroom.

"I was already on my way to see Madre when she called me. She said you had locked yourself in your rooms and wouldn't come out."

Adrian took a sip of cold water. His stomach rolled, but he managed to keep it down.

"Who says it doesn't pay to get out of bed in the morning?" He forced a look of stoicism that belied the pain squeezing his lungs with an iron grip.

Everleigh's gone.

When he'd left the chapel that day fury had guided his steps. How could he have been so stupid as to let his guard down?

Seeing his mother in the hospital bed, pale and hooked up to an IV, had brought those terrible months after the still-birth roaring back. Not just the memories, but the pain—the vicious cycle of hoping that tomorrow things might return to normal, only to have that day never come. Other ghosts from his past—like the memory of that first day he'd woken up after Abuela's death and realized that he was truly alone—had taken hold of his tongue when he'd spoken to Everleigh and delivered one crushing blow after another.

"...loving you is worth all of that."

He'd wanted to pull Everleigh to him, hug her tight and never let her go. But just the thought of saying those words back to her had frightened him more than the thought of not having her in his life.

He'd done the right thing.

He'd let her go.

Hell, he'd pushed her away with such force there was no possible way she'd ever think of coming back.

He'd almost asked her to stay with him in Granada after they'd made love in the cottage. The thought of her going back to New York, of moving on with someone else, had filled him with a desperate possessiveness that had made him tighten his arms around her naked body.

By the grace of the powers that be, he'd never gotten the chance. Everleigh might have the courage to risk her heart, but he didn't have the courage to risk his. He'd allowed himself to feel—just a bit—when Isabella had invited him to lunch. Allowed himself to hope that maybe they could move forward, even repair their relationship as Everleigh had with her father.

That little bit of power had devastated him when he'd gotten the call from the hospital—had left him frantic as he'd tried to ascertain whether his mother was alive, in a coma, paralyzed, or any of the other possibilities that had taken away his control as fear had poured in.

What would happen if he gave Everleigh the power to hold his heart in her hands? She wasn't the type to purposely hurt him. Hell, even Isabella hadn't meant to in this case. But it hadn't taken away any of the panic that had chased him all the way to the hospital…the dizziness that had nearly knocked him off his feet as he'd raced through the corridors to her bedside.

His original conclusion was right.

Emotions had no place in his life.

Neither did Everleigh.

So he'd focused on a task he could measure from a distance: Isabella's healing.

The surgery on her wrist had been successful, the concussion officially labeled as mild. And, despite his demands that Isabella remain in the hospital for a week, she'd displayed a stubborn streak and insisted on returning home to recuperate.

The Cabrera men had descended en masse upon the house. His father had flown in from England the day of the accident. Antonio had followed a day later from the Bahamas, and Alejandro had arrived late last night—after Adrian had started chasing his sorrows to the bottom of a bottle.

Because no matter how much he told himself that Everleigh had just been an intense fling, that anything he'd felt for her would fade over time, his heart refused to listen.

Alejandro crossed his arms. "Seriously... What's going on?"

Adrian faced his brother and leaned against the bathroom counter. He'd been hungover before, although it had been some years since he had entertained a headache this bad. It didn't even begin to compare with the ache in his chest.

"I screwed up."

"How?"

The words lodged in his throat. His heart still told him Everleigh wasn't a mistake.

"I slept with Everleigh Bradford," he finally forced out. "I got in too deep. I ended it. She's back in New York."

He turned, expecting his brother to be ready with a joke or an offer to introduce him to some bikini-clad model. Instead, Alejandro's eyes widened.

"So, is the mistake that you ended it?"

Adrian's hands clenched into fists. "No. I never should have let myself get so deep in the first place."

"Is this because of Nicole?"

Adrian scrubbed his hands over his face as he stalked over to the hook by the shower and pulled on his robe.

A derisive snort came from his brother. "I called that one."

"Congratulations." Adrian rolled his eyes. "Nicole's a small part of it, but..." His voice drifted off.

Alejandro and Antonio both had good relationships with their mother. They would have had to be dense not to pick up on the tension between him and Isabella over the years. But was it fair to disclose what had happened? To alter how they saw her?

"I imagine a large part of it is me."

Adrian's head snapped up. He stepped out of the bathroom to see his mother standing in the middle of his room. Dressed in lounge pants and a T-shirt, with her wrist bandaged and her hair pulled up into a bun, she looked pale. Tears glinted in her eyes.

"I am so sorry, Adrian."

He stared at her. Thirty-three years he'd waited for an apology. And now that the words had been uttered he didn't know what to say, what to do, how to feel.

"I'll leave you two alone."

Alejandro nodded at Adrian, kissed their mother on the cheek. And before Adrian could say anything he was alone with his mother.

He'd expected to feel resentment, frustration, even anger when they finally talked. But all he felt was the deep-seated fear that had sprouted that day his mother had come back from the hospital without her baby and wound its ugly roots into his soul. The fear that there was no explanation for his mother's rejection save one. He wasn't enough.

"When I lost your sister..." Isabella sucked in a shuddering breath. "I fell into a very deep depression. Every time I saw you..." Tears spilled over and streamed down her cheeks. "It was a reminder of what I'd lost. I was in so much pain, so focused on what I didn't have, that I couldn't see the amazing son I still had."

Each word made Adrian's throat tighten. The fear shuddered, loosened its grip just a fraction as hope bloomed in his chest for the first time in decades. He kept his face smooth, unwilling to let her see the effect her explanation was having on him.

"When your *abuela* offered to take care of you I was so exhausted... Your father was busy traveling, and I felt like I couldn't ask for help—that it would make me look weak. Losing a child...it wasn't talked about back then. I should have told him I needed help..." Her voice trembled. "I felt so alone... But it's no excuse. I'm your mother and I should have... I should have been there for you."

Adrian's fingers curled into fists. He'd never considered the role his father had played after the stillbirth. Or in this case hadn't. Yes, his mother should have asked for help— but, *Dios mío*, she'd just lost a child. His father should have been there for her. Knowing that his mother had suffered from the same loneliness he had, the same unfulfilled desire to be comforted in her darkest hour, wiped away his anger and resentment and left him adrift in a new reality.

She sat on the edge of bed and brushed the tears off her cheeks. "When I got pregnant with Alejandro I was so terrified of losing him I barely got out of bed. By the time he was born you didn't seem to have any interest in anyone other than your *abuela*. Something I fault myself for," she hurriedly added. "And so I focused on your brothers, developed the kind of relationship with them that I wish you and I could have had. You were so young—"

Her voice broke again and she started to sob.

Before Adrian could stop himself, he crossed to the bed and sat next to her. Isabella turned and flung her arms around his neck, crying onto his shoulder. Slowly, he hugged her back. The gesture took effort. His heart was raging a relentless war on the death grip he tried to keep on his control.

After a few moments her cries subsided. She pulled back, her hands finding his and cradling them.

"After your brothers went to school I talked to your *abuela*. Whenever I saw you with her you seemed so happy that I convinced myself you were better off with her. When she died…" She smiled through her tears. "I couldn't have asked for a better mother-in-law. I missed her so much. But I realized it was my opportunity to make things right."

"Which is when you started trying?"

Isabella nodded. "I should have talked to you. But it took me years, and recently a lot of counseling, to even fully realize myself what had happened. And then I felt shame, knowing how much I'd hurt you… Every time you tried to talk to me I was so cowardly that I ran. And I just kept hurting you—until, I imagine, you stopped letting yourself feel. Not just for me, but for anyone."

Her analysis was all too accurate. He stood and walked to the French doors that opened onto his balcony. "I don't trust myself."

"I know. I didn't trust myself either."

He heard Isabella come up behind him. She settled a hand on his shoulder and, instead of shrugging it off or moving away as he would have in the past, he accepted his mother's offer of comfort.

"But what I've seen between you and Everleigh…the love you share…is worth taking the risk."

Love.

"Everleigh told me how she felt, but there's no way I could…"

In less than four weeks he'd come to…what? Lust after Everleigh? Care about her? "Care" didn't even begin to scratch the surface of the depths of his feelings for her. The ache in his heart when he woke up in the morning to an empty bed. The agony every time he relived turning away from her in the chapel and leaving her alone.

He'd told himself it was for the best—that he couldn't return the love she offered. But walking away had still been a cruel, cowardly move she hadn't deserved. Sometimes at night, when the house was quiet and a breeze whistled down from the mountains, he could almost imagine he heard her sobbing...just like he'd heard her cries the day he'd walked away from her.

Memories of the past month whipped through his mind—mental snapshots of all their moments together. Listening to her at the restaurant, trying to conceal how impressed he was. The level of trust she'd placed in him when she'd shared the true depths of her pain right before he'd taken her to bed. How he'd felt when he'd made love her— not just the desire that sent fire coursing through his veins, but the need to feel her, to sink into her, to never let her go.

The day of her interview, when he'd followed her out to the vineyard and she'd turned to look at him, he'd known. But the thought of what that meant—what *love* meant— terrified him almost as much as, if not more than, the possibility of making another mistake.

"It's only been four weeks."

"Your father and I fell in love in one night."

Isabella reached up, her hand hanging in the air for a moment before she tentatively settled her fingers on his cheek. His eyes grew hot.

"*Mi hijo*, please don't make the same mistake I did and let the past keep you from the present. I know we have a long road ahead of us. But if you'll let me, Adrian, I'd like to be the mother you deserve."

After all this time, was it worth it? To let his mother in would be taking a terrible risk...forgiving the woman who had dealt him so much pain over the years.

Yet as he replayed her words in his head he saw the horrible irony. He had sworn not to let someone else in, not to risk pain and heartache. And in doing so he had done exactly what his mother had done all those years ago. He'd shut people out, closed himself off—not out of strength and self-protection, but out of fear.

And he had rejected Everleigh as his mother had rejected him.

Rejected the woman who had seen past his pain and loved him—all of him.

He swallowed hard. "I would like that."

Her smile lit up her face, chasing away some of the fragility that still clung to her. "Thank you, Adrian. Now you need to eat. You look like *mierda*."

As Isabella called Diego and rattled off a list of breakfast items to be brought up Adrian stood frozen in place.

Dear God, what had he done?

Everleigh had brought out the best in him...made him want to be a better man. He'd found himself talking to his employees more over the past weeks, remembering the little details that made them human instead of just ID numbers on the payroll. And would the old Adrian have paid attention to Richard Bradford's condition and reached out to Dr. Pratt in New York?

Failure was not an option. He'd hurt Everleigh—he knew that—but she was his. The possibility that she might find someone else one day filled him with a jealous fury unlike any he'd ever known. If she moved on without him it would kill him.

Isabella waited until Diego had delivered a plate of eggs, lightly buttered toast and a chopped banana before she spoke again. "So now what?"

Adrian forced a bite of egg down his throat. "First I eat. Then I get her back."

CHAPTER TWENTY-ONE

WAS IT POSSIBLE for a smiley face on a pregnancy stick to be mocking?

Everleigh's fingers curled around the test. She closed her eyes, counted to three, and then opened them.

The face stared back at her, a wide grin stretched from side to side. With a sigh, she glanced at the other five tests scattered across the bed, each one saying the same thing.

Pregnant.

How was this possible? Adrian had used protection both times. But the test, as it boasted in pink bubble letters on the box, was over ninety-nine percent accurate. However it had happened, she was pregnant with Adrian Cabrera's child.

She dropped the test on the floor and let her head fall into her hands. What was she going to do? Adrian had made it clear he had no interest in her or a long-term relationship. He might have wanted a family once, before Nicole had gotten her gold-digging hooks into him, but he'd made it clear having a family now was off the table.

She'd have to tell him at some point. It wouldn't be right to conceal something like that from the father of her baby. But she'd wait a while, give herself time to get used to the idea of becoming a mother, and figure out exactly what she was going to say.

When she told him, she'd make it clear that she would raise this child on her own. The thought of taking money from him for their baby when he wouldn't be a part of its life made her sick to her stomach.

Or was that the baby? She'd only taken the test because, along with her period being late, there had been...

something—a feeling deep in her bones that her life had just been drastically altered once more.

Her hand drifted to her belly, her fingers settling on her still flat stomach. "Hi, baby."

Joy whispered at the edges of her pain. It would be hard raising a child alone, especially as she took on the new challenge of directing Fox. And yet the part of her that had yearned for years for a family of her own, yearned to walk barefoot through the vineyards on a summer morning as the sun rose and pluck ripe grapes with her child, thrilled at the gift that had been given to her in the midst of such heartbreak.

"Hi, baby," she said softly again.

Tears pricked her eyes. She was going to be a mom. She could do this. She would be the best mom she could be, and she'd make sure this baby knew every single day just how much she loved it.

Gravel crunched outside. She rose and walked to her window just in time to see her dad pull up outside the farmhouse. He hopped out of his car with a spring in his step that brought a smile to her face. She hadn't seen that kind of energy in him in months.

When the Cabrera plane had touched down at Fox Creek's airport a week ago she'd finally called her dad. Every time she'd tried before—on her way back to the house to pack, on the limo ride to the airport, in the air—her throat had closed and she'd come so close to crying she'd barely been able to get out a request for water to the flight attendant. But when her dad had picked up the phone it had been to tell her he was still in New York and wouldn't be home until the day of the party.

"I'm sorry, Ever-girl. I thought you were going to be in Spain until the day before," he'd said.

"Change of plans," Everleigh had responded, in as bright a voice as she'd been able to manage. "There's some stuff

I need to do here before the party and…" Her voice had nearly broken. "It'll be wonderful to see you, Dad."

He'd invited her to spend the week with him in New York, but the thought of returning to the city where she and Adrian had first met had filled her with such sadness that she'd made excuses and returned to the empty farmhouse.

For the first time ever, the sight of the rolling hills sweeping up to the wraparound porch had failed to produce that wonderful sense of homecoming.

Home, as she'd found out the hard way, was no longer a place. It was people. People like her father and, whether he wanted to be with her or not, Adrian.

She'd have to tell her dad…maybe right after her first doctor's appointment. The thought of her father not being there for her baby's birth, for her baby's first steps, first words, threatened the tiny amount of happiness that contemplating motherhood had brought her.

With a muffled curse, she swept the tests into the drawer of her vanity and hurried downstairs.

"Dad!"

Her dad turned from hanging up his blazer and beamed at her. "Ever-girl!"

She skipped the last step of the stairs and flung herself into his arms. He hugged her back with unexpected energy, his tight embrace soothing some of the raging turmoil inside her.

"Dad, you look amazing," she said as she pulled back.

Her eyes drank in the sight of his face, fuller and tanner than when she'd last seen him, nearly a month ago. Unlike on the day he'd told her the winery was on the verge of bankruptcy, when his clothes had hung loose on his too-thin frame, today he sported a polo shirt that, while still big, seemed to conform more to his chest and his shoulders.

"What have you been doing?" she asked.

"Everleigh…"

His hands settled on her shoulders and the smile he gave her temporarily chased away the negativity of the past week.

"Everleigh, I'm getting better."

His pronouncement hung in the air for a moment, too good to be true.

"But... Dad, how?"

"Adrian Cabrera."

Just hearing his name was like having someone reach into her chest and squeeze her heart with a vicious twist.

"Adrian?" she repeated.

"He met a hematologist—Dr. Nathaniel Pratt—at a fundraiser in London two months ago. Dr. Pratt started a clinical trial last year, for late-stage leukemia patients. Out of the nine patients, eight are now in remission and one has seen a marked reduction in leukemia cells." Her dad's grin broadened. "I started the second round of his trial the week after you left and, Everleigh... Everleigh, my cancer cells are shrinking." He squeezed her hands. "I won't know for another two or three months if I'm going into remission, but it looks good. I have more time—more time with you."

She wrapped her arms around her father's neck. Relief zapped the strength from her limbs, rendered her speechless. He returned her hug with such strength it brought on even more tears. Tears, and a horrible, selfish sadness.

Adrian had once again proved himself to be more than he thought he was. How could he not see what an incredible man he was? To give her father this incredible gift...

She buried her face deeper against her father's shoulder. This was not a time for sadness. Only joy.

She didn't know how long they stood like that in the foyer. But, whether her dad lived another year or another ten, she knew she would always remember this moment.

At last she pulled back and wiped the tears from her cheeks. "I can't believe it."

"I can't either."

He reached out and smoothed the hair back from her head just like he had when she was a little girl.

"I can't tell you how sorry I am about Fox, Everleigh. I know it was your dream, and I screwed up."

She shook her head. "I learned a lot about myself in Spain, Dad. You were right. I wanted Fox for the wrong reasons." She blew out a frustrated breath. "I don't like admitting this, but I think it would have turned into an obsession instead of a passion. Being director and having the support of Cabrera Wine will make it enjoyable, instead of a stressor."

He smiled. "So, Mr. Cabrera turned out to be not as big or bad of a wolf as you thought?"

Her cheeks heated as memories of just how big and bad Adrian Cabrera could be flared in her mind.

She swallowed hard. "Cabrera Wine is more than I gave it credit for," she said finally.

"Then tonight will be even more of a celebration."

He pecked her on the cheek and then, like a little kid, spun around and grabbed a large purple box tied with a satin ribbon off the chair by the front door.

"And to commemorate my incredible news and your new job, I brought you something special."

Everleigh bit down on her lower lip to keep yet another wave of tears at bay as she read the elegant white script across the top of the lid. "'Annabelle's Boutique,'" she said out loud. "Dad…"

He nodded, grinning from ear to ear. "I remember your mother was going to take you shopping at this store in New York to pick out an evening gown for your trip to Paris. If it fits, I hope you'll wear it tonight."

She leaned up and kissed his cheek. "I'd be honored."

Everleigh stood in front of the mirror later that afternoon. Normally she didn't think of herself as attractive, but here, in this moment, she felt truly beautiful.

The gown her father had picked out for her made her feel like a princess. Violet silk crossed over one shoulder and wrapped around her waist, before flowing down past her hips and along her legs to the floor. The bodice and the skirt, which kissed the top of her silver heels, were dressed in violet lace and sparkled with tiny crystals sewn into the delicate fabric.

Some of the girls from the winery had coaxed her into traveling into Fox Creek and having her hair and make-up done at the local spa. The stylist had teased her hair into golden curls, gathered them at the back of her neck in a loose chignon and pulled several tendrils down to frame her face. But the one thing Everleigh had insisted on was a natural look for her make-up. She loved dressing up, but she still wanted to look in the mirror and see herself looking back at her.

Her hand drifted once more to her stomach, as it had at least a dozen times throughout the day. She'd tell her dad this weekend about the gift that would grace both their lives just after Christmas. Between Dad's incredible prognosis, her new job and being able to raise her child in the family farmhouse, she had been richly blessed.

Which made her feel even more ungrateful every time thoughts of Adrian intruded and triggered heartache. How could she possibly be so unthankful as to want even more?

She whirled around and walked out of her room, her head held high. Each click of her heels on the hardwood amped up her confidence.

Tonight would be her first time seeing Adrian since their disastrous parting in the hospital chapel. Hopefully, it would also be her last. She'd write him a letter next month, with proof of her pregnancy, ensure he understood that he was off the hook and then continue on with her life.

Her dad whistled as she walked down the stairs.

"You look beautiful." Wistfulness tinged his smile

as held out an arm. "Your mother would be proud of the woman you've become."

Everleigh returned his smile. "I hope so, Dad."

If she could be even a tenth of the mother to her child that her mom had been to her, then she would consider herself lucky.

The drive to Fox's tasting room and the attached newly constructed event venue took less than five minutes. The parking lot was already flooded with everything from Porsches to rusty pick-up trucks. She'd insisted that all of Fox's employees be invited to the gala, something Jade and the marketing team back in Granada had heartily endorsed.

The venue had been designed to look like a white barn with evergreen trim. The double doors were thrown open, with wine barrels standing guard on either side topped with pots overflowing with geraniums, azaleas and red carnations—a nod to Spain's national flower. Inside, the rafters were draped in lights that created a warm glow. The far side of the barn had been constructed from glass and overlooked the north acres of Fox Vineyards, now lit with a breathtaking reddish-yellow glimmer from the setting sun.

Everleigh had collaborated with Calandra's assistant to hire in outside waitstaff, so all the Fox employees could truly enjoy the evening. Servers moved among the guests, offering glasses of Fox's Chardonel and Cabrera's Merlot.

Her dad squeezed her hand. "Truly magnificent, Everleigh. You're going to lead Fox on to great things."

She'd started to smile and thank him when the temperature of the air went from cool and relaxed to sizzling hot. Her spine straightened, and before she could stop herself she whipped her head around.

Adrian stood in the doorway, power and confidence etched into his broad shoulders. He spoke with the young woman next to him—a beautiful redhead dressed in a poison-green gown that clung to every sensuous curve. Well, aside from the folds that fell away from the generous expanse of thigh revealed by the slit in the skirt.

Adrian said something to the woman that made her laugh, one hand going to her slender throat and the other coming to rest on Adrian's arm.

Jealousy and agony clashed inside Everleigh's chest, squeezing her lungs until she could barely breathe. The father of her child, the only man she'd ever loved, had found someone else in less than a week. Any romantic notions she'd seen in Adrian's face, felt in his touch when he'd taken her to bed, had clearly been imagined by her own desire.

"Everleigh?"

Her father had followed her line of sight, and he frowned when he saw her looking at Adrian. "Is there something you want to tell me?"

Somehow she stretched her lips into a smile. "No. Why?"

He looked between her and Adrian, his frown deepening, his eyes suspicious. "So there's nothing going on between you and Adrian?"

"No," she answered. "He's attractive, but we have nothing in common. Besides, he lives in Spain and my home is here."

She was dancing around the truth. There would most definitely be a reckoning when she shared with him who the father of his grandchild was, but for tonight she needed to pretend that Adrian Cabrera was a generous business acquaintance who had given her father the chance of a longer life and Fox the gift of another chance at success.

Before her dad could ask any further questions, she kissed him on the cheek and plunged into the crowd, putting as much distance between her and Adrian as possible. She'd have to see him again later that night, when he joined them on stage to deliver the speech his public relations department had crafted. But until then, the less she saw of him, the better.

Her hand drifted to her stomach once more. Pain threatened to choke her and send her into another fit of crying. If today was any indicator, she was going to be very weepy throughout her pregnancy. And seeing the father of her child, the man she loved, was not helping her errant emotions in the slightest.

She walked up to the bar and ordered sparkling apple cider. As the bartender handed her the glass, a shadow fell over her.

"Everleigh, right?"

The Spanish accent lingering beneath the words put her on alert. She glanced up to see a bear of a man with the same dark hair and deep blue eyes as Adrian grinning at her.

"Yes," she replied coolly. "And you are…?"

"Alejandro Cabrera. The middle brother."

She raised her glass to him. "Nice to meet you. I hope you're enjoying the party."

She started to walk off. She'd had enough Cabreras to last a lifetime. But Alejandro grabbed her hand.

"Before you run off, I have some questions for you. About Fox and the direction you're going to take it in."

Her eyes narrowed. "Aren't you in shipping?"

He shrugged, a playful smile belying the sharp alertness in his eyes. "Can I not be interested in my brother's business?"

Oh, he was up to something—no doubt about it. She turned and looked out over the crowd, but Adrian had disappeared.

"Did Adrian put you up to this?"

Alejandro's hand flew to his chest. "I'm hurt, *señorita*, that you would automatically jump to such a negative thought."

"I'm sure," she replied dryly, desperate to escape. "Fine. You have five minutes."

182   HIS BILLION-DOLLAR TAKEOVER TEMPTATION

"Excellent." He glanced up at the loft. "Isn't there a balcony that overlooks the vineyards?"

"Yes."

"That sounds like the perfect place for a private conversation."

She led the way upstairs and down the length of the loft, with Alejandro close behind. What had Adrian sent him for? Did he want to make sure she wasn't going to cause a scene tonight, the way Nicole had when he'd ended their engagement? Just the thought that he might think her capable of such horrid behavior made her sick to her stomach.

They reached the door that led out to the balcony. Alejandro opened it for her.

"So, what did you…?"

Her voice trailed off as the door closed behind her, followed a second later by an audible click. She grabbed the handle and gave it a tug. The bastard had locked her out.

She leaned over the railing. The venue was perched on the edge of a hill, with the ground sloping away from the stone walls into the vineyards below. There was nothing to climb down, and even if there was she wouldn't risk falling and hurting the baby.

"I can see why you love it here."

She froze. That voice—that sinful, wonderful, sensuous voice—washed over her. Slowly she turned.

A large deck had been built off to one side of the balcony, boasting a collection of high-top tables and chairs. She'd expected it to be crowded with guests, because it offered the most incredible views of the countryside.

But there was only one person present, hands in his pockets and fire in his eyes.

Adrian.

CHAPTER TWENTY-TWO

ADRIAN STARED AT Everleigh hungrily, his eyes drinking in every detail. He'd thought her stunning at the Merlot release party in New York City. But the gown she wore tonight inflamed his desire to new heights. His fingers itched to tear that scrap of silk from her shoulder, peel the dress off her and bare her skin so he could touch every inch of her.

The last three days of waiting, of planning, had been sheer torture. In each move he'd made since taking over Cabrera Wine, each deal he'd gone after, he had been filled with confidence that he would get what he wanted. Failure had never been an option.

But now, standing before the woman he loved and seeing the mistrust and banked anger in those violet eyes that had haunted his dreams since she'd left, he knew true fear.

Fear that she would reject him as he'd so cruelly rejected her.

Fear that after tonight he'd never see her again.

He nodded out toward the vineyards. "Your father took me up there when I first visited. But that was in the early afternoon. It's truly stunning."

"It is."

Her tone could freeze hell over.

"What do you want, Adrian?"

His hands curled inside his pockets—the only way to stop himself from reaching out and smoothing one of those loose, silky tendrils of gold from her neck before he covered her lips with his own.

"I want…" *A life with you. Children. To wake up to your face every morning and make love to you every night.* "I want to apologize."

"Excuse me?"

"I treated you horribly at the hospital."

The memory of how cold he'd been to her, how callously he'd spoken of their lovemaking and the bond they'd developed, had made him experience shame like he never had before. He'd made mistakes in the past. But this time he'd made a deliberate decision and brought unimaginable grief on the woman he loved.

"Well…thank you. How is your mother?"

He suppressed a smile. It was one of the many things he loved about her: she cared about his family.

"On a fast road to recovery and reveling in my father being home. He's waiting on her hand and foot. I'm fairly certain a dozen roses have arrived every single day she's been home."

Her lips twitched. God, he wanted to see her smile again, to smooth the lines of worry from her face and chase the shadows from her eyes.

"My dad told me what you did for him." She softened for just a moment. "Adrian, no matter what's happened between us, I can't thank you enough."

"I'm glad his prognosis is positive. Dr. Pratt is a pioneer in his field."

Gratitude shone in her gaze. But he wanted so much more than her gratitude.

"But my apology is not just about that time at the hospital." He breathed in deeply. "I talked with my mother. I learned a lot about what happened when she lost my sister."

A wistful smile crossed Everleigh's face. He wanted to kiss that smile and make sure he was the last man ever to do so.

"We've talked a lot these past few days. I have a better understanding of the pain that drove her to do what she did." And he'd realized that he had blamed his mother for everything, while giving his father a free pass. Something else he'd have to confront eventually.

"I'm really glad, Adrian."

"My mother told me she was hurt so much by losing my sister that she couldn't see what she had right in front of her..."

He took a deep breath. His next words would give Everleigh the power either to make him the happiest man alive or plunge him into a despair worse than anything he'd ever experienced.

"I did the same thing, Everleigh. I was so hurt by my mother's rejection—more than I think I even realized. When she started trying to reconnect, but refused to explain why, I felt like she'd validated my conclusion. That I wasn't good enough. That I couldn't be loved. The more she tried, the more it felt like a cruel game of getting my hopes up only to put me right back where I'd started when she wouldn't answer my questions. Every time I asked she disappeared for days...even weeks at a time. I know now it was guilt and shame, but back then..." He swallowed hard. "I loved Abuela so much. When she died, and when my mother still refused to explain why she abandoned me, I stopped feeling much of anything because it hurt too much."

Everleigh's hand started to come up, but she dropped it back to her side. The small gesture gave him hope.

"Nicole awoke that old need in me to be loved, but for the wrong reasons. After we broke up it reinforced my belief that opening myself up, feeling something for someone else, would only result in pain. I equated feeling more than casual lust for a woman with weakness."

Temptation got the better of him and he reached up, brushing a strand of golden hair off Everleigh's face.

"But you don't make me feel weak. You make me feel

strong. You make me want to be a better leader, a better man."

The urge to feel more of her overpowered his good sense and he took a step toward her, capturing her hands in his before she could turn and run from him. She didn't pull away, but she lowered her eyes.

"What we have…what I feel for you…is so much more than I've ever felt for anyone else."

Slowly, ever so slowly, she raised her head. Her gaze met his, those violet eyes gleaming with unshed tears that twisted him into knots.

"You hurt me."

Those three words pierced his heart. He brought her hands to his lips and kissed her fingers. "I did. And if you can forgive me, Everleigh, I will spend the rest of my life proving how much I care about you. How I feel about you."

"What *do* you feel for me, Adrian?" she whispered.

He brought one hand up and gently cupped her face, touching his forehead to hers. "I love you, Everleigh Bradford. I love you, heart, mind and soul."

With that proclamation hanging in the air between them, he leaned down and pressed his lips to hers.

The world stopped. And then she threw her arms around his neck and kissed him back.

The tenuous hold he'd been keeping on his passion snapped. He crushed her body to his and lifted her off her feet, his tongue sweeping between her lips to stake his claim on her once more. She moaned into his mouth as her fingers tangled and tightened in his hair.

"Everleigh," he whispered, "be my wife."

She froze, and for a heart-wrenching moment his panic returned in full force. He tensed his arms, trying to pull her closer, to hold her as tightly as he could for as long as he could, even if it was just for this one moment.

Then her hands came up and rested on his jaw. She

pulled back, and the happiness behind her smile was so intense it nearly blinded him.

"Yes!" She laughed, the jubilant sound sending a rush of pleasure through him unlike any he'd ever known. "Yes, Adrian!"

He kissed her again, desire, love and joy pounding through him. He didn't deserve her love—but, dear God, selfish man that he was, he wasn't going to let her go again.

"Everleigh, I'm so sorry," he whispered as he rained kisses over her face.

"I forgive you. Oh, Adrian, I'm sorry you experienced that pain again. I would have never, ever wished that on you."

How did he deserve a woman like her? To care so much about him after what he'd done to her, after he'd driven her away?

"My mother and I still have a long way to go," he said. "And my father and I will have to work some things out, too. But, Everleigh… I want you to be a part of our family. The whole complicated mess. And I can't imagine being with anyone but you. We'll make this work," he hurried on, not wanting her to have a second to summon any doubts. "You can still lead Fox, we can split our time between here and Spain, and anywhere else you want to go in the world."

An excited sparkle lit her eyes. "Even Paris?"

"Every weekend if you want."

A frown crossed her face. "What about kids?"

"I think we should start on that right away."

A delighted laugh escaped Everleigh's lips. She grabbed his hand and slowly drew it to her belly. His fingers settled across her flat stomach and he raised an eyebrow.

"We already have a head start," she said. "About a month."

For a moment he stared at her.

Pregnant? With his child?

He looked down, floored at the thought that a tiny being was growing inside the woman he loved, right beneath his palm. If he'd thought himself possessive before, it was nothing compared to what he felt now—the need to protect both Everleigh and his unborn child, to let them both know he would never abandon them again.

"Are you happy?" she asked.

His gaze snapped back up to hers. "Everleigh…" His throat constricted. "I don't deserve this. I don't deserve the happiness you've given me."

She clasped his face in her hands and kissed him on the forehead. "None of that. I love you. You love me. What more do we need?"

He held up a finger, reached into the pocket of his pants and pulled out a box. He stepped back and knelt down. Her hand flew to her mouth and her eyes welled with tears.

"You need a proper proposal and a ring on your finger." He flipped the lid up. The red coral gemstone, set in a circle of diamonds, sparkled under the light of the sunset. "This ring belonged to my *abuela*. It would honor me, and her memory, if you would accept it."

Everleigh nodded, a smile stretching from ear to ear even as tears spilled down her cheeks. Adrian slid the ring onto her finger just as the sun disappeared behind the horizon. Then he stood and pulled her against him once more, not wanting to spend a second away from her.

"It's almost time for our speech," Everleigh whispered between the kisses he continued to press to her lips.

"Considering that I would like to announce to the world that you're officially mine, perhaps we should pull your father aside and let him know first?"

"Let him know he's gaining a son-in-law and a grandchild?"

"Yes." He winced. "And we have to call my mother. She'd be furious if a crowd of strangers found out before her. Although she's the one who gave me the ring." He kissed the tip of her nose. "She knew, just as I did, that you're meant to be a Cabrera."

She smiled up at him, her eyes radiant and her face glowing. "How do you say *I love you* in Spanish?"

"Te quiero."

"Te quiero," she repeated.

"Te quiero, Everleigh. *Siempre.* Always."

* * * * *

MILLS & BOON

Coming next month

SECRETS OF CINDERELLA'S AWAKENING
Sharon Kendrick

Almost as if he'd read her mind, Leon caught hold of her and turned her round, his hands on either side of her waist. She held her breath because his touch felt *electric* and he studied her upturned face for what felt like a long time, before lowering his head to kiss her.

It was…dynamite.

It was…life-changing.

Marnie swayed in disbelief, her limbs growing instantly boneless. How was it possible for a kiss to feel this *good*? How could *anything* feel this good? At first there was barely any contact between them – just the intoxicating graze of his mouth over hers.

He deepened the kiss and began to stroke one of her breasts. Her nipple was pushing against her baggy T-shirt dress towards the enticing circling of his thumb. Was it that which made her writhe her hips against his with instinctive hunger, causing him to utter something in Greek which sounded almost *despairing*?

The sound broke the spell and she drew back – though in the faint light all she could see was the hectic glitter of his eyes. 'What…what did you just say?'

'I said that you set my blood on fire, *agape mou*. And that I want you very much. But you already know that.'

Well, she knew he wanted her, yes. She wasn't actually sure about the blood-on-fire bit because nobody had ever said anything like that to her before. And although she liked it her instinct was not to believe him because even if they were true, she knew compliments always came with a price.

Yet what was the *point* of all this if she was just going to pepper the experience with her usual doubts, and spoil it? Couldn't she have a holiday from her normal self and shake off all the worries which had been weighing her down for so long? Couldn't she be a different Marnie tonight – one who was seeking nothing but uncomplicated pleasure? She had always been the responsible one. The one who looked out for other people – with one eye on the distance, preparing for the shadows which inevitably hovered there. Wasn't it time to articulate what *she* wanted for a change?

She cleared her throat. 'Would you mind speaking in English so I can understand what you're saying?'

She could hear the amusement which deepened his voice.

'Are we planning to do a lot of talking then, Marnie? Is that what turns you on?'

Something warned her she'd be straying into dangerous territory if she told him she didn't *know* what turned her on because she'd never given herself the chance to find out. But while she didn't want to lie to him, that didn't mean she couldn't tell a different kind of truth.

'*You* turn me on,' she said boldly and something about the breathless rush of her words made his powerful body tense.

'Oh, *do* I?' he questioned, tilting her chin with his fingers so that their darkened gazes clashed. 'So what are we going to do about that, I wonder?'

Continue reading
SECRETS OF CINDERELLA'S AWAKENING
Sharon Kendrick

Available next month
www.millsandboon.co.uk

COMING SOON!

We really hope you enjoyed reading this book.
If you're looking for more romance, be sure to
head to the shops when new books are
available on

Thursday 10th
June

MILLS & BOON

THE HEART OF ROMANCE

A ROMANCE FOR EVERY READER

MODERN

Prepare to be swept off your feet by sophisticated, sexy and seductive heroes, in some of the world's most glamourous and romantic locations, where power and passion collide.

HISTORICAL

Escape with historical heroes from time gone by. Whether your passion is for wicked Regency Rakes, muscled Vikings or rugged Highlanders, awaken the romance of the past.

MEDICAL

Set your pulse racing with dedicated, delectable doctors in the high-pressure world of medicine, where emotions run high and passion, comfort and love are the best medicine.

True Love

Celebrate true love with tender stories of heartfelt romance, from the rush of falling in love to the joy a new baby can bring, and a focus on the emotional heart of a relationship.

Desire

Indulge in secrets and scandal, intense drama and plenty of sizzling hot action with powerful and passionate heroes who have it all: wealth, status, good looks…everything but the right woman.

HEROES

Experience all the excitement of a gripping thriller, with an intense romance at its heart. Resourceful, true-to-life women and strong, fearless men face danger and desire - a killer combination!

To see which titles are coming soon, please visit

millsandboon.co.uk/nextmonth

JOIN US ON SOCIAL MEDIA!

Stay up to date with our latest releases, author news and gossip, special offers and discounts, and all the behind-the-scenes action from Mills & Boon...

 millsandboon

 millsandboonuk

 millsandboon

It might just be true love...

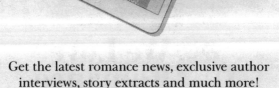